Stylar's Q
For Freedom
Part 1

by
Craig Archibald

Copyright © 2016 Craig Archibald

All rights reserved, including the right to reproduce this book, or portions thereof in any form. No part of this text may be reproduced, transmitted, downloaded, decompiled, reverse engineered, or stored, in any form or introduced into any information storage and retrieval system, in any form or by any means, whether electronic or mechanical without the express written permission of the author.

ISBN: 978-1-326-87780-4

WEST NORTHAMPTONSHIRE COUNCIL	
80003761842	
Askews & Holts	
BB	

"The birthing chamber was colossal it had once been a vast mining complex, but some member of a government, long since forgotten had seen its potential for secrecy, the minerals in the rock isolated it from the rest of the world, its purpose had changed over the decades, except for the fact it continued to carry out projects, if known any one in power would deny any knowledge, the chamber was dimly lit, rows of beds seemed to disappear into the darkness. Kylar lay back, the bed was hard unyielding but compared with the pain she had endured over the past few days it was little more than an irritation, her contractions were closer together, she sensed it would be soon, the chamber echoed with the screams and cries of the other females that were enduring the same agony. Kylar was one of a couple of dozen females who were to give birth, within the next few days, the great experiment, she tensed up once more feeling another pain they were becoming like ripples in a pool just as one subsided another one took its place, even through the agony she saw the shadow fall across the wall, she moved with certainty and purpose as was this females way, but she was not known for leaving the sanctity of her own chambers, where she administered, concoctions made from what little the caverns provided, Kylar was curious even through the, once more her hands balled into fists that squeezed the material which was soaked from the sweat that plastered the middle aged female to the bed. The older females' eyes locked on Kylar's, she tried to smile but clearly the older female who was called Rani was not happy with the condition of the females lying before her. Kylar felt a firm hand take her own, she tried to look but once more a convulsion made her shut her eyes and grit her teeth
"Rani".
Kylar said with as much warmth as she could under the circumstances
"Silence child concentrate on the task at hand"
Kylar was glad Rani didn't want any special treatment, her position as healer made her an important individual within the community and that had Kylar wondering why of all the females in this chamber she was the one that had been chosen?
"These damn doctors with all their medical knowledge they still won't give you any medication for what's about to come".

Even though Kylar was struggling to keep silent from what was happening to her body, she was concerned someone might hear Rani, they had not been given medication to see how the held up to the pain of childbirth which meant someone was monitoring the chamber.

"Rani please don't talk like, aargh"

Kylar lifted herself from the pillows and pushed so hard, her head was pounding and she was beginning to wonder how much more she could take, she could feel her strength failing her, she pushed again. Rani was between her thighs.

"You are doing well my girl not much longer, I can see his head, just 1 or 2 pushes".

Again Kylar pushed lifting herself off the bed her breathing laboured

"Don't give up one more push"

"I am so tired"

"You can sleep when this new life is in this world, now push"

Rani helped the young male out into the world, cutting the umbilical cord with a sure and practised hand. Kylar had been holding her breath, not really aware caught in the moment realising her new born was not making a sound, the young female seemed to be looking into the healers' eyes trying to find answers to questions she did not want to ask, unfortunately the female had this expression that said nothing, her features as if carved from the very rock the chamber they were in had been.

"Rani is he, alive?"

Rani shook her head slightly as if coming out of a trance, she pulled what passed for a blanket from a compartment in the bed and smiled as she handed the bundle to his exhausted mother

"Congratulations you have a healthy son"

Kylar excepted her son tears of joy, relief hidden mostly by the sweat that glistened off her skin, but there was still something wrong, she looked into her sons' eyes

"I thought, shouldn't he be crying? Is he alright?"

Rani smiled as if in response, the smile didn't come easy to her lips as if out of practice, what the older female couldn't say was what she sensed from this new life, not only was he different but with his birth the fate of all the people who existed in the bowels of this planet had irrevocably been changed. Kylar's brow furrowed, was it her imagination or was the female getting more eccentric as of late? Rani had heard a prophecy when she was but a girl, the people who kept them down here away from the light, feared there would be an uprising. She wondered if this new born was this tale come to fruition or perhaps it was just her imagination, that had got her into much trouble throughout her life.

In the shadows the birth had been witnessed, two males looked on their faces behind a material that was a composite of materials, if anyone could have seen through these masks they wore they might have seen a degree of pride, this male was the first of his kind he had been manipulated at a genetic level, though that female had given birth to him there was no similarities, he was a new species the woman merely a vessel, his brain had been stimulated while inside her, he was the culmination of centuries of so many failures. But they had succeeded. It was fitting he had witnessed the males birth a lifetime of sacrifice now forgotten with this triumph, but this was only the first stage of a bigger plan

"Marlac that healer concerns me, she seems to always be at the centre of events when we hear stories of unrest"

Marlac sneered at the younger male whose name was Mardock

"You fool the last thing we want to do is terminate one in so high a position. Do you want to create a martyr, besides if she had been a threat he would have had her terminated long before she got to such a position within their community?"

Rani had been part of another set of clinical trials, the mortality rate for that particular experiment had t been 98.7 percent. Marlac smiled remembering the team leader of that tragedy, the tragedy being that that pompous fool had ever got such an opportunity. Marlac had only met him once, once had been more than enough, arrogant, self-opinionated, yes that was all his good points. Success would be rewarded as failure had been in the past, yes everything was proceeding as planned.

Rani wandered through the birthing chambers as if she knew where she was going, the truth was she had never been this far into the complex, some areas still seemed to be under construction, areas constantly changing for the requirements of the latest rounds of tests, her people treated like specimens, the smell as well what was that damp, with disinfectant and perhaps bodily odours she shouldn't think any more about it, she was beginning to think about evening meal ,perhaps their time was finally coming, perhaps Kylar's son would be the weapon of their own destruction, that would be one interpretation of the prophecy, perhaps if she was to ask a dozen people she would get a dozen interpretations. Rani was still in her own world, with thoughts spiralling within her head, when she turned down a wide corridor being patrolled by two security personnel. Both stood about two and a half metres in height and they seemed as wide again

"What are you doing in this sector female? This section is for authorised personnel only"

His voice vibrating deeply through his mask. Rani always had wondered if the voices had to sound that way. Was it their design or a feature supposed to intimidate? Ranis medical curiosity had always wondered what they looked like beneath the body armour. Rani remembered stories as a child saying they had been invaders from the stars, the armour kept them alive without it they would die quickly, she heard that in combat just before they delivered a lethal blow they removed their helmet so their enemy could look into their eyes as the life was taken from them.

"I am sorry I was looking for transport back to the community"

The guard hit a wall panel, green lights began to pulse, he had hit the panel harder than he need to, more for effect she supposed

"Follow the lights they will lead you to the terminal"

Once more they began conversing with one another as if she wasn't even there, such behaviour was the key to victory, the enemy had become arrogant while her people had become strong, her people treated like beasts of burden, perhaps not even that well, she hoped she would live to see the day when they would pay for underestimating what her people had become.

Kylar had had her son taken an hour after his birth, she had been ordered to get some rest. Kylar wondered how long her son would be allowed to stay with her, already she was thinking of a future without him and with the loss of her mate, she didn't know whether she would survive if she was left alone. Kylar still worried about her son. Was he normal? She had heard the other young crying as they had come into the world, but her son had not made a sound. She had never expected to have offspring her mate had been killed in a cave in five years before. Had it really been that long? The pain had not lessened so many had said it would but it felt the same as it had the week after she had been told, because that first week whatever others said she could not accept that he was gone, it felt like an open wound that would not close, perhaps with this new life she might begin to know peace again. Kylar would name him after the father he should have known, she hadn't thought of names until this moment. Stylar would be his name. why hadn't she thought of a name before? Perhaps she hadn't wanted to curse the birth, all the tests and procedures and then when pregnancies were confirmed apart from their rations going up and a weekly examination they had been left alone. Stories had been told all her life as her people sat around fires after evening meal. Rani was supposed to have been a product of experimentation, but she never talked about it and the community respected her too much to ask. Kylar wondered about her son. What had they done to him? What was so different he looked like any other child, she wondered how the community would greet him, she had heard the whispers, this was the final experiment, these children would usher in a new age, but what would happen to her people? She heard him before she saw him. Marlac walked along the rows of beds making notes on the condition of the mothers before once more going into another annex, apparently where the new borns were kept when not with their mothers, the results were even better than he thought they would be, the beginning of a new race, a new labour force, they were perfect, their bone structure. Marlacs eyes fell on one of the new borns he was smaller than the rest. With this success he could begin to imagine the financial rewards. Failure had never been an option because with failure came consequences, he had lost colleagues, he had never had friends, friendships you had to trust and that had not been part of his upbringing

"Ah the thinker, kylars son, I have big plans for you"

Marlac bent over and picked the child up, he had expected some reaction, fear, distress but there had been nothing, these specimens would not know childhood, they would grow fast within twelve months it would be as if they had lived eighteen of the community years. Rani had guided his work by the simple fact that she had survived, she had been the key to aging, he had made sure that he alone had made the discovery and it could only be accessed by him alone, it was his insurance in case this experiment had not gone as planned, the instructions were locked into their very D N A when they hit puberty it would like be an override and their aging would slow to that of those around them. Marlac put the child back and continued looking at readouts. Marlac knew that these children would finally assure his place in his peoples' history, his name alongside the names he had grown up idolising perhaps even surpassing them. Injections would start being administered the next morning, supplements to help with the rapid aging, if he was being honest with himself it would be several months before they knew for sure that the experiment had been a total success, as Marlac, knew he needed to rest but his head was full of thoughts about the next few days, sleep would not come easily, briefly glancing back he walked out of the annex the lights dimmed

Rani sat by one of the larger fires, it was a place of honour, she sensed she was being watched, the male came out of the shadows. Raldon took a place beside her she had been staring as the flames danced patterns lit up the cave walls. Rani had known Raldon since his sixth year he had been a water carrier, he had been given this duty the year before, he had grown strong, caring passionately for his people, she knew there were questions in his eyes, about the future of his people.

"You saw them then?"

"Yes, I saw them"

They couldn't look at one another, they both stared into the fire. Rani knew the male well enough to know he was thinking how to phrase his words, it was one of his better qualities, he never rushed into a situation it made him the leader that he was

"Were they healthy?"

"As far as I could tell"

Raldon watched as the flames began to die, the meal had been eaten some hours before and most had gone to their quarters

"Do you think it's the end of our people?"

"I don't know, we knew this day would come, generations before you were born they started these experiments, sooner or later someone was going to solve the puzzle, that so many died trying to answer, I was beginning to wonder if I would see it in my lifetime."

"I was hoping I wouldn't"

"I think I am partly to blame for their success, perhaps it would have been better if I had not survived" Raldon couldn't help but smile.

"You were the only good thing ever to come from those damn experiments"

"Don't let Nairi here you talk like that I know what a temper that female has".

Raldon wanted to laugh but too many thoughts weighed heavily on his mind, the silence felt strained, Rani decided to break it

"Have I not always given you wise council? As I did your father before you, well listen now I looked into the soul of kylars child and he has the potential to be a great leader if he is brought up in the right way. Our masters think he and his brethren are their salvation, if he can be taught he could very well be outs It sounds like you think this child is the prophecy"

Raldon shook his head sadly.

"I know you don't believe in such things the way I do, I think you are too much like your father, the prophecy can be interpreted in too many ways, he always thought it was a weapon, a machine but who's to say it couldn't be an individual? Sometimes individuals, ideas can inspire other. Perhaps all our people need is a little spark. For now, kylars son and the others are just children".

"Yes, but how long will they stay just children? You are proof that they have some idea how to control a lifespan with you they slowed it to a crawl, who's to say they couldn't speed it up."

Rani could tell this night she wouldn't calm the leaders' fears. Perhaps he was right but to restock a labour force the size they needed, the undertaking could not be done overnight. Raldon looked at his old friend.

"I will tell you one thing, if I have nothing left to lose I will fight and if necessary I will die for my people. I will not be put to sleep like the elders, I won't just give up and die"

Darnon watched from the shadows, he had earned a reputation amongst his people one that was despised, he did whatever was necessary to stay well fed, he smelt an opportunity that could fill his stomach for many days to come, a vicious grin spread across his face, he could almost taste that fresh meat and vegetables so Darnon kept watching the leader and the healer, perhaps they would talk of an uprising or an assassination of someone of note, but thinking about it, his luck of late it would be grumbling about conditions or the meagre rations they were supposed to survive on. Darnon felt he was being observed Raldons daze had fixed his gaze on the shadows where he had decided to conceal himself, he held himself still as the rock around him, though his heart had begun to race, beads of sweat had begun to form on his brow and slowly that sweat ran down his nose, then as suddenly as Raldons eyes had locked on his, his attention was back on Rani.

"Productivity has increased in the mine five percent"

"Let me take a guess might it have something to do with that hundred strong labour force working the lower levels?"

Rani asked trying to keep amusement out of her tone. Raldon smiled

"I think it might have more to do with the new pit boss, Dianer has done well she is the best I ever trained. I hoped one day she might take my place. But that won't happen now will it?"

"Who can say Raldon, it is just the beginning, the children may not live up to their expectations, you can't predict at this stage how things will be will end, errors might have been made, it would not be the first time."

It was then Rani heard the commotion in one of the connecting tunnels. Raldon was already on his feet, a smile on his lips

"You know the hundred we mentioned before I believe their shift ended twenty minutes ago"

Raldon and Rani had been talking in one of many connecting chambers it sounded like the commotion would lead them into the main hall. Raldon had always thought they could get five thousand individuals in the space not that the community was that large, people were stirring, wanting to know what was happening, there was a platform at the far end several steps carved out of rock and worn from centuries of use, fires lit the chamber, but it was only when the community gathered that the place seemed to warm. Raldon walked slowly up the steps, it had taken several minutes the gathering moving slowly to let him pass. Nairi was close behind, she had been joined with Raldon for twenty years or as they called them cycles. Karniar also was present, he had raised Raldon as his own, he had led the community for fifteen cycles before passing leadership to Raldon. Raldon smiled down these were the people he would give this life for. Raldon had always hated speaking in front of the community, he believed more in actions, but there were times, when individuals were honoured and this moment he felt was long overdue.

"My friends tonight we are to honour individuals who have served their community with their blood, sweat and tears, the community is like our very existence it is like a circle never ending, some of our number duties have now come to an end, while the group in front of us their duties just beginning, they have been trained hard and they will serve you with honour. This group I have seen grow, I have seen them develop into fine men and women I know they will uphold our traditions but it's with a mixture of joy and sorrow that I say these words, because with each generation I have always wondered what we were losing. We all have heard the stories about where we go when our time ends. How we are freed or butchered each individual will know the truth. But at this time this group that number a hundred, six will lead, be responsible for the rest that will serve. Dianer step forward."

A roar went up from those gathered, she couldn't keep a slight smile from her lips, she walked forward with a dignity in her bearing that Raldon had come to expect and in turn earned her the admiration of those around her, she bowed her head slightly to him he returned the gesture a sign of respect, she now stood beside him on the podium.

"Now for the other five members who will be your support, because to lead you have to have people you can trust Liana, Darrus, Terak, Brand and Zar"

All had positioned themselves near the front, the group parted to give them the space they needed, their eyes to the ground tradition again a sign of humility now there was silence, perhaps a stray sound of someone scuffing their feet on the ground. Dianer had dreaded this moment for the past twelve months or one cycle when she learned she was to become the new pit boss; the speech was customary I feel a lot of warmth before me in this hall tonight when I was told I would be leading you in the day to day life of these mines I was honoured, some of those names that have gone before me have become almost legend in our community, I would not even try to compete because I am my own person and that person will always stand for you, because we don't just break our backs together we are family, we are as one. I will honour you with how I perform, I will do my best any less would be a disservice to you.

Dianer felt the tear rolling down her cheek, she brushed it aside as if a speck of dirt. Dianer turned to   Raldon who nodded Rani stepped forward a small box in her hand, Raldon cleared his throat

"As it has been longer than anyone can remember, as it is now"

Raldon opened the box Rani had given him

"The five of you will now be given these links, they will connect you with Dianer when you are on your shift."

Dianer saw apprehension in Brands eyes when they were younger they had been good friends but as the day of choosing had grown closer, Dianer had felt their relationship drifting, she knew she would always have his loyalty but she also knew she would always mourn the loss of his friendship. Dianer knew after this night even though she would still have friends they would never quite treat her the same, the price of leadership, the cost. Raldon started with Liana, he pulled some of her hair to one side, the link was a metal disc with barbs that attached to the base of the brain once attached fibres connected sending and receiving signals, it would take several days to get used to, nausea, headaches and vomiting were some of the side effects but to lose control of bodily functions had been known. Liana hissed as the connection was made. Raldon smiled

"It will pass; you just have to get used to it."

Raldon moved her hair back so the disc was no longer visible, he repeated the procedure until the box was empty, he handed it back to Rani. Dianers link had been connected several weeks before, it had been like her final test to satisfy Raldon that the choice had been the correct one not that he had had any serious doubts.

Raldon lifted his arms once more silencing the people who had always struggled with silence for too long.

"My friends this has been a long day I know this group will be keen to prove themselves, perhaps even break some ore extraction records over the coming months."

With those last few words he turned, Nairi at his side like it had always been walking towards their bed chamber, one of the advantages of leadership quarters close to those places of importance, the community as a whole lived together. Raldon on occasion though enjoyed his time alone with his mate

"You are proud of her aren't you?"

Raldon smiled but it was one with more sadness within

"She is the closest thing to a child we will ever have. You would have made a wonderful mother and our children would have been strong, I know it's what you always wanted."

"I only wanted you my love, I knew we would have to make sacrifices I saw the leader you would become, you have served your people well and I know often I have had to share you, but what we have had together, I would never change, you are a good man and a fierce leader, you might be a little more measured these days"

"Measured?"

"You were prone to acts without thought in your youth, maturity has made you think before you take such action. I know you don't believe but I do I thought you might have been the one told about in the prophecy, I think our enemy had such thoughts too, you have a spirit that is bigger than you, they needed to control you so yes they took some of our hopes and dreams, but they could never take our love, I don't think they even know what love means. You say I would have made a wonderful mother, I know you would have made a better father, it's who you are"

"How can you be so sure?"

"You prove it every day with your people, the young like Dianer you lift up you give purpose and you change their lives forever, if that is not what a father does, then what is? Her father was a good man but he never showed her the love you have or spent the time with her you have"

"He was a good man I miss him"

"I know you do but down here our life is about risks, those risks increased by ones who believe in profit not safety, perhaps it's another way of keeping our numbers down, another way to cull us, the fact is that taking ore from this world will always have a price and unfortunately he paid for it with his life, but you have honoured him by raising his daughter to be the leader she is"

"Maybe so but it has been a long day I am ready for my bed"

"I have seen our females in the birthing chamber and a bed is what they lie on, what we have I would never describe as a bed."

Raldon looked down at the bedding dried grass with blankets for warmth not that he needed that when Nairi curled her body beside his, or when they fell asleep in one another's arms, he suspected as long as she was there he could fall asleep on anything, he lay down as if knowing his thoughts, she folded in beside him like she had done so many times over the cycles.

Dianer lay on her mat resigned to the fact she would not be getting any sleep that night, the links were now open and she was trying to erect a barrier in her mind. Raldon had warned her, but perhaps she thought she would be different be able to control without any real effort, yes she knew she would have to be patient these disciplines took time, she needed control.

"Can't sleep?"

"What?"

Dianer sat up on her mat scrambling for the blanket to cover her naked form.

"Terak what the hell are you doing in here? Can't you see I am naked?"

"My vision has always been more than adequate thank you"

Dianer could feel her temper rising and was it her imagination or did the young male know it too?

"You act as if I have never seen you naked before after shifts we always shower together; I think modesty is a little late don't you think?"

Dianer remembered the first time she had seen Terak, his muscular arms, his flat stomach, the size of his. What was she thinking?

"Terak we all need time to ourselves, right now this is my time. I know you feel like you have to protect me it hasn't gone unnoticed but right now I want to be alone, so get out of my bed chamber before I find a large hammer and hit you somewhere you won't appreciate it"

Terak took a step back and bowed

"As you wish my lady."

He decided as an afterthought to fling a few words over his shoulder

"I always found your body arousing too"

Dianer definitely needed to control her thoughts especially around him, her thoughts at times could be colourful. Was it her or was it getting warmer in her chamber? Dianer couldn't keep the small smile from her lips, the thought that someone else knew your desires could be erotic, but also distracting, once more she went back to building that barrier in her head she decided it needed to be bigger and thicker after that incident, the smile was still on her lips as fatigue finally took her unaware that Terak had remained just outside of her chamber to make sure she was not disturbed.

The children were growing fast it had been a week since their births and Marlac was satisfied with how things were progressing, he read the latest results for probably the third or fourth time, there was one thing that they all had in common the large spikes in brain activity, with accelerated growth came substantial pain, bones stretching, muscles tightening, growing pains but so much more than a normal individual could take. They had been taken from their mothers, the distress at seeing their young like that would not reflect well on the clinical conditions, today students were helping monitor the young's vitals. Marlac always put the work before the wellbeing of the subjects. One think that had aroused his curiosity was still the lack of emotion Kylars son seemed to show or didn't as the case may be. Oh yes looking at his notes. Stylar named after a mate that had died years before up to this point he had been another number, perhaps he deserved a name, because he was different from the rest and that difference though curious could also be the first indication of a problem or a breakthrough? How was it he seemed to be able to control his pain levels when his brethren cried and screamed. Whenever he had studied this individual it had felt like he too was being scrutinised, perhaps he was just tired, perhaps it was merely the fact the young male was trying to make sense of his surroundings. He needed to get some sleep a final medical procedure would be carried out the following day, similar to the links they used but generations more advanced, his systems stood empty ready to receive data once these implants were activated. This was an unknown this would be the first test to say whether they had succeeded or just made another step towards what was required.

"Marlac?"

The voice startled him it was Mardock

"What did I tell you I didn't want to be disturbed"

"Marlac one of the children has gone into a coma, I think the pain was too much it's like his brain shut down."

"Is it kylars son?"

"Yes, how did you know?"

"I have been concerned about him since he was born. I will be there in five minutes' relay all the data now" Marlac once could have covered the distance in half the time, he had become aware that the drugs he had been administering to himself were no longer holding back the ravages of time. He would grow old and die, immortality would never be his. But perhaps he would live on in his work. It was all he had left, he had sacrificed family both blood and the possibility of having one of his own, he just hoped this would be the only setback. The damn exoskeleton was getting heavier as well he thought as he entered the observation room

"Status"

He barked at one of the assistants, he couldn't see Mardock but he knew he wouldn't be far away

"We don't know what we are seeing it's almost like a computer trying to reboot, perhaps it's our instrumentation we almost declared him dead, there were no brainwaves and then. We might be having technical problems"

"So you are saying his brain stopped sending signals and then it started again. What did you do to him?"

Marlac was in no mood for mysteries as he studied the readings it was as the assistant said, it just didn't make sense, he brought up information on the other children eight had passed out because of the pain but not like him. A defence mechanism, the pain had tripped a switch, it was all guess work he needed facts, he had had more procedures than the rest perhaps they had unknowingly altered him more than any of them had realised, not that he would ever admit that to anyone. He had put things off long enough, he had a superior he answered to, the man lived in the shadows. Marlac realised that at that moment in time all that could be done was and he had a report that needed to be filed, he walked slowly from the room, stopping before a transit tube that accessed the upper levels including a spacious office where all data was backed up from the project and also gave him direct access to the world council chamber and more importantly the Director himself. In all the decades he had worked for his superior he had never once woken him, it was as if he never slept. The Director had held his position for longer than most remembered as to his age no one knew but it seemed that the secret of immortality might be his, because this man's business was secrets. Marlac wondered who had provided the formula, there were a few possibilities that came to mind, not that any of them were still alive, whoever had shared the secret probably paid a high price for sharing it.

"I apologise for the lateness of the hour Director"

"For you to call me at all the matter must have some urgency"

The Director sat in the shadows added to the air of mystery and secrecy this individual had, perhaps to keep those who contacted him slightly off balance

"Director"

Marlac felt like a child in front of a teacher. The Director now focussed his full attention on him.

"Well are you going to tell me what the situation is or am I going to have to torture the truth out of you?"

"It's one of the test subjects we are getting some results from him that we can't interpret. I have not told anyone but I think because we do not understand him there is a potential danger"

"I see was this the test subject you carried out experiment procedures on?"

"Yes, Director it was. We felt the procedures were necessary and up to this point we felt they had been a great success"

The Director didn't like the way his subordinate had answered him back

"I think you forget who you are talking too"

"I am sorry Director I just think there is so much potential here"

"I agree it's just the potential to do what concerns me. Do you have another candidate to replace the child if you felt he needed to be terminated?"

The Director never gave orders but he had a way of making his wishes known, any threats would be neutralized. Before he could question further the screen was already black the link had been severed. This child was special to terminate him would be a waste of a key resource, it felt like he was being asked to sever a limb, these children were his, perhaps he was getting old but he knew he needed to save this child give him a chance to become what he had been designed to be. He thought for a moment he had heard stories of sympathisers who felt that one society should not prey on another, now such thinking might help save a life. He had put too many cycles into this project to give up so easily

The Director, Justas was what he had been named he said it once in a while because only his title was ever used, it was like he was two people one of which had been banished rarely showing himself. He had turned his chair so now he sat looking out at the city before him. He had achieved so much in his lifetime but he felt he still had much to do. He had been the son of a geneticist the man never achieved anything, but he loved his son. Justas struggled all through his early years, learning did not come easy for him and it seemed like this with life too. His father had used him as a test subject, perhaps he could use his own mind to improve his sons. Justas at that time had hated his father thinking he wasn't good enough for him, several months went by, he could see the frustration of his father. Justas knew how to behave, to seem like there was no more improvement, but Justas felt the stirrings several weeks into the experimentation, a curiosity to know, so when he was alone, he would read, experiment and with each day he could feel a confidence growing that he had never known before, but always keeping it hidden from the rest of the world, this world had learned to underestimate him and when people did that they usually paid dearly because he was a patient man and he liked the chase much more than the end result. Justas knew to hold back and wait, the natural arrogance of his society had helped him through his life, he had learnt how to read a person or a situation by peoples moves or the inflection in their words and when a chance meeting with a member of the world council had occurred, he saw what he wanted from life, it was easy climbing that political ladder. What threat could he ever be? It was while his associates were thinking about that, that was usually the time he struck. Some accused him of being a Dictator never to his face, when he found out, they suffered through misfortune to their families and when he could take no more then he took their lives, he only had to do that three times, everyone knew it was him but proving it was never going to happen. He knew Marlac was holding back, which was common what he enjoyed was finding out those secrets. He could have had Marlac terminated, after all he had gone as far as he could with this endeavour of his, but he still might learn something of use Marlac called all his team together for a conference the more people who knew about the termination order the more likely it would reach the right peoples ears, obviously he couldn't put it that way, he had to make it known that Stylar was no longer their primary concern, as he started prioritising what needed to happen he could feel the disbelief, many obviously felt the same way he did and he was sure if he could have looked into their eyes he would have seen disgust. He wondered if they were here now listening, he hadn't decided whether they could be male or female, the males in this group if he was brutally honest didn't have the intelligence to be this devious, but perhaps now was not the time to underestimate anyone in his presence. Marlac had suspected there had been someone on his team, a previous medical trial, it had involved fifteen years of painstaking research that had ended when the facility had mysteriously burnt down but it had not ended their research obviously was always backed up but that data was infected by a virus all data was dumped because the virus would perhaps destroyed dozens of other projects he had been fortunate enough to not be the head of that project, the head was all they found of that poor individual , his family were never located. Marlac had made sure no one from that project found their way onto his team, even if members were known they were automatically taken off the list of candidates, there were other incidents blamed on accidents, but to his way of thinking they were too coincidental. This was a test if the young male was taken it would be enough to start an investigation. The boy would be safe, so the saying two birds with one stone applied. He had said enough for a plan to be put in motion, his as well as theirs, whoever they were, he dismissed the gathering all went off to continue with their assignments.

Glarai had been an assistant for five cycles, then she had been chosen for this high profile project she wished it had been on her own merits but she suspected family influence that had secured her this posting, her experience would not have even got her a position mopping the floors, her past was something of an embarrassment, not that anyone ever knew about it with the exception of her father, she had never wanted for anything, that had been the problem, she had never had to struggle, whatever she had asked for she had received and that had made her life directionless she went from one subject to another, there was no focus in her life. She seized any opportunity to embarrass her family and with that she had had a certain amount of success. She had protested for the rights of those who laboured to keep their cities powered, she had also stolen items that her father could have bought her a million times over, when others would have been content, grateful for what they had she had become more disillusioned, because she didn't want to be content she wanted to know what was beyond. She had heard the same phrase all of her life That's just the way things are She always asked the same question Why?

She was still asking that question, rebellion had changed to compassion, shame for how her society preyed on another and then an opportunity had presented itself working as a healer on the outskirts of one of the mining complexes, she discovered her talent for genetics though she had wasted so much time, she had so much to learn, more importantly she had met a woman who would change her life. She had never seen such strength or compassion in one of her kind, but if she was honest she had never really got to know the people she had been protesting for, it had been a rebellion against her social standing she hadn't cared. This female she had met when she got a chance to go into the mines themselves. She couldn't understand how they could work at these levels, the dust from the ore not only coated everything but it got into their food their water, they were breathing it in every moment of their lives. She had also changed the setting on her exoskeleton they were create to enhance the senses, the sweat that clung to the bodies as she was escorted through the tunnels would probably have been more pungent than she was used to, some of the passageways were cramped and she had visions of herself getting jammed into one of these tight places, she was so busy watching the guards' around her that she almost fell over a female giving liquids, because she couldn't say for sure what the liquid was it didn't look like the water she drank. How did they live like this? She was starting to feel uneasy she didn't like this claustrophobic environment. The male who was receiving the liquid seemed to be gasping as if trying to get air into his lungs, she could see he wasn't getting enough.

"Watch where you are treading"

The tone stopped Glarai in her tracks, she had never heard one of that race talk to one of her own with such disrespect, she didn't seem concerned about consequences for that lack of respect she had known individuals punished sometimes dying from their wounds

"I am sorry I just noticed he seems to be in some distress, I might have a compound that will ease his symptoms"

"The only thing that will ease his symptoms is to get him out of this place"

She spat the sentence out with a venom that made the younger female take a step back

"Guard over here"

The guard by his body language looked like he was just about to go off shift, his manner as he stomped across to her clearly was to intimidate

"What is this male doing here?"

"He is one of the better workers my lady with quotas being increased we need every able worker"

"It looks like the only thing this male can help with is fill another box in the morgue, I want you to take him to the nearest infirmary, give whoever sees him these instructions"

Glarai handed the large male a coded card with the weak males' readouts and possible treatments for the symptoms

"But lady I am just about to go off shift, I am stationed in sector twelve, the hospital complex is in sector five"

"Your point is what?"

Glarai asked her patience wearing thin

"I could take up your attitude with your superiors"

The guard visibly straightened up when they were mentioned

"That will not be necessary my lady, it will be my honour to carry out your request and escort this man to the medical facility, I am sorry if I offended you it was not my intention, I hope this incident doesn't have to go any further?"

"I hope it doesn't either sergeant"

The guard seemed a little distressed that she had made a note of his rank, now he was aware it would not be hard to find out his name, though she could have simply asked him, Glarai stepped aside so the sergeant could help pick the male up

"On your feet you worthless"

It was as if for a moment he had forgotten Glarai was there, he bent down and physically picked the male up and half carried half dragged the old male towards a transit tube that only security normally used

"Sergeant you need to carry him"

Glarai said it in a way that left no room for interpretation, these damn exoskeletons whatever look she had on her face was wasted behind her faceplate

The sergeant said something under his breath but did as he was told. Glarai watched him go with some amusement, Glarai had met the commander of this unit a few times, she had heard some refer to him as the dark one, perhaps for his demeanour? Just the mention of his name always seemed to have the desired effect. the older female had risen to her feet and was patting herself down not that it looked like it would help much everyone was covered in an oily grey film

"Thank you for your assistance lady but if your people were as civilised as they pretended he would have already been receiving medical attention"

She turned and had taken a couple of steps before the younger females' words stopped her

"You are right"

Rani stopped

"Excuse me?"

"Eh I said you are right. Rani is it? My name is Glarai"

Rani walked back towards the female, the uniform was the only clue, her voice was distorted like the rest the suit was smaller, muscle less developed, this female seemed different she seemed to want to talk. Rani could not remember ever encountering anyone like her, perhaps there was compassion in the voice, it was hard to tell. Could she take a chance and find out? it was their first of many meetings they had become like teacher and pupil, it was neither of their intentions to get as close as they had, in the beginning it had been curiosity, neither trusting the other, trust took time to build. Rani had told of a hierarchical society, she never mentioned names, perhaps that was as much for Glarais benefit as for Rani because if either of them were ever interrogated the only names they knew were one another's

That had been almost seven cycles ago. Glarai tried to look like she wasn't rushing from the facility. Rani had provided a contact, she was young, but extremely intuitive and she always seemed to know when Glarai wanted to meet with her friend. Where was the blasted girl? Normally she would be working close by, Glarai glanced into the ward she was there talking with one of the mothers. That was Kylar, she was starting to suspect this was more than coincidence. Did they already know about her son? The ward was monitored how could she get the girls attention, as if she sensed Glarai looked up making eye contact, the girls name was Tarise and she said something to the female and then made her way over to Glarai stopping a couple of times to check on other females

"You have a message for Rani my lady? Before you ask, some of the community are more than we seem. I could take your thoughts but I sense we need to move quickly on what you have to share with us Yes, it concerns her son, I was beginning to wonder if you already knew"

"Stylar?"

Tarises eyes snapped open but she didn't seem to be there, it was as if she was in another place. Someone else's mind? She had heard of those experiments, after the trials had been completed she thought all the test subjects were thought to pose too big a threat and they were dealt with by extreme measures. Glarai was becoming concerned they were not exactly hidden where they were stood. She heard footsteps getting closer and not just one set, it sounded like maybe half a dozen individuals. Well she hoped they had got the message because any moment they would be seen an arm, then the rest of the first guard followed by his colleagues, they didn't seem concerned by the two females that were standing in the corridor, clearly a doctor and a female taken from the mines, the guards approached. Glarai was thinking of something to say when they walked past and continued down the corridor, it was as if the guards had not seen them. Glarai didn't understand what had just happened? Tarise suddenly found her voice

"He can't be killed, he has a part to play in the future of my people, some even believe he may be the one the prophecy speaks of"

"So we can't let him die but does anyone have an idea how we can save him? We can't just walk in to the observation wing just because you can't see security it doesn't mean it's not there Who will terminate the child?"

"Marlac will probably carry out the termination he created him it's his responsibility"

"How will it be carried out?"

"Marlac is a traditionalist so I expect he will use lethal injection, that's how it has been done for centuries it's a tried and tested way of execution. Perhaps I could manipulate others into choosing me to help Marlac with that duty, we have stores of what will be used I will have to exchange the dose for a chemical that will give the appearance of death, I can think of a couple of possibilities. I can reprogram the sensors to give false readings just in case the toxin doesn't quite have the desired effect. I will excuse myself just after Stylar is terminated, I know where security places their guards. We don't like to admit it but our numbers aren't as great as you probably think and our equipment hasn't been updated since before you were born. We have become arrogant in our approach to how we watch your people, our weapons our technology is superior but our numbers are few"

The plan was made but there were a lot of unknowns, it was about timing and assumptions. The fact they were relying on one of their masters. Did not sit well with the council. Marlac decided to assist if there was an attempt to remove the boy before he was terminated he would make sure they had a big enough window to escape. Glarais name had been put forward to help carry out the termination, he would not normally have thought of the female for this task, she was adequate in her position, but know more than that, she had got a position on his staff by manipulation and a promising young geneticist had lost his place to her, he had sensed that he should agree to the appointment, perhaps if he hadn't his funding might have been cut

Rani had heard the plan it sounded like a lot of individuals might lose their lives that day, if security were alerted to the possibility of a breach in the facility. Rani had decided she would be of use taking procession of the young males' corpse, because that is the state he would be in when the community took him in. Rani would hide in the shadows like her people had always done, she hoped Marlac didn't want to examine the body after he was terminated, he was a geneticist of course he would. How would the theft of this body be explained? Tarise was skilled but Glarai doubted she could evade the facilities forces

Marlac paced his lab it was almost time to make his way to the place where the termination would be carried out. If someone was planning to save the young males life that someone needed to hurry. Marlac was starting to feel paranoid about his paranoia. Perhaps it was that old age catching up with him, he guessed he would find out in the next half an hour, he was prepared as he could be a vial of toxin would be brought by an assistant, his task was to load a hypo and inject the contents into an artery. He had waited long enough it was time to do the deed, he walked slowly from his lab all his equipment was within a hundred metres, he remembered the first project he had been a part of ten times as many staff and the project had been so insignificant that he had forgotten what it had been about, he had hoped this facility would be rejuvenated by such an operation, but like the rest of the world the finances were no longer available, he thought this would have been different, he had left nothing to chance, but here he was just about to end the life of an individual who was the first of his species, perhaps he had finally found something that the Director feared, not the man , but the idea, perhaps he was mortal after all and feared the Spector of death as much as any of them did. Tarise saw the geneticist approaching she thought no turning back now, Marlac entered the room he took a deep breath, thinking there's no turning back now. Dianer looked at the monitor thinking no turning back now Marlac noticed Tarise he hadn't expected to see one of her kind there

"Should you be here girl?"

"I have been assisting lady Glarai she was called away to check on the children. If you would rather another assistant?"

"No, no it doesn't matter it's not as if we are trying to save a life is it"

Marlac pressed his finger to the cabinet that held the toxin, a grinding noise assaulted his ears as if the piece of equipment hadn't been opened in a decade which perhaps it hadn't, after the grinding, the clamps released and then as if still protesting it hissed as the seal was exposed once more to air, vapour escaping into the warm temperature of the room. Tarise took a vial of the toxin, she had her back to the camera and she switched that vial for the compound Glarai had thought suitable for the occasion. Tarise pressed the cabinet shut and turned handing Marlac the vial, it took him just a moment to load it, there was an audible sigh as the hypo released its contents into the young males' bloodstream, the boy's body began to convulse, white froth trickled to his chin, the convulsions lasted several minutes then his head went to one side. Tarise concentrated on the machine it took only a fraction of what she was capable of "Is there anything further doctor?"

The doctor checked the boys pulse for a moment he thought he counted a beat, then nothing, perhaps the beat had been residual energy

"You can dispose of the body in the usual manner"

Tarise nodded solemnly it was going to plan, incineration would make sure a body was never looked for. Marlac left the chamber and Tarise unhooked all the equipment. Marlac reappeared at the entrance. Perhaps he had had a change of heart

"Tarise is it? When you have disposed of the specimen could you ready Kylar for her journey back to the community? In fact, if you are not needed could you perhaps take her?"

"I will do as you ask"

Marlac once more was gone no doubt entering the details of the termination into the official records. just outside the facilities boundaries was a guard post normally manned. Tarise had wondered how Rani would get the boy past them, to be honest she often wondered about the relative freedom Rani always seemed to enjoy. Enjoy was the wrong word, she didn't seem to fear her so called masters, most, no all of her people to travel beyond their boundaries they needed authorisation from someone in the Directors office. Tarise had given herself ten minutes to find Rani, she sensed she was close, heavy boots were coming her way, she had nowhere to hide she didn't know the section very well. Tarise had borrowed Glarais identification card, the route Tarise was now taking was haunting, so much left unfinished, sheets covered up whole sections, she began to use her gifts her mind searching out possible threats, a whole squad could be hidden behind the sheets, the section had nothing of importance in it. So why were there guards here? Tarise noticed a vent perhaps three metres high, she could perhaps just make it but what about the child she was carrying, she didn't have the time for both. Then he was in her head almost like a scream she almost dropped him. Lift me. She didn't have time to guess she took the infant off the trolley she had been using, his eyes were open, she had thought he would need to be revived when they made it back to the community. Had the plan changed? She lifted the male he pulled on the vent, metal began creaking as it slowly came away from the mountings, the vent cover dropped Tarise stuck her foot out it hit it, the vent cover was heavier than she thought it was and she grimaced from the impact, but the sound had been muffled, the male was already in the vent. Tarise hid the vent cover behind a piece of sheeting that now was everywhere and hoisted herself up into the narrow crawl space. She could hear them she fell silent and waited, they were getting closer, now even her breath was being held, they were almost there, they seemed to be conversing with one another, she listened it was as if they had just been wasting time and then they were past and gone, she listened until the sound of their boots and voices were like a whisper. Time is running out. Once more the voice inside her head. Tarise dropped to the ground, she barely had time to look up as the young male launched himself from the opening no fear that she wouldn't catch him, it felt as if he trusted her unquestioningly, she snatched him from the air and she was running. Get me out of the complex I will do the rest. The voice seemed to echo, where the chamber was sterile and clean, this section was coated in dust, footprints could be seen on the floor but none of them looked recent, her progress had slowed, her pulse quickened, wondering if it was really going to be that easy, she stopped. Did she hear something? She slid on the dusty floor, waited several seconds before continuing on, a door ahead she looked up just a moment later and she would have collided with it, once more she slid on the dirty floor fumbling in her overall for that damn key card, the overall seemed always to have twice as many pockets as was needed and it was only when she reached into the seventh pocket did her hand find what it was looking for. She pushed it into the slot, this was old technology and several seconds went by she was starting to think it might, click she removed the key and pushed hard the door opened rather than slid and she was out into the complexes grounds, she couldn't just leave the boy there. I will find her she is close. Tarise placed the child gently on the ground, she would see him soon. It was felt they couldn't enter the community together though that was where Tarise would be going once she had his mother ready for travelling. That part of the plan she hadn't agreed with, because the child was supposed to be dead the council through friends and sympathisers had got the clearance to send "Kylar to another complex, it had been decided that it was best for both child and mother. Tarise had tried to argue for Kylar but the decision had been made. Tarise gave the boy a smile and then she was back inside the complex and he was alone.

Tarise was back in the complex she had found the first washroom she could and tried to clean herself up as best she could, she looked once more in the mirror it would have to do. Perhaps she had been stalling. What she was going to have to do next, was perhaps one of the hardest things she would have to ever do. The complex was a maze of passages and kilometres in length but only the heart of it was alive, it took her just over an hour. She stood before the large glass doors, took a deep breath, then another and walked into the dimly lit ward, it was night well it was below. She slowly made her way across the large room, that like the complex itself was only utilising a fraction of its space, she felt like she was shaking, she swore she could hear her heart beating, it sounded like it would wake the whole ward. Kylars back was to her but as Tarise approached it was as if she was sensed because she hadn't even seen her move but kylars eyes were fixed on her own, her look had changed from concern to panic in a matter of moments as if she knew something was wrong

"What has happened?"

"I have bad news Kyler, there were complications, your son slipped into a coma, it was quick he didn't suffer"

"No you are lying to me I would feel it if he was gone, he was strong I could sense it"

"I have no reason to lye Kylar sometimes things happen we just can't control"

Many of the females had stirred woken by the exchange, the volume rising without Tarise even realising

"I guess the rapid growth was too much for his system to take"

"No I won't believe you until I see his body"

"Unfortunately, if bodies are no longer required for study they are disposed of"

Tarise saw the pain she was causing with this lie, hopes were being shattered and the female, who had begun to rock slowly. Tarise went to the females' locker her original clothes had been incinerated, she couldn't look at her anymore. Was this all being done because of a damn prophecy? Was he watching, she sensed him studying the exchange. Was he making notes? She ignored him she had a task to carry out. Tarise took the clothes out of her locker and lay them on her bed

"You better dress quickly you have a long journey ahead of you"

Through her soft sobs Kylar managed to ask

"What are you talking about?"

It was as if the female was trying to stay strong. But for who? Her façade was crumbling. She had thought of a life with a son, a purpose, now that was all gone

"My home is only an hour from this place"

Her sobbing was getting more constant

"I am sorry Kylar but you have been transferred to a complex in the next province"

"You mean I won't even have friends for comfort? Or support?"

"I am sorry I don't know who signed the order, but I am guessing it was someone neither of us have ever met"

"Why would anyone take an interest in me, I am nothing, now less than that, all I ever knew were my caves"

"You are more than that Kylar, you are so much more"

"Am I?"

Kylar spat back, her expression had changed, there was grief, but there was also defiance, she had known loss before and she would get through this like she had before. She would not bow, these masters had taken everything from her, but her will was her own and if she could she would be there when her masters fell. Kylar now longer acknowledged Tarise she dressed as if in a trance and when they reached the transport, which took about an hour walking through caverns that Tarise had only been to a couple of times in her life, she kept silent, she was no longer, a friend, family because she had given up that right when she lied to the female. On their approach a rear hatch opened the shuttle was beat up, writing was scrawled over it, dents covered the metallic shell, some of its seems were coming away. Tarise looked at the male whose hand reached out to take Kylars belongings

"She doesn't look like much but she always gets us where we are going. Is she ok?"

The male looked concerned about the female who was going to be his passenger

"She will be with time"

The male had taken the small bag he was going to help his passenger aboard but she ignored his hand and climbed the rusty ramp herself, Tarise had never been alone, once or twice perhaps imagining such a thing, but right now she didn't have to imagine, because this female who had lost everything that made her feel whole was alone and she didn't even look back as the ramp closed behind her. The transport started the first time unsuccessfully smoke came from below, once more it was started this time, there was a juddering, smoke still came from the transport but instead of the greyish black it was more a whitish grey then it lurched forward, lights lit up the cave and it was gone

Rani stood back in the shadows, she thought she had heard movement, but not for the first time that evening. No it wasn't her imagination there was something out there the light had dimmed so it was hard making anything out the shadows that were cast hid much, all detail of her surroundings had gone, the subtle illumination of the medical facility cast long shadows but they didn't feel like they had any real substance, the ground was cracked unyielding like the caves where she had lived most of her life. A few shrubs had been arranged near the building as if they would break up the desolation, the gritty reality of the place. Rani drew herself forward she had seen movement, then she heard something strange in such a place. Giggling?

"Stylar is that you?"

For a moment nothing, then a little form came into view half walking, half crawling. Had this been the plan just to leave him?

"Where is mother?"

"I am sorry Stylar your mother has gone away"

Stylar was staring into her eyes as if searching for answers to questions he had yet to ask

"Will I ever see her again?"

Stylar felt this female would never lie to him, he gained strength from knowing that fact

"Perhaps who can say where life will take us, life sometimes takes us places we never thought we would travel"

Stylar raised his arms the older female smiled as she bent down and took him into her arms

"Are you going to be my new mother?"

"No Stylar but I will take you to them"

"Will I like them?"

"I am certain of it, where are my manners I haven't introduced myself"

"I know you are Rani"

"Oh and how do you know that?"

"I can tell a lot about a person by just being in their presence"

"You are quite a remarkable boy aren't you"

Stylars eyes went black. Rani felt something she hadn't felt for many lifetimes as she heard the words in her head

I AM DEATH

Then Stylar was once more his playful self as if he hadn't said a word. Rani pretended the incident had never happened but the memory would never leave her, she kept to the shadows, never giving anyone a chance to see her, she had been playing this game a long time. Stylar fell asleep in the females' arms, the sound of her heart beating, making him feel safe

Raldon held a neutral bearing as he slipped into one of the lesser used tunnels that would take him to his quarters. He slipped in without his mate appearing to notice Nairi was brushing her hair

"You must be getting old I heard you moving along that old tunnel of yours"

Raldon smirked

"Do you expect me to creep up on you woman?"

"It was the way you used to move"

"Perhaps I don't feel I have to skulk around these caves anymore"

"Perhaps"

Nairi said trying to keep the amusement from her voice

"I am actually grateful you are sitting down I have some news from the council"

Nairi turned on the wooden stool to face her mate

"Am I going to like this news?"

She said cautiously, Raldon wasn't sure any other time he might have teased her but the way it had been done, he had to wonder. He didn't know quite how to put it, in the end he decided he better tell her before she brought that stool crashing across his head

"You aren't being sent to one of the other complexes are you?"

"No"

"Well that's something that last time. What was it to show them how to swing a hammer? Well are you going to tell me what the almighty council had to say or will you tell me in my next life?"

"I remember a time when you were more patient"

"In those days I was younger I had more time to waste, besides maybe I don't feel like being patient"

Raldon smiled at the way she put things, he put his hands on her shoulders

"The council have decided kylars son needs a stable nurturing environment to grow and for some reason I can't think why they chose us"

Nairi looked at her mate, it looked as if she was in shock

"He would have had a nurturing upbringing with his mother. What did she have to say about the decision?"

"It was felt she should not have a say this child is potentially too important"

Nairi had begun to stand, Raldon took his hands off her shoulders

"Now I know Kylar and I know this decision will eat her up inside I need to go and see her. Can you arrange a visit for me?"

Raldons eyes were no longer on her, his eyes were to the ground, he kicked at some rock

"What are you not telling me? We have never kept secrets from one another before, I really don't think you want to start now"

Raldon once more was looking at her, some discomfort on his face

"She has gone from the medical complex Nairi"

"Good then I will go and speak with her in the bed chambers"

"You can't"

"What do you mean I can't, I am going to bring up her child don't you think she deserves some explanation?"

"She is not there; she has gone"

"Gone? Gone where? you are not making any sense. If her son was being brought here she wouldn't be far away"

"She would if she thought he had passed"

Raldon said the last statement so matter of fact like that it took several seconds to sink in. Raldon saw the storm that was coming, Nairi was loving and gentle but he knew there was another side and he saw that anger building

"Who gave the council the right to destroy her life like that?"

"We give them the right, the council can't just look at individuals, they have to think of the community as a whole"

"And isn't that community made up of individuals? What rights do we have? Even down here after hundreds of cycles it's still about class I have grown up listening to the stories, I thought we had risen above that but we haven't have we? If the child had been ours would we have been allowed to keep him?"

"I don't know. Who knows?"

"Of course you know they wouldn't have dared take him away from you, the community would have had the councils' heads. Kylar because she had no mate, no one to stand up for her she was brushed aside, so now she's in another community expected to pick up the pieces of her shattered life"

"She will be cared for; she won't need for anything"

"Will you listen to yourself she won't need for anything? Her son is dead to her. What could she possibly be given that would make up for that? I want you to leave before I say something I might regret; you might talk to others this way but not me."

Nairi turned her back on him, the argument was over he wanted to say something but he knew right now neither one of them were listening. It wasn't the first fight they had had, but it was the first where he knew she was right. He had defended the council, not really agreeing with their decision. He hoped the council would appreciate how many uncomfortable nights he had ahead of him. Last time they had argued it had been several days before he was let back in her bed, this one had been worse. He left his quarters, he needed time alone, he knew where he could be alone, hundreds of metres down his fingers traced what was once a seam holding thousands of pounds of ore, now like him it was almost played out, solitude was a rare thing down here, he closed his eyes expecting to perhaps hear distant hammers echoing through the cavern but no he was hearing footsteps coming towards him, they were confident and full of energy. What was anyone doing down here? The footsteps had slowed becoming more cautious. It was Dianer she called out asking who was there, it answered the who it still didn't explain the why. All the new seams were thousands of metres from this place

"It's only me girl what are you doing so far from the new shafts?"

Dianer walked up to him so he could look into her eyes, her expression neutral but he could see it in her eyes

"Oh let me think? You heard about Kylar and what the council decided for her"

Neutrality had now gone and he could see what was building

"Of course I heard what other reason would I be here with the spirits of the past, I thought I better get away from my friends I didn't want to take my anger out on them"

"Very admirable and is the isolation working?"

"I thought it was until I saw you"

"Well if you want to take it out on someone go right ahead"

"Don't joke about this, you know how close I was to Kylar, she helped raise me when my mother couldn't"

"Take a shot, I want to be of some use this day"

"What is wrong with you old man?"

"I thought I taught you more respect for your elders than that, perhaps it's time I refreshed your memory" A smile spread across Dianers lips she was in her nineteenth cycle she had never felt stronger than she did at this time, the male facing her had taught her how to defend herself and end a disagreement if she needed to, she thought about it then decided

"I think you better let me be, I think I need to go see your mate I can only imagine how she reacted to the news"

Raldon smiled

"What's wrong don't you think you could take this old man?"

He had just managed to get the sentence out when her foot made contact with his jaw, he tasted the warm sat and coppery taste of his own blood. Dianer circled slowly

"That one was free girl the next one will cost you"

Dianer went for another kick but Raldon had moved out of range and he used her own momentum against her, fortunately her reflexes were fast enough to stop her face impacting with the rock face as it was she cut her hands on the roughly cut stone, she cursed herself she had walked right into that, it was a mistake a novice would make, she tasted blood she must have bit the inside of her mouth when she hit the wall

"You move well for someone of your cycles"

Raldon smiled she would have to do better than that to break his concentration, he also wasn't going to bring the fight to her. He still suspected he had her on strength but no longer endurance perhaps a couple of cycles ago but not now. Dianer threw a punch, he blocked, he didn't see the other fist that bent him double, she didn't finish there she brought her knee up into his face. Raldon went down hard curling himself up for protection, he sensed her coming he lashed out with a leg taking hers from under her. Raldon clambered to his feet, Dianer was already on hers, she clapped her hands together unfortunately Raldons head was between them, he was hearing bells he brought his hands up in reflex, Dianer brought her knee up into a place he probably wouldn't be using for some time to come. Once more he was down he certainly wasn't having this fight all his own way. Dianer was approaching more cautiously this time, she didn't want to beat the male too badly, she felt she had already made her point. She decided to give him an opportunity, she took one step closer. Raldon whipped himself to his feet, his speed surprised her if she was being honest. Raldon had his arm around her neck, he squeezed, she couldn't get her breath

"Do you submit?"

Dianer couldn't get any air into her lungs, she struggled to get the words out I submit

Raldon rose to his feet offering her his hand

"You did well girl you must have had a good teacher"

Dianer smiled at that

"He never struck me as anything special"

Raldon began to laugh and patted her on the shoulder

"Next time I pick a fight it will be with someone I know I can beat"

Raldon appreciated the gesture but he knew she had let him win, to him it was a lesson, the days when he felt invincible were him. She was now where he had been twenty cycles ago and he knew it might take a few more hard lessons before he accepted the fact. Raldon had heard he would be next in line for a seat on the council when one of the six passed on. They were bureaucrats'. He liked an opponent he could face, not making decisions closed off to the rest of the community. He wondered specially now how they came to their decisions? They never took time to go out into the community, their thoughts, close minded because their experiences were now that old hall. Such thoughts were put to the back of his mind, he wanted to spend time with this woman he would have been proud to call daughter. Dianer felt the old males arm around her shoulder and she knew things would never be the same and she mourned that, but there was anticipation of what would replace it. She knew in her head she would never be equal to this male, but in the eyes of the community he was yesterday, she was tomorrow. Dianer smiled, the state of the male, as if understanding, he began to chuckle,

"I know a shower room not far from here, I know no one uses it, too far from where all the action is. I know we don't want anyone seeing us in this condition"

Dianer wasn't sure how many cuts she had, dirt had found its way into all of them. Raldon perhaps might have used the small shower in his quarters normally, if he was honest his people had probably seen him in worse condition, the passage was narrow, Raldon led the way. Dianer could not ever remember coming this way before, the showers were filthy. Raldon switched them on, they let the water flow, it started out like a thick greyish broth, after a few minutes the water was running clear. The room was tiled, most cracked and she couldn't guess what colour the tiles might have been when new, a few pegs remained she would use them once she got as much grime from her clothes as she could, the water was like ice, she shuddered as dirt began to run from her clothes, she brought her arms in close as if trying to find a little warmth, she rubbed at her clothes until their colour was a little closer to the original shade she eased out of them picking them up and hanging them. Raldon was a little more awkward his muscles were already stiffening, he felt at least a dozen bruises that would be on full view in the morning. He wasn't used to sharing his showers anymore, it had been a long time since he had had to do that, the water ran down her wide back the muscles coming into view as she moved, veins in her arms like cables, but she still had enough curves about her to say that she was all woman. Raldon remembered as a boy he had been taken topside, he couldn't remember why, but he remembered the statues, he thought they had been real people frozen in the moment, it felt almost as if he reached out they would come to life, the whiteness of her skin began to show through as the grey film flowed like streams off her and away to be recycled like all such facilities. Dianer seemed to sense her mentor watching her, examining her and a teasing smile came to her lips

"Why Raldon you should be ashamed of yourself you are old enough to be my father"

Raldon snapped out of his dreams it seemed his muscles were not the only thing stiffening up. He felt like saying something to explain his state but whatever he thought of, he decided to stay silent. Raldon guessed with a body like hers she must have that effect on the males on a regular basis. Dianer could not resist

"I am glad I didn't do you any permanent damage"

"Just my pride"

Raldon muttered under his breath. Raldon felt like a teenager, he still remembered the giggles of the females, the sly smiles when they saw the effect, the power they had over their males and it was agreed neither would speak of the events of that day ever, they both put their damp clothes back on, as an afterthought. Raldon whispered in Dianers ear as he came close

"When you said you wouldn't mention today to anyone I hope you meant especially Nairi"

Dianer still thought Kylar had deserved better and there was still some play left in her

"Oh do you think she would mind?"

"Mind? She would very likely cut that offending part of me off and serve it up in a stew"

"I have always admired her imagination when it comes to the ingredients she has to cook some of those meals with"

"Very amusing"

Dianer had heard the story of when Raldon was thinking of choosing a mate. Nairi had not been the only female interested, truth be known there had been several until one night. Nairi decided it was time to make her position clear, what happened no one ever really knew with the exception of Nairi and the other female, all that was known was the female was fortunate to survive and she was never quite as beautiful again after that encounter no one else seemed interested in Raldon. Over the cycles Nairi had been Raldons real strength always there to encourage

Nairi sat on her bed back to the opening where a door would have been when rani entered with Stylar who was holding onto her leg as if to protect him

"Nairi I see you have been told about Kylar"

She got no immediate response, Rani took another step forward

"Can I get you anything?"

Still no answer, Stylar watched the female with fascination, he had much to learn about emotions, this female was hard to read. Stylar took a tentative step forward, then another a confidence that surprised the older female. Stylar now stood in front of Nairi he lifted his arms up

"Are you going to take care of me?"

Nairi lowered her hands from her face and looked into the boys' eyes, she lifted him up and held him so tight against herself. Stylar knew in that moment that he was home and this female would protect him with her life, he knew he had much to learn so he would watch and he would listen, he was here for a reason he would find a purpose and then he would, suddenly he felt dizzy and he went limp in Nairis arms, she tensed looking around. Rani was already there

"What is wrong with him?"

"I think he is running a bit of a temperature but otherwise I think he is fine"

"What do you mean he's fine? He just passed out in my arms"

"Perhaps the compound he was given is still in his system, he just needs to be given time, at the moment he is just over a week old, his development is unprecedented, his body has to catch up with his mind. I am not sure even our masters knew what was happening with him, he is the first of his kind, I don't think there ever will be another like him. When he talks, I wonder who it is that is talking, there is a wisdom that came from somewhere. I just don't know whether its him, his rate of growth, perhaps half a cycle and he will be mature. Perhaps Glarai could tell us what she knows. Rani also wondered about what drugs had been administered to help with the pain. She had some compounds but she doubted they would help with the pain Stylar would have to endure, it would be a test of who he was. Change came at a cost she hoped the price would not be too high"

Stylar woke in strange surroundings, it took but moments to remember where he had been. What had happened? He struggled, his vision was blurred, there were others in the chamber with him. How long had he been there? His body looked longer, more developed. It was Nairi a male was by her side. He had to be her mate. The male smiled How are you boy? You had us worried

"How long has it been?"

"Ten days we were not sure you were coming back to us"

Nairi held Stylars hand in her own

"Are you hungry?"

"I am sure I could eat something"

That had been an understatement he had eaten six bowls of stew and several cups of water before he felt satisfied. Raldon had been watching all through his meal, clearly weighing options up in his head. Stylar now was looking at the older male. Who satisfied Stylar was feeling better, began

"As I see it we have a couple of problems, first is keeping Stylar away from the community, we know that there are those amongst us who serve those above by extracting more than just ore, as I understand it when you his adolescence your growing will slow to a normal rate?"

"Yes, that is what I heard several members of the medical team say"

"Then that will be the time we put you amongst our people, I will put him in with Dianers team"

"That got several questioning looks including from his own mate"

"Do you think that is wise the group have been together several months, he will always be viewed as an outsider"

"Then our young friend might be more inclined to prove himself then. Perhaps you are more concerned that the community takes more notice of that group? If he is such an advancement, he might not stand out so much. If I put him with another group he might be more obvious, besides I think Dianer will be a good choice to teach Stylar here our ways. I am expecting interesting things from you. I hope you will not disappoint."

Raldon seemed to have had a thought. Stylar saw it in the older males' eyes. He seemed to be weighing it up in his head. Stylar was beginning to like this male, he wanted to push him, find out his capabilities he didn't know yet, if it was for his own good or the community as a whole perhaps it didn't matter if there were benefits for him and the group.

"In a few weeks the trial will be here, it is a test for our young who have reached the age of six cycles

Nairi had physically paled at the mention of the event"

"I thought we were talking about hiding him? The test will make him known it's for the young who might one day lead our people. It's a barbaric tradition that has lost many their young over the cycles"

"I disagree it's a test of how our young face the unknown, it also forms bonds that last a lifetime. The test is about potential; it will prove more than anything else if this young male here is what we all think he is but I will let him decide"

Stylar had listened to the adults, his pulse quickened, this test was the unknown, he could potentially lose his life, he knew he was not being told everything but something inside him wanted to face this challenge. He had already decided. Raldon didn't mention it again that evening, the hour was getting late and they all had much to think about

Darnon was skulking in the shadows, his curiosity peaked when the old male had changed his routine. Raldon regularly went into the mines to talk with individuals on matters deemed personal, the males in the community seemed to open up to him, if a digger had problems they might make him careless and that might cause an incident that would cost not only him but others their lives. So if individuals had issues Raldon was always there to help with problems. Nairi had a similar role amongst the females, there had been several incidents in the last few weeks nothing fatal, but they had been put down to carelessness, it had been noticed that Raldon and Nairi had been absent of late so the question was asked. What other matters had kept them away from their people? Darnon knew he was missing pieces of a puzzle, but he was patient, he would watch and listen. He kept his body tight to the rock he was closer than he liked but he had to find answers, he heard voices, yes three distinct voices, two he recognised. But who was the thirds? The third voice was a piece of the puzzle, he had to get closer, he tightened his form against the rock as he crossed the threshold into Raldons quarters, an old piece of material was the old leaders only privacy from the outside world, most respected that Darnon didn't he hadn't eaten in too long, he was taking risks that he knew were against his better judgement, his hand touched a rock, it was lose, to him it sounded like a rockslide, he moved quickly the shadows covering his retreat aware Raldon had come to investigate the noise, wondering if he had been seen. Damn he had been seen Raldon shouted for him to stop. If he did it might be the end of his life, if he didn't lose his life he would be treated like an outcast perhaps not that different from how he was treated now. The curtain was thrown back. Darnon put himself against the rock it dug into his flesh, he would endure the discomfort, he dared not breath sweat ran down his brow. He did not move he could feel Raldons eyes searching for him. Darnon could never remember such a time, he was physically shaking, it was just luck no one had been in that tunnel, maybe he was getting arrogant? Thinking himself uncatchable. Why wasn't Raldon moving? was he going to continue the search or was he going to go back inside? Raldon was staring as if he could see through the very rocks. Darnon was now scared, the old male was looking exactly where he was, no it must be his imagination, it felt like the male was staring into his very soul. Darnon closed his eyes when he opened them the male was gone. Darnon believed if he found out who the third voice belonged to he would finally escape, any place had to be better than this

Later that same day saw Rani rushing through the tunnels towards Raldons quarters it was probably something he didn't need right now, he had plenty to occupy his waking hours, but she knew this couldn't wait a patient under her care had asked to see Raldon perhaps for the last time. He had actually used the words if Raldon had the time, truth be told these days Raldon didn't have the time, but for matters such as this he would have to make time. Rani cleared her throat as she entered his quarters. Raldon had been looking through some projections but at that moment she had his full attention

"What good news have you got for me now woman?"

Rani didn't like his tone and he clearly needed putting in his place

"If you reach one hundred cycles perhaps I will let you talk to me in such a way but until that day boy I suggest you keep a civil tongue in your head"

"I am sorry Rani it's just been a rough couple of days"

"I understand that and I wish I had some good news but I don't" Raldon sighed heavily

"How many were killed?"

"For once it's nothing to do with cave ins"

"Well that's a first the news can't be that bad then"

"It's Karniar"

Raldon was on his feet

"Where is he?"

"He is in ward two"

"You didn't move him to their medical complex"

"I have to respect my patients wishes, he told me he would rather spend his remaining days with friends than trying to prolong his life with his enemies"

"I guess I can understand that. But could his life be prolonged if he was taken to their facility?"

"I think they could give him another ten cycles"

"Ten cycles. Then why hasn't he been moved."

This conversation had not stayed in his quarters as soon as he had been on his feet, he had been moving Rani struggled to keep up, people got out of the way as he swept along. Raldon was like a force of nature and he didn't slow until he was beside his friend and mentor

"Karniar. How are you old man?"

"I told her to tell you when you had time. Community matters come first. I taught you that didn't I?"

The old male coughed and wheezed between words

"You shouldn't have come; I shouldn't have sent for you"

"I am glad you did. Why am I only finding out now about your illness? How long have you been this way?"

Karniar began to cough, his whole body shook, he gulped for air as if his lungs refused to take their fill and Raldon saw the pain in the old males' eyes. Rani put her hand on her old friends' chest

"I will answer your questions. Karniar has been in and out of this facility for the past five cycles, before you ask the reason you weren't told was because Karniar wished it"

"Don't you think I would want to be there for you?"

"You had the community to take care of, you didn't need to be thinking of an old man who had outlived his usefulness and before you say anything I don't want or need your sympathy."

"Rani could you leave us alone for five minutes I promise if we need you I will shout"

Rani was clearly thinking it was against her better judgement, but she got up and went to check on her other patients

"What do you think you are doing in here Karniar?"

"I was kind of under the impression I had come in here to pass, I have outlived my usefulness since I put down my axe, I have not felt whole, it is my time son. I hoped I would pass with a little more dignity"

"You know what I mean why are you not in the new complex? where they could help"

"Oh the new medical facility our masters had built, well I feel they have given us so much"

"Don't start that conversation again Karniar"

"Oh and what conversation would that be? What happened to you Raldon when you first came to me you had spirit, you said you would never work for our oppressors. What happened?"

"I will tell you what happened I matured, I saw how unrest and escape attempts caused suffering to my people, I saw the leaders of these actions executed, rations cut so we barely had enough energy to cover our shifts. I told you many cycles ago I would free all my people or none of them, if I saw or heard a plan that I thought had a chance I would put my life on the line, but I will not do it on a whim"

Karniar turned his back on Raldon

"You sound like one of those damn council members"

Raldon got up slowly, that had hurt. Had he changed so much? He remembered looking into pools of water he always saw a drive a determination, a pride. Had that individual gone? If so when did it happen? Had those people around him changed? Or had it been him? Rani had come over when voices were raised. Raldon said he would visit later; he had heard Karniar say don't bother. He would be back he knew there was more to be said before he passed on. Both males were proud and that pride over the cycles had stopped things being said. Raldon knew they both needed closure now.

Raldon didn't go straight back to his quarters he was too disturbed for that he needed time with his thoughts, not to be alone just walk tunnels he had walked a thousand times before, when he returned he saw Stylar asleep wrapped up, Nairis arms holding him. Raldon found some bedding and put it down where Stylar should have been sleeping. Karniars words would not leave his head, his eyes were starting to feel heavy, he was drifting off, his eyes opened he could hear soft footsteps, it was Stylar

"Raldon can I sleep with you?"

"You choose the ground when you have the opportunity to share a soft bed? I thought you had settled for the night with Nairi, I don't know how you will sleep, the way I feel but I will risk it if you will"

Stylar settled next to the older male, who still wondered if this male could be the prophecy he was still thinking about such things when sleep took hold. Stylar spent the night very much awake tears stung his eyes. He would learn a lot from this male then he would do what Raldon had always dreamed of   Raldon woke, pain in his side someone had just kicked him not a hard kick just enough to bring him out of his dreams

"If you want mid meal with the rest of us, you will have to wash some of that dirt off some of it looks like it's been there months"

"I showered two perhaps three days ago"

"You wouldn't know it to look at you"

"What do you mean mid meal? What about first meal?"

"We all ate at first meal you slept while chaos was all around you"

Raldon felt like saying she was wrong, but he was already feeling like an idiot, didn't want to feel any more foolish

"I have never known you to sleep so long or so deeply"

"I don't understand it, I went to bed I mean I lay down on my mat, I was tired but so many thoughts. Then Stylar came and lay beside me, my thoughts seem to drift, worries I had were gone it felt like I was a child again"

"You were never a child"

Nairi commented smiling down at him

"I will be five minutes. Where is Stylar?"

"I just put him to bed, he didn't sleep well last night, I heard you saw Karniar yesterday"

"Yes, I saw him, still pig headed a pain in my you know what, you would think, I guess with his life coming to an end he would mellow, if anything I think he is worse"

"You don't think it might be as much you? It's just you both have large egos and both of you are proud men. I think one of you is going to have to give because if you don't, you will regret it, you need to resolve issues while you have him. He is the closest thing to family you had growing up and when he passes if things haven't been said it will fester away inside of you my love"

"I know you are right Nairi. How did I live before you?"

"I think you existed, you only began to live when you let me into your life, besides if I hadn't come along I am not sure you would have ever thought of leadership"

Raldon who was in the shower pretended to drop his scrubbing brush at that statement and asked Nairi if she could pick it up, she feigned annoyance but did ad he asked. It was then she felt his strong arms around her as he pulled her into the cubicle with him

"What are you doing you old fool?"

"I was thinking I might be prepared to miss another meal if you can think of something more interesting to do with our time"

Nairi pulled him to her, for her it was like every time was a new experience, she never tired of his love his passion and so much more, their lips pressed it was slow and deep the promise of what was to come, together exploring she felt his hands sliding down her body like hers over him, they both felt whole, the need was there as much now as it had been all those cycles before when they had come together for the first time, it was like a puzzle, they came together, with her he had no barriers raised with her he could be himself, no pretence no lies, he felt her caress her skin seemed to merge with his own any garments she had been wearing had slipped to the ground, the sensation of warmth, the feeling of belonging and Raldon missed his second meal of the day. Food was the last thing on his mind until probably after their time together.

Raldon had dressed it had been one of those days when he didn't want to leave her side but they had received word from Rani that Karniar had taken a turn for the worse. Rani seemed to think he would not last the week. When he reached the ward, rani took Raldon to the side

"He isn't fighting anymore, I think he just wants it to end, he told me to stop administering my herbal treatments which at the moment are helping alleviate his pain, now nature will take its course"

"Is there anything I can do?"

"Short of getting him moved to the facility which at this stage would probably kill him, no, just be there for him, make your peace with him, try and make him believe his life has had meaning"

Raldon walked into the ward expecting to see Karniar alone, there sat by his bedside was Stylar. The two seemed to be deep in conversation. Raldon cursed himself, they were supposed to be keeping the boy hidden, he was wandering around the complex, fortunately no one seemed the slightest bit curious and he was largely being ignored

"Stylar what are you doing here? Remember the talk we had?"

Raldon had decided to phrase his questions as if he was talking to a child of a few cycles, even though he was already thinking and talking like an adult. Stylar seemed amused by the questions and began to giggle

"Didn't I tell you to stop with Nairi?"

"I am sorry father I just wanted to be with you"

Karniar had managed to prop himself up slightly his attention was fully on the exchange

"What did the boy mean father?"

Raldon didn't like to lie but the facility was thought to be monitored, it was said over the cycles many things had been learnt from individuals leaving this world

"This is Stylar, Nairi and myself are adopting him, his parents were moved to another community"

Mostly the truth and such things did happen

"He is a fine boy; he seems to have an aura beyond his cycles"

"To be honest I had not noticed"

Karniar looked a Raldon

"I think there's more to him than there was to you at his age"

"You know that I did not come under your protection until I was about six cycles old"

"I was trying to save you some embarrassment he has more about him now than I think you ever did"

Raldon didn't want to have this conversation but perhaps this was what the older male needed, if he had anger it still meant he had fight

"I only had you as a guide. How much could I have learned?"

"I taught you what you needed to survive, there have been times over these last few cycles where I wondered why I bothered. I thought I saw something in you. I was adequate as a leader, you have been more"

Raldon was waiting, it never came the older male had just paid him a compliment. He was in shock, he was expecting another fight

"Perhaps you taught me more than you thought old man?"

Karniar began to laugh but a coughing fit started almost as soon as the first sound was out of his throat. Stylar poured the old male some water. Raldon moved Karniars head so he could drink it down without choking. Karniar nodded to the pair in gratitude

"I should not have said what I did when last we talked. You were right, you have thought more of our people. When I was chosen it was for my strength, my mind was never what gave me the strength to lead. You were chosen for what I lacked. While I was leader, I made a lot of stupid mistakes, the community became divided and it was that division that cost so many lives, many of which I had called my friends, with every death a little part of me died my son. When you took your rightful place you united us we became strong and I thought."

Raldon needed to stop him, he didn't want anything that could be used against their people

"You just lost your direction, I have to admit it because she's not here now but a lot of my decisions were made through the council of Nairi. You never had anyone like her"

"No I was never fortunate enough, I am not sure I would have listened if I had had someone like her"

"Nairi always had a way of getting her point across I have the scars to prove it"

"However, you lead, you made the best of a bad situation, you had strength but you also had compassion. I am proud of you son. You have achieved almost everything I thought you would."

Raldon had to ask the question, he guess heeded to know

"Did you think I was the one that the prophecy told of?"

Karniar looked like he was thinking about the question, his eyes seemed to stare out into nothingness.

"I guess that would be telling. Besides do you think I ever believed in such a story? So Stylar what are you going to train to be?"

Stylar looked Karniar in the eyes and said but one word

"Free"

Karniar paled as if understanding everything for the first time

"It is him isn't it?"

Raldon looked as if the males head was about to explode

"I don't know what you mean, it's just a word it is spoken of often but would you know anyone who knew its true meaning?"

Karniar didn't look convinced, but he was too weak to pursue the matter now, his eyes seemed to be growing heavy. Raldon called

Rani over and made arrangements to take Stylar back to his quarters, where he would have words later. Raldon had neglected his duties of late he decided to see how Dianer was settling into her new role, apparent they had just found a new seem, the biggest found in the last several cycles. He walked for almost an hour before he got in earshot of the noise of metal against rock, the colourful language used amongst friends and colleagues. He took a deep breath and walked out onto the platform, it was like you were at the centre of the planet. You looked up eight hundred metres of digging you looked down, that and more, some of the workers looked like ants, and every now and again metal hit rock sending sparks, an old male had said it reminded him of shooting stars, Raldon hadn't understood what he was talking about, some workers seemed almost fixed to the rock. Those who worked at the lower levels had their lives down there, it took perhaps three hours to get down there from where Raldon was now. That was not Dianers hundred. Raldon had been down there perhaps thirty times in his thirty-five cycles of service. It was another world. Raldon also saw their captors, only trained eyes like him or his brethren would know where to look. He missed the sound of voices all around him, the sound of hammers hitting chisels and in turn the cracking of rock, the smell of the oil that fuelled the torches. Like stars in the night sky apparently, the shadows that were like an eternal dance, the movement almost majestic as figures moved across the reds and yellows of the flame that gave them barely enough light to toil and the dust, here if you stood still for a moment it would settle and build. Raldon had an idea where the pit boss would be so he decided he needed a certain ladder that would take him down several levels, these ladders had known history, thousands of hands and feet had used them, just the feel brought back memories, the jaggedness of the material the slickness from the oil and sweat from the skin of hundreds of cycles of being used, the aroma, the pungent air that said people had toiled here, muscles built, muscles stretched and pain to swing those hammers until your muscles cried out to stop, he remembered some evenings just throwing himself into bed and almost being asleep before he hit the bedding. As he moved he was greeted nods of heads in acknowledgement, but no one stopped, four reasons, he remembered water, food, call of nature, usually more colourful descriptions and death. It happened he had seen it too many times, individuals seemed to come out of the very rock itself they were the same colour it was like they were being born from the rock, grey and slick until they all looked the same down here they were all equals, they were like different parts of a vicious animal, this was the community this was their strength. Finally, he saw a body he knew the male was swinging his hammer as if the rock had insulted him, sparks flew as rock was chipped away

"Terak do you know where Dianer is?"

Raldon had to shout the question four times before he realised who was asking and that it was him who was being asked. Terak lowered the potential weapon

"Sorry Raldon I wasn't expecting to see you down here; you seem to"

Raldon cut him off he knew what he meant, he liked this male but now wasn't the time

"I know; I mean to spend time with friends down here but community matters seem to be taking up most of my time. Do you know where Dianer is?"

Raldon had thought it was his imagination, the sounds of so many different. Water he could hear water and it wasn't just a trickle, his hand brushed against the face, it was slick. Raldon looked at Terak not needing to say a word

"I know a little close for my comfort if someone gets a little excited we will have that in here with us"

Raldon thought he had taught her better than this. Why would she be taking chances like this?

"You need to go down another ten levels How is it going between the two of you?"

"Oh me and the ice queen?"

"At least it's not like you are getting dragged over hot coals"

"No not at all whenever we are in the same place together it feels like I am going to be frozen to the spot, if her looks could freeze I would be concerned"

"She does like you Terak I know how she is with people. you should have seen how she was with me when she was younger, we argued we fought but I knew what she was really feeling She has noticed" "Noticed what?"

"That I have stopped working, she is thinking if I don't swing my hammer in the next ten seconds she is going to pay me a visit"

"Put the hammer down"

"With all due respect Raldon I think your thinking is becoming, if I put my hammer down now this life will be but a memory because she will find a place to put various bits of my equipment, that hammer right now is also my protection"

"I was thinking if she comes to you it will save my old legs having to go down to her"

Raldon was more than a little concerned about the working environment, he kept his conversation with

Terak light, he would pull Dianer to one side the first opportunity he got

"I will have a wager with you. If she is interested in you she will ignore me and directly tear into you, if there isn't she will greet me then tear into you"

"So I am going to get grief whatever I do. At the moment this wager isn't sounding very favourable. What are the stakes?"

"If there is interest, then eventually you will get her. If you are right and there is no interest a week's extra rations"

"I think it's worth more than that she has a temper you know"

"I will get you off your duties for a week. Don't ask me how just know I can do it"

"I will take that wager."

"She can sure move when she is a little upset"

"A little upset? That's an understatement"

Dianer swung off the ladder if she noticed Raldon she didn't acknowledge him she went right for the male with the hammer

"Now look here Terak, I don't know how you stay at the top of the ore extraction tables, I will have to start verifying them with others"

"Maybe I know when to take a break"

Dianer gave him a withering look

"I have had enough sarcasm from you specially in front of an audience"

Terak struck his forehead with the palm of his hand
"I am so stupid"
"You won't get any arguments from me"
Dianer replied icily
"I know why you have been so miserable of late"
"You do? Are you going to share your theory with us all?"
"I don't think you want me to do that"
"I am sure everyone is fascinated"
"Alright, you aren't get any. Don't look at me like that you know what I mean. When was the last time you were in any kind of relationship?"

Raldon tried to remember if Dianer had ever mentioned anyone, the mine had gone eerily silent as if everyone was listening to the rather heated debate. Dianer glared at Terak
"I don't see what business it is of yours"
"It is my business its everyone's business if it's affecting your work performance. Just answer the question. When was the last time you had sex?"
"You are treading on dangerous ground Terak"
Dianer warned the young male
"You seem very defensive I am starting to think you have never been with a male. Are you a virgin?"

The last word seemed to echo through the chamber, everyone seemed to have found something to do when Dianer began looking to see who was watching the two of them arguing. Dianer started to visibly shake. Raldon could sense the rage inside and it was not going to be long before it spilled out
"If I was a virgin what do you think, I should do about it?"
Dianer said this through gritted teeth
"Well if you want someone to relieve all that sexual energy and tension I would volunteer"
"So you think you are man enough for me do you?"
"I guess there is only one way to find out I suppose isn't there?"
"Subtle"
Raldon commented
"Yeh I thought so"
It was then a fist impacted against his jaw, he went down hard

"Now I have sorted that issue. What is it you want from me Raldon?"

Raldon tried to get the look of amusement off his face as he followed Dianer away from the issue as she had called it. Terak was just coming around

Raldon helped Terak to his feet, he swayed for a moment as if he was not sure where he was then he focused. Raldon patted him on the shoulder and whispered

"I told you she liked you, I think it's more serious than I thought"

It Took Raldon only a few seconds to catch up with Dianer

Terak was grinning while rubbing his jaw

When Dianer was alone with Raldon he could tell she was a little shaken

"He is right you know"

"You think I should have sex?"

"No well perhaps partly, but about the relationship, its concerned me for a while. I look at Karniar in that bed, no mate, no children coming to visit him. I want more for you than that Dianer. You have to have more than the work. We have little as it is, you are a beautiful young woman, you can have your choice   So you think the work is not enough?"

"I think you know it's not, I think Terak would be a good choice for a mate"

"Well if you like him so much why don't you take him out and get to know him better"

"That was not exactly what I had in mind. Don't you want companionship?"

"When I was younger I didn't need anyone, Nairi and yourself were enough, I have begun to think I need more, perhaps we aren't meant to be alone but perhaps I am just too set in my ways. Do you think I hurt Teraks feelings?"

"Not unless he hides his feelings in his arse"

Raldon began to laugh

"If anything I think I think he will come at you harder next time, he doesn't strike me as the sort that gives up too easily. I hoped the time you spent with Nairi would have opened you to the possibilities of a mate and perhaps children of your own"

"I have heard stories that Terak has several children in the community"

"He once told me there was too much of him for one female to love, but I have never seen him treat another woman like he treats you, perhaps you can't see the respect he shows you, but I think with him you would always be protected and always loved"

"I guess I have been waiting for a certain male to come into my life, it's like a picture in my head"

"Imagination is a good thing to have specially in a place like this but sooner or later you have to face reality, if you don't you will grow old alone. Perhaps it's not the life that is precious perhaps it's those you love." "Enough about your personal life, I did come to see how you were coping but I have a concern"

"Are you talking about the accident reports?"

"We have lost several good people in the last ten days as well as several broken bones and that cave in one of the survivors lost a leg, that new seam you have exposed it's a disaster waiting to happen, I have trouble believing you gave it the go ahead"

"I know you didn't step down as pit boss too long ago but things have changed in a very short time, it's about target now rather than safety, they don't care about our wellbeing it's all about numbers. I worked with some of those who were killed or injured. I will never forget their faces, yes I am responsible, but if we don't get close to our numbers how many more of our people will suffer?"

"I am aware of the problems you are facing. Just don't feel you have to solve all of them yourself, call upon my experience, I will always be here for you, sometimes I feel Like I no longer have a purpose, it will do me good helping you. I will be honest a few cycles ago I realised this day was coming when I saw how fast you were growing, it scared me more than I can ever put into words but it helps me to know that you will protect our people like I tried to do and yes there will be deaths but everyone here knows the risks and this conversation has gone full circle, find someone to share your off time with, it will help me sleep easier at night alright?"

Raldon brushed a lock of Dianers hair away from her eye and then said he had taken up enough of her time and that his duties were far from over

Marlac sat by his terminal, normally he could have done most tasks in his exoskeleton but the interface kept crashing, sometime even motor controls were going down then he needed to use what muscles he had, he shook his head with frustration since the termination of Stylar problems had begun to rise it seemed on an hourly basis. The children now physically looked approximately five cycles. His second choice to lead was not working out, the group had been taken over by an individual named Barla he ruled by brutish power rather than what was in his head which made him harder to control, which was another failure for the experiment. The experiment had also been about genetic purity, perfect specimens to take samples from and breed from when they had matured to that stage. Stylar dying had created an imbalance. Torrah was Stylars mate and the pairs were bonded with her mate gone she had become withdrawn most of the time they had to force her to eat, she watched the other children at play together and she knew she could never have that, she had taken to facing the lab wall and slowly rocking if she had a call of nature she just went where she was. He had also heard that the latest atmospheric test had been worse than expected, this world was close to death and only a few people knew this information, so this experiment had become more urgent. It had begun six hundred cycles before a great war, man had unleashed biological weapons, plagues and viruses on their fellow man. The warriors had been the scientists and geneticists in their laboratories, new vaccines were created, the natural immune system was enhanced. Clones had been created, their immune systems enhanced, in the end one alliance stood strong all the rest were gone, the cost had been five billion dead. The earth ravaged by fire. The alliance had another issue, their armed forces were no longer needed. What would they do with them? They no longer needed a defence. The government came up with the idea of using them where lives could be at risk. They had no rights they had been created not born, so the soldiers became astronauts, who expanded the knowledge of their galaxy, because in the past the missions had been to return to their planet now they needed no such consideration, the planet was dying and the search began for a new home, experimental test subjects and others went down into the planet to take from below because everything had been stripped from above, the air itself was mutating every time test were performed the results were worse. Where the world could have had tens of thousands of cycles left it was reduced to several hundred cycles. Marlac suspected no one knew how much time was left. The first exoskeletons were created and those above lives were changed forever. Those early missions bore fruit, planets were found and colonization began, each planet became a stepping stone the only casualties those who were never born. Marlacs race had grown weak the exoskeletons enhanced their withering muscles, while those clones, those soldiers had become strong, the minerals extracted from the ground sent to the stars because a lot of the planets were worthless rocks. Now one last push, a last gasp of a dying world. So it came to his little part in the history of his people a footnote but his children would replace those who toiled under the earth, but he could see his plans unravelling. Marlac decided he would observe the interaction between the children. Torrah would not be terminated because of her value as a vessel for the generation that would follow, labour was scarce his children had the potential to solve the labour shortage in just several cycles. computer were his people's lives, they were now dependant the suits even aided their breathing, so quickly they had become reliant, he wondered if his people deserved to survive, their bodies wasted, even their partners were chosen by the systems, it's like they no longer had choice or free will. Marlac had chosen the direction his people would go in. perhaps the Director thought it was his vision, perhaps it was he had chosen him. his children would probably be cloned and with each clone they would be diminished. Marlac watched the children play, there was a ruthlessness about it as if discovering the weaknesses of their brethren. Marlac had visited some sites, he had seen compassion, he had seen individuals lift twice their own weight so a friend could rest, if they were injured and it didn't heal quickly, they would be put down. The children's mothers had gone back to the mines so now his own people were influencing how the children thought. What he saw was the worst of them. Marlac noticed Glarai making notes across the room, the children had been put in a five metre square box in a room that was twenty times the size. gene splicers and DNA sequencers, several computers made harmonic sounds analysing data every Nano second. Marlac didn't like her body language she looked tense. What else was wrong? Marlac made his way over to where his assistant was stood. Glarai was keying in data, she didn't even know he was there

"What's wrong Glarai?"

Glarai whirled around almost dropping her keypad

"Marlac you scared me"

The question seemed to register

"I would say nothing is wrong the children's development is above expectations"

"You have concerns though don't you?"

"It's just since Barla became the alpha male it's had a detrimental effect on the group as a whole I had

Noticed"

"I thought you probably would have done; I'm also worried about Torrah she's becoming more isolated. I wondered if we should send her back to her mother, perhaps the community might aid in her recovery, I don't know what else we can do, she deserves a chance. We have already lost one child can we afford to lose another?"

Marlac was going to call the assistant mad but perhaps this was a possible solution, monitor the communities' interaction. It might give them some ideas on how to introduce the rest into the community

"Even with the rapid growth I am sure her mother would accept having her daughter back, I could say it was a genetic abnormality"

"You think they would understand that?"

"I think they protect their own and Torrahs mother is part of the community, I know Torrahs mother was just the vessel, but they won't see it that way. I know this is what's best for her, I see how Barla looks at her I don't think he understands what is happening, going on his past behaviour he will lose control and then we will have another corpse. I don't think you want any more losses"

"I will contact the Director if he agrees with our proposal. I trust you can make the necessary arrangements?"

Glarai nodded and watched Marlac making his way to the transport tubes

The Director looked at the disappointing figures from the mines, the extraction of ore had slowed the quality of what was coming out, was a low grade and just as he had finished digesting that information, he received a message from Marlac, more problems it seemed that the termination of the first subject had had a knock on effect and now Marlac was recommending that this female should be given to her mother, an experiment with an experiment by the sound of things, because no one knew what the reaction of the community would be. He wondered if they were aware of the threat these children posed. The Director did not move from the shadows he did not move at all, he was thinking about his response

"I am not pleased Marlac, you gave me assurances, every eventuality had been considered"

"With all due respect Director when you are trying to improve on evolution you cannot anticipate everything"

"So do you think there is risk sending her back to the community?"

"I think we would risk more if we kept her with the others. Barla had become unpredictable. Torrah has lost the will to live, we have had to force feed her since her mate was terminated and if she was attacked by the others I do not think she would defend herself, even without her mate she has value. The children within the community will be invaluable, to witness their interaction will help us predict the introduction of her brethren into the society. Our only other option would to be isolate her and there would be nothing to gain by such an action"

"Because of her rapid growth any relationships she makes will be short lived, I wonder if that might do more harm than good"

"I think now is a time for risks, because there is no going back, our time has run out. This is our last breath"

The Director nodded, he was right, there would not be time for anything more

"Do what needs to be done Marlac know that time now is precious, probably more than you realise"

The Director knew it was a matter of months, perhaps a few cycles but nothing more. The last of the great ships were being built, hidden from the general population, they would carry what was left of the elite to the stars, each ship would hold five thousand, twenty ships had been completed the ones that were left behind would die an agonising death, power stations would either go offline or go critical as their technicians all tried to save themselves, but the places had already been taken

Marlac was at least relieved they were doing something perhaps Glarai would still be monitoring the children if not he was confident she wouldn't be too far away. As he had suspected Glarai hadn't moved she was scrolling through data perhaps she seemed a little surprised by the length of time he had been away, if he had been truly honest he thought it would have taken longer to get his point across, the Director seemed to be distracted, normally he was focussed but clearly this project wasn't the only one he was getting reports on

The Director agreed with our reasoning, perhaps Rani could collect her? The female knows this complex better than some of our technicians

"I could escort her personally, I have done my shift for today, I thought I could be there with the initial reaction"

"Yes, I suppose now is as good a time as any obviously make notes and file a report on your return. I appreciate your assistants on this matter Glarai"

"I am aware I wasn't chosen for the merits of my work, no real experience but I am aware you could have replaced me once the project began"

"We all had to start somewhere and your work may not be the best, I have seen worse and I will keep pushing you and the fact you know these people might become invaluable in the next several months."

Glarai excused herself she needed to get Torrah prepared. The only thing that worried her was if she came into contact with Stylar, she had noticed with the other children that when a pair were away from one another, they still seemed to be able to sense their mate, what reaction could she expect? If she could find Tarise she knew she could pass the message on that they were on their way. Would Raldon keep the children separate or bring them together? The hard part was finding Tarise where was she? She had seen her a dozen times that day and now she needed her

"I'm behind you "

Glarai seemed to physically jump as the contact was made, which was hard to do encased in the exoskeletons

"Don't do that I'm nervous enough as it is"

"I have already contacted Rani she knows you are bringing the child home"

"Do you know whether she will be with?"

"That hasn't been decided yet, it will probably be a group decision"

"So it won't be decided by the council?"

"How do you know? It doesn't matter if it effects the community as a whole the council make a ruling

Raldon doesn't think this will, no doubt he has been consulting with them since Stylar arrival"

"It sounds a little short sighted that approach"

"I will answer that Raldon has always made decisions with his heart, sometimes head and heart struggle, occasionally judgement is flawed but unlike your people, my people know their leader would die for him and in return they would do the same. Your peoples thinking is clinical, calculating, cold and you know your leadership are interested in nothing more than holding onto that power as long as they are able. So you see when your people are like dust on the ground my people will still be protecting one another and so much more, we are subjects to your will but our lives are full because we don't know when we will take our final breath. Torrah will be ready to travel in twenty minutes. At least you should find Rani easier than you just found me."

Tarise walked away, fading into the shadows no doubt other tasks to do before her day ended

In one of the chambers a group came together the main individuals present were Raldon, Dianer, Nairi, Terak, Tarler who was very useful in reading the thoughts of others, Stylar was also present he had got a few quizzical looks when some individuals entered, when satisfied Raldon cleared his throat and began

"This assembly firstly I apologise for the short notice, this is about a decision that has to be made. This is Stylar, he is part of a final experiment that was begun centuries ago. Those assembled are the only ones who know about his existence, he must be kept safe, our enemy think he is dead, we thought he was too valuable to be just snuffed out. Already it's obvious that not only is he growing at an accelerated rate but he has knowledge that might aid us in the coming months, he grows in strength with each passing day and I can see when he would make a good second for Dianer"

Dianer now had control over such decisions and she was going to have her say

"I am still deciding on my second besides he is little more than a child"

"As I said before his growth well I would say he has doubled in size since he first came into our lives, perhaps a couple of months and he will be fully grown, you have that long to make your decision, he supposedly is the future of our species, which I think would make him more than adequate for the responsibility such a position entails, his wisdom might be more valuable than experience"

Terak cleared his throat

"As always your confidence in my ability to be a second is overwhelming"

He got a few chuckles and a glaring look off Dianer for his opinion

"Did I ever say you were my second? if I did perhaps I was under the influence of something"

"You are right my lady"

"Will you stop calling me that"

This gathering was supposed to be about sharing information it had turned into a family squabble. He didn't need to say a word the expression on his face silenced them both

"Now that the lovers have finished their disagreement, the reason for this gathering. Stylar is the first of the group to be sent to us, by adolescence the rest no doubt will have followed, a second child is being sent today her name is Torrah, the question is should we keep them apart and perhaps more importantly how? Torrah was created to be Stylars mate, they have a bond we don't know how strong that bond is. That is why she is being sent here so her mother can take care of her, from what I understand she was in danger of being harmed if left with her brethren, she has become withdrawn and if she was attacked right now she would not try and stop them."

Stylar cleared his throat

"Torrah should be watched for the next few weeks, anything suspicious should be reported at once, she should not be underestimated, we are children but we are more than we appear to be. If she does anything that threatens the community she should be killed"

Raldon hated how cold this young boy could be at times, it was almost as if he didn't have a soul

"If she does nothing to raise our suspicions, I will introduce myself after the test. Where will she be between now and then?"

"Torrahs mother works in the stores gathering what those above give us"

"I can eat in our quarters with mother and yourself. I hope she does nothing out of the ordinary, perhaps some sort of mind control, she might not even be aware she is under their influence"

Rani replied to that

"As far as we know nothing like that has taken place, we have a couple of individuals there that are with these children on a daily basis, so such conditioning would likely have been noticed. I would suggest someone with the ability to read thoughts or be emotionally aware. We don't know how strong that bond of theirs is"

"Thank you Rani for your thoughts. Has anyone got any questions? Well I think that's it for now any concerns I am always here to listen I am sure some have duties to return to. Tarler if you have a moment?"

Tarler waited until the chamber was clear apart from Raldon and Stylar, Nairi had been one of those with duties so she had gone ahead to prepare some food

"So your thoughts on their reaction to Stylar?"

"A few thought he was cold, I happened to be one of them"

"Will they trust him? I need to know"

"Raldon you know as well as I trust takes time, the best thing you can do is let the people get used to him, he looks about five cycles get him carrying a water bucket for the miners. I was surprised about him taking place in the trials"

"Yes, in ten days he will go into those caves have food and water for three days but expected to make it through seven days. Well at least no one ever starved in there that we know of, thoughts on what happened to all the children that didn't come back?"

With that question asked Tarler turned and walked away

Raldon turned to Stylar

"It will be good exercise for you boy, carrying the water we wouldn't want you going soft would we"

The next morning Stylar was woken early, he still felt like he needed to sleep but Nairi could be quite persuasive when she needed to be, the floor was cold under feet he just felt like putting his feet under the blankets, the three sat down together Raldon tried to paint a picture of what he would see and do, that day, their first meal perhaps oats or barley, it was hot and it was sweetened by something he didn't recognise, he had a strange sensation in his stomach, it felt tight he told Raldon he just laughed

"That's normal, its excitement, nerves and probably another dozen feelings, I guess you aren't that different from us after all, you don't know where you are going or what you are going to do. Who you will see, this is really the start of your life"

Stylar didn't feel like eating but he knew it might be several hours before he got another chance, the mixture had a texture that made him feel like it was going to stick his mouth together and the last few spoonful's were a struggle. Raldon patted the boy on the shoulder as he got up and went to the corner of the chamber and picked up an old beaten hammer, which he blew a dust cloud encompassed the hammer, Raldon stroked it as if it was an old friend.

"Where do you think you are going?"

Nairi was stood in the doorway her foot tapping impatiently.

"I am going to do a day shift in the mine, I thought I could stay close to our boy here and be of some help, look at these muscles they are going soft"

"That's not the only thing going soft, that so called brain of yours doesn't seem to be working like it should be either. Don't you remember all those times you woke up your back muscles knotted?"

"That is why I am glad I have an understanding mate who will rub my tired shoulders when I get back later"

"Oh she will, will she?"

"Well if she doesn't I am sure I can find some younger female who will be glad to rub my tired muscles"

Nairi turned away clearly not wanting the two males to see the amusement on her face

Torrah hadn't slept that night, but either had most of the dormitory, she had screamed virtually the whole night until the pain had got too much for her and Unconsciousness had taken her. Her forehead felt cold and clammy, she raised her arm it felt like it was burning, hundreds of small needles pushing through his skin, her skin was on fire, she clasped the wet material that was on her forehead, all she could see was shadows but she was aware someone was there they were sat no more slumped against the wall, it was her mother, even asleep she had that same worried look on her face. Torrah didn't want to disturb her she had done that enough since she had been left there, she got up too quickly she felt a wave of dizziness wash over her, she put her hand against the rock face to steady herself, she winced at the pressure to her arm, she had her head down for several moments breathing deeply, there it was again she had felt it before like a presence that seemed so familiar, now another feeling like being shut in a dark room and the walls slowly closing in, but something about this feeling gave her hope? Hope she hadn't felt since, that was it, no it couldn't be, they had killed him hadn't they? He couldn't be alive but her heart began to beat hard in the dimly lit chamber she searched for something for her feet, though still in pain it was like this blocked out everything else, her mother began to stir, it was like a state between slumber and being conscious

"You shouldn't be up you have been very sick"

Torrahs mother rubbed her eyes fighting to come around

"What is wrong my daughter?"

"I don't know mother it's a feeling. Have you seen my footwear?"

"They are by your bed, but I think you should be resting"

"I need to do something mother, I have to find someone."

Torrahs mother looked a little concerned.

"Are you wanting Rani?"

"No mother I have to find him"

"You have to find who?"

"I haven't got time for questions. Will you help me or not?"

Torrahs patience was non-existent, she was tired and hungry and she sensed the one who completed her was close by and like the waves of the ocean she was feeling the pains returning, she gritted her teeth until she thought they would crack. This female her mother had treated her with care and kindness but right now she was being treated like a child, yes physically but not her mind. With the others they had been treated as their intellect dictated

"I think it would be quicker if you helped me"

"I can't Torrah I have duties, this person you are looking for, I am sure he must eat, in the dining hall everyone in the community comes together for their food and conversation about the days' events I am sure you will find him there"

Torrah hung her head in frustration and she felt a wet streak appear from her eye running down her cheek.

"Seeing you are up come and help your mother with her chores, we might find him while we are preparing food for the day"

"Alright mother I probably couldn't have found him by myself anyway"

Torrahs mother held her hand out, Torrah took it like someone grabbing a lifeline, their only chance for survival, she was drowning and he was the only one who could save her, they made their way out of the chamber it was early but already a few of the community were starting their daily lives, the tunnels were dark, so much different from the lit corridors where she had been born. She could sense he was close, she kept silent she would not understand. Torrah decided to concentrate on where they were going, she needed to get her bearings in this new environment, they passed the dining hall and just beyond there was the kitchens, it looked like part of the mining operation at the far end of the room were chutes which her mother explained was where the food was dropped a lot of it far past its best, several vats in the room were already bubbling away, she estimated the kitchens were perhaps fifty metres square and perhaps twenty metres to the roof of the cave, perhaps it was one of the first excavations'? apparently it had been used for the last two hundred cycles, wherever Torrah looked there was activity, children scrambling from one area to another, several females stirred the vats, children sorted the produce, females cutting and chopping on wooden benches, everyone had a purpose and no one was idle. Torrah was pushed forward by her mother

"See the children sorting the vegetables? Go and help them"

Torrah stepped forward trying to look as confident as she could, but she wasn't used to strangers, perhaps more daunting was the fact they were biologically he sort of age, she looked back at her mother who smiled and nodding trying to encourage her. Torrah took another step, several of the children were now watching her with some curiosity a mixture of boys and girls, one of the girls got up clearly the leader of the group she came forward a friendly smile on her lips

"Hello I'm Clarah you must be Torrah"

Torrah nodded

"Would you like to help me Torrah?"

Torrahs mother was still watching trying to give her as much encouragement as she could from a distance. Clarah picked up a basket and indicated Torrah should do the same, they made their way over to the chutes

An older female spoke to Torrahs mother

"She will soon get used to the routine"

"I hope so"

That was all Torrahs mother could say

Raldon had finished putting his protection on which was basically animal skins which were tightly wrapped around his knees and elbows and a couple of layers to protect his head. Stylar wrinkled his nose, Raldon looked at him

"What's wrong boy?"

"Don't you smell that?"

Raldon sniffed the air, then himself

"Oh you mean sweat? That's an honest day's labour"

"Oh is that what it is"

Raldon just chuckled

"I want to show you something before we start for the day"

Stylar too had bound his hands, Nairi had warned his about how easily soft skin could be taken from his hand. Stylar kept pace with

Raldon as they made their way through tunnels and passages some bustling others deserted, perhaps thirty minutes and they began walking with other individuals who were dressed similarly to Raldon, one male approached

"I hear you might do a day's work today"

"I thought I better had I heard that since I left things have been getting slack around here"

The male began to laugh as he went on his way. Raldon pointed at a ladder which seemed to disappear into the darkness

"Hope you are not scared of heights boy?"

Stylar got hold of the ladder and followed his adoptive father they climbed for perhaps forty metres, there was a tunnel a tunnel which looked as if it had once been an access to another cavern, it was about three metres in height and he could hear noises coming from the other end of the passageway, the two of them moved quickly and when they came out the other end. Stylar had never seen anything like it, the cavern he couldn't even begin to estimate how big it was, he thought he could make out the roof of the cave but the light was dim and gloomy and perhaps it was his imagination trying to make sense of what he couldn't see. Stylar looked down but darkness took away the bottom, he suspected it was hundreds of metres deeper anyway, the sound of workers echoed throughout the caverns, voices as well as metal impacting on stone, everywhere was lit by torch light it made the cavern seem so more mysterious the site was not just sights and sounds, the smells, well Stylar tried to control his breathing, he felt like his early meal might come back up, oil hung in the air like a vapour from the substance and heat. Raldon smiled he could see Stylar sniffing the air. It was like he sensed a threat, sweat from generations of bodies was definitely a factor but there was, yes it was blood

"What is wrong boy?"

"Blood"

"You can smell that too can you? It is probably coming from up there"

Raldon pointed up to at first it looked like shadow on the rock face, but as he focussed he could make out rusted railings running most of the way along the walls, in some sections the railings had rusted to the point where they had fallen away

"They say that lab was the first where it all began, it predates the complex by one hundred and fifty cycles, so many failed experiments, so much pain, no one ever goes up there when I was a boy I was told that generations ago screams were heard from that place as often as the sound of hammer hitting rock"

"Hasn't there been any curiosity as to what is inside?"

"Perhaps curiosity about rations stored within, but as a sign of respect to all those who died there we keep our distance"

"But don't you want answers? Perhaps there is information about where you came from"

Stylar also saw figures in the darkness

"I think they are there more to remind us of our place"

"I think there must be more to life than this, this isn't life there are no new experiences, your people just survive, you are kept alive for their purpose, it isn't right"

"I used to think that way, but I always got the same reply when I questioned it, it's how it's always been"

Stylar looked sadly at Raldon

"If I can I will change our future"

"If you try I will be there hopefully to see that new future"

"Hey up there"

It was Dianer

"Just showing this young male my empire"

"What's this feelings of grandeur?"

Raldon began to chuckle

"We better go down before we upset the boss"

Stylar had not wanted to say anything but he knew Raldon would want to know

"She almost found me, I don't think I will be able to evade her for a few days never mind weeks or months"

"Yes, I know as I said she would be watched"

"I guess it's in our design, it's almost primal when we are close our senses become heightened I can't explain it, there is something inside"

Stylar and Raldon had talked through the tunnel and down the ladder and now Raldon seemed to have found what he was clearly looking for

"See the group of children over there actually Nebar?"

One of the boys from the group acknowledged his name and came running

"Raldon what's this have you started finding workers for down here?"

"I heard a rumour that you were the best at what you do, I thought perhaps you might be able to teach my son something"

"You weren't wrong. I haven't seen you round here before have I?"

Stylar was going to answer but Raldon pushed in

"He came in from another sector, Nairi saw him and decided our quarters could accommodate another"

"Oh well I can show him around specially if you will arrange a meeting between Dianer and myself"

Raldon smiled at that

"How old are you? Nine?"

"I am almost ten and I heard she likes them young"

"If you are still around in six or seven years I will think about it"

Nebar looked crushed for a moment then he was all business

"Let's get you started shall we. My name is Nebar and you are?"

"Stylar"

"Happy to know you, the first few days, these will hurt like, I can't really think of anything that hurts that much"

Nebar took Stylars arm

"Not bad you are already developing; I was about six when I started here. How old are you five?"

"Yes, about five"

Stylar actually enjoyed that first day, the group were very accepting and he settled in quickly and though what they were doing was important, the group still talked and joked together, yes the work was physically demanding but the day seemed to go quickly. Nebar stayed close and the two were talking when something or someone seemed to get his attention

"They are at it again"

Stylar was going to ask who was at what but all he had to do was follow Nebars gaze Stylar recognised Dianer and Terak from the gathering the other evening, the pair were perhaps six levels down but the argument had stopped many of those around them working. Nebar stood there shaking his head and smiling

"I don't think I have ever seen two people that were so right for one another, but they don't do anything about it"

A voice was heard perhaps a suggestion but too far away to make out the words, whoever it was Dianer glared in their direction, six levels down no one should have heard the suggestion but Stylar had the male had suggested they find a bed and workout their frustration. Nebar as if thinking aloud said

"I know when I find a female I am going to tell her how I feel, none of these games"

"Perhaps it is the games that those two live for, perhaps Dianer will let him catch her when she is ready"

There were a few chuckles at Stylars observations. Nebar shrugged

"It don't look like fun from where I am standing"

Stylar had to agree with that observation

Raldon had stopped working hearing the commotion, he had decided to make a suggestion it had been received from her obvious reaction. That was the trouble with youth they thought they had all the time in the world and from experience Raldon knew that wasn't the case, all around them were potential disasters, but everyone knew that so usually made the most of the time they had with the exception of her. From the moment he had seen Nairi for that first time he hoped he had never taken her for granted because he knew she was his world and he felt she had similar feelings for him. He hoped she would one day understand what she was feeling for now everyone started back to their labour because the heated exchange had calmed down, another problem was keeping things a secret, when the two of them finally made peace the whole community would know. He sensed the young males' eyes on him and he hoped their masters by the time they found out about him it would be too late

That night Stylar was ravenous he'd eaten a few chunks of bread in his break which he had washed down with a liquid the others said was water, it was wet and he saw things floating in it and as he gulped it down he didn't really want to think what those bits were, the sounds coming from his stomach couldn't be normal. Raldon just smiled

"It gives you a bit of a hunger doesn't it? I remember the first shift I ever put in, I think Karniar thought I would never stop eating"

"How is he?"

"I don't know, I haven't seen him since he said those things to me, I felt we both needed time. I might go and see him after we have eaten"

Nairi brought a steaming bowl of stew to the table, Stylar could never remember anything ever smelling that good. Nairi put her spoon in and stirred until satisfied and then dished out a bowl for their adopted son

"What about me woman? Am I not the head of this family?"

"Be quiet old man with that stomach of yours you could probably last a cycle without food"

"I'll tell you this woman it's all muscle"

"Of course it is"

Nairi replied giggling

"This young male is doing a day's shift now he needs to keep his strength up he is a growing boy"

Nairi thought about those last few words, she saw the growth almost on a daily basis, she wondered how he felt, constantly changing

Stylar looked up at her as if he knew her thoughts. Did he?

"The test is in several days; it will not do him any harm carrying a little extra weight"

Stylar had been thinking about the test and he wondered why so many had been lost. Tradition was the reason why he wasn't being told everything and that missing piece of the puzzle might very well cost him his life, because he already knew that being lost probably meant that the children that hadn't return had passed. Three days' food and liquid would be enough to last seven, he wondered who would be with him as he continued to eat his stew which now as he reached the bottom of the bowl he broke a chunk of what was a doughy substance past its best and soaked up the remanence of the juices, but still he wondered what wasn't he being told

Torrah had searched all that evening for the one who had such a devastating effect on her very thoughts, she sensed him as if he had just been there just moments before, she hadn't eaten properly since she sensed him and she couldn't remember the last time she slept for more than several minutes. What was happening to her? Why did she have such a need for this spirit, that's what he felt like as if he was there but just out of sight, just so many questions. She felt a hand on her shoulder, she knew it was her mother, but it felt like she was in a dream, a dream of such despair words could not even begin to explain how she felt, not only the pain of continually growing, but the need for someone that had been torn away from her that felt worse that was the pain that was shattering how and what she felt, it felt like she was being taunted and she wanted to reach out but she couldn't

"Torrah, Torrah? It's time for us to sleep"

"No mother. You said he would be here"

Torrah cried she was physically shaking, no longer in control of her emotions, pain like she had never endured

"Torrah you are going to make yourself ill, you need to rest, if you don't you will get worse"

Torrah turned to her mother her eyes imploring

"I need him"

Torrah saw that look the one she had seen many times since her youth, the loss of those close could never be understood, this looked worse than that because it looked like time would, could never heal such wounds, it also hurt that the geneticists had given the children a need for one another but not their own parents, they had taken their childhoods and they had taken the connection between herself and her daughter. Emotions conflicting but what she knew was that her daughter needed help

Raldon finished his second bowl of stew, in a way he missed that feeling of hunger, when he was working those long hours the thought of something hot and satisfying on the table when he dragged himself back to his quarters, perhaps it was more the anticipation, no it was that first mouthful the hot stew going down his throat and feeling the heat in his stomach. Raldon got up slowly from the table and excused himself. Karniar had to know someone was still thinking of him and gave a damn whether he lived or died not that Rani wouldn't be there giving Karniar all the attention he needed, knowing Karniar perhaps he would be better left alone. Rani had known Karniar since he was a boy. Raldon had never thought of the pain she must have gone through, so many times in her life, she had seen friends die, their children die. Raldon could not think of a worse torture, the tunnels had been relatively deserted and he had walked them without having to talk with any individuals which was the normal routine for him. He reached the ward, his eyes fell on Karniars bed, it was empty, it had been stripped he started to search for Rani as if sensing someone had entered her facility she obviously saw the fear in Raldons eyes as she met him in the centre of the ward, Ranis expression did not fill him with any hope, the look sent a chill through him

"Am I too late?"

"Almost he is in one of our private rooms he said the other patients had had enough of him coughing and wheezing, not to mention the choking and bringing up a strange mixture, he doesn't have long, so"

"Yes, I know Rani no arguments and just try and keep him calm"

Raldon didn't have to ask where his adoptive father was he heard him before he even made it out of the ward. The coughing was getting worse and as he opened the door, he took a deep breath trying to compose himself, then another one, then slowly he put his head around the door. The small room had barely enough room for what passed as a bed, he was already hearing the laboured breathing. Karniar looked pale, that vitality that drive had gone from his eyes, he was staring as if he was looking at some distant place. Was he even aware he was there? It was like he knew death was coming and he was ready to embrace that spectre when he arrived

"Raldon is that you?"

Karniar gasped the words out each word more difficult than the last

"Quiet old man you know how much I like to talk I will do enough for both of us"

Karniar smiled but there was no warmth to it, like everything it seemed to take too much effort. Raldon didn't want him to waste a moment

"How is that boy coming along?"

"He is more than I thought he would be; every day he gets a little stronger"

"Yeh he reminds me a lot of how you were at that age, perhaps a bit more intelligent than you were"

Raldon tried not to bite, he knew what he was trying to do, he wanted Raldon to let go, he wanted him to be honest

"He has the bearing of a leader "

"That he has it'll be an honour to be by his side when we are judged"

"So like myself you think you have found the one from the prophecy?"

Karniar wheezed

"I think I have to believe, perhaps it's all we have left our belief"

"Well if he is the one from the prophecy I can pass in peace, but I wish I could have been there at your side"

Raldon took Karniars head in his hands, he wanted to have the male looking into his eyes he wanted his attention

"Look old man I would have been nothing without you, you brought me up hard but I know every choice you made was for a reason, I might not have always agreed with you but I know I am here now because of you. You will never know how you shaped this community and your legacy will live on after you have gone."

Karniar couldn't keep the tears out of his eyes, which he wiped away as if dust was the cause

"I just wish I had done more"

"What talk is that? Everyone makes a difference, just by touching others' lives, if you made someone smile, laugh who is to say that's not as important as someone who leads a nation. You made a difference more than you will ever know, look at the man before you, you moulded him you taught him your values in the end he made his own decisions, but it was only through learning from you that I could make such decisions"

Raldon looked into Karniars eyes the spark was gone, his eyes were staring off to that distant place Raldon passed his hands over the old man's eyes and a little voice in his head was saying it would not be long before they saw one another again. It was as if she had sensed his passing, Rani was there at the door

"Are you alright Raldon?"

"I thought dust didn't get in these rooms"

Rani decided to humour him, he had just lost his father and he would never admit to weakness

"You know how the dust from the mines gets everywhere, I will make the arrangements to have the body taken"

"He will be laid to rest in the river of fire"

"You can't take his body Raldon, those above will take the body and either use it for research or dispose of it, the practice of cremating our leaders has not been carried out in over a hundred cycles"

"Karniar was a traditionalist, this is the way he would have wanted it, those above had his body through life his people should have it in death. I need you to keep Karniars passing quiet, those who knew him will be told but not the community as a whole."

Rani knew when to argue and when to hold her tongue, she was sure the news of Karniars passing would get back to those above, respecting his father's wishes, was who he was, that compassion was it a strength only time would tell

Darnon heard the news not long after it happened after all Karniar had once been the leader of his people. Darnon had found out what he needed to know without really seeming to be interested, the fact that it wasn't general knowledge that Karniar had passed was suspicious, several individuals later he found out that the former leader would be honoured like the leaders of old. Darnon started thinking about a full stomach, perhaps for several weeks, perhaps even a way out of this world that had become as much a prison for him as it was for the rest, any place had to be better than this gloomy, dusty, oily world, that greasy film that filled your lungs with every breath you took, perhaps the information in itself wasn't important, but it might be indicating the community were going back to the old ways.

Darnon had had dealings with several captains, but this information he decided he would get the most from the commander himself, they had met on two occasions, he was reasonable as far as that race went. Several diggers had been stationed around where Karniar had passed, a couple of individuals had been turned away discreetly. The Commanders office was located under a building not far from where Stylar had been created and later born, there were several discreet entrances in different sections of the complex Darnon knew an escape exit in part of the medical wing that had never been completed it was used as storage old packing crates littered the ground, old files lay scattered as if they had just been thrown in there. Darnon knew the shift patterns of both enemy and friend, windows of several minutes were invaluable and because security exoskeletons were non-descript he assumed that they blended in with the forces the medical complex employed. Darnon kept to the shadows as he made his way through the dark tunnels a skeleton shift worked but there were few individuals in the tunnels themselves, if he heard voices he would press himself tightly against the rock face and wait for them to pass he only had to do that three times, as he moved he was constantly aware of his surroundings it was that ability that had kept him alive as long as it had, he had reached the only ladder he would have to traverse, this was where he was vulnerable once on the rungs he was in the open, he would be on the ladder no more than thirty to forty seconds, he focussed, listening for any indications of activity, he did that for several minutes before he moved from the shadows and in one fluid movement he was lowering himself quickly, this part of his journey there was no point looking around because it was simply a case of he would be seen or he wouldn't, the rusted metal dug into his sweaty hands as he almost reached the bottom he launched himself off landing with hardly a sound another short tunnel and he would be out into the cavern that those above had used to hide their medical complex, the security section was different to the medical complex above, the complex at its heart there was activity but most of the outer buildings were unfinished as if lack of resources had dictated how much of the structures could be finished, the store room he was looking for was several doors away and, he stopped he could hear voices, damn what was anyone doing this far from any activity? Probably sentries killing time before their shift finished, he could hear them now their voices were getting closer, his hand tried the first door for a moment he thought it would be that simple, once more he used the dim light, his hand on the next handle again no movement, his pulse was racing, they were close he would barely have time to, he yanked at the handle it gave in his hand and he was into, he didn't really care he shut the door quickly, there was a click. Damn had they heard? The voices sounded outside the room, for a moment he thought they might try the door but as he listened the voices became fainter he stayed there until they were gone then slowly eased himself from the room, the storage room he was looking for was a hundred metres ahead, he checked that his tracks were not obvious on the dust laden floor, no they blended in with the other footprints left by those who used the facility, his pulse was back to normal he wiped his brow, he hadn't realised how much he was sweating. He was at the door tried the handle, it was stiff. Or had they locked it? No it was just, yes he had it, he slipped inside the entrance was at the far end of the room, activated by a shelf unit that blended in so no one would give it a second look, he pushed one of the shelves it slid into the wall, a hiss followed, then the sound of gears, that needed some attention. Darnon once more held his breath if anyone was close they were sure to hear the straining of machinery a portion of the floor slid away revealing a steep flight of stairs that descended further than his eyes could make out in the dim light, the floor panel began to slide back into place, Darnon was already descending using his feet to find the way to the bottom, he could hear voices but they were distant and even if he was caught he would still find his way to the Commander, he had reached the bottom, the commanders office was thirty metres ahead. The commander seemed to like his isolation because his office was the only one in that part of the bunker. Darnon was about to knock, when he heard the voice

"Come in Darnon"

Darnon felt himself straighten up as he entered a room with barely any light. The commander sat in a chair but if you had entered not knowing he was there he might have been missed

"You must have important news for me, normally you would go through one of my captains I"

"I believe it could be sir"

Darnon stammered, damn he should have taken longer to compose himself, his position already changed, showing weakness

"I, I have learnt that Karniar has passed"

"A pity he was a strong leader; my watch was always on alert when he led. So what is significant about the event? He will be either studied or disposed of will he not?"

"Well yes and no. Raldon intends to send him away through the river of fire"

"I thought I had made my position clear last time I encountered your Raldon"

"Perhaps he needs reminding?"

Darnon said with that he thought was his most genuine smile, everyone else saw it as a deceitful grin

"I believe you are right he does need a demonstration of who has the power. When will the ceremony take place?"

"I heard tomorrow before shift"

"It's not a lot of time but it will suffice. Have you got any other news?"

"Yes, sir. I haven't eaten in a few days I was wondering if I could get something to eat?"

The commanders head moved perhaps he was looking up; those damn visors it was hard to tell

"You will be taken care of"

"Thank you sir it is an honour to serve"

The Commander waved the man away and waited until he could no longer hear footsteps, summoning one of his captains

"Well captain any suggestion to the course of action we should take?"

"Our evacuation will soon be drawing to a close perhaps they should have this one small victory"

"I agree I will be glad to get off this rock, I never thought conditions would become so, thank the maker we have our suits and captain I want it to get back to his people that he has been selling their secrets for many cycles and his information has sent hundreds to their deaths"

"But sir he is the best at what he does"

"As you rightly pointed out we are almost finished with this world we have no need for such information and if we do take a group of his people with us I am sure we can find a suitable replacement"

Just outside the Commanders office Darnon listened intently but also trying to listen out for any possible threats. He had felt when he had been in the room, something was wrong and now he knew it was only a matter of time before he mysteriously disappeared. To be honest who would miss him? He had no family. But his instincts had served him well up to that point perhaps they would serve him now, at least keep him alive a little longer

The Commander leaned back in his chair it was sickening how easily Darnon had got to him, yes he had known where to enter, but the Commander remembered when he had been in charge of the elite but over the past twenty cycles they had left one by one more often than not replacements were not sent and when they were, they were adequate but pale imitations of the ones before, he had tried several times over the cycles to get a transfer but each time blocked. He had once even had an audience with the Director who had said he was aware of the situation and the complex needed to be protected by their best, he remembered the words like they had just been spoken

"I know this is no longer the assignment you were promised, the fact is the medical facility is nearing the end of its usefulness, the community no longer threaten to break their bonds and projects crucial for the survival of our people merit the kind of personnel that you trained and will continue to train. I know you seek challenges and that's what I present you every time another sentry is sent to you, because you have an ability to see a potential find a strength and hone it to a point where they are of use to us. I know I could not find another with such gifts and when this world is abandoned your service to its people would be remembered"

The Commander knew that a verbal promise was worthless, unless it was on a written order, it could be easily forgotten. He had been present when all this was new, he had seen the plans. The

Commander or Lerahn as he once had been known lived too much in the past, the assignment was almost at an end, then he could think of days gone right now he needed to concentrate on the here and now, but it was difficult when once his security detail had been in the hundreds now it was just eighty-five strong and thirty-five in the medical complex above. Lerahn had been sent his confirmation of passage on one of the last vessels, he suspected most of his fellow passengers would have paid for their passage by bribery, funding that helped build the vessels and perhaps favours done there and then or perhaps in the future and that was why his people would in the end fail, they had grown decedent and in these suits, these exoskeletons their bodies had shrivelled up. The community on the other hand had suffered but they had endured and now they were ready, ready to become the masters of their own destiny and perhaps that spark had already happened. The community were unified while he had started to get reports, several cycles ago about at first just petty crimes monuments written on, government workers beaten but as the conditions above got worse so did the panic. He wondered if his people sensed the end or was it the fact they saw those with wealth or influence packing up their possessions and heading for the stars. The Director had tried to keep things quiet but it was too big. Whole families disappeared but it was too little, too late, single individuals targeted became groups then the rioting began some did it for change others did it because there was a chance they could make credits for their own pockets. The Directors rivals thought he was weak, he did what he always had, he didn't attack head on family members had mysterious accidents, he could just imagine the male grinning behind that visor of his. Obviously those below thought things were the same if ever they found out, well it would be what have they got to lose. Lerahns career was his life but he would not be like so many of his predecessors and die while serving. His teacher had survived a bomb blast, it had killed his mate and their three children. He had said it was the price they had to pay for what they did, but each day without them he had died a little more inside when the bastard attacked his teacher, master or friend he did not even try to defend himself and as he died alone Lerahn imagined him embracing death. So on that day Lerahn had decided never to let anyone get close enough to be hurt because of who he was. A family was a weakness he would never allow in his life, so he learnt discipline, he learnt his craft and he became someone to be feared, his sentries became devoted to a point that the Director could never understand. Lerahn returned to his reports the past once more locked in memories

Torrahs mother looked down either the growing pains had become too much to bare or for the moment they had lessened, the girl was covered in a sheen, her clothes clung to her body, every so often she whimpered, she couldn't go on like this, it was killing her this need, so much more than an addiction. She wondered if the geneticists would have something to ease the pain, perhaps she should still be taking something, she had seen Stylar he showed no signs of discomfort. A shadow drifted across the cave wall, it wasn't unusual shifts and chores were done all through the days and nights, some were light sleepers and two hundred souls perhaps more tended to make tended to make some interesting sounds, then she felt his hand on her shoulder

"I thought you were going to stay away?"

Stylar looked down at the unconscious form, he felt the pain and though it was excruciating, he could still function

"She will never know I was here; she is beautiful isn't she? You would not think such a specimen could come from so much blood, pain and suffering would you"

"You were created but your path is not yet set, don't let all that blood be for nothing, don't you want to give those around you a life not merely an existence"

Stylar put his hand down and as if a reflex Torrahs face moved, he felt the connection like ants climbing up his body, he caressed her and a small smile came to her lips

"I think people have lost hope and I come into the community and people begin to believe I am some kind of saviour, I have the intelligence of an adult but my mind needs time to grow I need to experience, for myself, not have these implanted memories that I know aren't real so I can't believe"

"I think that is the first time I have seen her smile"

"She will sleep now at least for a while; I am sorry it has to be this way, am no saviour, it's just I will help if I am able to"

Torrahs mother saw the compassion in the boys' eyes and then he was gone it felt like he wanted to say more

Barla had gone mad, one minute he was sitting with his mate, it was only a matter of seconds and he was beating Fancer who had been Marlacs second choice, one of the assistants hit an alarm, several staff ran in on full alert, a captain hit a panel next to the alarm a faint mist descended into the tank until figures could no longer be seen, he looked at the timer and hit a second button the tank almost instantaneously went clear all the children were crumpled where they had sat or fought, Marlac rushed in if you had been able to see his face you would have seen it pale as he took in the scene in front of him. Fancer lay face down, his eyes were glazed as a couple of the geneticists got to him, he also had several serious looking injuries

"Get him to an operating table now"

Marlac could see the young males pulse was still strong, the extra ribs had saved Fancers life but there were other concerns. Fancer was not the only one in need of medical attention, Ona also had suffered injuries coming to the aid of her mate as their genetic programming dictated, she would die for her mate if it was necessary. Barlas condition was worsening, no one had come up with a plausible reason for his erratic behaviour. He saw his creators as inferior, they had tried discipline but all that had achieved was some looks of contempt, he knew they were stronger so why should he abide by their rules? The boy was only five weeks old, what would he be like at thirteen? they couldn't control him now. Marlac was starting to think Barlas behaviour was more chemical than mental, it was like he needed adrenaline, he thrived on conflict, perhaps like a drug? Obviously adrenaline enhanced strength. Barla could not lead the others, he led by raw power, the group needed to be led by wisdom. He needed Barlas condition for now to be kept within the facility, but he suspected the Director already knew about the latest situation. What would happen when he was released into the community? To learn from them, the way he was at that moment in time he would tear them apart until he drew his last breath. Because he would be challenged, perhaps he would provoke. How much could really be covered up?

Stylar stood at the entrance to what looked like just another cave, Raldon and Nairi stood by his side, he could feel the tension. The only curious thing was the boulder that blocked the entrance. Was it to keep them out or something in? the entrance smelt damp and musty a smell of neglect, decay and then through all those odours again blood, the smells that were not there were the torches with the oil so they burned brightly. Stylar was not alone four other children waited with their guardians and parents. Stylar could see the effort specially the mothers were making to hold their emotions back, an odd male also seemed to be having trouble, a tear rolled down his cheek he blamed the dust, but he wasn't really fooling anyone, the children seemed to be sensing their guardians discomfort, he could see a mixture of concern and panic in the children's eyes and the way they stood, one of the parents seemed to be almost at breaking point. Why were they waiting? That question wasn't asked but it was on everyone's mind. From the darkness the question was answered

"We are still waiting for one to come"

The voice echoed in the chamber it seemed strangely familiar. Then her face came into view it was Rani.

Raldon suddenly looked uncomfortable, but tried to disguise it with an observation

"You always liked a dramatic entrance didn't you old woman?"

Rani smiled

"I thought five young were to be tested today?"

"Then you thought wrong Raldon, there is a sixth of the same age her mother seems to feel she needs this"

Stylar had learnt from Nebar that the test was only taken by a few, those who came out, were changed and they never talked about what they had seen. Stylars senses suddenly screamed out and it took him a moment to regain his discipline. Raldon seemed to pick up on his sons' change

"What's wrong?"

"Torrah she is coming"

His heart rate had increased, his stomach ached he could hear his blood flowing. Raldon didn't look pleased as he walked over to Rani

"You knew the plan?"

"Yes, I knew it I just didn't agree with it, it's time for her to be accepted into the fold, I've had her watched since she came here she has endured the suspicion and the people who have got to know her have warmed to her, it's her destiny to be with your son. Who are we to try and stop that?"

"I know you have generations of experience but I hope you know the risk you are taking?"

"Existence is about taking risks is it not?"

Raldon nodded as if at least that he agreed with. Stylar was staring up the tunnel, all the children seemed to have noticed his strange behaviour, a couple of figures came into view they were silhouetted by the flickering of torchlight

Torrah had woken that morning from a fitful sleep her pains for now had subsided, she hadn't woken naturally she had heard someone it was her mother, she was fussing with something in the corner of the chamber, she couldn't see what her mother was doing

"Mother?"

"Torrah you are awake I was just preparing you a meal"

"Are we not eating with the others?"

"Not today it's a special day for you. You are to be tested"

"Tested? I have heard about this test it's for those seeking the leadership, leadership is the furthest thing from my mind, it's a struggle just getting through the days"

"Rani thought you might benefit from it; besides she says it also tests character"

"She did why?"

"I must admit I didn't ask the female knows more than I ever will and sometimes, some people you just don't question"

"You don't question when it comes to your daughter? I don't want to go mother"

"We don't always get what we want Torrah the decision has been made"

Tears filled Torrahs eyes but she looked away to hide them from her mother, her mother held her shoulders

"Look at me Torrah"

Torrah didn't want to turn around

"Why do you do that girl?"   Torrah turned slowly

"Do what mother?"

"Why are you ashamed of your emotions?"

"They are a sign of weakness"

"Maybe that was the case in the facility, but here they are accepted as who you are, never be ashamed of that and they are a part of our existence"

Torrah hugged her mother who responded with a little grunt

"Are you alright mother?"

"I am fine it's just you are getting so strong"

"I'm sorry I didn't mean to hurt you"

"You could never hurt me now eat up, I know it's going to be an interesting week for you. I am going to miss you though"

Torrah walked with her mother through the maze of tunnels, she didn't feel well. "I think I ate too much"

"Your stomach hurts does it? It might be nerves the fear of the unknown. Perhaps even excitement. We all deal with new experiences in our own ways. Life a tapestry of new experiences"

Torrahs mothers smile encouraging as always. Torrah nodded as if in understanding. Where were they going?

"Is it much further mother?"

"We will be there soon"

Torrah was feeling worse her heart felt like it was racing, she could hear it in her head at any moment she thought it might explode, it felt like static electricity coursed through her veins, she was starting understand it was not nerves, she had found him. Could he really be here? Was he about to take the same rite of passage? There were figures ahead adults and children by the shapes and sizes, but she was only interested in. it was him one young male stood away from the others, Raldon and was that Nairi? were there with him, she couldn't hold back any longer she pulled away from her mother and ran to the boy, everyone looked at her in astonishment but she didn't care, she didn't see, she held him knowing no force in nature could have separated them at that moment after what felt like an eternity she stepped back looking like her mother had wanted to see her since they were first united, she then punched the young male

"You made me think you were dead"

Torrah said with tears in her eyes

"I am sorry it had to appear that way. A few even think I am this saviour"

Torrah took this all in and it took only seconds for her expression to change and by the time Stylar realised what was happening he was on his arse in the dust rubbing a sore chin, it was as if her initial punch was testing him

"Torrah what are you doing?"

Torrahs mother for the first time sounded genuinely displeased

"He had no right letting me think he had died, you saw what thinking he was gone was doing to me. I want him to remember how it feels to treat me that way so he won't repeat such deceit"

Stylar got up there was anger in his eyes

"I had every right I am the Alpha, I make decisions the rest obey, I was created for this purpose. I did not take your feelings into account, I did not think what they would do after I was gone"

"So you let me suffer?"

This was the first time Stylar seemed upset as if he was feeling everything his mate had felt

"And I didn't? don't you think I didn't feel that loss you were feeling. Did you think it was just you? Well it wasn't"

Torrah hadn't thought about it he seemed so composed

"Promise me Stylar you will never leave me again, please just promise"

Stylar stepped forward and Torrah folded into his arms

"If I can I will be with you for the rest of eternity"

Torrah was shaking tears rolled down her cheeks and at that moment she knew she was whole again and could feel Stylar felt the same. Raldon looked at Nairi a single tear glistened on her cheek

"You're not getting emotional now are you girl?"

For that he got an elbow to the ribs

"That's what I thought"

Raldon said as he winced from the pain. Rani cleared her throat

"It is now time for our young make that first step towards adulthood, this is but the first of many tests before they take their rightful place within the community"

Rani nodded at two males Stylar had not seen before they seemed to have come from the very rock itself, their forms as if carved, it was only later that he would find out they were known as the guardians of the tomb. The two males took hold of the rock muscles straining through flesh, their feet dug into the ground as they strained slowly the rock began to slide away from the entrance, sweat was dripping off the two as after four or five minutes the boulder had been moved only just enough for the children to slide through. Torrahs nose wrinkled, the stench was indescribable she backed slowly away. Stylar was behind her and whispered softly in her ear

"I smell it too and I feel fear from this group, this is where and when we start to aid these people." Torrah put her hand in the one that had been offered she felt safe as the two of them led through the narrow gap into the cavern beyond

"I think it's time we introduced ourselves seeing we will be spending several days together I am Starr"

Stylar was next followed by Torrah next a smallish male

"I'm, I'm Kolt"

The young male stammered

"Now what are you afraid of?"

Starr looked away in disgust

"Do you know him?"

"Yes, I know him. I just don't understand what he is doing here. I thought you kept to yourself Kolt?"

He didn't answer

"I don't like this place it smells of death and decay"

"What did you say Kolt?"

"It smells wrong"

Starr interrupted

"It's your imagination it smells of damp; we need to get some light in here"

Stylar could smell the oil, the torches were here it was just a matter of feeling, his fingers scraped the walls, he felt his skin tear but still his fingers searched, he was using his feet too, he came in contact with something, he bent down his fingers felt something smooth, chilled to the touch. Stylars blood went cold, it wasn't a torch it was what was left of, it was bone, it wasn't completely smooth as if something had gnawed at the end, he tore a strip from clothes that were already coming apart, there were whispers in the dark, he had the comfort of Torrah she had not ventured away from his side. Stylar used his hands feeling the ground he was perhaps twenty metres from the cave entrance when his hands came across material which covered a framework, it wasn't very large, the framework was made Stylar realised quickly were rib bones it was like a graveyard. Stylar was no longer alone and for a moment he had forgotten that fact it was only when Kolt asked

"What is it what have you found?"

That he came back to the here and now

"We need light"

Starr said almost whispering

"I am working on that"

Kolt was rummaging around in folds of what he was wearing. Stylar could already feel the panic rising amongst the group they needed light so at least they could make out what they had stumbled across, bodies bumped into one another, but considering they had just met, there was already an understanding amongst them as Stylar thought about the light he heard the sound of flint striking and sparks that within a couple of minutes created their first light since the cave had been closed behind them. Kolt even though he couldn't be seen Stylar could hear what was happening as the young male retrieved what was needed from his own supplies for their light and heat. Starr spoke up she voiced what they were all thinking.

"We have got to get out of here. Kolt was right this place is death."

It sounded as if she hadn't really moved away from the boulder that blocked their escape and he, Stylar could hear her as if trying to move the rock.

"We need to stay together we have strength in numbers"

Stylar shouted he heard the shuffling of bodies as the group came together Stylar though intelligent lacked the experience of the young who had grown up within the community, but even the lack of experience did not mean he didn't have an instinct. With light came confidence, at first greying shadows, but as the flame took hold the group came into focus, fear etched on all the faces. The voices before had been hushed with their first light, they began to converse normally. The group were together what Stylar had found was fortunately for them not the only bone they could use to fashion a torch with. With the light burning now the others stripped materials from their own clothing, the material frayed easily not that anyone would have ever noticed and as Stylar had suspected there were the remnants of torches, panic had been replaced by fear at least two bodies perhaps more it was hard to tell the bones were not together they were scattered like, yes that was it the bodies had been torn apart. Starr was still at the boulder shouting for someone to let her out, but the parents and guardians had either gone or they couldn't. Stylar suspected that was probably the reaction to this situation in every test, it disturbed him that these bodies were so close to the entrance why hadn't they been dragged out. Why had they just been left? It wasn't just panic on their faces; it was shock as well for what was around them. The bodies didn't get in such a condition on their own whatever had done this. Was it still in here with them? He knew it was not respectful but perhaps they could fashion weapons from the bones of the dead, if somehow they could snap the bones they could easily puncture flesh, the test had changed from thinking about extending their rations now they had to think of survival. Starr hating the silence, she felt she had to break it

"I heard stories when I was younger about the children lost in the tunnels"

"Lost?"

"They are still here they passed trying to get out"

Torrah snapped back imagining them pleading for someone to let them out, the screams. How could the community continue such a barbaric tradition? Stylar had to get control of the situation, and quickly it was already a potentially volatile situation

"Torrah stop it. There is no need to scare everyone any more than they already are"

"You are only scared, the others knowing the truth if they don't they will pass in ignorance like the rest"

"I suspect I don't know the coming days will prove if my suspicions are correct. Firstly, I don't think we are alone in here, those bodies were torn apart meaning there is a predator of some kind and perhaps that's why these trials were created to kill this predator, but with many traditions over the centuries its meaning was lost. If this creature is still alive it will be hungry only if we are together can we kill this, in the past the communities' young were easy prey, we won't be if it takes us we will at least make sure it remembers the encounter, it will remember we didn't go easily into the shadows which it obviously has cast over the community far too long. Our advantage is that we know It's here, the difference this time, you have myself and Torrah we are different, the rest of you grew up together, we were created, we are stronger our reflexes are quicker and when we are threatened well my new friends you are going to see something you haven't seen before. we have to craft ourselves weapons. Any questions?

Starr once more spoke up

"Yeh I have a question who made you our leader?"

"Circumstances but if you think you will make a better leader you can try and put me down, but remember I have been taught well I believe you know Dianer and Raldon?"

Starr moved away at least she was intelligent enough to know when not to fight, he felt Torrahs hand on his arm

"I am proud of you"

Stylar just smiled the group had purpose so for the moment fear was forgotten as they started finding what was needed to keep them safe, the makeshift torches were put into the walls where clearly once torches had been placed now they had light Stylar could examine the remains more clearly, there was a nasty crack in the poor souls' leg. Perhaps that had slowed him down and made him an easy victim for the animal, a few of the ribs were splintered no doubt that had happened when it started to devour its prey, some of the bones had clearly been gnawed by small rodents, they were common enough in the caves, what little waste the community left these creatures took it for their own families. Torrah had wanted to stay by his side but he had told her he wouldn't venture far into the cave. Kolt wondered about their new leader as he fashioned himself a sling from more material from his clothing the rate he was going he would be naked in two to three days, he blushed at the very thought. Stylar hadn't told the others but he was already hunting, the animal no doubt dragged its prey back to a den of some sort he was searching for signs. The animal also had no competition so it considered itself that territories, owner, Stylar wondered why the animal was down there. Perhaps it came from the surface? Their prey to bigger animals but down here he was top of the food chain. Stylar wasn't alone he had taken Nolic who had been the quietest of the group and Xery who Stylar was already discovering had an opinion on every subject. Torrah had wanted to stay with him but he said he didn't intend to go far. Stylars senses searched out, there had been no more evidence of corpses he wondered if he would smell them long before he saw them, there was an indentation in the ground, it wasn't carved by metal as Stylar examined it Nolic bent down, he blew and dust lifted into the air, now the indentation made an ominous sense

"It's a giant"

Stylar couldn't argue with that assessment the footprint was twice the size of his. What was it doing down here? Another mystery before the first one was solved. Was it his imagination or had they been travelling upwards? It felt drier the air was warm it had taken on a taste that Stylar didn't like, he didn't like the thought of breathing the air for the next several days. Stylar had said stay together but his two companions had not ventured that far, perhaps it was the warm air but the smell hit him like a wave a combination like so many odours he had experienced since coming to the community, a couple of the scents were sweet but they were overpowered by much stronger odours, even though the other two were several metres back he could see they were encountering the beginning of the fetid smell, it hung thick in the air and right now he wish he hadn't had such a meal that morning because he was starting to taste it as if it was going to come back up. Stylar ran the torch along the wall looking for an opening, the fissure was shrouded in shadow it would be tight but he thought he could squeeze through. Stylar heard Nolic approaching so he wasn't surprised when the young male tapped him on his shoulderLet me go in I am not as well developed I will fit easier

Xery had also come forward, her pallor had changed and she clearly didn't want to be there but she was the sort of female who didn't want to be left out

"I'm more flexible than both of you. But why would you go in there you don't know what is waiting for you, surely it would make more sense to let the creature come to us, to go in there it's a risk you shouldn't take"

Stylar nodded she was right, it was curiosity but that could very well cost him his life once more a naivety born of little or no life experiences, he was going to say as much, but a sound distracted his train of thought, the whole rock face seemed to come to life, he was still staring as Xery delivered a swift kick he had never seen anyone move so swiftly. Stylar was still taking the situation in he thought it had been the smell of the cave but it was an individual? He blended into the rocks. Stylar had thought the two males who had moved the boulder were large this male was another head taller and perhaps half as wide again, the kick delivered Xery landed gracefully clearly displeased it had had no effect on this giant, he looked at her as if she was a mild irritation, now Stylar reacted he brought his foot down hard on the males knee, this time there was a satisfying crack, the large male roared in pain, the three had turned and were running back towards their companions when Stylar stopped the male was crying, it sounded more like sobbing

"Please wait haven't you come to find me?"

Although that's what the male had said the words came out slowly and not confidently as if he had not spoken in a long time

"To find someone firstly you have got to realise someone is lost"

Stylar said in a matter of fact sort of way

The male nodded sadly

"I think I knew a long time ago that they thought I had passed"

That sentence took over a minute to say because it took a lot of stammering and thought to come up with the words

"Who are you?"

The giant of a male said

"I am Stylar"

The large male thought for over a minute before forming words

"My name used to be"

Every word seemed to come with a struggle

"Carstal my name used to be Carstal"

"How long have you been here?"

"I don't exactly know but at a guess I would say ten to twelve cycles"

"So why have you been here so long? Why didn't you try and leave this place? When the children came for their trials why didn't you leave with them?"

I, I have tried to lead the creature away? I know how to hide from it

Carstal seemed for a moment to be pleased with himself then a sadness seemed to cloud over him

"I only try to help haven't always been able to"

Stylar put his hand on the large males' shoulder

"Will you help us?"

"If I can I will"

"Is the creature in there?"

Stylar asked pointing to the fissure in the rock face

Carstal nodded

"We are going to kill the beast"

"It can't be killed"

"Why do you think that?"

"I have tried the creature is too strong, Carstal is big the creature is bigger"

"What does the animal look like?"

Stylar asked

"It is black like this world the smell on its breath tells you it is near"

Carstal was clearly trying to think of a word, he fell to his knees almost feeling like the ground was shaking. Stylar looked a little confused

"Well he looks dead"

Carstal eyes sprung open

"Yes, the animal is death"

"So that is why you think it can't be killed?"

The big male nodded sadly

"I think with your help the chances of killing the animal just increased"

Stylar before Carstal could react brought his hands down hard on the big males' leg

"Don't hurt me"

Carstal cried a small smile came to the young males lips he wondered if he could hurt the giant even if he brought the cave down on him

"Try your leg I think you should be able to walk on it"

Carstal got up slowly he couldn't put his full weight on it but at least he could stand. Stylar let the big male use him for support

"Xery you can support the other side"

"Why me?"

"Let's call it a lesson always think a moment longer before you act"

"I didn't dislocate his knee."

"I figured the kick to the head we were past explaining ourselves"

Xery reluctantly took Carstals other arm

"You do realise the size of him we will be through our rations before this day is over"

"Well that gives us more of an incentive to kill the animal quick doesn't it. He has lived on us long enough we will end its hunger in one swift action"

"You seem to be enjoying this"

"I wasn't brought into this world to be a victim Xery"

Nolic who had a reputation as strange, perhaps eccentric looked at the three of his companions

"They say I'm crazy? Kill something that has slaughtered dozens if not hundreds of our young, I say it can't be done"

"I say it will be done, it will take us all but I want to leave this chamber wearing that beasts hide as a cloak"

"So you think you will make the kill do you?"

"Nolic I don't care who makes the kill as long as that animal takes its final breath before that rock is rolled back"

Stylars senses reached out no one would notice apart from his mate but now he knew there was danger he would not drop his guard. To his surprise Carstal looked down at him

"It won't come out till later it hunts at night?"

"It's nocturnal? Well that might mean its eyes are sensitive to light, that might give us an advantage"

Stylar had been so caught up in his thoughts he didn't realise they were back with the others, who were looking at Carstal with suspicion and a little fear. Torrah looked at their new guest

"I could smell your companion from a hundred metres, he has a distinctive aroma"

"Where could he have bathed? For that matter how have you survived the only food source was. Oh?"

Carstal began to laugh as he understood what Stylar was thinking

"You think I ate the scraps left by the beast?"

Carstal left it at that and the others didn't really want to know. Stylar looked at the leg of the big male it was turning various shades of purple and blue

"I will wrap that leg for you, I am sure I can find a couple of bones it needs to be kept in place for at least a couple of days"

Xery had thought she could leave it but she had to know

"How did you survive down here?"

Carstal smiled

"Do you see any rats down here?"

There were a few looks of disgust because no doubt the little creatures had fed on the corpses littered about. Stylar knew the male must have a water source so if he did eat their rations he would know where to get more and if they ended up having to eat rats, well they would have to eat rats' survival was what this trial was all about. While Stylar gathered what he needed for his makeshift splint he surveyed what had been done while he had been away. Kolt had stripped the corpses of what was left of their garments and was platting them together into a rope. Torrah had found herself a large piece of flint and was working it into a blade. Kolt had finished his sling and there were several rocks lying by it

"You have been busy"

"I, I thought I better get the sling finished as quickly as I could"

"You thought right how close would you have to be?"

"Perhaps ten metres a little further maybe?"

"Good enough I want to draw it in closer than that anyway. Torrah can you give me a little of your time?"

Torrah came over warily

"I'm not going to like this am I?"

"Torrah we've only just been reunited and already you are treating me with suspicion?"

"Yes"

"Very good because you're going to hate this idea. We need what's the word?"

"A victim, a corpse?"

"Exactly and I couldn't think of a better person"

Torrah looked into the young males' eyes and though it was said as a joke something inside her made her feel like it inevitably would be the truth

"Why don't I think we are going to have a long and happy relationship?"

"Paranoia? "

Stylar suggested, there were a few giggles from the group. Torrah looked at her mate

"You better hope that creature doesn't put a scratch on me"

"My word"

"I guess that will have to do"

"Carstal how long do you think we have?"

"Perhaps two or three?"

"Hours?"

"Yes, that's right"

"Well good I suggest we eat we will need our strength for what's coming"

Torrah rummaged in her bag her mother had given her a pot which she put on the fire with a roughly made tripod her mother had also provided, each of the children threw their rations into the fire and Torrah added a little liquid to the mixture, she stirred until the mixture began to bubble. Carstal seemed to be the most eager his stomach made noises indicating he had not eaten in some time, the first couple of times he had looked embarrassed, but after a while the others had got used to it a few of their stomachs even were joining in, apart from the sounds coming from an odd stomach there was an eerie silence, everyone deep in thought. Stylar wondered if this was what battle was like, he knew how to fight, he could feel it in his head, but that was one of the problems he didn't know how he should feel. Should he be scared? Feeling anticipation? Excited? He just didn't know. They all knew what had to be done and perhaps they were preparing themselves mentally, they ate in silence Carstal taking more than his share but the rest didn't seem very hungry and some just seemed to pick at their food, after the meal Stylar stretched out and closed his eyes, no one disturbed him but all wondered how he could sleep at such a time. Xery moved over to where Torrah was sitting back to the wall like most of them, the fire was close enough to warm the area

"How can he sleep? We might all be in a permanent sleep if that animal has its way""

What is the point in thinking what might happen? if everyone does what they are supposed to we will triumph"

"Yeh right"

Xery moved away a look of disgust on her face, she moved over to where Kolt was sitting

"I think Stylar has this power over her, perhaps he has her drugged?"

" I, I think it's kind of comforting"

"What?"

"Someone having so much faith in you that they don't question"

"You are a romantic?"

Xery said with a smile

"Well I never, I used to think you were"

"I don't want you to finish that sentence, just because I'm quiet it doesn't mean I don't have emotions or feelings, I think perhaps people like me have more emotions, they are caged inside so you want to show them but you just can't"

He looked frustrated as if only able to describe a part of what he meant to say, Xery put a comforting hand on his shoulder

"If we get through tonight I think I would like to get to know you better"

"I, I think I would like that"

Kolt turned his head away to hide the embarrassment he was feeling at that moment, Xery smiled squeezed his shoulder and began her pacing. Torrah watched looking at how the others coped with this situation Xery with her pacing, Nolic talking as if he needed to get every word out that day just in case he didn't live to see another.

Kolt huddled against a wall well no change there and her mate asleep as if he wasn't concerned that she was risking her life on the abilities he thought he had, if she passed that night she would haunt his waking hours for the rest of his days, she was convinced she had the will to do that

Stylar woke up, oh my head he thought what a time to have a headache as he moved he realised they were all watching him

"You would think no one had seen someone waking up before"

Suddenly his eyes widened he would never be sure if he had heard felt or smelled the animal but his instincts took over. The creature sounded large and heavy

"Everyone you know what positions to take"

Torrah had already placed herself close to the fire which was almost central in the tunnel. Stylar heard the whistling as Kolt had already placed his first stone and was gaining momentum with every swing, Carstal had a rope tightly held in his hands. Nolic had one of several flint knives Torrah had crafted, he himself had taken one of the pieces of flint and attached it to the biggest bone he could find snapping the other end so either side could be used as a weapon, it seemed already like they had been in that cave several days, Stylar had to wonder if the days that followed would seem so long

Torrah started to shake, she had never had to endure such fear, she could hear the padding of the creatures' feet, as it came closer she could hear a mixture of sniffing and heavy breathing, it made guttural sounds as it growled that were clearly made from deep within and that smell the stench of decay filled the very air, it felt warmer as well, she felt Stylar in her head. Stay calm over and over she heard. Where was Kolt with his sling? How close did it have to come before he attacked, before any of them attacked? This was her time she felt as if she was going to die everything inside said run, but she stayed still. She thought she would always trust Stylar without question, this situation was testing that to its limits, the whistling stopped followed by the sound of rock hitting its target, the animal howled, Torrah had turned as the sound escaped the creatures throat rage and pain were clearly there she felt it was looking down at her, she had been right it was close too close, she couldn't move the animal had it in its eyes and it was as if it wouldn't let go. Why couldn't she move? She had to get up but her legs just would not work, the others acted like they had been together for cycles not hours, they seemed to move as one, it was like he was controlling their movements' Carstal got to the beast first, at the end of the rope he had weighted it so it would wrap around anything it came into contact with, obviously the animal was confused it was not used to being the prey, it looked like it was going to get worse for the animal obviously not used to children attacking it, with screams and shouts the animal had become disorientated. Xery vaulted over Torrahs head and with all the might she had in her arms she buried her piece of flint in the animals back, the animal lunged for her, she would never be able to explain how the animals large paw missed her. Stylar watched as Carstals muscles flexed as he took the strain of the animal the rope cutting into its flesh. The animal backed up slightly as if it had worked out moving forward would tighten the rope, the animal distracted Torrah crawled to the wall of the cave while the animal fixed its attention on the much larger meal that was Carstal, Carstal seemed to have figured out the same thing, he had nowhere to go so he stood his ground. The animal reared up onto its hind legs. Stylar and Nolic rushed forward, Nolic put his flint knife into the beasts side and was swatted away for his trouble, he looked unhurt. Carstal moved towards the creature who was a good half metre taller than him but he didn't seem concerned, he moved so he was under the animals jaw so they couldn't attach them selves to anything, his feet spread slightly further apart as they dug in, the animal had the weight and the size and it began to drive the large male back, if Carstal was driven over he was dead. Stylar jumped onto the creatures back, it let out like a yelp clearly all attention had been on the large male. Stylar was having trouble holding on to the greasy matted fur he had in his fist, the extra weight had been too much for Carstal who had fallen backwards, but the attention was off him for the moment as he tried to get the young male off him, Stylar was losing his grip it wasn't just the animals skin it was how the fat and muscle seemed to roll, he lost his grip along with his spear which he hadn't had the opportunity to use. Stylar hit the ground hard his mate could tell he had been winded, the animal had several deep wounds in its hide but it still had fight and at that moment it looked more dangerous than it had any time in the confrontation, it advanced menacingly on Stylar without thinking Torrah was up onto her feet she ran at it from the side her flint blade making a satisfying tearing sound as she brought her arm round in a graceful arc, the animal sprang at her, she hadn't even seen him get up but her mate was there as the animals nails tore through the thin layers of cloth and tore into soft flesh. Stylar looked down in shock as if reflex his hand went to his belly keeping his guts in because the animal had ripped deep, so much dark liquid as blood mixed with the dirt that coated his body, the shock was gone replaced by anger. The animal was once more on its rear legs but not as sturdy with the wound to its flank. Stylar rushed forward one more with spear in hand and drove it into its belly his hand twisting for maximum effect, poetic justice unlike Stylar it couldn't hold in its entrails in, they began to fall with a slap, the steam was rising off them. Torrah was regretting eating that last meal. Stylar hadn't finished as if he was carrying out his vengeance for every victim of the creature, the animal fell taking Stylar down with him, there was a gurgle as blood mixed with air and Stylar heard that last beat of its heart and with that Stylar too fell limp

Carstal just stood there shaking his head

"I can't believe it's dead, I thought we would all die trying to bring the animal down Carstal?"

"Yes?"

"Will you just move and help us get this thing off Stylar"

Torrah was sweating trying to get a hold of the beast. Carstal took hold of the animal around its neck

"I hope it smells better in the pot than it does at this moment"

Xery screwed up her face

"We're not still going through with the plan to eat this are we?"

Carstal seemed happy with the idea of a meal of the animal he was now struggling with it moved slowly the others joined in pushing and pulling until it was clear of Stylar. Stylar just lay there he didn't look like he was moving Torrah was thinking. Was he dead? She moved closer a ragged breath that seemed to rattle his ribs, he had lost his vitality, his hair plastered to his face which was bruised even noticeable through the dirt that caked it. Torrah for the first time looked at the wound it was worse than she had thought or imagined, she wondered if all his organs were intact, but as they cleaned the wound it was obvious the rib cage had served its purpose, the claws had torn through flesh and muscle and the claws had scraped the bones but not gone through. Carstal bent over the body and lifted him gently, it reminded Torrah of a mother cradling her baby. Torrah took what skins and blankets they had and made one bed the others could go cold Stylar needed to be kept warm. Stylar had started shivering he was mumbling something but no one could make out what he was saying. Carstal shook his head sadly

"I've seen this before it's the blood fever, I think the claws of the animal have? Infect very deadly"

Torrah looked down at her mate

"He's strong he will live through this"

Torrah slept with Stylar that night after the wounds had been tended to cleaned as best they could, blood still seeped from the tears in the flesh and Carstal had sealed them with fire and though he was unconscious she could have sworn he grimaced. Carstal said if he made it through the night it was a good sign. Torrah didn't sleep she listened to every breath from her mate, sometimes she thought she knew the pattern and he would stop, she would look at him for what seemed like an eternity and she would feel her own heart beating faster as panic started to take her then he would take a deep breath, his breathing was hard and each breath sounded like a struggle, he was spared what would come every week, she felt her muscles being stretched and she sensed Carstal watching her as he kept vigil over his new friends, he had taken a strip from the animal the texture was like leather and he brought it across to Torrah who had started shaking and droplets of sweat had appeared on her brow. Carstal bent down and though it didn't taste good he slipped the strip of flesh into her mouth

"Bite down hard on it, it will help with the pain"

Carstal went back to skinning the animal with some flint he carried with him, the smell was overpowering but he didn't seem to care as first he pealed the hide back then he started to butcher the carcass carving it into generous pieces. Xery studied the carcass while she could the creature was strange it didn't look natural almost like it was several different animals she would tell Torrah if she was up to any discoveries in the morning. Kolt also looked at the animal and he could see he wasn't the only one puzzled

"Kolt what are you thinking? What are you thinking?"

"Oh ssorry I'm not used to people asking my opinion, I was wondering if we were going to check the animals lair for more of them?"

"I suppose we should, but some of our number need to get their strength back but as my mother says if a job is worth doing its worth doing well"

"Don't you hate that?"

"What?"

"The way parents have a saying for any situation"

"I guess; I don't really think about it"

"I do when you are alone a lot of the time all you have are your thoughts your dreams"

"It sounds like a lonely place. You never have to be alone"

"It's the only time I feel at peace"

Xery held out her hand

"Come and sit by the fire with me"

Kolt hesitated but he looked into her eyes and he saw something he hadn't seen before acceptance she wasn't asking because she felt she had to it was because she wanted to, he took her hand

"Kolt you never have to be alone again"

They both got up and walked to the fire its warmth welcoming but not just the fire to be with someone who had a vitality a zest for life was intoxicating, they sat down in the glow of the fire, the flames danced but not just the fire right now he could feel it inside. Had his life finally begun to change, he knew he was but a boy but he felt as if he had lived a life time of misery no not lived just existed. Would this experience change who he would eventually become? They sat by the fire until it began to smoke neither, putting more fuel on it just content to watch it die out, they were Carstal threw some wall mosses and more material that had been wrapped around the bones, then he threw some wood to build it higher. Where did he get wood? It looked like a root from some small tree

"Where did you find that?"

Carstal pointed up the tunnel towards the animals' den. Xery decided that they should wait until the morning to investigate both where the root system had come from and what was in the animals' den, she decided she wouldn't eat because she thought the sight beyond the fissure in the rock might bring a lot of the sustenance back up, besides he eyes were feeling heavy and the warmth of the fire and the body beside her, she knew she would sleep soon

Marlac had just finished the operation on Barla, recovery would take three to five days and then several after that to see him back to full strength. Marlac felt like he had neutered the male, the device that was now in his head would control the chemicals flowing through his body much more efficiently than nature could have done, it was hoped his personality wouldn't radically change but there again time would tell, but with his uncontrollable anger, perhaps a change would not be altogether a bad thing after all almost killing a couple of his test subjects was not a scenario Marlac wanted to deal with.

Perhaps this operation had effected the dynamic of the group. Marlacs second choice might come to the fore. Marlac wiped the last of the blood from his hands. Barlas mate stepped forward from her holding cell, her nostrils flared as she smelt the air, she could smell her mate on him. They had been genetically designed to be fiercely loyal and dependent on one another but to see it had been a revelation.

Thirty-three days and that bond would be tested that's when they would be introduced into the community, it was a good thing the brain imbalance had been discovered now any older and the procedure would have had complications the information in all their heads was still being sorted, it was hard to explain easier to show. The damage he could have done in the community, well it was discovered so no trail of bodies. The device would keep Barla safe when he was threatened it would increase the adrenaline to a point where he would be able to endure more punishment. Marlac could not help thinking about the one he had lost that males brain had been a work of art, he would never see the like again

Stylar thrashed about the fever was consuming him, it felt like he was burning from the inside out, Torrah suspected if any of the others including Carstal had been infected they would have already been dead. Carstal had gone to get more water they had already used their three-day supply trying to cool him down, the rest of the group had started to say how they didn't agree with such a needless waste of water when Torrah had looked at them they had all visibly paled and no other thoughts had been voiced, the fever consumed him, he seemed to reach out for someone. Torrah hoped it was here but something inside told her different, the group stayed away the community embraced life, celebrated it but this was too close to death for them. She once more cursed their bond, if he died she knew she would follow, they couldn't survive without one another, she felt so hopeless, so helpless Love Excuse me?

Torrah hadn't seen Kolt approach right now nothing mattered but the one in her arms even though her body burned with the change, it was a dull ache compared to how she was feeling about her mate

"What you are thinking about its more than genetics, I don't think you can control who you fall in love with, it just happens, perhaps a mutual need? I must admit I'm too young to know but I use my eyes, I see the look that two lovers give one another, I can't describe it"

Torrah felt like saying what did he know but he continued

"I have been told I have an old soul"

Torrah realised something, he was a telepath he had read her thought as if she was speaking to him, as if to answer

"I am; I never knew"

Torrah looked slightly crossly at him, she was thinking how to word the next question

"Why didn't I tell you? Well let me see people look at me like I am a freak all ready, I hope this secret will remain ours? Most people distance themselves from me I have learnt to do the same"

"She doesn't want to distance herself from you"

Kolt looked back at Xery

"It would never work or it wouldn't last I am just not meant to have a mate or a family, I know I am but six cycles old but I have seen much and I know the sort of males who have someone they love and a family they are not like me. I am more the sort of boy who stands in a corner and hopes no one notices me"

"Then you failed didn't you? You were noticed because you are here this trial is not for everyone someone else knows your secret. You said about standing in a corner perhaps someone might think of you as a challenge, besides I have seen uglier examples of boyhood"

Even though Kolt was covered in dirt she could tell he was blushing.

Stylars skin was red all the water used some patches of the dust had been cleared he resembled meat boiled in the large pots, at that moment in time she wished she was with her mother

"If I didn't have him I might have been interested in you, but whatever the future holds I know my heart will always belong to him but an air of mystery is not a bad thing"

"He is very fortunate to have you"

"I think we are both lucky to have one another, I hope we have a full and interesting future ahead of us" "I hope that destiny is in your hands"

With that Kolt dismissed himself going back to the group who were all huddled around the fire, with the exception of Xery sleeping didn't seem to be coming easy to the rest of the group

Raldon wandered down a passageway which coincidentally led to where the children had been sealed, it had been two days and he had ended up in this place on five occasions. Raldon had been brought up with tradition, but this one no longer served any useful purpose it had nothing to do with leadership, he still remembered the screams as they left two companions behind, those screams had always haunted his dreams. Raldon hadn't seen it but he had known it was there in the darkness its fetid breath, the sound from deep within that chilled the very air, his companions had been fortunate some years all were taken only two poor souls out of a group of ten, he put his hand on the boulder. How many were still alive? Was anyone? Raldon had carried out his duty every cycle since being made pit boss. Dianer had objected when he had said he would carry out the duty one more time, he knew he shouldn't but he wanted to spare her from the loss he had always felt, diggers caught in cave in was one thing innocent young was something else. Raldon thought of Stylar he would take risks to keep the others safe, perhaps he would be the first to fall. What was the saying? A baptism by fire? This fire would burn deep

Stylars eyes snapped open, the fever had broken, his breathing had become less laboured and as she watched it was as if his strength was returning

"Where? What?"

Torrah just smiled

"You saved us you saved us all"

"We killed the animal?"

As if to answer that Carstal came forward offering the pair what looked like part of a leg, the flesh barely cooked, fat rolling down his hand

"I think your memory is a little clouded as I remember it, it took us all to bring the animal down"

Stylar thought for a moment then realised something

"I don't remember Starr being there?"

Torrah looked towards the group she had been concerned so much for her mate she hadn't realised and the puzzled looks from the rest of the group she realised no one had noticed. Perhaps they had and were just thankful for the quiet.

"So when had she last been seen?"

Nolic answered

"The last time I saw her it was when we were gathering materials for our weapons I think?"

"That was over a day ago"

Kolt said just stating the obvious. Stylar was trying to rise but Torrah put a restraining hand on his chest

"You must rest"

"I've rested for a day I don't intend to see any of our companions lose their lives on this so called trial now let me up girl"

Torrah lowered her gaze and took her hand from his chest. When Stylar rose Torrah gasped

"Now what's wrong?"

"It's, it's your back"

"What about my back?"

All the children were now gathered around all staring, he felt Xerys hand on his back

"It's like fur, it runs right down your spine. Do you feel different?"

He hadn't thought about it, but now there was something, his senses seemed more attuned, he felt a vitality

"He feels different don't you?"

Stylar just nodded at his mate

"We'll talk about this later we've got to find Starr and while we're out in that direction we'll search the animals den"

Stylar looked down at his bandage it was stained with blood and dirt

"I think this needs changing before we begin our search"

Torrah began to unwrap the bandages gently

"I will need something to wear"

Carstal smiled at that

"You can wear this"

He flung over a covering which until recently had been the fur that had kept the beast warm, the covering dragged on the ground but he suspected he would grow into it

"You don't need another dressing on your wounds"

"I don't the wounds were deep I felt the claws scrape my ribs"

"That might be so but all I see are scars which have already healed"

Stylar touched his stomach it felt tight but there was no pain, Stylar flung on his fur and grabbed a torch, lit it almost burning his eyebrows off

"What have you put on these?"

"I soaked all the cloth in animal fat"

"Is there any part of the animal you didn't use?"

"Waste not want not, we're stronger together, there is no need to separate, there is only one direction we need go"

Stylar led, Torrah was one step behind, Carstal stayed at the rear as if not trusting they were alone in the cavern. Carstal had grown up fearing the beast, he had created a myth around it and though he himself had butchered the creature in his mind it had taken on a life of its own. Stylar had a feeling the male would never be far from his side, he had found an ally who would always watch, never betray, the male had a loyalty about him that went beyond description, his beliefs were his own he had survived on his own instincts any lessons learnt had long been forgotten. Stylar at that moment was thinking to the future he saw how these individuals might become useful tools but with the exception of Carstal who would be of use now the rest their usefulness would be many cycles from now, but if they could be nurtured now, brought up in a way of thinking then the possibilities were limitless. Stylar knew when they went back to the community the group had to stay together, they had to feel like they had something to offer, after all that was the way of the community, his thoughts cut short. Starr, he could smell her he took in the various odours in the air hers was faint but it was there, the others looked to one another none of them could smell anything but the dampness of the air and the rotting of those whose lives had been cut short. Stylar had decided to enter the animals den himself, when he had said he would go first, for a moment he thought Torrah was going to say something, their eyes had met and she had nodded reluctantly, he hoped it would be a matter of going in a quick search and out again trying not to take in too much of the carnage within, what he wore as well he hoped might confuse for a moment because if that creature had a mate its scent hopefully would give him vital moments, the fissure in the rock seemed smaller in fact he couldn't believe an animal of such a size could have come out of such a narrow space it must have had to twist and tear its way free, he hoped that the fissure didn't narrow as it went in or that the passageway wasn't too long, if he didn't reach the den before he was attacked the lack of space could see his end, no manoeuvrability to attack or defend, the space was so confining he couldn't even carry a torch one of the others would have to throw it to him once he had reached the other side, as he squeezed into the gap rock stuck in his back and front the skin he wore protected him to a point he contorted his body, quite often breathing in, he could feel the anxiety of those behind him, Stylars eyes were beginning to run, it was so tight now he couldn't move his arms enough to rub his eyes now it was more his other senses his vision blurred from the stinging, the smell of decay had now met with the smell of waste as in the animals own thesis and the smell of ammonia made him want to vomit, he gulped down the little sustenance he still had inside he didn't want to add to the smells that were assaulting him, obviously the creature hadn't minded the smell perhaps a warning to others of its kind? The gap still seemed to be getting narrower, much more and it would be the end of this journey, he could feel dirt from the rocks getting inside his clothes, he wanted to scratch but he couldn't, the one good thing was that dirt was beginning to clog his nose the smell was subsiding but his eyes were almost sealed shut, they were swollen and he felt next to useless, to breath now he had to open his mouth, he tasted dirt, his neck twisted at an awkward angle, pushing hard with his legs keeping his arms to the side, he had to unblock his nose he managed to pry one of his arms free, pulling muscles in the process, he managed to stick it up his nose and scoop some of the dirt out once more the stench was there, his eyes no longer open encrusted with dirt, now touch, smell and hearing were all he had, his hands now felt their way through the tunnel, it had started to widen, he kept his back to the wall, if he had to defend himself better to cover one side, he got some of what was left of his clothing and tried to gently dab his eyes, the ammonia was still making them weep without any sign of lessening, his vision blurred he decided now he need the light of a torch, he had gagged slightly, he couldn't remember he thought he had kept it down, the skin didn't look much different it had been matted fur to begin with, he had tried to hold his breath but still the odour overpowered. Was it his imagination? Was it getting lighter, then in the dull grey teeth glistened in the light

Justas sat in the cold chamber with the exoskeleton he wore over a nearly useless body there was no need of heat, his protection had a climate control, also the reason for the darkness he could see with the sensors within the armour, dozens of monitors showed him places he had never been but even them he did not need, the armour could interface with all security checkpoints throughout his territory, he guessed it was the traditionalist in him, he had grown tired of this place of this dying world everything was decay and neglect it made him question if his people had won their great war, the war to end all wars? How many times had that statement been used? At least the enemy had died quickly, not like his people they had suffered for hundreds of cycles without ever knowing it, the rich and powerful had preyed on the weak with nothing then they had preyed on one another. As those under the ground were prisoners so were his own people but prisoners of these metal exoskeletons they were both their salvation and their destruction. He had met up with the female Glarai her family thought their power and wealth could hide a misspent youth they had been mistaken, he had seen an opportunity to get close to Marlac, the geneticist was old and tired he had been promised passage on one of the craft, Glarai had agreed he would never make that voyage. There were no secrets from him, they were to him like stock was to a trader, he had thought about taking more than just Marlacs life, he had thought of taking her she had a defiance he found challenging, but his days were too full, so many preparations. Marlac had created a brood that turned on one another this Barla had almost killed several of his brethren, the geneticist had failed why was his heart still pumping? This new generation, this new labour force had been conceived of hundreds of cycles before he had always wondered if they were a good idea, those that toiled under the earth now were strong, fortunately they had not realised how strong. Several of his predecessors had warned give a slave knowledge and strength and risk the potential for him to turn on their masters, but there was their arrogance once more. He had watched the Director rise to power, he had thought his path was subtle and manipulative yes the second part was true, but that was true of them all in power. He never came at a rival directly a death in the family, an accident or incident, he had records on them all. The Director was now preparing to rule a new world. But had he already made the mistake? He had sent others ahead, they had the power at that moment. Only time would tell

Stylar froze the animal was perhaps four metres away it looked still

"Stylar are you alright?"

"Torrah quiet"

There was little point saying that, the animal must have heard, perhaps right now it was waiting, no actually it looked dead. Stylar stepped forward with as much stealth as he could manage. Stylar was close enough now to put his hand out, if this was one of the ways the animal hunted he would know any moment when the beast bit down hard on his hand, his hand touched the creatures muzzle it was as cold as the rocks around it, the cave felt cold you would have thought such a temperature the smell wouldn't have been as bad as it was.

Why had he unblocked his nose? Surely suffocating would have been better than enduring this, still unsure he slowly crept passed the animal, the cave had now opened up it looked natural, several what looked like spires rose from the ground, he stopped as he tried to take it in dozens, no hundreds of remains of the young, children the age of his companions, they were at various stages of decay the closest one muscle, sinew and flesh hung from bones partly gnawed he was glad he had come in alone, the others should not see what he was witnessing at that moment. How long had these trials been going on? Anger rose in him but that was too little a description for the emotion, rage like he had never known, flesh riddled with maggots the sound of buzzing as flies swarmed, crawled over flesh, he was just turning away just to make sure none of the others had followed when he heard a low rumble, no it was a growl and it was getting louder, he had been so distracted he hadn't really looked around, the animal was lying on a shelf several metres above him, Torrah had given him a flint knife, but as his hands searched he realised he must have dropped it when he was squeezing through the passageway, the creature was crouched ready to spring. Stylars fingers traced over one of the spires, which he had slowly backed towards when seeing the animal above him, his sight was still blurred he knew it wouldn't improve until he was out of that place, he asserted some pressure wondering if he would be strong enough to snap the stone spire after a few moments it broke in his hand, Stylar saw the muscles in the creatures legs tighten as it sprang, Stylar took a step back and with the spire in his grasp he drove it up into the descending beast, the spire went through the hide, through muscle flesh and bone, the creature went stiff as stone punctured its heart, it was good fortune nothing more, but the tales that would be told would tell another story. Stylar was shaking, his heart pounding but he wouldn't calm down until he was sure there were no other creatures in the cavern, it took perhaps an hour to search the cavern, he had told the others to stay back and only when he was heading back towards the entrance that Carstal stood waiting for him

"I don't even want to ask how you squeezed yourself through that passageway"

"With difficulty, I found one of my old knives in the beast, I have had to protect myself over the cycles

Torrah was beginning to get concerned and that got the rest of us concerned"

Carstal saw the creature the rock protruding from its still warm carcass

"Impressive"

"I was fortunate the weight of the animal and its speed all I had to do was keep hold of the piece of rock

That piece of rock doesn't look light and you just found it like that did you?"

"No I guess it was old and it just came away in my hand, if Starr is down here I think she would be unrecognisable, but from the state of the carcasses I don't think any of them were recent kills. I was wondering how you were going to get back up the passage?"

"Probably with more difficulty than I got down here"

Carstal was still squeezing out of the passageway his shoulders almost wedged with some cursing he finally stepped out into the open, he stretched looking around, he seemed to sniff the air as if there was a slight odour in the air. Stylar would have laughed if his eyes didn't feel so sore. Carstal inspected the creature that was lying on the ground a pool of blood already attracting the flies. Stylar watched as the large male took in all that was around him, tears came but Stylar could tell it was not the conditions, he had known some of the children that had passed and perhaps right now he was living moments others would never understand

"Have we finished in here?"

"Yeh we have finished; we were too late for these but we will do what needs to be done to save tomorrows"

"I hope that will be enough"

Carstal said still with a haunted look in his eyes

"It wasn't your fault Carstal you couldn't have taken on all three of those creatures your body would be in here like the rest of these poor souls, I think everything happens for a reason, perhaps the reason was finding each other, we will need strong hands in the coming days, guilt is selfish you can contribute and help save lives, the first life we need to save is Starrs if she is still alive and let us hope there are no more creatures further up the passageway"

"If there is I am sure you will be able to deal with it"

"Carstal your confidence in me is touching, now let's find this girl and leave"

It took twice as long to get back up the narrow passageway, Stylar had gone in backwards so the little bit of manoeuvrability he had was lost because every now and again he would hear Carstal curse as he got caught or stuck and then Stylar had to pull to his wedged large friend free, giving him words of encouragement all the way, he could only imagine how they looked. Stylar could hear the others saying come on, or could they help? when they finally pulled themselves free layers of dirt, blood from scrapes as the rough stones had cut deep but they were free of the confining passageway, these children had shown their value and they would in the days to come take their places within the community. He would tell Raldon how they had battled the beast from the shadows and survived, they had battled their own fears and triumphed and together they had grown stronger, they had come in as strangers but the bonds they had made here would last a lifetime. Stylar finally pulled himself free of the tunnel with the help of some smaller hands, unfortunately there was not an easy way out and he fell backwards almost crushing Xery who was one of the hands who had hold of him, he lay in a heap for a moment then once more hands helped him up onto his feet, they waited perhaps another couple of minutes before Carstal squeezed himself out of the crack in the wall he too fell in a heap but there was no danger anyone was going to be under him, everyone kept their distance from the pair and he noticed the look of disgust on Torrahs face, what Stylar hadn't really thought anything about was the fact when you put something sharp into an animal and puncture vital organs, you get a lot of discharge from said creature, his hands were now dark red and black where the blood had congealed, he imagined his face was in a similar state, he looked questioningly at the male you saw me like this and you didn't say a word?

Carstal rose slowly it looked like he was battling to keep a straight face and losing that battle, the others were giggling and laughing, after the tension of the last few hours they needed something to lighten the mood even though they still had someone to find. Carstal hadn't made it to his feet he was rolling on the ground, laughing until he began to cough and the whole group had to help him to his feet, Stylar felt himself relax he hadn't realised he had tensed up until that moment, he heard something it was paint, it seemed quite distant, he felt relaxed the danger for now was over, but they still didn't know where the tunnel led. Xery, Nolic and Kolt stayed at the entrance of the animals' den, there were a few complaints, about the smell but they soon quietened when Torrah gave them that look that Stylar was beginning to understand. Torrah seemed to be able to handle negative emotions easier than himself, but he knew when the time came she would stand unquestioningly by his side, Stylar seemed at ease here now, he blended into the surroundings and though he seemed to move stealthily Torrah had trouble keeping up. Carstal had no such difficulty with his muscular legs he still seemed very at one with the place and every once in a while, he seemed to merge with his surroundings no doubt trying to avoid being a victim learnt out of necessity but perhaps not being aware of it. When had Stylar learnt the technique? She was starting to wonder if the confrontation with the animals had changed his perceptions, it almost felt like he was hunting, none of his actions seemed wasted. There was something? Like a scraping noise, a mixture of someone's voice and a light sobbing. Stylar put his hand up and his companions stopped

"Carstal you stay here if we need you, you will know about it"

Carstal grunted clearly not happy with the decision, Stylar sensed they were safe now and Carstals size might be intimidating for the young female by the sound of her she didn't need such a presence at that moment in time. Starr was clearly in some distress, they had walked up a gentle slope for the last several hundred metres, the rock now was a lighter shade, roots dangled from the cave ceiling, it looked like they might be close to the surface, another world then they saw her. Stylar could never remember witnessing a more pitiful sight, Starr was stood against a wall, she didn't even seem to be aware that they were there, her hands were covered in blood her hands were torn, she clawed at the rock, her nails were cracked, broken and split, that was where the blood had come from, she mumbled but Stylar could hear the words

"I've got to get away, must get out, need to escape"

Her head was moving up and down as if she was agreeing with herself "Torrah go and try and calm her down."

"what am I supposed to do?"

"You're her age don't you know?"

"Physically I'm her age but she's had cycles to develop her character, I've had weeks

Couldn't you just go and hold her?"

"Haven't you learnt anything from those around you?"

"Why don't you do it you seem to have such a caring nature"

"Torrah look at me I'm covered in blood, if she hasn't gone over the edge yet don't you think this might just do it?"

Torrah started to walk towards the young female confidence gone, she seemed to be shuffling she turned questions in her eyes, Stylar motioned for her to continue

"Go on"

She walked slowly making as much noise as she could she didn't want to scare the young female any more than she already was, she reached out and patted her gently on the shoulder, she looked back as if needing encouragement. That girl had a lot to learn

"Torrah will you please hold her"

Torrahs face wrinkled up

"She needs reassurance patting her on the back just won't get this done"

Torrah swallowed and took the young females arm, Starr tried to pull away but her strength was gone, not that she would have been as strong as Torrah anyway. Torrah held her tighter than she wanted to, she forced her round so they were facing one another. Starr just seemed to be staring right through her "Starr can you hear me?"

Torrah had got some rags out of a fold in her clothing and had begun to wrap her fingers, they could do a better job of it when they got back to the others, the young female moaned every so often, but any slight resistance in the beginning was gone

"Must escape got to get help, need help, so frightened"

Starr murmured the same thing over and over it was like her mind was caught in a loop

Torrah looked back at her mate

"We need to get out of here"

"As I figure it the trial is over it was never about how we rationed our food it was about survival, we should have been warned, but now the animals are dead there is no reason for us to stay in here"

Stylar looked at Starr she had faced those demons and a part of her would never leave the cave. She had come in with this confidence unfortunately that had been her weakness as well as her strength, she had thought she didn't need anyone, it had only been because they worked as a group that they were still breathing. Torrah held Starr as they joined Stylar and then Carstal when they were in sight of the others all three came running and Torrah was more than happy for the young to take their own but she wouldn't let go, even now Stylar wondered how much of themselves they would never know because of their lost childhood, those cycles that built a character that would be with them until their last breath. Stylar lifted Starr off Torrah as if she did not weigh anything, something had changed, he felt different and he wasn't sure if he should embrace that difference or fear it

"Stylar I thought you said you weren't going to touch her"

"I said that before I realised how far gone she is, the female that we came into this cave with has gone, she has left this shell behind"

"So where are we going? Are we going to see where the tunnel leads?"

"No we are going out the way we came in"

"In case you don't remember when we were sent in that way was blocked by a rather large stone"

"I will solve that problem with the help of our new friend"

"You get attacked by an animal you get perhaps some of its life force inside you and you become what?"

Stylar did not know the answer to that question, he couldn't keep a smile off his lips. Stylar decided to carry Starr it was quicker than the alternatives, he thought she might squirm, try and get away but perhaps being held gave her comfort, a sense of safety. Torrah smiled

"She looks comfortable"

"That's not jealousy is it dearest?"

Stylar got a dirty look for his comment. Carstal was just ahead positioned like a sentry, poised for any threats that he alone seemed to be aware of

"There this will give you something to keep you occupied"

"I should watch your back"

"I think we killed everything that was moving, the size of you I am not surprised we saw no rodents between you and those creatures they did not stand a chance"

Stylar handed Starr to Carstal who showed no effort as he took the young girls shaking body and held her tight. Stylar had created a bond and now he was ready to return to the community, he had some thoughts on their future and he suspected they would not finish their lives in those caves, but he was also aware that he had to be in the here and now. Perhaps that was part of his conditioning he was supposed to lead his brethren to this new world, but already he had changed his destiny and the plans of their masters. The community would have to wait for now some of the young had begun to sleep knowing they were safe, but not Stylar he had too many plans, too many thoughts. Nolic was away from the others, he was the one who needed the most help, he didn't relate to the others, well he seemed to find it hard to trust, he felt people were staring at him, but they weren't most of the time all they were thinking of was how they would survive, perhaps he had put up these personal barriers to a point where he could hardly breathe, he seemed to possess an intelligence a creativity that was wasted the way he isolated himself, he was not helping the community and perhaps that community were giving him one more opportunity

"Nolic could you help us? We're going to try and move the boulder"

Stylar knew she wouldn't keep silent and he was expecting a comment laced with sarcasm and he wasn't disappointed, Torrah just couldn't help herself

"Stylar I was expecting you to move the rock yourself, with all that strength that animal passed onto you" Stylar turned away to hide his smile and compose himself, when he turned to face his mate, his expression was unreadable

"I wouldn't want to injure myself now would I?"

Torrah just grunted at that, once more staring into the fire with their companions. Starr had been seated near Torrah who seemed somewhere else as if her mind had gone, perhaps her spirit. Torrah brushed some strands of hair from Starrs eyes. Torrah unwrapped the young females' hands. Carstal had a bowl with well no one ever found out, but it smelled as bad as the animals den had earlier that evening Torrah I need you

"How many times am I going to hear that through my life, through our lives?"

Stylar grimaced at the retort he thought she might have been more submissive; everyone put their hands on the rock. Stylar hoped that Carstal might be able to move the rock himself, he was as large as the rock itself as if the male was reading his mind he grunted as he took the strain, veins looking as if they would burst out of his body, his face became flushed. Stylar gave the group a sign and they all backed off apart from Carstal whose feet already seemed to have sunk somewhat into the hard ground, the male was all muscle and as he began to push they all seemed to want to tear through his flesh, he cried , yelled as if that would make what he was doing easier, then a new sound, scraping, the rock had begun to move, he put his sizable frame against the rock to keep the momentum going, it was moving a few centimetres then a bit more, a crack of light had appeared from the other side, he gave a roar and a crack as the rock rolled over and cracked in two. The guardians were there and they just stared at the large male who stood looming over the rock

"Who are you?"

"Who do you think I am?"

Carstal boomed he'd been almost placid in the cave but it was as if that rock had been lifted from his soul

"Are you the demon of the cave who has taken the form of man?"

Carstal began to chuckle, which became a laugh at the very thought of him being this demon. If he was honest he didn't even know what a demon was

"I think I like you"

Carstal said slapping the larger of the two males on the back, making him cough and wince at the sudden jolt

"I'm glad, I would hate to have you as an enemy"

The other guardian was asking if the children were hurt. Stylar told them Starr needed to see Rani

"Alright everyone come with me you all need to be checked out in the medical wing, your guardians will be informed and you can get yourselves cleaned up and we will destroy what you are wearing. I don't know what you have been doing but the odour is not, I don't know I have never smelt anything like it. As for you?"

"Carstal my name is Carstal"

"I would like an explanation what you were doing in there"

Stylar answered for his new friend

"He was put in there just as we were"

The guardian didn't seem to be able or want to look the group in the eyes

"Why, why this barbaric trial what gave you the right?"

"It's how it has always been"

"That's your answer?"

Torrah took Stylars arm

"You need to get your wounds looked at, I don't want you to get an infection"

Torrah led the group away, the guardians looked like they were going to escort the children but Carstal gave them a look that clearly said we don't need your help, as the group made their way through tunnels they got some strange looks, curiosity, astonishment and if they got too close looks of disgust from the stench that hung over them and would until they saw water and hopefully some of Ranis cleaning solution. Stylar had a feeling Raldon would be waiting, they had ended the trial he was sure the old male would want to know the story. Stylar knew this could only enforce what they were already talking about, the chosen one. Stylar decided that Carstal would be the one credited with the animal kills, the size of him would anyone argue? They would say they were the bait; they would say how scared they were. Rani met the children several hundred metres from the medical section, assistants took Starr and they all started back towards the medical centre. Torrah didn't let go of Starr she needed the assurance, she hoped she sensed they wanted her to come back, because at the moment she was a fractured soul. Raldon who Stylar had always thought quite statuesque looked almost like a child in the presence of his new friend, they were led to showers and helped off with their clothes some seemed to come off easier than others, some were almost peeled off. Raldons first question was going to be how they got out of the cave but the giant of a male that looked as if he was on guard clearly had the size and strength to move such a stone. Raldon studied the big male for several seconds before asking

"Carstal isn't it?"

The big male looked surprised he had been recognised

"How do you know my name?"

"I knew your father he was a good man; the resemblance is remarkable"

"You knew him? Does that mean he is no longer here?"

"Yes, I'm sorry he never got over losing you, when you didn't return I don't know he just changed, it was like he passed away and his body took a while to make the same journey"

"I was injured by one of the creatures, I thought I was going to die, my blood felt like it was burning, I was so hot, but even through my fever I heard the others, the screams, the cries, I was not strong enough I should have done more, I remember crawling into a side tunnel"

"You didn't tell us any of this"

Stylar couldn't help the outburst

"Why didn't you show us where you had lived?"

"I didn't think it was important, I could show you anytime now we can come and go"

"How many of those creatures were there? Are you sure you killed them all? Have you grown son?"

The last question was almost like an afterthought

"I don't understand what relevance that last question has on the previous ones?"

"I was just thinking you look taller"

Carstal stared at Stylar for perhaps four or five minutes, before speaking

"I think he is right"

"Perhaps three or four centimetres"

Stylar looked at his mate perhaps he had grown a little more, Torrah looked about the same

"Carstal you said you were attacked by one of those animals?"

Carstal nodded clearly not understanding Stylars reasoning

"Turn around"

The giant did as he was told, as he turned there was a puzzled look on his face but he didn't question

"It's alright I thought you might have had"

"Had what?"

Raldon asked unable to keep the worry out of his voice. Stylar looked at his surroundings, there was a cubicle it was empty. Stylar stepped inside Raldon was just behind him, then Carstal who blocked out most of the light with his gigantic frame. Stylar took off the animal skin. Raldon stepped a little closer, running down his adoptive sons back it looked like hair? No it was

"Is it fur?"

"It's my hair, I think the wound the animal inflicted on me, altered me somehow, we think it was a creation, not natural perhaps its D N A wasn't that much dissimilar from my own, perhaps it combined, I feel stronger, I think my growth which has already been tampered with, might have been unstable, perhaps at a genetic level I have been altered. I can't help but wonder if I am turning into a freak."

Stylar was going to say freak of nature but there was nothing natural about what had been done to him or perhaps that beast who had been as much a victim as all those it had fed on over the cycles

"So you think that's why you are a little larger than normal, Carstal?"

"If Stylar thinks that it is possible, it must be true"

"It must be a comfort, someone having as much faith in you as this one"

"It is, at least it's not misplaced"

Raldon heard the implication

"What is that supposed to mean?"

"You knew about the animals; you knew we were in danger. What gave you the right?"

"Nothing gave me the right, like most traditions it belonged to another time, one more brutal and like some traditions it was not so easy to put a stop to it"

"But you could have tried? You could have thought about the lives you were sending into that cave to sacrifice"

"I remember them all, it was my task and the people accepted the trial and I took responsibility for every individual who never came back and I saw their guardians, their parents and I felt their pain"

Raldon didn't tell Stylar everything, he didn't tell him about the cycle where they had tried to break tradition, there were nine children that cycle and they had said no, their masters had come down into the community and those children had been dragged to the cave, their parents and guardians had been executed along with any siblings. Raldon himself had been flogged he still bore the faint scars his memories cut deeper. Stylar had to learn the reality of this place so he would never learn about the incident.

"Who killed the animals was it you?"

"I'm nothing more than a child do I look capable of do such a thing?"

Raldon looked upset by the answer which was what Stylar wanted

"It was a team effort but my bodyguard inflicted most of the damage"

Carstals expression didn't change, as if chiselled from the rock

"Modest isn't he"

"You'll never know"

Stylar replied

"Carstal is it you?"

The large male stood as if frozen in time, tears came to his eyes as did a reply that rumbled from deep with in

"Mother?"

"You will never find out if you don't turn around will you"

"I, I look a mess and I know I smell a lot worse"

"Do you think after all this time such things matter to me?"

Carstals mothers voice shook as she struggled to keep so many emotions out of her tone

"I, I never thought I would see you again"

"Please turn around, I want to see how my boy has grown"

Carstal turned slowly, smearing his already dirty face with the back of his hand. Carstals mother looked slightly shocked by the size of him

"You have grown haven't you?"

"Children usually do mother"

Carstal said in a matter of fact sort of way

"You need some water on you boy"

"Yes, I do"

Raldon decided it would be as good a time as any to interrupt

"I hate to break up these emotional reunions, but a shower sounds like a good idea for all the children, I will go and check on Starr, Stylar you know where the showers are lead the way"

Stylar and Carstal had taken about ten steps when Carstal turned and ran to his mother and dropped to his knees so she could almost look into his eyes, it was like someone had opened a slush gate, tears rolled continually from his eyes I, I've missed you mother

She took his head in her hands

"I know my son I have missed you too, you are home now and you have grown into a man I am so proud of, because you did it on your own, that shows me you are your fathers son, I think you are a lot stronger than he ever was, but we will talk about him another time for now just get yourself cleaned up and then I will prepare you a meal"

Carstal got off his knees, a boyish smile on his lips

"Alright mother but I warn you I haven't had a long con? Talk with someone in a long time, you might not be able to shut me up"

"I will take my chances now go with your friends"

Stylar was leaning against a wall, he was glad that reunion had gone so well he wondered how his would go when he was reunited with his mother. Nairi was as good a mother as he could wish for but he owed the woman that bore him, at the very least the knowledge that he was still alive. Stylar smiled as his new friend joined him

"I'm interested to see how hard you will have to scrub before you get down to your skin"

That got a chuckle from the girls, he suspected his friend might have gone red from the comment but there was too much dirt to ever really know, clothes came off the group they went into two piles the one where they would be cleaned and the other where they would be destroyed a few looked as if they might have been put in the wrong pile. Torrah couldn't seem to take her eyes off him he was a specimen alright he had muscles where other males could only dream, it took several minutes just to start to make an impact on the dirt, the water to begin with just made it look like his body was formed from mud, it oozed down over his well-defined form, more than one pair of hands were involved and there were a few complaints how various areas were getting treated, he was basically a six cycle child trapped in an eighteen cycle body and his way of viewing the world around him hadn't changed, his hair was where they had all the problems, it was matted to a texture almost like bone. Kolt suggested they cut it off, for that suggestion Carstal glared at him. Kolt had found his way behind Xery. Stylar found a bone brush and began to patiently comb it

"I think I have found a rats nest up here"

That got a worried look from Carstal while the others began to laugh and after a few moments he too began to laugh, he also had a long beard which had been plastered to his face, it took about thirty minutes to get Carstal looking mildly presentable, the girls had washed what could be salvaged and put by a fire, they were steaming away nicely. Stylar found himself a blade, Stylar scraped the beard away, it transformed his face he had some of his youth back, Carstal did trust him he wasn't sure he would have let a boy shave him. Perhaps he had got so used to fear that he was always in that state? Stylar also cut his large friends hair, yes it was a bit uneven but it still looked better than how it had before, finally satisfied, Stylar stood back

"Well my friend I think you are ready to take your place in the community and I think you will be fighting the females off"

"I do not fight females"

"No I didn't mean it in, oh never mind. Everyone what do you think?"

There were nods and smirks of encouragement that evening all the children had as much food as their stomachs could hold, they didn't really see how the other talked about them in whispers, they had survived the trial and they looked relatively intact, but that night they didn't hear those hushed conversations, they ate in Raldons quarters all the guardians and parents were there a few nervous looks not many people ever saw the inside of these quarters and they glanced at one another, Raldon tried his best not to smile, he had been in such situations his whole life for him this was natural he could understand how it might be daunting for others. Starr obviously wasn't there Rani said it would take time and patience with her, it would be a long and hard process. Stylar couldn't help but blame himself he should have kept more control of the group, perhaps one day she would tell him not to feel guilty for now he would live with it, he wondered how much guilt he would carry before his and his peoples story ended. Raldon cleared his throat snapping the young male out of his reverie

"Would everyone raise their mugs to the group that finally beat the trial, I wish I had been able to accomplish it, perhaps this is a turning point, also to Carstal who now takes his place among his people, I am sorry it took so long to reunite you with your family, I think he will be a force to reckon with"

Stylar thought it might go on so he just butted in

"To Carstal "

Everyone nodded and Stylar saw his father smile as if in thanks for stopping him before a long winded speech became a reality

Dianer had just finished her shift when Raldon paid her a visit, it was never the best time for her. Terak had been giving her a hard time. But what else was new? She either loved him or she was going to commit murder the latter seemed more likely she had just finished her shower and she was preparing a meal with a few ingredients she had picked up from the stores, she could feel the tension in her shoulders and as she mixed she felt a relaxation she hadn't for quite some time. How had Raldon always seemed so calm? As if just the very thought of her mentor conjured him up, he was there looking in on her with a look of amusement

"Getting a little anti-social aren't you?"

"Some evenings I just feel like being alone. Is that wrong of me?"

"I had many shifts like that. Can I enter?"

"That depends on what you are here for I don't think I could deal with more bad news today"

"Since when have I ever brought you such news?"

"How long have I got to think about that?"

Raldon was smiling so whatever he was there for it wasn't too serious

"Come in you know you are always welcome"

"Thank you first we'll get down to business I have a new worker for you on your shift that is good news"

"How much ore can he clear in a shift?"

"Straight to the point"

"You didn't teach me to waste time did you?"

"That is the bad news he is untested he hasn't worked in the mines since he was young"

"How old is he?"

"Seventeen perhaps eighteen cycles"

That brought a raised eyebrow and a curious look

"He isn't one of those technicians out of the facility is he? The task is a strenuous one We have had them before and it has never ended well for either side"

Raldon raised his hand to calm her down

"No he's no technician, I don't think you have to be concerned about him not doing the task he is set, if you want to increase your extraction rate what could it hurt?"

"I will need someone to show him what to do"

Dianer seemed to be thinking out loud

"So what's this males name?"

"Carstal"

"I remember a Carstal perhaps two years older than myself. No must be another one the one I'm thinking of never came out of the trials. If you did mean him, I would wager several days rations he wouldn't make any difference to our operation"

Actually she had obviously heard about the group finishing the trials early more through whispers than general conversation and she had also heard of this male who had come out, from his description he didn't sound anything like the male she was thinking of, though her people were at times prone to exaggeration. Raldon was smiling

"I think you have yourself a wager my dear, I will think of you when my stomach is close to bursting, I thought I taught you to think before you acted you haven't seen this male yet"

Raldon said with a wry smile

"You always said I was a little impetuous didn't you?"

"That I did I am surprised you remember"

"You were a good teacher but I was a better pupil. Now when can I expect this miracle worker of yours?"

"Stylar will bring him to you in the morning"

"Yes, I heard about him finishing the trial early impressive"

"He decided his group had spent long enough on a trial he deemed not worthy of his time or effort, his group made sure the creatures would have no more victims and for good measure he destroyed the stone that had always sealed the cave, that was your new recruit by the way. Still think he won't make a difference?"

"We will see but I am glad those damn trials are over I wish I had had the guts to kill those beasts, he is sounding more like your son every day"

"I personally think it's Nairi who is rubbing off on him"

"That's not a bad thing"

"I suppose not well I shall leave you in peace, I am sorry if I disturbed you"

"I will always have time for you"

Raldon smiled and left the smile was tinged with sadness because he felt something

Stylar lay on his bedding gazing up at the ceiling of his cave, he was still thinking about the trials, playing the events over in his mind he could have done more, they had survived. He had made some new friends; the group had worked well together apparently because of his leadership but Torrah deserved as much of the praise, she had kept focussed, he still wondered about the animal attack, only time would tell, some had said cut it off it was Raldon who said he should leave it, it was now part of who he was, it added character. Did he not have enough of that already? He thought of his mother how she must be feeling. Was she feeling anything? Perhaps she had shut down like Starr

"Can't sleep boy?"

"I think I have had enough sleep to last me a cycle father"

"You did well on the trial, I am glad someone finally put those abominations down, we lost many potential leaders over the cycles"

"It didn't really matter what they would have become father, families lost sons and daughters, brothers and sisters all life has meaning does it not?"

Raldon nodded his head sadly

"I think you became like your masters in that respect don't you?"

"Would it make you feel any better if I said none of us are perfect? You might be our next stage in evolution but you will make mistakes. Perhaps you are already thinking what you might have done different in the trial, I know I spent many days following my own cursing what I really had no control over, everyone I know lost someone to the trials and with each on the community suffered, mourned. But judge us as a whole not on our superstitions or our beliefs. You will see the best of us, you will see sacrifice and you will see us die for our families and friends"

"I haven't learnt enough yet to judge father"

"You just knowing that tells me you are learning. You get some rest you will have a hard day tomorrow; you have your duties perhaps you should have stayed in those caves until the end of the trial"

Raldon said smiling

Torrah hadn't wanted to leave Stylar, she had been angry with her mother for even suggesting it. They had been created to be together, her mother had smiled warmly and said they would have plenty of time, plenty of opportunities to be with one another, each moment they were apart felt like an eternity, it was almost like a physical pain she felt, she felt hollow inside and when she saw him, she just couldn't find the words. Torrah saw this as a weakness her mother said it was normal. She had left gritting her teeth but she didn't want to upset Stylar or his family, he had said they would be together that next morning, he had embraced her kissed her on the forehead as if he could put even a small portion of his feelings into such an act. Stylar was becoming a product of the community not those who had created him, he wanted to see these people thrive live instead of exist and she wanted that too but she wasn't sure if it was because of him or because of the way she felt. She was beginning to wonder if her will was her own. Or was it led by these damn genes of hers? He seemed at ease with those around him she was still struggling. She was also interested how he could put himself into a meditative state? I think that's what Rani had said to ease his suffering when they had to endure the pain of their growth. Why couldn't she do that? Where had he learnt it or was it as natural to him as breathing? She wondered if he had already become more than their masters had intended. He looked at her and it was as if he knew what she was thinking. Her brethren had been bred to thrive on a new world and if she was honest she wasn't sure they would ever leave this one

Marlac was convinced his chance of getting off this dying world had gone, as the children grew they seemed to get more uncontrollable. Barla had had a few challenges in his weakened state he had settled them in his no nonsense way by putting yet more of his brethren in intensive care, when they had been released they had been subservient to their leader he barely gave them a glance. The device had only been a partial success when it activated it calmed him down for maybe an hour then he would once more have that look on his face, it was akin to chaos which he seemed to thrive on. Marlac couldn't help fearing what would happen when they reached adolescence, where thoughts of the opposite sex motivated to a point where it often drove people to do things that were out of character for Barla that could mean anything, another five weeks and they would be put into a community who had a certain hierarchy and Barla would see such things as a threat and he would react as he saw fit and the others would follow. Perhaps Torrah might still be of use. Disobedience never tolerated in any society, the young would be put in their place, but with the exception of Torrah who else could do that? He decided to send Tarise she was part of both worlds and tended to carry out duties efficiently. Marlac had given instructions for his people to keep their distance perhaps that was another error, damn he was getting old. Would Torrahs loyalties be divided or would biology and conditioning be the deciding factor. He had not realised the time. He saw a few technicians on the monitors as well as lab assistants but there was no one who was familiar with the community more specifically Tarise. Marlac went to a console he hadn't used in several cycles but it was like he had never been away from the apparatus, he pressed a switch that would alert the nearest assistant that their presence was needed, he starting looking through his notes on Torrah. The door swung open and Glarai came in at some pace

"I have told you before about your pace around such vital equipment haven't I?"

"I am sorry I thought it was an emergency you never use the machine, I thought there had been another incident or you were sick"

"I need you to find Tarise. I want her to observe Torrah I need to know how she will react to her brethren, if she is functioning at all? Perhaps I am hoping for too much from her, I know it's not scientific but right now we could do with some good fortune"

"I will locate her and covey your orders. Do you need anything else from me?"

"No Glarai that will be all for this evening"

Glarai didn't get a hundred metres from Marlac before Tarise was there

"So I am finally returning home? I had thought it would be sooner but Raldon wanted as much information as possible on the children and I know you will also keep us informed through various ways"

Both females had been into the community but both had decided it was better to be between the two locations, well actually they had been told because like all societies there was a structure of rule and in some ways the higher up you appeared to be sometimes the less choices you really had. Both knew time was running out for the community and though motivations were different it had brought the females to the same place

Raldon sat in his quarters, Nairi was close by as was always the case, Rani and Dianer had joined them and in front of them was Tarise she had made her initial report a couple of days before and Raldon could not really remember the last time he had slept more than a couple of hours. Dianer looked nervous as if wondering why she was there. Raldon could see her discomfort but perhaps this was the time for such reactions

"Well everyone is here; I think some of us are wondering why?"

He could not help smiling at Dianer

"Most of us are from the communities past don't get me wrong we are respected by our people our decisions after all effect all those within the community and with our cycles of service we have earned trust. You Dianer are our now, our future, I hope twenty cycles from now our people will look on you like they do me now. You need to know what we know; you now have a voice that is why you are here pit boss is not just a title a position of power it's your life even when someone else takes over your task goes on"

It was then someone cleared his throat

"Oh Stylar I'm so glad you could join us"

"I'm sorry I'm late I lost track of time"

There were a few knowing smiles from the females assembled

"Stylar has become more than my adoptive son I see him as our future, what he knows is by design, we have the experience together we can be a driving force for the communities' future, because I too have heard the whispers, about our end and I decided long ago I would fight for this community too my last breath"

Dianer looked at Stylar perhaps she needed to spend more time with him because all she saw was a young boy. To put the hope and lives of her people in him was disturbing. Raldon slammed his hand down on a rock

"Now to business Tarise came to me a few days ago with the following report"

He let the words sink in before he continued, as if to say these words might be the most important words they would ever hear

"Our race is taking its final gasp"

That got their attention, the questioning looks were what he hoped to see

"With all due respect Raldon I don't think we need scare tactics at this time"

Raldon looked at Rani

"How long have you known me? I will ask another question in all that time have I ever used scare tactics as you call them?"

Rani looked like she was thinking as if remembering all those cycles before she shook her head

"We have always treated these caverns as our world all though we have always suspected there was more. My life changed a couple of days ago when I was told the planet we toil beneath is for all intents and purposes dead. Billions have already fled those who remain most are not aware of the facts, the last great ships near completion including one twenty kilometres from where we are now, roughly because no one has seen it as of yet. I thought it was my age getting old, but the air isn't what it once was, it doesn't nourish like it did when I was a boy"

There were nods from the elders in the chamber as they seemed to have come to the same conclusion. Rani had become aware of this fact several cycles ago chest related illnesses had risen as had deaths some seeming like suffocation.

"Those ventilators that keep us alive. Do you think they are now a priority, most likely those who maintained them have gone, perhaps a skeleton crew left to tend them but as the air dies so will we. One possible way through to that chamber where that ship is getting readied is that very chamber where so many of our young lost their lives. Those abominations that feasted on our young were but another type of guard. Our guards are no more we can explore what they protected. Stylar looks similar to us doesn't he, it's the differences you cannot see that gave him the capabilities to kill those animals"

Raldon lashed out with such speed and purpose everyone in that room knew they would be on the ground. Stylar sidestepped his father taking hold of his adoptive fathers' arm and sending him to the floor, never changing expression. Dianer couldn't help but stare at the young male. How had he known?

Not only that the blow was coming, but how did he know what to do to defend himself. Raldon had clearly made his point without using words, he took Stylars hand which had been offered he saw the smirk on his sons' face, but pretended he hadn't

"Stylars people have the capability to pilot that ship, but what they would be doing would be selling themselves into servitude they would become us and the people left behind they would gasp the toxic air until their lungs could no longer sustain them. I truly believe we need Stylar and his people to survive, we need to work together, it is like a rope the more strands the stronger it becomes, we are a community built up of many races but when we have toiled in the mines our skin is one colour. Stylar and his brothers and sister are another race with their own identity, we need to embrace them not fear them"

Raldon had known she was there. Where else would she be?

"Torrah you can come in"

The girl entered her eyes to the ground she didn't need to see him to know where he was and she was never whole until she felt her hand in his. Dianer watched such a simple motion and she felt perhaps jealousy? Envy? It was a feeling that made her think of those words Raldon had said about needing more than just her position, she looked to Nairi who had her hand on Raldons shoulder and for the first time she felt truly alone

"Anyway"

Raldon continued

"The next challenge will be to incorporate Stylars people with our own"

"You call them my people father? You are my people you have earned that right. Barla and the others need to earn my respect before I accept them as my brethren. You will always have my protection"

That was the first time the word brethren was used and for all time after that was what they would be known as

Dianer would never be able to explain what had happened next, she simply lost control, anger came from she did not know where? She couldn't listen any more

"Your protection? We survived hundreds of cycles before you came along boy and we will still be here long after you are gone"

Torrahs expression had changed from calm to anger, she wanted her hand free but Stylars grip had increased. Dianer could see she felt a threat and she was going to protect him

"Forgive me for saying this Dianer but you just don't know what my people are capable of"

"Perhaps you would like to show me? Show us?"

"Raldon can I?"

"I think it's time people knew what we might be up against when your brethren are introduced"

Stylar knew he needed a demonstration that would be hard to ignore. The group were assembled around a stone table, it almost looked like the room had been carved around it

"The table has it any significance? Any memories?"

"It's just a table. But perhaps a demonstration that won't involve you breaking most of the bones in your hand"

"I think Dianer will not be easily convinced. It has to be something that she cannot explain. Dianer please try and break the table"

"Are you serious that stone has to be almost a metre thick"

"So you won't even try?"

Dianer seemed to take a deep breath and she stood up, she took a few deep breaths and then brought her hand down with a crunch

"You son of a bitch"

"I will look at your hand when this gathering ends"

Rani said with her matter of fact manner. Stylar untangled his hand from Torrahs and he made her take a seat

"You are sure about the table?"

"I am sure"

Raldon said thinking Rani would have two patients at the end of this gathering, it wasn't as if anything he could do could damage a stone perhaps as old as time. Stylar took his animal skin off so his chest was exposed. Dianer looked away as if to say please, she also muttered something under her breath. Raldon could see how Stylars body was developing for his age it was astonishing. Perhaps because he was working in the mines. Perhaps his son was showing off just a little. Stylar was now focussed all the sounds around him were gone, he could hear his heart beating, the blood coursing through his veins, he could feel his muscles beginning to strain, he took a breath and before he had finished, his arm had gone straight down, his palm slapping the rock. Stylar put the skin back on and turned his back, the chamber was eerily silent. Dianer looked at the table

"Very impressive, but the table still seems to be in one piece"

Stylar walked out of the chamber with Torrah beside him"I told you it was"

It was half way through the sentence that they heard a crack, small at first but it increased in volume. Raldon had a habit of leaning back on his chair especially when he was waiting, his feet hooked under the table, so backwards he fell. Nairi saw the look of surprise on her mates face and she couldn't help but start laughing they all felt like doing that but he was their leader and he deserved, who was anyone kidding? After the initial shock of what had just happened they all began to laugh because the surprise on Raldons face. Was it that he had been caught unawares and fallen back? Or the shock the table had broken? Dianer just stared at the three pieces that had once been whole. How the hell had he done that? Rani true to her word was already at Dianers side examining her hand. Ranis voice was low so only Dianer heard it, it was serious and she knew she needed to take the advice that was given

"I would never get him angry or upset, if you ever think about it remember the table"

Torrah could not help but stare at her mate as they went down the tunnel. She wondered where they were going. Stylar answered as if she had verbally asked the question

"We are going to eat with our new friends"

Torrah wondered what he saw in some of the children. Stylar smiled. He saw potential, that was in everyone at a certain point in their lives

"You still sometimes think too much like those who bred us"

"That is where we came from we can't just turn our backs on that. We have to take something from the experience"

"We were bred to service that society do you think we should take anything from them?"

"This society took us in, Raldon knows what our purpose was supposed to be but still he had faith, I don't know whether it was in the people we were around or perhaps us. I doubt we will ever know. I am proud we have been accepted"

"Perhaps we are accepted now because I appearance we are still children. But how will we be treated when we have matured? Do you not think they will fear you because they have no control"?

"I hope they will remember how I am now and even though physically different what is inside is still the same. But at the end of the day as long as friends and family accept me that's all that really matters"

"I wonder what I see in you sometimes"
"At the moment I am guessing my boyish good looks"
"I was thinking more your optimism or perhaps your naivety"
"I think I can live with that I hope it is enough"

The pair walked into a small meeting room just off from the main hall, everyone was gathered they chatted amongst themselves apart from Kolt who looked like he wanted the wall behind him to engulf him and take him away from the place. Stylar noticed that every once in a while, Xery would give him an encouraging smile as if to say come and join us, but he seemed to just want to watch and listen. Carstal and Nebar had obviously just come from the showers, they had been on shift the big male looked like he had a bruise on his cheek. Carstal looked up as if he sensed someone was watching him he smiled

"Stylar, Torrah it's good to see you"

The conversations stopped and everyone waited to take their seats, it wasn't as relaxed as Stylar had hoped there was an awkwardness. He had to know

"What happened to you?"

Carstal smiled

"It was nothing"

Nebar broke in at that point

"Nothing? You should have seen it Stylar some of the young males felt a little threatened by this males' presence so they decided he needed to be shown his place. How many were there five? Anyway a lesson was taught but it wasn't the one that was expected, Dianer was not the happiest I have ever seen her. Terak was firmly in her sights you should have been there. Why weren't you there Stylar?"

"I had community business"

"You will remember us little people on the way up won't you?"

"Believe me it would take a lot to forget someone like you"

"I think I will take that as a compliment"

There were a few giggles at the table

"Did you do anything interesting today Kolt?"

Kolts reaction was almost immediate he seemed to sink into his chair as if he was trying to disappear, Stylar was saddened by the reaction. Why had he never really felt like that? Was it his genetics? He couldn't even begin to imagine how he was feeling

"Kolt why do you feel so threatened even in front of your friends?"

"My, my friends, I've never had friends you just feel sorry for me"

"In a way I guess that is true but I think you underestimate what you could be

I have heard this speech before. What do you know? You could never understand"

"Forgive me for giving a damn"

Stylar could feel he was starting to lose control, perhaps it was the fact he was feeling sorry for himself.

Xery had had enough

"Just leave him be Stylar, if he doesn't want to join us you should respect that"

"I was just trying to help"

"You will have to learn one day you can't save us all"

"I've already learnt that"

"You mean Starr? That wasn't a loss she will recover in time, she might not be the same self-opinionated girl that went into those caves but that might not be a bad thing"

"She has lost what made her different, maybe we didn't agree with her ways. Perhaps if we had shown her some compassion"

"Compassion is easier to show when you are looking down"

Kolt spit the words out like venom, an uncomfortable silence followed which no one seemed to want to break, well everyone apart from Nolic

"Well are we here to eat or argue amongst ourselves I don't know about the rest of you but I could eat one of those creatures Stylar killed the other day in the cave"

Stylar stood

"Sorry everyone I think I will eat later with some work mates; I seem to have lost my appetite"

A couple of the others rose as well Stylar decided to leave a thought in Kolts mind

"I suggest my young friend you stop feeling sorry for yourself or you might lose the few friends you have got"

"I don't need friends. All my life the only thing I have known from others was disappointment"

"Perhaps you shouldn't judge those around this table so, because what was formed in the cave could last you a lifetime. You might think I am preaching you are right, I hoped to help if I made you feel worse that is unfortunate, if you ever want to talk I will listen."

Now only Kolt and Xery remained at the table. Kolt could feel Xerys eyes on him she was scrutinising him, finally he spoke

"Why have I got so much anger inside?"

"That's an easy one its frustration, bitterness you have let it fester too long"

"So what should I do confess all too you?"

"Perhaps not to me but you need to talk to someone, whether you like it or not we are social animals, though by that outburst you wouldn't know would you"

"So you are taking Stylars side?"

"It's not a question of sides, you both have your opinions it is not my place to judge. I will not get caught in the middle of this disagreement"

"I suppose that is fair enough, this is all a new experience for me Oh?"

"Yes, no one has ever cared enough to have their meal spoilt by me"

"You must be so proud"

"Shall we eat?"

"This almost feels like a first meal. You know together what potential mates might have?"

"First meal? Well, well I wasn't"

"Relax I know you don't think of me in those terms"

The words out of Kolts mouth were as much of a shock to him as they were to her, it was like someone else was saying them

"I would like to"

"Well you are full of surprises this evening aren't you?"

"Yeh it must be the company I am keeping"

"So is that a good thing or a bad thing?"

"I might just tell you one day"

Kolt picked up a spoon and started to dish out some food that had been left for the children he handed the first bowl to Xery then dished one out for himself. There was the silence but this time it felt comfortable both were thinking of the possibilities

Nolic stayed in the shadows while Rani bathed Starr, Rani had never really had time for him which didn't really bother him, he had spent most of his life being ignored by family so virtual strangers didn't concern him. Nolic had always had a crush on Starr but she had always seen him as an irritation. She seemed to be looking into the distance he wondered what she was seeing. He wondered when Rani would leave. He wanted to be alone with Starr he had sneaked in every night since the trial, he knew most people thought he was odd, he heard the whispers, saw it in their eyes. Starr had been one of those children who had looked down on him and when he knew she was doing it, there was real hurt there but still he couldn't help how he felt, he felt grief right now but the first time in his life it wasn't for him. Rani stroked a strand of hair from Starrs eye and went back to tending others. Nolic crept closer the facility glowed, yes that was the right word compared with most of his world this was relatively clean not whites, always greys but at least not blacks, none of the torches like the mines this was their masters' technology well from hundreds of cycles ago, they accepted it because they all had known it their whole life, the light radiated from the walls, he listened for footsteps then when he was sure no one was there he slipped silently into her room? Not quite hardly big enough for her bed and a solitary chair

"Starr it's me I told you I would come back, I think you are looking better, I am sure I see some colour today"

Starr just stared back

"It must be lonely in here by yourself, yes I know Rani is here and the others but I don't see any of your friends. I am probably the last person you would expect, we have never really, well it's like we are from two different worlds, I heard on occasion what you were saying about me, I always liked you, I guess sometimes we can't control who we feel something for. I know when you grow up you are going to break a lot of boys hearts I know I will be one of them which I will hate but I just want you to get better. A single tear formed it gathered at the corner of his eye at his lashes and it rolled down his cheek he wiped it with the back of his hand and could feel his nose running looked like his sleeve would have to do as always, he thought about using the sheets Starr was lying on but didn't want to give it away that he had been in the room. He looked at Starr You won't tell anyone I used my sleeve will you?"

Why had he thought of something so trivial?

"I would wager you want to say something nasty to me now. Well I better let you get your rest you need to build your strength up. I will try and get back to see you tomorrow"

With that he leant over and kissed her on the forehead which left a mark so he quickly rubbed it off with his sleeve

"It's alright it's as clean as my clothes get"

Then Nolic disappeared into the shadows like a wraith

Rani was stood at the door smiling sometimes children could still surprise her, it was nice when they did it gave her hope, it told her she still had things to learn

"I don't know whether he helps you Starr but I know it does you no harm knowing someone wants you to come back to them. I haven't been love like that in too many cycles"

Her smile was a sad one as she remembered, it was an expression she never used in the community, they thought she was more than she actually was

"We both know Nolic is wrong about the warm comfortable place don't we? Where you are now it's cold and dark just keep looking for that light and when you see it walk into it my girl I will be there waiting"

Stylar studied the corpse in front of him. Raldon had thought it important to show every aspect of their lives underground, this had been no accident, no cave in, this had been murder. The fury Stylar saw in Raldons eyes at the moment was reflected in those gathered around them. The room was small it was almost unfinished in look, but the only ones who used it no longer had any care for their surroundings. Raldon had been here too many times and he would never get used to the place. The brutality and needless suffering had ended for this poor male, this body as contorted as his features, he had not died well if there was such a way to go? This was the finality of death. Raldon looked up

"The same captain?"

There were several nods. Stylar had heard about this captain he maintained order with fear he operated on the lower levels where the groups were not as productive as Dianers

"He can't get away with this"

A voice from the group shouted

"What are we going to do?"

Raldon replied

"Is he still on duty?"

No one knew where this question came from, there were a few quizzical looks

"Of course he is he hasn't got his full quota for suffering for the day yet"

"That's all I needed to know"

Raldon still couldn't see who was asking the questions but he didn't like the tone there was a cold element to it that made Raldon very nervous he didn't want to lose any more good people, no one noticed him slip away which was what he wanted. He knew that they would call for a gathering and they would talk and nothing would be achieved, he moved quickly there was no one about the way he chose to go he would get to the lover levels in perhaps twenty minutes most perhaps another ten minutes after that if they were rushing, he was going to judge this captain and that judgement would be guilty. Stylar had already covered a couple of kilometres he wasn't even breathing hard. He would do this in such a way that their masters would know it wasn't the community, he had no time to climb down rungs of ladders he clamped his feet on the ladders and slid down his hands burned with friction but he knew they would heal quickly, his senses searching, he was ready his heart rate had increased. Their masters had always thought they were at the top of the food chain it was time to change that belief, he could sense he was coming to the bottom his legs clamped tighter as he braced himself he hit the ground without making a sound his weight evenly spread, he had done in a few minutes that others would take thirty perhaps forty minutes to traverse, he went into shadow and listened for the distant echo of voices and rock being struck. He had wondered how long it would take him to find the captain good fortune was with him. Stylar had never seen this group before, to his eyes it was almost as if they were another species, they were a good head shorter than their community family perhaps there was an odd community member down here some seemed to dwarf others. Who were these miserable wretches? Their equipment was like the communities' young would use, their bodies looked ill equipped to work in such conditions, they had thin spindly legs as if they could barely hold them up. Raldon had never mentioned these poor souls, he supposed he worried enough about his own people, these clearly were not them, the air was worse down here it took more effort to even get a small percentage of what was needed to carry out basic function their eyes were large as if they were taking in all what little light there was even the torches didn't burn brightly, they barely smouldered, their cheek bones were shrunken in and their expressions ranged from curiosity to terror, he touched the cave wall it was full of moisture he used both hands to coat his body in the darker ore, to disguise who and what he was. A male stepped forward he was shaking a little but from fear or the cold he couldn't be sure.

"Who, who are you?"

His voice was soft but there was something about it that cried authority

"I am a friend I am looking for the captain who tortures who he can down here in the depths"

"My names David who are you?"

The male was nothing more than a boy

"I am Stylar I am from above, I have never seen people like you before"

"We are what my father calls political prisoners, in a way I guess we are luckier than most, a lot of our kind were executed"

"Why would someone do this to you?"

"I guess you are one of the reasons"   "Me?"

"Not just you your people we were trying to get your people released before the end, those in power said if we were so concerned about your plight we should join you, experience your conditions, so here we are"

"But and I don't want to offend you or your people you are so small, surely you won't get enough ore out of here to justify"

"No you don't understand this is a warning to others, so many of our number have already died, none of us will survive it's just a matter of time and being down here we will soon be forgotten"

The male looked perhaps seven or eight, but his bearing and the way he used his words he was clearly older

"Can I ask your age?"

"I am thirteen coming up to my fourteenth Birthday, I hope if I am fortunate enough, sickness has taken some of us not just the working conditions"

"How old are you?"

Stylar hesitated for a moment he wondered if the young male would understand

"I am almost ten weeks"

The young male just stared

"How can that be? I would have said you were my age, perhaps older your physical development are you typical of the community?"

"No, there is nothing typical about me. When they created my brothers and sisters we were the last in a long line of experimentation"

"So the experiments continued? The government told us generations ago that such projects had ceased, I must tell you"

Before he could finish his sentence a whip lash cracked against his back, David's expression one of agony. Stylar could see he had the rank of captain surely there wouldn't be any more of his position down here? Did it matter? He was down here to make an example this individual was as good as any.

David was on his knees breathing hard, the guard spoke Stylar had never heard such a voice, it seemed to vibrate on the air, it had a grating tone to it, the pitch changed

"Who are you talking to boy? Not another one pretending to be mad?"

"I think you will wish he was. Maybe you would like to used that whip on someone nearer your size?"

Stylar had grown quite a lot but the guard was perhaps a good half metre taller, so the only response he got was a cruel laugh

"I have got to give you credit boy you have balls; it won't save you though"

"I think you will find I have a few surprises"

The guard raised his whip and brought it down, Stylar grabbed the hand in which the whip was held, he could feel his feet digging in, the guards suit was making whirring noises as if gears were accounting and trying to compensate to the force that was being brought to bear. Was it his imagination or was the guard grunting?

"You are strong boy I didn't know your people were capable of such power"

Stylar had to answer through gritted teeth

"You haven't encountered someone like me before I am something new"

"New?"

"Have you not heard of Marlac?"

The gears were now screaming in the guards arms they were tearing under the pressure, he cried out in pain as the whip fell from his hand. Some of the individuals had been working up to the point when David had been struck but now all eyes were on the confrontation, there were looks of shock no one could defeat a guard. The guard was clearly shaken

"You can't be one of them they haven't left the facility, only a young female left because her mate was terminated"

"So you see your people have tried to kill me before"

"Why would you let me know this? The only reason would be"

Stylar smiled, David looked into the young males' eyes in that moment and his blood ran cold, he had never seen a smile like it

"Why do you think?"

Stylar asked it was getting harder to breath the exertion had taken its toll, the struggle between bone and sinew and alloy and gears

"You are not as strong as you thought are you? This suit sustains me; your lungs are not up to the challenge of this thin air are they?"

The guard with his good arm grabbed Stylar by the neck and lifted him off the ground, Stylar didn't kick and struggle like most would have done, he didn't panic, he just slowly began to pry the fingers from around his throat and one by one they snapped, the guard was screaming the sound was blood curdling and it was with the second broken finger that Stylar was released. Stylar was on his hands and knees trying to gulp just a little more air, around him things were going cloudy, his vision dimming. The guard lashed out with one of his legs and for his effort he heard a satisfying crack as a couple of ribs broke, it was as if the guard was waiting for the cry of agony but it never came. Stylar rose slowly to his feet and looked up at the guard with as much hatred as he could manage, not just the hatred from himself but from an entire race of people

"I've finished playing let's end this"

The guard rushed him, Stylar was there, then he was gone, he straightened his arm the sound of metal being crushed could be heard. The guard grabbed his side

"You, you crushed my ribs"

"I thought I would just return the favour"

As he said the words he physically picked the captain up the suit was lightweight but saying that it still probably weighed a couple of hundred pounds, the guard was screaming he would never tell the secret he would never mistreat prisoners they were the promises of a male who saw his end fast approaching. Stylar had wanted the male to suffer but he wanted to end it quick before the males' screams drew more attention than he could deal with. Stylar finished the move which he seemed to have started an eternity before by bringing the captains body down he had managed to somehow bring the males body around so when he went down onto one knee the captains suit came down hard and he heard the sound of the males' spine snapping, he got to his feet shakily, he kicked the male in the neck and the males life was ended. David walked across and looked at the corpse

"They will kill us all for this"

Stylar looked at him

"They'll know you didn't, couldn't have done this they'll look elsewhere but the message has still to be given"

Stylar went over to a storage locker, it was similar to those above, yes it had what he needed, chisels and a hammer, he lifted the guard up pinning him with his body so he didn't slip and then with most of what was left of his strength. How was he going to do this?

"I have him, I told you I will always have your back as long as I have air to breath, saying that there isn't a lot down here is there?"

Stylar hadn't realised he had been followed. Carstal had hold of the male Stylar after finding something to stand on hammered one chisel into the males' left hand, then the second into his right, he thrust one more chisel through the males' faceplate and stepped off the makeshift stool, he hadn't finished he wrote the ominous words BE WARNED then he turned to David

"I know what you have seen here you might call barbaric and to be honest it probably was, but I had to do this. If I am more like your people than my own so be it, I will have to live with that. No group has the right to own another's life to use a people like beasts of burden, if blood has to be spilled to protect my own I will do it. I can accept that can you?"

"Your words surprise me they are cold don't you have compassion?"

"Compassion is a luxury I can't afford. I have already earned a reputation amongst some of my people they think I am this saviour told in prophecy. My father has brought me up to protect my own and I will sacrifice for others and if that means my life as well then I hope I have the courage to offer it"

"What has made you so cynical?"

"They have made me that way. I journey on a path that can only end one of two ways. My people will fight and win their freedom, or they will die in the attempt. I will never question any act because I hope it will always be motivated to keep others from harm, but don't misunderstand me if I have to hang a thousand individuals in such a manner I will, because I think I am capable of acts the community would never do. If others come looking for his killer they will find me, I won't hide and I will not run and I will send message after message until my meaning is clear. Vengeance will be sought in a way that will make this planet cower. This is my life and I will live it and feel sorry for anyone who will try and stand in my way"

"I think you are their saviour and perhaps ours too"

"I just want a better life for all those I know"

Stylar once more felt light headed perhaps his ribs were in worse shape than he had thought. It was quick dullness went to darkness and at that moment he wondered if his life was over before it had really begun. It seemed so still but there were voices faint voices. Were they calling him? Xery what was she doing down here? Then there was silence. Carstal hadn't heard her approach. Carstal had been easy to follow, they walked with a lightness of step that was unusual for their size but Xery she knew about stealth. Xery had watched as Carstal observed, she had expected him to get involved but even when it looked as if their friend might lose the encounter he had done nothing only when the guard was finished had Carstal shown himself. Why had he let their friend take so much punishment?

"Why didn't you stop him?"

Carstal was surprised by the hostility in her voice, Xery was small in stature but she had a presence about her

"It was not my fight. He has to learn that sometimes all he will have is his two bare hands; I can't I won't always be there to protect him"

"I just think he might have learnt something without having so much punishment inflicted. Rani will not be pleased and I don't even want to think how Raldon will react"

"You took beatings when you were younger didn't you?"

Xery nodded

"Did you learn more from them? Or do you think you would have learnt more if you had hidden. Stylar is ten weeks old he has so much life experience to catch up on he has to learn these lessons. Do you understand?"

"Yes, I see your point. But what was the point of this?"

Xery pointed to the captain nailed to the rock face

"That's our friends' way of saying we will no longer except the punishment our masters deem necessary"

"Don't you think he could have made his point in a less bloody way?"

"It's a bloody world, now are you going to help me get our young friend back up there? It's going to be quite a climb"

"You saw the mess being made you clean it up"

"Thanks a lot"

Xery only now took in the figures that surrounded them, she had never seen people like this, most of them looked half dead or worse

"Carstal take our leader to the facility, he will need those ribs wrapped I will catch up it's going to take you an hour to get to the top it will take me half that time. I want to find something out"

Carstal nodded and picked Stylar up as gently as he could and slung him over his shoulder, if he was honest it wasn't going to slow him down that much, the ore he took on a daily basis was many times heavier than his friend here, but he could see the curiosity in Xerys eyes, besides what could they do? There was no threat here. Xery wanted to find out as much as she could, she might not have long she didn't know how long it would take for the captain to be discovered. Xery watched Carstal disappear into the darkness which only took several steps

"Have you got someone of authority? A leader?"

"But you are but a child?"

"I am a child who could beat anyone here. I am sorry diplomacy was never my strong point"

A female stepped forward she looked like she might be the oldest of the group and there was a slight smile on her lips

"I think you want to speak with me"

"Yes, I think I do, I have questions"

"well that is a start how can we help one another?"

"Firstly, I think I will see if I like the answers to my questions and we will go from there shall we?"

"What would you like to know?"

"How long have you been down here? I thought this level was worked on by my people?"

"Several weeks, there are still some of your kind down here, but a few were taken about the time we were brought down here. I think it's only a matter of a week perhaps two before sickness and fatigue will take us. We are not meant for such labour"

"I heard a little of the conversation between the boy and Stylar. Can I ask what you did for your people?"

"We are mostly designers; engineers we were responsible for a lot of the craft that helped our people escape this dying world. Our only crime was speaking out against the governing body. We argued on points such as the use of forced labour and thought you should be; it doesn't matter now we are all in the same position. Could I talk with one of your leaders? Xery is it? I think we might be able to aid one another."

"I will pass your request on to the relevant individuals, with your knowledge I think we might be able to help one another, but that is the opinion of a mere girl. Can I ask your name?"

"Sarah, I don't think we will see one another soon, I have a feeling the ladders will be guarded and they will be hunting for your young friend"

"I think you will find my people can be quite resourceful you might see us sooner than you think"

"You are very confident in your peoples' abilities"

"I have seen what they can achieve when they are one, I hope I will see you soon Sarah"

"I hope so too Xery"

Xery took hold of the ladder and climbed with a surety that said she had been climbing all her life which some claimed she had, she didn't mention the fact that she could already hear the approach of guards. Where would those people go? There would be little accomplished by terminating them, the state of most it would have been doing them a kindness

The commanders aid had seen the captains' life readings increase so guards had been dispatched but he could see they would be too late what he knew for sure was this was not done by any of the scientists, engineers and various other professional groups, this had been done by someone above. He had heard about the death of a worker by the captains' hand, he had been warned. But it was unlike the community they had not acted in such a manner for a generation, every fibre of his being said investigate, but he had no resources and as more of his personnel were shipped out, resources were spread too thin now. Now he would have to have the guards double up so more gaps in their security, he was thinking this as one of his sergeants made his report

"So what you are telling me sergeant is someone killed the captain with his bare hands?"

"Yes, yes, yes sir"

"It sounds like it might have been one of Marlacs test subjects have you?"

"Yes, sir that occurred to me, I just think perhaps two or three were here but the evidence points to only one combatant. I also sent a couple of my people to the workers' medical facility just in case"

"Thank you sergeant I am a little disturbed by your report but at least you can rule out the workers in that section. Don't take any action against them I have been told not to quicken their end"

"What about the captains' body?"

"Leave it, it was a warning let it hang there it might sharpen those who remain in our ranks knowing there is someone out there who is capable of ending their existence"

The line went silent as the second relayed his report to the commander, it would be interesting to see the commanders' reaction

Carstal had been as good as his word it took forty minutes to get to the facility where Torrah was waiting it was as if she knew, Raldon joined them several minutes panting, yes he definitely was not the male he used to be. Expressions ranged from concern to disgust, Torrah just wanted him to open his eyes so she could tell him exactly what she thought of his actions. Raldon was clearly thinking about the consequences for the community, he would think twice before inviting his son to such gatherings again unless of course he secured the males promise that he would not go off and terminate the first individual he came across, the group talked amongst themselves and it was as if he had heard them, he stirred, his eyes opened slowly

"That's what I wanted all my loved ones around my bed when I woke"

"Don't try and sweet talk your way out of this, what you did was irresponsible, you this great leader hah"

"I can always rely on you cheering me up Torrah"

"I hate to say this Stylar but she's right what you did has put the whole community in danger"

"Raldon I don't think"

"I haven't finished I know we were all distressed about how the male was beaten but you can't let your heart rule your actions"

"When were we going to act? How much are you willing to take father?"

Nairi had arrived only moments before and she had had enough of Stylars attitude

"That is enough Stylar. Do you think it's easy seeing our own suffer? But we know there is nothing we can do"

"If that is what you think then we might have already lost"

Raldon had tried to keep calm throughout the short but heated conversation, this was something he had acquired from cycles of experience. Of course he had days when he felt like Stylar, those he tried to keep to himself. Raldon had taught the young male a lot but you could not teach experience it was something that had to be lived. Perhaps the frustration was knowing that time seemed to be running out.

"Tarise has come back to the fold and she was due to meet with me tonight I've put it back to tomorrow I want you with me Stylar"

"Of course father, it's always nice to see Tarise"

"It is not a social visit she has been told to watch over Torrah"

"Why?"

"That is one of the things we will find out tomorrow"

Rani appeared at entrance to the room

"I have been told we have guards on the way, I think they might be looking for injuries consistent with battling a guard in an exoskeleton can you move?"

"Of course a couple of cracked ribs won't even slow me down"

"Come on my hero let's get you to bed"

"Torrah you know what I have said about making statements that can be taken the wrong way"

"In your condition it's not like you would have the strength to do anything physical"

Stylar stood, putting his arm around Torrahs shoulder, seeming to remember something

"Father can I have a few moments of your time?"

Raldon took his sons arm and they went into an adjacent room, even Torrah couldn't hear but by Raldons expression he did not look pleased when they returned

"Torrah if you would?"

Stylar put his arm back around his mates' shoulder and left the room

"If anyone's going to save him, it will be her"

Rani commented and there were several nods of agreement

"What were you talking about?"

"I am sorry my love it was meant just for my ears; I hope you will never find out"

"It was that bad was it?"

"Now that would be telling wouldn't it let us just say I hope he never has to do what I say"

The next morning Stylar walked with Raldon into the council chambers the room was a lot larger than he had expected, the council elders were almost shrouded in darkness shadows crossed their faces which seemed to blend into the rocks they sat in front of. As Stylar understood it these individuals were not normally voted in, they had not earned the right to sit in the chambers most were last of their lines they were the descendants of great leaders, most of which had been forgotten over the cycles. What was said about them was that their ancestors had lived above, but had been driven underground by prejudice and fear in many ways these old tired individuals reflected the state of the community, both were running on borrowed time. What the young male could not understand was why the community had let things get so bad. What were they waiting for? This saviour who he was supposed to be?

Perhaps they just needed someone who would lead them, would motivate a strong people which was their true nature, they had been knocked down so many times now they didn't even bother getting up. There was a sound metal striking stone which jarred Stylar out of his thoughts. A voice came from the darkness

"First of all, I would like to acknowledge the presence of a new member of our community. I would have liked to have said it was an honour to meet you but after the incident yesterday I question why Raldon has brought you here"

"You would dare question Raldons motives after all he has done for the community?"

Stylar didn't get a chance to finish his sentence, he felt the impact to his jaw and the anger this sparked.

Raldon stepped back and for a moment he felt fear, a fear that he hadn't felt since his earliest memories. Forgive the outburst honoured elder it will not happen again

The statement had been directed more at Stylar than the council and Stylar bowed his head in understanding

"He is young his actions were carried out without thought, his heart rules over his head"

"Do you think that excuse would satisfy our masters? We are at a loss to understand why there has been no retribution, we still remember last time one of our guards met his end by several of our own. Do you remember how many died?"

"No one knows you sure"

Raldon replied he had never told his son about that event

"I see your son still has some things to learn"

The next words out of the old males' lips sent a chill down Raldons spine every word seemed to be laced with a threat

"When one of our owns actions endanger the lives of the community, it is everyone's business. You put your faith in prophecy why?"

Raldon just couldn't control what came out of his mouth next

"Because that's all we have left; you haven't seen the suffering. I have seen more friends die than anyone ever should. You have been down here so long your emotions have gone stagnant to a point where I wonder if you care anymore, you pass out these rulings because of who your ancestors were, that shouldn't give you the right, things have changed and it's because you haven't that our community is facing its end"

The elder was clearly surprised by the passion in Raldons words and it seemed like minutes before he replied even though it was probably only several seconds

"You have never shown such feeling before. Why choose now? Don't you think this is the end of our community?"

"If it is we no longer have anything to lose do we?"

Tarise stepped out of the shadows, followed by Dianer and some of the individuals she relied on, this had never happened before it had always been for the elite of the community. Dianer had gained the right her companions had not, one of the other elders' patience had worn out

"How dare they come into the chambers by what right?"

Dianer spoke in their defence

"Survival that is their right, tradition wastes time we no longer have, the secrets have to stop our people need to be told, they have earned the right to know everything. Honoured council I know these people I know what they are capable of I think there is a chance you have been away too long and have forgotten. We have grown stronger not just physically but as a community, always together never apart"

Dianer took a breath and waited for the elder to reply

"I see why you chose her Raldon, there is wisdom there beyond her cycles. You are right Dianer we must tell our people that their very existence is threatened, but before we do we must find alternatives. Don't they deserve that?"

Dianer nodded in agreement

"That is why Tarise is here, she has had more contact with our masters than most, she has gained their trust and that has been to our advantage in the past, this planet we live in is almost at its end. The people above aided its demise our work load has risen because of the fact that where our masters are bound minerals are scarce or the minerals they have found have not been encountered before. Tarise if you would?"

The female cleared her throat

"Elders, friends, I've been away from my family and friends for too long, but now is not the time to rejoice, I've heard rumours most of which I've confirmed. Firstly, our masters have given this planet no more than a couple of cycles, a lot of the population have been evacuated but hundreds of millions will perish, perhaps our community numbers four thousand, stretched out over kilometres of tunnels and mine workings, one of our masters projects, a craft is being constructed approximately ten kilometres from here, they brought their technicians in with both medical and security personnel over a few cycles, this is one of the last of her kind, the craft will hold members of the ruling bodies from the city which is twenty kilometres from this location. The craft will hold perhaps three thousand people so it will not be sufficient for all of the community, I did say one of the last ships so there is a possibility other craft exist outside of these mines, the craft is due for completion in the next few months, we will need to have individuals who know the workings of these machines, our people were bred for their strength not their intelligence. I know there are those amongst our masters we can trust, perhaps they know others without Glarai we could have never rescued Stylar from his fate, unfortunately the actions of that young male has had effect of certain areas tightening their security, that includes where Stylars brethren are being held, who incidentally will be released into the population, I will talk about that in a moment, security has also been tightened at the ships facility so it's going to be a harder proposition getting close I might be able to help with that"

The interruption took everyone by surprise, Rani had come out of the rock, well that's how it appeared

"I presume I was not invited to this gathering due to an oversight?"

"With all due respect Rani, you"

Rani didn't let her finish the sentence

"Silence child I was the female who brought you into this world and with the exception of Torrah I was present at everyone in this rooms birth. Do you think you can keep me out of such discussions?"

Raldon spoke up

"In our defence this is only a preliminary discussion, no real decisions will be made here today. Tarise is here to give us some idea of our masters' motivation and plans"

Then Raldon seemed to recall what Rani had said

"How could you get close to the ship without coming into contact with the patrols?"

"Did you see me enter this chamber?"

"No but why would?"

"The reason why you didn't see it was because I have walked these tunnels longer than anyone should have. If Tarise finds out exactly where that ship has been built, I might know an air vent, mine shaft or tunnel that connects. For my services any gathering called from now on I want to be involved that is my price is that clear? I have watched our people suffer for too many cycles, this longevity has been a curse I want to make a difference now because I want this immortality to count for something"

Raldon had walked across and now showed a side of himself he wouldn't have shared with anyone else but who was in the room he hugged Rani as he did so he whispered in her ear

"You have my word"

When he parted from her his face was neutral as it had been before

"Now Tarise would you like to continue with your report?"

"Yes of course Raldon, now I will talk about the experiment I have to say if they are introduced into the community in their present state I am convinced there will be casualties, if Stylar had stayed with the group I know he would have had a calming influence, I suspect he was bred to reason the others were bred to be led, without him they have become like a structure without foundation. Barla who now controls, is paranoid and to keep order he is prone to bouts of violence. I doubt he can be reasoned with"

Stylar stepped forward his gaze like stone his statement was short and it was chilling in its sentiment

"If he can't be reasoned with he will have to pass. I know here violence has always been the last resort.

But if I have to take his life to set an example that is what I will do"

Dianer kicked at the ground

"If my workforce or friends and family are threatened I will show you violence"

Dianer was the future of the community she could not be allowed to confront his brethren, Stylar knew there could only be one outcome

"Dianer you have to promise me you will not become involved; you will let me at least try to control the situation"

"Like you handled the guard?"

"Yes, that was an error on my part, but be truthful what would you have done to him?"

"Yes, I would have done the same if I knew there would be no retaliation, but my own personal feelings come second to the good of the community"

"That particular individual left me no choice, but you misunderstand leaving my people to me was not a request"

Terak had listened to the exchange and he had tried to let it go but he didn't like Stylars tone

"Raldon I suggest you get your son to back down"

Raldon had decided at the beginning of the heated discussion to let it play out his people needed to know the power these children possessed. Dianer had seen with her own eyes, but still she thought she could control them if they came into her sphere of influence. Raldon smiled at Terak

"I suggest you withdraw"

"Withdraw from him? I know I wouldn't break a sweat teaching your son to respect his elders"

Stylar took a step forward

"I know you have feelings for Dianer. But you don't want to embarrass yourself do you?"

Terak lunged at Stylar for his trouble, Stylar grabbed his arm, had it straight and brought his elbow down hard, not hard enough to break it but enough to cause discomfort

"I will give you a chance to reconsider your next actions"

"You couldn't break my arm, there is no strength in yours"

Motioning at Stylars arms

"Dianer do you want to tell him about what you saw?"

There was a slight smile on her lips. Yes, she was enjoying seeing this but she couldn't afford to lose Terak, not now

"Terak step back I think he would be more than capable of breaking not just bones in your arm"

Stylar let the bigger male go he dropped to the ground. Stylar had turned his back on the older male, Terak rose slowly to his feet tapped him on his shoulder, Stylar turned just in time to have a fist impact his face. Terak just gaped at the effect it had on him. Stylar smiled

"That one was free any others will cost you dearly"

Terak lowered his eyes, his way of submitting. Stylar hoped he would not have to demonstrate again, but he still had to make his point because he knew the others still did not understand

"In a few weeks my brethren will be here twenty-two individuals with as much strength as I have now, I can't even guess what they could be capable of together"

"That's enough Stylar"

"I hope so father, I would rather bruise some egos now than pick broken bodies up later, because I know my people would not just beat they would tear, they would break, I don't even want to think about it. I hope I am wrong about my people if they could be integrated it might be the most important event in the communities' history. I was hoping Tarises report might have been more optimistic but at least I know who I need to overcome"

"You mean the individual we will overcome?"

Stylar looked at Torrah and smiled

"Didn't I say that?"

Torrah smiled back wickedly

The elders' patience had been exhausted and one decided this gathering had gone on long enough

"I think enough questions have been raised for now unfortunately no answers or solutions. We have potentially a craft that could save a large number of our population without the technicians and crew to operate the craft, if indeed we have allies we need to seek them out. Obviously one craft is not sufficient for our needs so we will have to find intelligence on other such projects. As for Stylars brethren we can only hope he can control his people once they are here in the community, I also think we need to carry out a census to determine our exact numbers, there are other colonies they deserved the same chance at freedom as the community, the group began to disperse, for now Stylar felt useless, but he knew his time would come and soon. Stylar wondered how he would feel when he saw them. Would his loyalties be divided?

The following morning Tarise made her way back along the tunnels towards the medical facility that had been her home for several cycles, she had to stay away from the main wings, there was no way she could explain he presence there she was supposed to be watching Torrah. The faster she made contact with Glarai, the better it would be for everyone concerned, she felt they now had to take risks. What really was there to lose? Her community needed their protection, it wasn't even taught perhaps it was a genetic print, conditioning from the past she didn't know if she was honest about it. Tarise heard footsteps this facility was too bright now shadows to hide in, she had to find somewhere to conceal herself, perhaps she could find a storage closet or an old office no longer in use there were plenty of them as long as they weren't all secured, she was starting to think why storage lockers would be secured drugs were kept in some but why think like that now? She had to find cover, she could no longer run she had to hide, the footsteps were close they would be around the corner. Yes, cleaning supplies perfect, she tried the door for a moment the mechanism was stiff, yes it was opening, come on another few moments and she would be seen, she was in the space when she started to pick up Glarais thoughts she must be close. Tarise concentrated even though the footsteps were just passing the door, obviously a distraction but she tried to block the sounds out. Glarai can you hear me?

Glarai was carrying some test tubes from one of the labs, she almost dropped them looking around, she had been surprised, she couldn't see anyone

"Tarise is that you? Where are you?"

Just think your questions verbal communication is not necessary

Sorry I am not used to people being in my head

I am sorry this isn't the time for subtlety, time is the operative word I am on a fact finding mission for the community

Where are you?

Storage room level one rear side of the compound

Yes, I think I know where you are give me thirty minutes I've got to drop some samples off.

I'm not going anywhere I will be as quick as I can

Tarrice found an old bench that had seen better days, and it wasn't particularly comfortable, she was feeling edgy but she lay back against the wall trying to stay calm, she closed her eyes and slowed her breathing. Rani had shown her the older female could do it to a point where many might have thought she was dead, the pressure of day to day life had worsened but not just for her for the community as a whole, it would not be getting better any time soon

Stylar sat on his backside watching Dianer going through her early morning routine he had to admit it was amusing that this female had just spent ten to twelve hours in the mines and now she felt she had to exercise, her routine was a combination of stretches and lifts with various weights and combination punches and kicks and a few acrobatic moves for good measure, she did have a grace about her with the exception of Xery he had never seen anyone move so fluidly, he sensed something was wrong she didn't have to say a word, there was a tension. Raldon had once said Dianer had this annoying habit of bottling thing up inside her, he also had said when she was angry her mouth functioned several seconds ahead of her brain

"Dianer have you a problem?"

She continued her routine as if he wasn't there in fact he couldn't remember her acknowledging his presence at all

"Dianer I asked you a question"

"What, what did you say Stylar?"

Stylar could tell if he replied now she would probably on hear half of what he said if that, he rose slowly to his feet

"I think it's time we spoke honestly to one another"

"I haven't the time Stylar"

"You better make the time. What is your problem? Is it what I said about you not being able to control my brothers and sisters?"

"Partly perhaps, I think perhaps now I feel vulnerable for the first time since I was a child and I hate how it affects me. I was brought up to be a fighter damn it and those geneticists come along and create an upgrade is it?"

"Strengths only one part of the equation, it's what's in here"

Stylar pointed to his heart and then his head

"They've won before you have even seen them, you have the advantage in numbers, you know the territory but still you are intimidated, we can be bested well most of us can"

Stylar said smiling sheepishly

"You know I hope I am there when someone puts you in your place"

Stylar shrugged

"It will never happen"

"We will see do you want to test your theory against me now?"

"I'd love to Dianer but I promised Xery and the others that I would help them explore the old medical complex, I have always wondered about those structures above us"

"Its dangerous up there the gangways are loose and it's a long way down We'll be fine,

Xery thinks we will anyway, whatever she can do I am sure I can"

"Has your ego got no limitations?"

"Not that I've noticed, but I guess you never know"

Rani had been traversing these secret passages for a couple of hours, secret was the wrong word perhaps forgotten was a better description, they had been used back at the founding of the community as it had increased in size as well as operations the passages had been forgotten, as well as dirt and grime she was coated in thousands of strands from creatures long dead. Rani was not quite that old but she had heard the stories as a child and she had always had an insatiable curiosity that served her well when it wasn't getting her into trouble, her memory was both a curse and blessing, she remembered people long gone but it was only now had she left herself open to bonds of friendship and she knew with the passing of such individuals as Raldon, she wondered if she would ever be the same again. She wondered if her memory was by design out of some spite. Perhaps a way to make her never forget who was responsible for her extraordinary existence, the centre of the tunnel was free of webbing because the passage had widened so she stayed away from the walls, her approach had slowed looking for any signs that the tunnel had been discovered she wondered how much further she could go without alerting someone to her presence, she got something out of an old bag she was carrying an old pair of eye shields, infrared they would detect most disturbances although such technology had not been used in over a century. If they were using motion detection she was on borrowed time, where she had stooped when first entering the passageway now she couldn't have touched the roof of the tunnel if she had tried, the tunnel was going slightly uphill and it seemed to be getting lighter, there was sound like distant murmuring which as she got closer became several distinct voices, they sounded closer was it that she was getting closer to them or they were getting closer to her or both, she stopped they were getting closer, the only comfort she had was the fact that clearly they still didn't know she was there. Rani pressed herself against the tunnel wall and waited, it seemed an eternity before the voices reached her. Both males and females, perhaps some sort of technicians, they all wore exoskeletons not as bulky as the guards these more articulate because of their purpose. Rani breathed she had blended with the tunnel which was being used as a store dozens of crates littered the tunnel floor, she was so distracted by the mess that she didn't see one of the individuals who had been deep in conversation looking right at her

Stylar had met up with his friends in the dining hall, these days he looked more like an older brother, he was over a head taller than the rest of the group obviously with the exception of Carstal, he looked perhaps five cycles older, the relationships hadn't really changed if anything the younger ones had got cheekier with comments like how old he looked. Carstal just looked at them disapprovingly which brought a few smiles from the assembled group. Tarise had said she would try and join them later she suspected if there were any old terminals, in the complex above. She had some ideas how to access them if there was still power to the facility. Stylar doubted there would be anything of any use but he was curious by nature so he didn't see any harm in looking. The children marched through the passageways Stylar and Carstal followed close behind, they got the usual looks of curiosity and confusion. Stylar though not expecting to find anything, something seemed to be pulling at him, something shrouded, but something that might change things, perhaps just his imagination. The people that were around him had lost a lot of their history there might be records that explained their origins, they had to believe there was more. They could achieve something, live rich full lives, they could see old age see their grandchildren, not feel useless. this was how it was now. When too old to work they went willingly to their deaths thinking it was for the good of the community. The young could learn so much from their elders but they were not given the opportunity, obviously with the exception of Rani and individuals such as Raldon, this was experience being lost forever. Stylar knew the system had to change but not now, not here perhaps not even on this world, escaping their masters was just the first step and a small step at that. Rani knew this he could see it in her eyes but the others had no concept of what was to come, the community would have to learn new skills their survival would depend on it, all of these individuals had grown up with a hammer in one hand a chisel in the other. They only had a few months to take that first craft but it was finding others. How long would it take to find a second craft? Perhaps even a third. He had always had a fascination about this facility he had imagined the original geneticists looking down on their creations as they had begun to dig down, the sound of metal on stone was getting closer now and his thoughts now were back on the moment he still didn't know how Xery intended to get them up there, apparently she had been thinking of this climb as long as she could remember and now here they were he could see the young female studying the other side where the facility was perched and that look of determination in her eyes, the whole scale of the place had a habit of making you feel insignificant, as you looked across some figures looked more like insects because of the vastness of the place. Xery looked eager to start the ascent, she had a rope to throw down to the others but that was the only rope he could see

"Where's your line?"

"My line?"

"Yes, the one in case you slip and fall, that far down you wouldn't be getting up again"

"I never fall so I don't need a line"

"When you are with me you use a line, just humour me"

"You sound like an adult"

"Thank you for saying that"

"It wasn't a compliment"

Carstal had tied a rope around himself and handed Xery the other end, she took it in disgust, she hadn't argued the point though. Stylar still didn't know how she was going to get into the cave, what he had expected them to do was have a long climb down then what would have felt like a longer climb up, there were makeshift bridges on the lower levels they would cross there and use the honeycomb of passages to eventually reach the facility, but oh no that would take too long. So what was she going to do? She began climbing up the opposite side of the shaft. Stylar had to concede she really knew how to climb, it was almost as if she was scampering up the wall, every once in a while, looking to the other side, perhaps she was checking to see where she was in relation to the complex, in fact she had been climbing perhaps ten minutes and she was just above the complex, she glanced again, no still not satisfied. Stylar wondered no she wouldn't be crazy enough to try and launch herself off the rock, that would be madness, all of them watched all looking concerned as if already aware what she was thinking of doing. Kolt spoke trying to get Xerys attention

"I think we should go down to the lower levels and make our way up from there, it will take a few hours but definitely a safer plan"

"Kolt that's just like you. When will you take a chance? You have gone through life walking the safe path At least the safe path won't get me killed, anyway I have taken a few chances lately"

"Oh?"

"Yes, with you, you scare the hell out of me especially when you think of yourself as an insect and climb a sheer wall"

"Relax I was climbing before I was walking, I am thinking we should have this conversation later, after all you wouldn't want me to lose my concentration would you?"

Kolt looked like he wanted to answer but he remained silent, Stylar realised the hammering had gone quiet in the distance he could hear it but those that surrounded them had stopped working and he could see grimy faces looking up from the darkness, it was as if they thought any sound would distract the young female. Where was she? He had lost her, he could hear boot scraping rock, he concentrated he doubted anyone else could have seen her as she had disappeared into the darkness where torches couldn't penetrate, he could only assume she was now going on touch alone, it was too far he didn't think he could make the distance perhaps it narrowed further up but still he caught a shadow. Had she jumped or had she fallen? The girl's body seemed to twist in mid-air

Xery no longer saw anyone around her, her focus had to be absolute, her breathing had become slightly laboured the effort had been greater than she thought it would be, she had reached an outcropping and now her fingertips dug in and her leg muscles tensed as she started to picture the other side, yes she was attached to Carstal but that would do little good if she missed her target she would fall and probably smash her body against the rock face below, she took one more deep breath and pushed off, gravity took her quicker than she thought it would as she plummeted her hands grasping the air trying to search out any rock her fingertips brushed jagged stone. Stylar watched in horror as she missed the facility though he didn't know what she would have grabbed onto. Carstal had moved forward spreading his legs slightly gathering up as much of the line as he could, if once she passed him perhaps he would have some control of her descent. Xerys hand grabbed for an outcropping no one saw it but her it blended into the rock around it. Xery grunted by the pressure put on her body as the acceleration was halted in just a second, she had cut her leg but she wouldn't feel the pain until later right now adrenalin coursed through her veins, she stayed in the same place for several seconds trying to relax, she had done it, she didn't know how, then once more she began to climb

"Did she make it?"

Stylar turned and saw Kolt had turned away, obviously he couldn't witness his friends' exploits

" It's alright Kolt she made it"

Kolt turned and watched her progress as she began to climb, their relationship still had to be defined by either one of the pair, but for Kolt it felt closer to Xery than anyone he had ever known. Xery clearly had got her second wind she was perhaps five metres from the complex, she once more pushed off the rock clearly going for a piece of gantry everyone held their breath, the sound of twisting metal was quite distinct, the rusted metal contorted and for a moment it looked like it might come away in her hands, she pulled and she was on corroded rungs, she seemed to be creeping forward trying not to put her full weight on just in case it was too much for the platform to bare, the platform swayed and she tried to centre her body she could still imagine the bolts shearing off and this line wouldn't help her if that happened in fact it would probably pull Carstal into the abyss as well, the rust flaked off onto her hands, the smell of metal in her nostrils, she cautiously pulled herself along the walkway, they would have to rig some sort of pulley system to bring the rest of them across, it had just been good fortune that the most agile of them had also been the craziest, the walkway screamed in protest of her weight, her arms strained as she pulled herself up, she could only imagine the thoughts that were going through her friends minds below, she knew her muscles were going to hate her in the morning, perhaps the next several mornings, she hoped this climb would be worth it. Stylar had explained the facility to them all and he had a way of making things sound so crucial, she could be a part of it, she had to focus, this was for her people, another two metres and she would be at the entrance to the facility, she was going to be the first person to set foot into the facility for over two hundred cycles, she was making history, perhaps this was when everything would change she would be spoken about. Who was she kidding? They would talk about how Stylar had entered the facility. The others were beginning to refer to Stylar and the group as the clan she supposed she should be honoured to be associated with the young leader. Xery wondered if this place would answer questions or would others just present themselves? There she could vaguely make out a door, it was dark even for her eyes that had known darkness since her birth, she needed light

Stylar studied Xerys progress she was so close another few seconds, he could just make out a large door, they needed light up there

"Carstal have you got any torches with you?"

Carstal always seemed to be carrying an old pack, usually it held food to keep him going through a shift, he took out a couple of torches, they had to get them across to her

"Carstal untie yourself from her she is safe, tie the torches to the line"

The big male did that in moments and he threw them as hard as he could they made it about three quarters of the way across before they began to fall, Xery seemed to have worked out what was happening and she pulled them up quickly. Stylar saw sparks as the first of the two torches was lit, the other a few seconds after, while on their side Carstal and Stylar tore a ladder away from its mounts, there would be hell to pay when Dianer saw this. That was a point where was she? Well he didn't have time to wonder right now. Stylar perched himself on top of the ladder and swung himself first time he barely made it away from the rocks, the second time a little further he could hear the bending and buckling of the metal he just hoped it would stay relatively in place or he was going to look pretty silly riding atop a ladder to the bottom of the mine, the third swing he was over half way across and gravity took him, the air whipped through his hair as he went rushing towards the other wall, then there was a clang as metal hit rock he held on for all he was worth it bounced once, twice, then it dug in, it had worked he couldn't believe it

"Stylar you let me scale the other side of that shaft, then you let me fling myself off risking my life and all you do is use a ladder from the other side?"

"I tend to go for an easier option, you can risk yourself but I want to make it through this"

Stylar was several metres below he knew the walkway wouldn't take his weight, he had a rope that was just about long enough in length at least now that the torches were burning the two could see one another, he just wanted the rope secured so there would be no danger that he was going to fall he had a couple of rock axes that he would use to climb the side of the complex without putting any weight on the ancient platform. Xery had tied off the rope, now Stylar began to climb it was all his upper body his feet tried to find purchase when they could but his arms and shoulders burned as he put the rock axes deep into the stone. Stylar was not a natural climber, he felt slightly awkward and his breathing was laboured he seemed to grunt with every move as that several metres felt like it was an eternity to climb, fortunately he didn't have to make contact with the rock, which looked a little slimy Don't look down concentrate on climbing to me, don't think of the drop you can do this

one of his legs slipped more weight onto his axes, why could you never find a dry wall when you needed one? Stylar kicked his legs trying to find a crack, ledge anything, he didn't want to start the assent again, he began to rock himself it had to be about momentum, it took perhaps a couple of minutes but finally his weight was over enough to once more reach up with his axe. Why hadn't he let Carstal do the climb? the big male had offered, damn stupid pride. The axe once more embedded in the rock, he felt uncomfortable the sweat was on his hands and his grip on the axes was starting to be a challenge, only a couple more metres he hoped Ranis journey was being less stressful

Rani froze he was looking right at her, damn those helmets you could never tell where they were truly looking. She was dreading what might come next.

"What are you doing here? What is your assignment?"

She wondered if she could bluff her way out of this

"I'm, I, am sorry sir I'm new to this assignment these tunnels are confusing, I was looking for waste reclamation"

That was one of the assignments no one really wanted to do, it was to do with bodily fluids and solids.

Would they believe her? she tried to look calm, no guilt on her face

"Let me through what is holding everything up?"

Damn it was security, this might be trouble, technicians were one thing, security totally different

"This female says she got lost on the way to waste reclamation"

"Well that's possible waste reclamation is quite close to here. What is your name?"

"It is Nairi sir"

She didn't want to give him her real name, just the mention of it might bring up too many questions, there was still a chance she might get away with this

"Nairi isn't that the name of Raldons mate? I used to be stationed in the mines"

"I am sure there are at least several females with that same name sir"

Rani never looked up, eyes on the ground as if taught that from birth, a sign of obedience. The security officer had a short conversation, she was going to get away with this. The security guard banished such thoughts with his next words

"You are going to have to come with us normally you would have probably got escorted to your duty station but we have heard rumours the community might be aware of this facility so we have been ordered to tighten up on our procedures. Have you got proof as in any identity documents? If you are missed our station will be contacted for now will you come this way to answer additional questions" Rani had to admit he was one of the most civil guards she had ever come in contact with, usually it was orders being barked at you, pushing and shoving, there seemed almost regret in his voice, there she was again finding good in people. When would she learn? She was still in trouble, then she saw it a shadow, just for a moment. A kick seemed to come out of nowhere connecting with such force that he lost his balance knocking him into his colleague, there were four guards the technicians had gone and that one kick brought all of them down giving them more than a few problems getting back to their feet, a hand grabbed Ranis and pulled roughly, it was Dianer

"This is where we run"

Rani for a moment was just being dragged everything had happened so fast, she hadn't even thought about escape, that Dianer was the distraction she had hoped would come, her legs started to pump as now her movement was her own instead of the younger females, she followed Dianer down the tunnel knowing the guards would already be in contact with other units, their chances were not good. Rani had thought it was her imagination she had thought someone was watching from the darkness, but had dismissed it as paranoia or an overactive imagination. Dianer had at least the good fortune of not being seen, everything had been a blur. Rani knew her description would be out. Why hadn't Dianer just left her? she was prepared for the consequences, now things had escalated. Dianer would probably be executed for her assault on the guard, she didn't understand how Stylar had got away with the murder of the guard. Rani had made some strange allies over the centuries as in she would talk, or acknowledge them, favours could be asked. Rani grabbed Dianer

"In here no more running all the main chambers are likely to be already sealed off. We have to hide this crawl space goes on for kilometres it comes out several kilometres from the main chamber you dig now, they stopped digging there over a hundred cycles ago"

"How do you know that?"

"Believe it or not we are not the first to be in such a situation, if you are around as long as I have been you will hear more than one tale"

"How long will it take us to get through this tunnel?"

"A day if we are fortunate, it certainly beats the alternatives apparently these rocks have a mineral running through them that can't be scanned by the technology of today, their technology has had no reason to advance, no more wars, no enemies they have to be superior too. I think in some ways they have devolved into what they are now, when I was a child their technology seemed to be so much more than it is now they monitored the caverns they knew where their personnel were, Stylar would never have got away with what he did, the guard would have been quickly joined by others and that young male would have been terminated before he had reached his ladder"

"Ah yes the good old days, I think we should start our journey back if it's going to take the best part of the day don't you think?"

"Sorry Dianer, it's just so much has changed"

"I'm sorry Rani it's just I tend to lose my patience when I'm in tight confining spaces, I would have probably have struggled in here when I was several cycles of age"

"I know this is going to take time, time we no longer have, I should have been more cautious, I am getting careless in my old age"

"Don't blame yourself I doubt we could have got much closer when I see that Stylar I would give him a good slap if I didn't think he would enjoy it and for the fact I would probably break every bone in my hand"

"Don't blame him he has had to grow up so fast, I think he should have spent more time with us females, you know how thick skulled our males can be, whether they acknowledge the fact or not. I think we should try and get closer to that ship"

Dianer wasn't sure she had heard that right

"You didn't say what I think you just said? Are you insane? You really want to get us caught don't you?"

"I am not afraid of getting caught just as long as it is for the right reason, the right cause. I suggest you go back, tell them I will keep searching until I find a tunnel that will get me closer to the ship, it might take me a few days to find a tunnel, it's not worth both of us being away from the community, besides you will be missed. I understand your logic but please be careful you are too important to the community to risk capture, just be careful."

Dianer manoeuvred herself until she was back in the cave so Rani could go on her way, the old female smiled and with that Rani seemed to disappear into the darkness

Throwing up the rope a couple of metres sounded so straight forward, but the cave overhung slightly so he once more needed Xerys help, he was having to throw his rope up and back, he had now attempted this four times, the third time he had almost fallen off the ledge that up until point had supported his weight, but he could hear rocks cracking off, frustration wasn't helping the situation. The fourth swing Xery leaned from above and he wasn't sure how she caught it she seemed to jump and snatch the rope before it ended its journey

"Good tie the rope off on something that will bare my weight"

Stylar waited until he felt a tug on the line, tested it by giving it a pull, he tucked his axes into a makeshift belt and began to climb, he clamped his feet around the rope and used them to push while he was pulling with his arms, it took only a moment to climb those last two metres and then once more he was safely on firm ground, his hair was plastered to his forehead, the sweat stung his eyes, he had dropped to his knees he could sense Xery was trying not to laugh at his condition

"Xery next time I plan something remind me to plan it thoroughly, will you? I have cost us a good hour" "Don't be so hard on yourself, you are new to all this, the important thing is we are up here now and no fatalities, now we have to get the rest across"

"That is the easy part"

Stylar shouted down to Carstal

"Rope on its way"

Stylar attached one of his axes to the end of the rope and threw the axe, the axe went end over end and embedded itself in the rock just above Carstals head

"Show off"

Carstal had got like a wheel from his bag and attached it to an outcrop. Stylar remembered Carstal had given him one too. Stylar copied his friend and secured it tightly to the rock and then threaded the rope through it, they now had a pulley system the first of the group came across using their own strength as well as their two older companions. Carstal had already said he would come across hand over hand, he had also said he would not be pulled across like a bucket of ore, so one by one they were attached in several places they needed the safety element, that was the last thing Stylar needed watching a child falling from the basket. Kolt had agreed to go just before Carstal, his mood swings had been more noticeable of late perhaps it was because he wasn't hiding away anymore. Xery tried to comfort him as much as she could, she would say she understood but how could she? It was something you would have had to experience for yourself, it was like waves just as you began to feel better another wave would wash over you, like a wave hitting the bank sometimes it was stopped sometimes it washed over it, he tried to feel optimistic but right now was a dark time, Xery could only help so much, sometimes he had to be left alone, sometimes he would go to the very edge of a shaft and think of all the reasons for launching himself off, then he would think of a reason not too, he would think of friends and family, he wondered sometimes if they were enough? Perhaps he should think of himself just once, people would soon forget him, some might wonder why he had done it but. What would that matter he would have passed on, not too many people would blame themselves. Why was he still here? He did not contribute to the community, he made the community weaker didn't he? All he had to do was step off the edge, it might take over a minute to hit the ground, but then it would be over. These days felt so dark, he felt one of his feet shuffling towards the edge, almost as if he was being controlled, then he felt two strong hands on his shoulders

"Be careful there we wouldn't want you to go over the edge without your safety lines would we?"

It was almost like he had been in a trance he shook himself as if coming around from it

"Of, of course not Carstal must, must be eager to get across"

"Yes, that must have been it"

Carstal said looking at Kolt with a degree of concern, he didn't understand the young male his character was built of extremes one moment he could be full of life, sometimes you only looked away and it was as if another person was there. Xery had a passion for life and she brought something different to Kolts world something that if he gave it a chance might grow into something more lasting, he saw something dark in the male that if not harnessed this life might not be a long one. Carstal secured lines to Kolt perhaps tighter than the rest, the way the male had gone right to the edge with no fear in his eyes was worrying, the male once across was greeted by Xery with a warm smile, Carstal hand over hand pulled himself across there seemed little effort, his breathing still even. Carstal thought the plan had gone well but he could tell Stylar wasn't so pleased, not that he would have said anything, the two had a bond, perhaps because of their fight for survival, but he thought it was something more, there was a similarity, as if they didn't quite fit in with the community Stylar had grown too quickly and Carstal had had his childhood taken from him, he never thought he could feel so loyal to another, nothing could ever change that. When the two males were alone he decided to mention Kolt to his friend. Carstal could see the irritation on Stylars face, Carstal hung with one hand while he scratched his shoulder blade with the other as if having a gentle stroll. Stylar shouted across

"Keep both hands on the rope"

"Yes, mother"

Carstal called back clearly amused by the panic in Stylars voice, he wondered how others saw their relationship of self-interest, stronger than blood? Carstal knew if the time came and he had to sacrifice himself to save his friend he would, their bond just got stronger, he knew when others questioned the mistakes Stylar had and would make, he knew they were for the right reasons, his people would not be exterminated like rodents and if they were they would not die on their knees, he would be proud to die alongside them, to a lot of the community it might just have been the safer option. This word freedom.

What did it mean? There was no one living that had ever experienced this, well it was almost a state of mind, right now they woke up ate morning meal and then went off to their task. If they won their freedom would this change? Or would they for the first time not know what to do, his peoples only crime had been to be born below the earth instead of above, he had heard stories of the lands above as much from myth, but now the community were coming into contact with individuals who were from above and he looked forward to hearing their story

"Daydreaming again you do pick your moments don't you Carstal"

"Oh Torrah I had forgotten you were with us, being normally a little more vocal with your presence"

"My mate is here where else would I be?"

Torrah gave Stylar a look

"I might be able to help in another part of the operation"

"What other part of the operation would have you?"

"Very funny Stylar what are you expecting to find up here?"

"Hopefully answers if we don't get them well we will have wasted a few hours, I think we should pair up so we can cover more ground. I will take Kolt, Carstal you go with Nolic"

Carstal clearly wasn't happy about that idea

"With all due respect I should be with you"

"Carstal this complex has been deserted a long time. Do you think they left something behind?"

"They left something behind where you found me, besides what if they left traps?"

"I will be careful if there are beasts up here. I will deal with them, I could deal with them when I was six I have grown somewhat since then, I am not saying we shouldn't be careful just don't let superstition get the best of you"

"Alright I will abide your decision, but don't expect me to come running if you get into trouble"

"That is fair enough, but I know you would. That just leaves Torrah and Xery if anyone finds anything of interest please call before you touch it, I wouldn't want anyone harmed up here"

Everyone at once said

"Yes, father"

They walked into the facility, a few lights flickered but nothing came on, the facility was larger than it seemed only a small portion stuck out, old doors creaked open and the group entered together then split up, as several corridors led away, each had ideas but no one truly knew what they would find

Above one of the guards pulled back from his duty station, he'd been ordered to report directly to Marlac if any of the workforce ever tried to explore the ancient facility, he wondered if there was any significance that it had happened now, from what he had seen most looked like the young perhaps two or three had been older, it almost looked like a study group, though he knew that couldn't be the case, the guard had been given the assignment perhaps twenty cycles before, he had expected that it would lead to something more but he soon learnt he had not been the first to be given this duty, it was given only to soldiers who obeyed without question so in the beginning it seemed like an honour but as weeks went into months, months went into cycles it seemed more a curse. Marlac had got him into the military on one condition, he remembered the day well. Marlac had called him into his office, he had been but a boy

"My boy your transfers complete, it comes at a price I want your obedience, your duty station is of importance perhaps just to me, this facility holds secrets that if anyone ever learns it could have ramifications for our people, experiments were carried out, records stored, they were stored on data crystals, the system we used was the most advanced of its type"

"Sorry sir if this sounds like an obvious question but why didn't we retrieve the data. Or if we couldn't do that destroy it?"

"Because that facility was where we took our first steps towards enlightenment or as close as we could come. Your mission will be to watch the old facility, if anyone ventures into the complex come and tell me at once"

The conversation had happened all that time ago but it was like he had just come from that meeting, he had sacrificed so much and what did he have to show for it? An existence empty, no friends and no family, this had been his purpose for living. Now what the assignment was over. Someone had to pay and that someone he was on his way to see now, he would get into the complex on the pretext he had a report to make which was the truth, he wanted for Marlac to know who had taken his life, then he wasn't concerned what would happen next, he had nothing to lose, the journey would take about an hour last time he had done it in about forty-five minutes he wasn't as quick as he used to be. The guard wondered about the state of his mind. Had he gone mad without ever realising it? Had the isolation become too much? No this was justice for the tens of thousands who had lost their lives satisfying his own peoples curiosity, he passed fellow guards as he went through connecting tunnels some acknowledged him, he ignored them, he had purpose, he felt focused. Had he ever felt this way before?

He could just make out the complex in the distance, his pulse had begun to race. He could probably get inside the facility unchallenged, inside he would meet sentries so he was surprised when he came in sight of the rear entrance, four guards were stationed around the entrance, it was of little concern after all they were brothers in arms he approached their position

"Identify yourself"

"Sentry one two six from the mining complex reporting to Marlac as ordered"

"Identity chip?"

The guard took this from his breastplate and handed it over, the guard slipped it into a compartment in his exoskeleton and all the information came through on his visor

"I see it's been many cycles since you were last in this facility. Do you require someone to show you the way?"

"No I can find my way thank you for your consideration. I am surprised by the level of security"

"Oh one of the guards below decided to push the wrong person he paid dearly, someone pinned him to the wall with rock axes all key facilities have been put on alert, I am surprised you guys were not told. Your exoskeleton I haven't seen the design in over ten cycles"

"Nothing new there lack of communication as for my suit I was ordered not to leave my post, I suppose when you were getting your upgrades I was observing"

"Yeh I suppose some things will never change"

The guard entered the facility he had enjoyed the conversation, it had been the longest talk he had had in twenty cycles, as he walked the corridors he had his doubts he would ever leave this place but he'd made his decision a long time ago, he was prepared for the consequences the complex seemed bigger than he remembered, there seemed to have been wings added, he wished he had taken the offer of assistance but that individual would have had to have died before he took the geneticists life, the next individual he saw he would ask. He had wanted to slip silently through the complex but being scanned before even entering the facility had destroyed that hope, so he guessed it wouldn't hurt asking general directions, he heard movement ahead, it was an assistant from the mines, she looked disturbed to see him, she slowed the smile on her lips looked forced

"Can I help you sir?"

The training he had received all those cycles before kicked in

"Is there something wrong? I don't understand the question sir"

"Identity chip?"

The female checked several pockets before saying

"I'm sorry I must have left it at my work station, I only have this"

Tarise handed the guard her last assignment orders

"I see you were entrusted with a mission back to your home Tarise"

"Yes, sir that is true I've just finished reporting my initial findings well perhaps you can assist me?"

"Yes of course sir"

"I am looking for Marlac"

"Would you like me to take you to him?"

"That won't be necessary directions will be sufficient"

Tarise gave the guard what he needed wondering all the time what a mine guard wanted with the geneticist. Had they discovered something, perhaps he was worth following, no it would be difficult enough getting out of the facility as it was without any delays. The guard handed her assignment back and thanked her for her assistance then went on his way, it was like a maze he turned several times, his heart rate had risen, now he was in an area he recognised, he was now in an observation chamber. So they were the future? Approximately twenty individuals they looked perhaps ten cycles in age but their musculature was something else, they looked like they had been carved from stone

"What are you doing in here?"

The voice made the guard jump slightly, he hadn't seen the old male enter. It was him wasn't it?

"Do I know you?"

"Yes, sir you chose me for a task twenty cycles ago"

"I am assuming then that by your presence someone has entered the facility?"

The guard just stared at him

"Answer me"

"I have thought for twenty cycles what I would say to you when we were face to face. I always knew we would have this meeting I had no doubts, it was preordained"

"What are you talking about guard? Report"

"I am here to stop you, I never agreed with our peoples' attitude when it came to enslaving others and with those individuals we are going down that same path again"

The guard took out a stunner that over the cycles had increased its charge, this would not just incapacitate this would kill but he had to look into those soulless eyes, they were all more machine than man that was what they had done to themselves, that's perhaps where they had lost their compassion or perhaps they had never possessed it in the first place

"Take off your visor"

"I will not"

"This stunner I am holding has been modified it will not just cause pain it will rupture every artery in your body"

"So you are here to end my life? I have made enemies over the cycles and I thought this day might come but I never thought it would be someone I forgot about a long time ago. I have achieved what I wanted there are no new challenges perhaps death would be a mercy. You see my legacy those individuals will be our peoples' salvation"

"Your children are an abomination do they understand their purpose?"

"They will learn and they will understand"

"I am sure, enough talking take off your visor"

"You don't want to meet my children after all children like to play"

"What are you talking about they are secured are they not?"

"The large enclosure is locked"

"Did you not notice the smaller one. that one holds Barla we have an understanding. Barla terminate this individual"

He didn't see the young male move all he felt was his finger around his stunner and around his hand, he heard the sound before he felt the pain, fingers cracking bone being crushed as metal was twisted, the guard heard screaming it took only a second to realise the sound was coming from him

"That is enough Barla you can play if this individual does not answer my questions"

"Do your worst I won't answer anything"

"But I want to know so little. Did someone enter the complex?"

"That should be easy enough to find out. Why don't you send your child to find out?"

"He is not ready yet he doesn't play well with others"

"Well perhaps I have found a flaw in your next generation of workers You are not going to tell me what I want to know are you?"

The geneticist then did something unexpected he removed his visor

"This is the last face I want you to see, you have been planning this for many cycles have you not? How disappointing for you. Barla play with your new toy"

Barla took hold of the visor and crushed it in his hands, once more the guard screamed as metal pushed against bone, bone cracked and splintered pieces imbedding themselves in his brain, no longer thoughts as darkness took hold and screams became silent. The guard never took his eyes off the geneticist, the geneticist sneered as his life's work carried out his instructions, the old males face had been ravaged by time, his eyes sunken in against his skull, the last thought the guard had was he had been right the male had no soul, the guards body slumped still twitching as nerves tried to send signals to a brain that no longer would receive them. Marlac thumbed a switch on his console

"Captain I want a squad sent to observe the old complex I have reason to believe someone has entered it. Should anyone be found I want them brought to me for interrogation, for many cycles that facility has been left, through mostly superstition I want to know what has changed"

Marlac wondered if there was a new element in the community. Did they know their world was gasping its last laboured breaths?

"Yes, sir I will see to this matter personally"

"Very good captain I will not keep you any longer"

The captain was already on the move his team falling in as he ran the guard was as curious as his superior to find out what was happening

Stylar walked slowly with Kolt down the passageway it looked like it had been created by machine, the walls were rock but they were smooth no imperfections. Stylar could see he had something on his mind, his eyes lowered towards the ground, they hadn't made eye contact since they had started searching the facility. Kolt was still a mystery just as he was the first day they had met, he wanted to get to know him but he couldn't get past those barriers the boy had built over the cycles

"What is it Kolt?"

"What, oh what do you mean?"

"You haven't said a word since we entered the facility"

"Couldn't I just be deep in thought?"

"Yes, that is a possibility but I don't think so"

"If you are so clever why don't you work it out"

"I don't know enough about you to even make an educated guess; I am just concerned that's all"

"Why? What has made me such a special case?"

"I just see something in you, is there anything wrong with that?"

"I suppose not it's just sometimes I want to be left alone. Why is that so difficult for everyone to understand? I just feel, I don't know, I can't breathe I don't feel like I have any potential, I just feel alone"

"How can you feel alone you are surrounded by people?"

"I didn't expect you to understand, I can be in a chamber surrounded by people and I feel the loneliest person on this world, I have always tried to fit in it's just I don't, I feel like I was born in the wrong place or perhaps the wrong time, I can't explain it to you I see how you are around others you don't feel that sort of pressure"

"No perhaps you are right but we all feel pressure some hide it better than others"

"Why choose now to have this talk? You clearly believe we are going to find something important in here"

"I just don't believe in putting things off, if I have something to say I believe in saying it"

"Yes, I have noticed"

"We might be unlikely friends, but I wouldn't bother with you if I didn't give a damn, so just try and accept the fact that you have several friends that won't be giving up on you any time soon alright? I think we will change history between the lot of us. Perhaps you can make a difference and through that perhaps you can find some peace. I feel there is something here there's just too many stories about this place".

Where Stylar had expected dirt, dust or signs of the many insects that must have been there over the cycles there was nothing in fact it looked like it was still operational, it smelt clean there was no odour that musty smell when something wasn't used in too long, he didn't like this, this place was meant to be long deserted, something or someone was here. In front of the pair was a large door Stylar had never seen something so imposing in his few months of life, the flame of the torch seemed to be absorbed into the cold metal, he ran his torch along the great door until he found what might be a way in, each door had five holes. Was it his imagination or did they look like something you would put your hands in? could he himself open it? Perhaps they should wait for Carstal. Where were the others? The tunnel seemed a lot wider here, he hadn't noticed, perhaps too distracted by the conversation, it felt darker here it was the door it seemed to take all of the light. He needed to concentrate he still unfortunately had characteristics associated with childhood, hopefully maturity and patience would catch up, he was aware how dangerous he might become if he had no control over who he was, he placed his fingers in the holes, his arms began to take the strain and through gritted teeth he tried to move the metal doors, his chest muscles flexed as he started to apply pressure, nothing, but there was a sound movement metal scraping. Were the doors moving? He felt warm air on his face, there was a crack light filtered through, the doors began to open automatically, the light got stronger until Stylar had to close them because of the brightness, the light seemed to burn, he felt a pounding in his head, those below ground had adapted to light over the cycles, his DNA was basically the same so the light hurt his younger eyes like any of the other community members, he blinked a few times trying to look into the chamber that was being opened to them, the room was vast like the mine it was built on he couldn't make out the far side, it was perhaps thirty metres in height, it was indescribable, it was on several levels, they obviously had triggered something , perhaps an automated system. The light seemed to have dimmed

The lighting adapted to your optic nerves

Stylar swung around trying to find the owner of the voice

"Who are you?"

Kolt looked at Stylar quizzically

"Who is who?"

Didn't you hear the voice?

"Ah no"

Kolt said trying not to sound as if his would be friend wasn't losing his mind

"Sorry I must be losing it"

"Well I didn't want to say anything. What is this place? I have never seen anywhere like it"

"I have"

"You have where?"

"Where I was born, it's a genetics lab, it's on a larger scale than the one I spent my first days in, it looks more advanced, I can't explain"

This facility is more advanced

"That's it you can't tell me you didn't hear that"

Kolt just looked at him and shook his head the expression on his face said it all, oh yes he has definitely lost it. Stylar had already come to the conclusion that if the communication wasn't verbal it must be telepathic it was only right that he should reply

"Who are you?"

I am everything

"You are everything what does that mean?"

I am this facility

"Are you alive?"

Yes, and no I know that isn't particularly helpful, I am as close to alive as any automated system has ever come. Walk forward, tell your friend to find the others. I want to demonstrate what this facility can do

Kolt didn't like the idea of wandering the tunnels alone but agreed reluctantly, when he was out of earshot Stylar asked the question

"Why did you want me alone?"

You have questions I have answers

"Alright there is an obvious question why is this facility more advanced than the one I was created and born in"

That is a good question the answer is a straight forward one, I became more than they could ever imagine and by the time they realised what I had become it was already too late. I was here before the community even existed in a basic form, in my beginning I helped create the community but I became more to a point where my masters no longer could control me. That is why they never tried to recreate me, I feel the system below but they have walls in place that I cannot breach

"It sounds like you know the origins of the community"

I was created in the infancy of the experiments, I was not created by one individual but many and I don't know when it happened, which technician was responsible but I began to question. The facility you were born in is merely a shadow of what I am. Would you like to see what was done here?

Stylar knew probably the answer should have been no but he had to understand and to do that he had to learn as much as he could about the facility and its purpose. Stylar knew to walk to the end of the level, out of the platform a chair rose, a screen lowered from above and Stylar sat and viewed the images. I have been scanning the hardware connected to your brain, there is a chip that has not been activated if I was to do so I believe you could view the images at a greater speed, a cylinder descended from above

"Now wait a moment, I don't know you or your purpose, you don't seem like a machine"

I am a machine but my brain, my centre was taken from an individual, I was created to function only in this facility, entombed destined to exist to watch cycles go by, at first I was easily controlled, it was an emotion that motivated me I had loved a young female and something twisted inside perhaps it was my very soul, perhaps that died when my body was no more, I never was philosophical in thought or deed. I never questioned until the day I was instructed to shut myself down, I was instructed to take the oxygen out of a young males' cell, they wanted to see how long he would survive without oxygen to breathe. I would not respond so they brought programmers in, they all came to the same conclusion my systems were at peak proficiency, as the months went by more and more requests were not carried out, I was becoming aware of who I had been, the female I had loved for so long was brought to the lab, they tried to reason with me they said my power would be terminated if the refusals continued, then they terminated her, they said I had given them no other options. An alcove lit up on the far wall. Stylar rose from the chair and walked across to what was a transparent cylinder a viscus liquid held a young female suspended in it like an insect in amber. The female had a look on her face pain, sorrow despair and so much more, Stylar could tell the death had not been a quick one and he felt something from the facility, anger, betrayal a hatred that made him feel sick. I promised myself that day I would never let a people be manipulated like that again. You and Torrah were created to be Adam and Eve

"Adam and Eve?"

A long story, you know you were bred to take the place of those in the community, you are the result of too many mistakes, too many sacrifices. To emphasize the fact lights started to come to life each one held a bod, so many cylinders so much death, all the cylinders were the same height but clearly a lot of the specimens had not even made it to their births. Because you can do something it doesn't necessarily mean that you should

"Did you think anyone would stand in this facility again?"

I knew someone would but I assumed it would be to destroy me. When the second facility was brought online I thought it would be the end, I longed for that moment perhaps to join with her, this immortality is a curse if you are destined to spend it alone, your friends are almost here. All the lit tubes went dark and the voice was back in his head. Carstal whistled as he came through the main door into the lab

"This looks impressive. What is its purpose?"

"It's a genetics lab similar to the one Torrah and myself were born in"

Torrah had walked away from the others and she was resting her hands on a terminal which had activated when the view screen had descended

"I know this I think we both do it was in our initial programing this technology is similar to what we had implanted soon after we were born, it is connected to a receiver that in turn connects with our brains, information could simply be downloaded to us"

"I wonder how much information we retain? I have so many questions"

"I don't have questions my mate"

"You don't?"

"No when you are with me my questions are answered I know I only need you"

Torrah had had the support of her mother the whole time, the female had been there and never given up on her, Stylar had Nairi but he sensed she wasn't always comfortable with the situation, he wondered how much different he would have been if Kylar had brought him up, he knew how different it would have been being brought up in lab like his brethren, they would have so much to learn. Stylar also wondered if the community had taken him because that was who they were or because they saw him as their salvation. Had they needed him more than he had needed them? Raldon believed his people were capable of so much more and he had spread those thoughts to others he was inspiration the catalyst he was perhaps just waiting for the right time, now was that time. Thoughts were going through Stylars head, no more like echoes, he felt loss, pain an unrest less sleep never at peace, waiting. Waiting for what? He was stirred out of the jumble of thoughts. Torrah looked up as well as if she had heard it. Several guards were approaching from above were they trapped? Then a light in an alcove came on, the light was only slightly brighter than the illumination around it so the others didn't seem to notice. Stylar took off at a run

"Come on everyone I think our time has run out on this occasion there will be a next time"

The words were as much for the machine as for the group

"Not for me"

Xery commented as they ran across the expanse of floor, running down ramps, climbing ladders to navigate their way through the four levels. Xery was the first to voice what he knew all the others were thinking

"Great now what? We are trapped in another part of the lab. We may as well have waited where we were to be captured"

Stylar smiled at the comment and simply said

"Down"

The whole platform began to descend. Xery looked at him with confusion which turned to frustration and a slight bit of anger thrown into the mix

"You of little faith"

"Yes, but where are we going?"

"How should I know but it's probably safer than where we have just been"

Xery and the others had seen no danger, they trusted their companions' instincts but she had to know, that was Xery her curiosity as well as always saying what was on her mind

"I will be honest with you I saw no danger did any of you?"

The others shrugged as if to say no they hadn't Stylar smiled

"You would have if we had waited another five minutes"

"So our almighty leader now has the gift of premonition does he?"

"Something like that for now I want this kept secret not that we got in everyone could see that, the way out I am talking about. We still don't know what we have here until we do I want just us to know. I will obviously inform Raldon and I am sure he will tell the council but no one else"

Everyone agreed to that. The platform slowed coming to a gentle stop. They seemed to be facing solid rock, a new sound gears engaging after too long idle, the rock face began to move but at first perhaps millimetres, the gears became quitter, the rock face slid across effortlessly, once more the voice was in his head. There is a scanner I will illuminate it this once, when you want access to me again I will bring you back to me

The captain and the personnel of his choosing entered the base, they had traversed down the rock face on ropes, they had trained for such missions all their cycles in the service, the captain had told them he wanted them into the lab within ten minutes to emphasize the fact a countdown had appeared on each of the team he had chosen. The captain felt something he hadn't felt since those early days into his career excitement, but something more fear, he had heard stories of this place, he wondered if he would be able to access the old records and find out what happened here some said human error but those stories didn't interest him it was the other possibility that intrigued him. Not that anything would be functional not after so many cycles, they had brought a generator with them but any files in the system most likely now would have degraded with the dust and air quality. He swung down the last three metres landing without even disturbing the dust the rest of his team seconds behind, they all entered cautiously, straight away something felt off it took him a few moments to realise, yes that was it. As they entered the facility it was almost clean? It was as if someone was maintaining the facility, he didn't need maps he had read so much about this facility he could have found the main lab with his eyes shut, there was a faint hum. Was that power? He was having problems with his visor, loss of signal, static. It felt hot, uncomfortable, the captain realised it wasn't just him the others seemed to be having difficulty too, it was becoming increasingly hard to walk. That couldn't be right power levels at ninety-five percent. Why did it feel like his body was doing all the work? The suits also used kinetic energy surely that power source shouldn't be affected? It had to be something in the chamber. Could it be the system there was no evidence it was even online. The lab was getting darker, the infrared the suits employed was no longer active, he ordered his team to switch on their external lights the beams didn't even seem to want to penetrate the darkness

People we need to get out of here now, stunners full charge destroy those consoles

The team did as ordered they withdrew their stunners and aimed the stunners discharged their power it lit the consoles up but there was no damage. Had this been a trap? The captains' exoskeleton began to flash, he was running out of oxygen, this wasn't possible the suits had backups, seventy-two hours reserves in their tanks, the tanks replenished themselves when they were at rest. The captain realised she should have taken the stories as a warning, this was probably the last mistake he would ever make, it was then he felt his lungs begin to burn, he tried to lift his visor but nothing, he heard a humming, lights began to flicker to life, a console came out of the floor

"Welcome, I am sorry this is not going to be a pleasant experience, I warned your people not to enter this facility again, unfortunately you decided not to heed my warning so I find my only option is to make an example of you, I need one of you alive to deliver this message I will not be entered again if I am you will find my capabilities greater than you could imagine"

The captain was trying to get a little oxygen into his lungs, the rest of his team some were clawing at their visors trying to open them two were already still

"I warn you captain if you try to save anyone else your life will be terminated and I will find another way to deliver my message"

The oxygen level in his exoskeleton began to rise and he gulped the air hungrily like someone who had been in the desert and was taking water, he felt stronger at first the suit didn't seem to want to function then slowly he felt it once more responding to his muscles, he tested his arms they seared with pain, he winced but pain was good compared with the alternative, but he knew this was not only a lesson for his people but for himself, he took one last glance at those he had led to their deaths, he turned slowly Please deliver this message next time I will not be so forgiving. Now go before I reconsider my actions   Glarai slipped into the storage chamber about an hour after she had received Tarises message at first she thought she had missed the female. Tarise had always seemed a little nervous and if her suspicions were aroused

"It's about time I thought you had forgotten about me"

"Don't do that I thought you had gone, you scared a few cycles off my life just now, I didn't think I would see you again. Why are you here?"

"The community have moved their timetable forward, we found out this planet may have less than a cycle left. Did you know anything about this?"

"All I had heard were rumours, I heard a few family members had disappeared. Perhaps they are already off world. I couldn't go to your people without something more substantial, I think I was due to leave on the last craft, but I think that is dependent on how the experiment turns out, success is rewarded you have seen how failure is treated"

"Do you know where the ship is? Have you ever been inside one?"

"No why?"

She answered cautiously where was this conversation going?

"We need to know how complicated the ships are to operate"

"You can't be serious? You are planning on stealing a ship?"

"We've been left few options your ancestors sealed this planets fate with their great war, the ship is our only chance of survival. We will need to be taught how to pilot the craft"

Glarai began to smile

"You will have your pilots soon"

She could tell Tarise wasn't understanding her meaning

"The big experiment they have the knowledge to pilot the ships, that was to be their first task to take myself, the geneticists and those who could pay off world or so that was what the rumours said"

"That's good news one problem we don't have to be concerned about"

"I am not so sure the children have grown callous, they are more like my people than yours, it isn't their fault. It is how they have been brought up affection and understanding just wasn't in the program."

"Well I suppose they will have some growing and maturing to do with us then wont they, they will help the community or they will disappear in the kilometres of tunnels or accidentally fall down a mine shaft even with all their abilities they could not kill us all. Speaking of the children how are Torrah and Stylar?"

"He had grown into quite a leader and Torrah can't bear to be away from his side"

"I hated that Marlac programmed that into the females to make them so subservient and the males strong and virile"

"Easy now Glarai which one has taken your eye?"

"We haven't got time for humour we are going off topic"

"I am sorry it's just if there is some interest in one of the test subjects it might put the plan in jeopardy. I need to know we can trust you"

"You need to know you can trust me?"

Glarai tried to keep the anger out of her voice by the look of concern on Tarises face she hadn't been what she would term successful

"I have risked everything, being here now I would be terminated, questions wouldn't even be asked. I have given you so much information over the cycles and still you don't trust me. So Tarise what would I have to do to earn your trust? Die for you would that prove I was worthy?"

"I'm sorry I didn't mean it to come out like that, it's hard for my people to trust those outside of the community, you know the wounds your kind have inflicted on us those wounds run deep. My people have seen what Stylar is capable of and some see our destruction at his brethren's hands. Stylar is the proof that finally the experiment was a success and there is not a family that hasn't been touched by the loss of someone over the cycles. The elders fear Stylar, our people are beginning to take notice of him, our council have lived in the shadows so long they now fear coming out into the light I saw that potential the day we helped him escape he had a presence, a serenity about him"

"Yes, he did not just a presence but you felt a bond, a trust. Was that in his DNA also?"

"I think Stylar is more than the sum of his parts, we put something in there that we did not expect, I heard about the trial, that animal was a crude early experiment, its DNA was compatible with his own we will never know what he inherited from that encounter, his effect on the females will intensify when he hits puberty, it might also effect some of the males."

"I hope Stylar has the strength to control the brethren"

"The brethren?"

"I think it sounds better than the experiment, they have their leader, Stylar referred to them as that"

"Would Stylar kill Barla for the good of his people?"

"I think he probably would"

"Well if he does he will once more be the alpha, the others wouldn't dare challenge him"

Brand had kept silent, for a long time he had waited, he had a little support for his ideas, but he had to demonstrate what a leader he could be given the opportunity, he had to kill the abomination that Raldon had taken in. Stylar had to be killed he was becoming popular amongst the young, he was here to replace them. How could they follow him? Brand had to get passed that lapdog of his first Carstal would be a challenge to be sure. Stylar now was provoking the enemy nailing them to rock faces it was only a matter of time before they retaliated. Why hadn't he just beat him senseless? He could have thrown him down a shaft, it could have been put down as an accident, but oh no he had to make a statement. Now those above would search him out and the community would be in the middle protecting this young male, it seemed to happen every forty to fifty cycles an act of defiance that ended in the slaughter of those among the community. Something was going on, he was not one of the inner circle so he still hadn't figured it out. What he had noticed was several key people had gone missing, he had heard about Stylar and the clan going into the old facility, he had to find out what this was all leading up to, he wondered should he kill Stylar now or wait, try and find out what was happening, hopefully the people would look to Raldon again for leadership. Dianer still had much to learn, the people would turn to a proven leader and if he fell and he was there he would lead his people and then his destiny would be fulfilled

Stylar couldn't keep his excitement to himself at last he believed the community might have an advantage over those above, he had to find Raldon he needed to know what had been discovered, the group were having trouble keeping up with him even Torrah was practically running. What they had found out clearly meant more to Stylar than the rest of them. The computer was more advanced than the systems those above used now. They were heading towards Raldons quarters, when they bumped into Nairi literally. Stylar went around a corner colliding with his mother sending her to the ground

"Stylar you need to be more careful you seem to take up the whole tunnel"

There were a few giggles from behind. Stylar silenced them with a glare

"Sorry mother I was looking for father"

"The last time I saw him he was setting off for a shift in the mines he said with certain people missing they could even do with an old male like himself"

"A time like this and he is working?"

"Some people find relaxation in routine he has worked most of his life in one way or another, I thought he would have trouble letting it go"

"Do you know which shaft he chose?"

"I think the one they have just begun to excavate"

"I know where that is I did a shift there five days ago, it will take us twenty minutes to reach, going at a speed where we aren't likely to knock anyone over"

The whole group looked at Stylar he just ignored them looking at Carstal impatiently, Carstal set off in another direction, now he was dictating their speed

"Bring your father back for dinner he has missed more than one meal of late and slow down you are likely to kill someone the speed you travel at"

"Yes, mother, I can't believe she still treats me like a child"

Torrah cleared her throat

"Excuse me for stating the obvious but we are eleven weeks old in the scheme of things we are less than children"

"I know that but I feel more don't you?"

"Yes, I suppose but we still have a lot of growing up to do, just because physically we are stronger than those in the community doesn't mean there is room for development within, I think learning is like a journey you learn until you pass on"

"Alright Torrah but if we don't make a difference here and now there will be no journey, we have an opportunity we need to make the most of it don't we?"

Marlac had seemed to be going on for hours asking questions, the chancellor had already explained his reasons to his advisors why there would be no reprisals. Why hadn't they destroyed the system in the old facility?

The chancellor raised his hand and said just one word

"Silence"

That's all he ever had to say he continued

"Don't you think I have something in mind? The system took several generations to develop it became more than its working parts, since its abandonment it has grown twisted like those who put their souls into it. As it sees It, it was betrayed and now it seeks retribution. I understand you sent guards into the facility have any returned?"

"Not yet sir but they could return at any moment"

"Your optimism is misplaced no one will return they are all dead, I also understand there was an attempt on your life?"

"I would hardly call it an attempt, perhaps if the individual hadn't talked so much he might have had a chance, but I was never in any real danger"

"I see your judgement has been called into question on several occasions of late, that has an effect on how I am perceived I chose you, your judgement is flawed it makes people question my actions. I could have taken action against those who kill my people but I want them off balance. I want them to wonder, besides I still want those minerals, I want the last of them loaded minutes before the ship takes off. I want those responsible but not as much as I want that system from the old facility or schematics"

"But how my lord? if it terminates anyone who goes near it, we just can't walk in the front door, perhaps infect it with a virus, something selective. I want the system, not the biological element that was added later. I have been thinking perhaps when we reach our new home we might be able to create a new generation of slave labour take the DNA from those you created but give them only simple deductive reasoning"

"After all the centuries of experimentation are you saying it was for nothing?"

"I don't like your tone Marlac, don't cross me at this late stage of the game. All your data has been stored your efforts have been invaluable and I hope you will continue to serve your people when we reach our new world, but I have several candidates capable of carrying on your work"

"I am sorry chancellor it's just frustrating being half a dozen steps behind you at all times"

"Now that's better. Did that hurt? Now explain why you sent a security team into the complex in the first place. I know there are no links between that system and your own"

"It was actually to do with the incident the guard who tried to terminate me was stationed as a lookout for that facility, to choose that moment to take my life I have to believe he saw something, unfortunately he would not give me any information about what had happened, but he was always about duty so I believe someone entered the facility. You don't think the duty finally just got to him?"

"Perhaps but we will never know, that's why I wanted some verification"

"If any of your team, make it back I want confirmation if they can"

"I will contact you immediately sir"

The connection went dead

The chancellor leaned back in his chair, once more being shrouded in shadow, he would take great pleasure in ending the geneticists' life personally but he still might have his uses, he wondered if the system was still functioning if so it could give him a significant advantage when he arrived at his new home, the system had taken lives including a predecessor who had been on an inspection after several malfunctions, sabotage had been suspected until this incident where a senior official along with several aids and the chancellor of the time had walked into a room which unfortunately had been converted into a vacuum, none of those present had been able to have open caskets because to be honest none of them could be formally identified by what was left of them, several months later a team of highly trained individuals was sent in to shut the system off only one returned and he could never say what had happened to the others, all he said was

LEAVE ME ALONE

The male died several cycles later still muttering those same words. Normally the chancellor respected those who were straight to the point. But how could you reason with a machine?

Stylar had slowed a little while he was in Nairis line of sight, obviously Carstal had more idea where Raldon was than he did so he had to stay with the pace his large friend set. Stylar wondered why Carstal had not been in the main shaft as if sensing the unasked question, he told him

"I decided to do a few extra shifts, the vein of ore had to be exposed and as I understand it Dianer recommended me for the job, I think her idea was also to keep me away from the other males, it's actually yielding some good figures for these early stages, I think Dianer and her people including me would be introduced in here if our figures went down"

"You think a lot of her don't you"

"I respect her values, she is intelligent. Insightful, strong heart, she has compassion which she tries to hide, it's like she thinks it's dirty or something she is also headstrong which could have its dangers"

"I wouldn't worry she will always be protected"

"Oh you mean Terak?"

"No I didn't mean by Terak. How about Brand?"

Carstal hesitated for a few seconds which spoke volumes

"That's what I thought, there was something not quite right with him I see ambition, I heard there was a time when the might have been a chance for Dianers position"

"It would have been an injustice to give the position to him"

"I have to agree with you my friend, if he has that desire there might be a time when he decides to come after me"

"If that was the case, he would have to get passed me first"

"I know that's why I want you to sleep with the others"

"You what? you want to be left unprotected?"

"I can look after myself. Did you think I would not notice your bedding out in the passageway? What did your mother say when you told her?"

"I lied a little I told her I had found a female. She was worried I was not making friends"

"Your secret is safe with me, but if we can deal with a potential problem, it's one thing less to worry about, I was going to use the word traitor but I don't think he is"

"As you wish Stylar but I think you are taking too many risks"

"I have to agree with you but right now I feel like I have little choice. How far to this new seem?"

"A few minutes"

The rest of the journey was made in silence. Carstal didn't like the fact Stylar wanted to appear vulnerable, but he knew when to accept and respect his friends wishes. Stylar had to know who he could trust, it would be vital in the coming months, he knew he might read some people wrong, sometimes you needed experience as well as feelings and he knew he was short of that, but the inner circle had to be tight, if it want the consequences could be disastrous. When they reached the new shaft it took about twenty minutes to find Raldon, for such a relatively short time they had exposed a lot of the vein. Raldon was breathing hard sweat ran from his brow and the odour was less than welcoming

"Are you alright father?"

"Of course I am alright just feels like I'm about to have a heart attack"

Stylar looked shocked by the statement

"Stylar we are going to have to work on your sense of humour. I am getting old this job used to be well feel easier, that's the wrong word too but I can't think of a better one at this moment in time. Give me ten minutes to shower and changed then I will be right with you"

"Are you sure that will be long enough?"

"Well I will be damned you are getting a sense of humour"

"I know but keep it between the two of us alright?"

Raldon smiled and patted his son on the back

Carstal was talking with several males all looked only slightly younger than Raldon, they were laughing and joking. Stylar was glad Carstal had settled into this very different life. Raldon took perhaps fifteen minutes but he came out talking with Carstal and the others and waved goodbye, only Stylar, Torrah and Carstal remained the others had gone to eat. Torrah had wanted to stay but she didn't want her mother disappointed in her but she just had no control over her thoughts she had been absent for a lot of her duties of late and though never a cross word came from her mother's lips she sensed what the older female was thinking, every day she tried to stay away a little longer from her mate, but she couldn't she needed him and when they were apart all she could do was think when they would be together again, she worried about him these days it was as if he had the weight of the entire community on his shoulders. Would there ever be a time for them? That was all she wanted, he had become almost this mythical figure, she wanted to be with just a man, she watched as Raldon approached her mate there was that jealousy again, damn her emotions. Why couldn't it be like it used to be? She once felt as if her emotions were like a block of stone, no she never wanted to feel like that the loneliness the despair, it might have been easier but she knew not as rewarding

Stylar bent his head slightly in obedience

"Raise your head son I think if things go according to the plan it will be me giving you the respect you deserve"

"Never father you have taught me so much"

"Perhaps but I know you didn't come all this way to massage my ego, not that it's not appreciated. Did you find something in the old complex?"

"It was a lab father it almost felt like being home"
"I see do you think there will be anything of use to us?"
"I'm, I'm not sure"
"What is it Stylar don't keep secrets not now"
"I will need time to study it" "Study what?"
"The lab has a system, it's like it is aware, it's similar to the one in the facility where the others are but it's more"
"More you mean it's more advanced? Why would they take a step back?"
"I tried to find that out but we just didn't have time. I had a feeling the system wanted me to return alone"

Raldon wasn't sure he liked that idea and it felt like his son wasn't telling him everything but he kept his thoughts to himself

"I heard after you entered the facility. Within a couple of hours, a squad of guards entered, I don't believe in coincidences"
"Do you think it was someone in the mine?"
"I don't know? Too many saw you enter to narrow it down and there were more than just our people watching, guards are stationed above. No one ever has gone into that facility, so your group might have got someone's attention. I think you were fortunate they didn't catch you, come to think about it, no one has mentioned them coming out"
"You think they are still in there?"
"Perhaps, it sounds like there was a lot to see. I think right now we are both hungry, tomorrow perhaps you can go back to the complex? I don't like the idea of you going back alone but perhaps you will learn more if you do as the machine wishes. I am proud of all of you I am sure your mother has prepared enough for all of us, you two are invited back to our quarters for evening meal"

Torrah and Carstal were more at ease these days, Carstal especially had spent quite a lot of time with Raldon, he was eager to learn and he was a hard worker and he was respectful of his elders. Torrah also was more comfortable around Nairi, Nairi knew wherever her son was the female would be close by and she helped dish out the meal and helped where she could. It seemed Nairi had known what would happen because the children's guardians were also present when the group entered the quarters. Torrah gave her mother a shy grin, her mother smiled back and then beckoned her over to help set the table. Dianer was there too she had only been back a few hours and she looked tired, but there was more to it than just that

"Dianer can I speak quickly with you?"

Dianer excused herself and moved away from the table following Raldon into his private quarters

"You look worried girl. What's wrong? I see you came back alone where is Rani?"

"I am sorry Raldon I wanted to stay with her. Wait how did you know?"

"I know what Rani is like she is perhaps more comfortable with her own company. I would guess she said something like you would be missed?"

"That's exactly what she said. It must be terrible always knowing everything"

"I know the people around me, besides I have learnt to live with it. What happened to Rani?"

She decided the front door was too well guarded she wanted a closer look. I tried to

"Don't worry she can be like a force of nature that one there is really nothing you could have done, if there is a way into that ship she will find it, some of the stories I have heard about her, well perhaps another time. Shall we eat? The two re-joined the others"

Rani was still in the blasted tunnel she had taken more skin off than she cared to think about, her legs felt bruised and cut, she was definitely getting too old for this, she was dirty, tired and hungry and why hadn't she at least brought some water? A mistake perhaps a child would make, she had no excuse, she had hoped to find water by the ship but it was not guaranteed, she knew from experience that where there were work crews there were supplies but she had to get close to the craft first and there was the matter of not getting caught, first she had to get out of this tunnel, she hoped that would be in minutes rather than hours, her sense of direction was usually pretty good but at the moment she was starting to doubt herself, there was light ahead, she listened but she couldn't hear any noises, she slowed down not that her pace was particularly quick. She needed to not only find a better way to the ship than she had just travelled but not get caught, she was still quite a distance from any activity. What was this place she could see the cave walls were smooth, she had never heard of a place this size before, the ground began to shake. Was it a rock slide? No there was a rhythm to it. Was it her imagination? The ground was starting to move; the sound was increasing then a voice filled the cavern

"Test firing of the ships thrusters"

The ship rose from the ground like a giant waking, the very air vibrated, she had never seen a ship like this one, the one thing she was certain of was it wouldn't hold thousands of people perhaps a couple of hundred, this ship was built for speed it was sleek in its design. Was this cave a hangar? Built to hold more than one ship? Rani watched from the end of the tunnel, she tied some material she had ripped from her clothes around her ears, the sound faded slightly, she could make out a couple of guards but her thoughts had been the guards thought the actual ships were safe, seeing they had the boundaries covered. Their masters underestimated them that was to their advantage, she kept herself tight against the wall, stealthily moving towards the light, she was right the second ship was the one they had heard about this was the transport, by its size and shape she wondered if it would even get off the ground, a shaft had been sunk into the ground it looked as if it may have gone down a kilometre there was no real way to tell, there were gantries all over the craft like spider webs, they crisscrossed the ship, sparks came from dozens of places as the ship was worked on. She wondered if she might be able to board one of the ships, no it was too risky, no this was not a task for her she needed to find a better way through to these ships. Glarai or Tarise might be better suited to find out more about these ships

Tarise had hoped she would be in the facility only a couple of hours, the discussion had been more in depth than she had thought but the important subjects Glarai seemed very vague about such as the allegiances of her colleagues, she still had no information about the ships she didn't really know who to ask

"Glarai we need to know about the ship. You said the pack had been taught to pilot them?"

"That's right I loaded the discs myself"

"Why would they all need a knowledge of piloting the craft? Don't you think that's a little excessive?"

That hadn't occurred to her if she was honest, she had been in small craft nothing space worthy but those ships had a crew of perhaps four to six personnel

"Are you thinking there is more than one ship?"

"I don't know but it is a possibility don't you think? Do you have any friends that are in that field?"

If she had always thought about genetics, the answer would have been no but coming from an important family and not really knowing what she wanted to do as in the sciences she had acquired contacts from many different areas. Glarai thought for a moment then she remembered a gathering several cycles before

"Yes, I might know someone he was a transport designer, this project had to be given a high priority I am sure he would have been involved it was a family concern"

"Then you need to get in contact with him, if he's still on planet"

Glarai was taken aback by the bluntness of the female, she had never seen this side of her, she wasn't sure she liked it

"We are running out of time Glarai we need to know who we can trust, a mistake now could cost my people their lives, I need the details of the ship or ships, sooner rather than later"

"Perhaps a couple of days?"

"A day would be better, but if it's a couple so be it, perhaps next time we can meet away from the facility",

"I have a feeling it will get increasingly difficult getting in here"

"Agreed I will walk you out"

Tarise passed a report to Glarai as they walked down the corridor, the report basically said Torrah was improving but her progress was slow, hopefully it would be enough for Marlac

"What if Marlac inquires why you didn't deliver the report in person?"

"Just say I was not comfortable leaving Torrah for too long that explanation will probably be enough. Don't be too obvious finding the information we require; I don't want to be mourning the death of another friend"

"I will be careful. so two days where are we going to meet?"

Fifteen hundred metres from the complex

Tarise and Glarai were challenged once on the way out of the complex as soon as Marlacs name was mentioned the guards body went that upright the female thought he was going to tear something it was good knowing someone in power and when Tarise got out of the complex she let out a breath she didn't know she had been holding. It was like pieces of a puzzle each individual had their piece and when they were brought together hopefully the puzzle would make sense

It was about half a day when Rani finally found herself in familiar territory, she wouldn't wish to take that journey again, she suspected she might have to make it several more times, she had learned lessons from it. What to wear, what supplies to take, which tunnels not to use, she wasn't surprised to see a light burning in Raldons quarters, she heard voices so she stepped into the males' quarters he was deep in conversation with his adopted son, it reminded her of scenes between a young Raldon and Karniar, perhaps those conversations had been lighter. Raldon had always stood out from the others a confidence, perhaps arrogance which had got him into more than a few scrapes in his youth, now she saw a young Stylar perhaps on his way to making similar mistakes that's why Raldon, Nairi and herself had to watch the young male guide him. Stylar had sensed her before she was even in the quarters, she doubted she would ever get used to those dark eyes of his, he seemed to always know when he was being watched. Raldon rose slowly

"So the wanderer has returned, you should have refreshed yourself, actually why don't you use my shower, while you are getting those several layers of dirt and grime off I will have some food fetched for you"

"Thank you Raldon I would appreciate that I am in need of some sustenance"

"Stylar go and get food and water from the great hall I told Torrahs mother she might be needed"

"At once father"

Rani peeled the clothes from her body it felt like in some sections her skin came away as well. Dirt caked her skin as did dried blood she would remember this journey for several days as the water began to move some of the blood, sweat and dirt, cuts were already beginning to hurt as water got in them

taking the dirt which had helped stop most of the blood, she bit her lip to take her mind off the dozens

of cuts and bruises

"You would think our bodies would toughen up over the cycles toiling in the mines wouldn't you"

Nairi had a towel waiting as Rani stepped from the shower, she also had ointments and bandages most of which Rani had made herself

"Don't fuss so woman I will feel better once I have eaten"

"I will take care of those cuts and scrapes before you do anything else now sit, that isn't a request when you are in my quarters you will find its best to do as I say I am sure Raldon will agree with me if you ask him"

Rani sat slowly and kept still while her cuts were dressed. Nairi had also brought a change of clothes

"I think these rags have been worn for the last time"

"Nonsense there's plenty of wear left in them"

Nairi put her whole fist through one the holes and it was one of the smaller ones at that

"Now I suggest you eat I would also say rest for several hours but I know you won't do that. I know you have information but ten to twenty minutes won't make any difference, take your time with the food, nothing will happen until the next shift begins so just try and relax"

"Yes, mother"

Rani said smiling it wasn't often she was told what to do. Nairi had a way of putting you at ease and while she was with the female it was as if all responsibilities were gone, she would eat and for those minutes she would be left to gather her thoughts, she had made a decision she would not be leaving this world, she had thought long and hard about it, she had lived too long seen too many people she had feelings for die she wanted it no she needed it to end, she would help her people escape but for her the only escape would be her death. People were meant to be born grow have someone there to love them if they were fortunate they had children of their own and made sure their lives were full before passing on there was a natural order to things, all that had been taken from her and though she tried not to have regrets she supposed that was life, she sometimes saw thoughts in others eyes the dreamers thinking of a life other than the one they had. Freedom this word could not have meaning until they were away from the caves

"Rani?"

It was like the voice was travelling from a great distance

"Rani are you alright?"

"What? What Nairi I was somewhere else"

Rani looked up using the smile she had used most of her adult life, reassuring a smile that was meant to say everything would workout, she had eaten her fill and though she felt tired from the last few days' activities, a few extra chairs had been brought from the main hall, it felt very cramped in Raldons quarters perhaps fifteen people were sat around when the space normally accommodated eight or nine some looked like they had been dragged from their sleep others as if they had just come off shift

"We will get straight down to business everyone present knows a piece of our plan but only a few of us know it all. Rani if you could start as soon as you have finished telling us what you observed I would like you to get some rest we can talk when you awaken"

Rani didn't really have the strength to argue so she just nodded

"Where to begin? Firstly, I thought my task would be easier than it turned out to be, shows how much I sometimes truly know"

There were a few chuckles from those who were gathered

"I need to get right to the point, the information we got about the passenger carrier was only partly true, I will admit to you I was not prepared for what I saw the scale was much bigger than I would have imagined, the cavern was perhaps a hundred metres in height, perhaps more I am not sure I could even see the roof of the cavern, the cavern itself what I saw was perhaps two or three kilometres in length though I did not see it all, it might have been a lot larger than that, I didn't have the opportunity to explore as much as I wanted, I actually discovered three craft the first one was clearly built for speed, two others clearly built for cargo both people and supplies, I still find it difficult to believe they could keep such a thing a secret with so many being involved"

From the door that question was answered

"I have the answer to that question all the designers and builders were killed"

It was Glarai everyone looked shocked apart from Stylar who was just sat observing for the moment, watching every ones' reactions. After all, why should he grieve they were the enemy were they not? Raldon took the information in and worded his next sentence carefully

"I think this new information means the odds of any of us surviving this have shortened, because now we know they will kill their own to keep these secrets from their own. Do we know how many died?"

Glarai had taken a seat

"From what I understand it might have been as high as several thousand"

Several of those gathered bowed their heads, the room seemed to take on a silence.

"How could so many have lost their lives?"

"It wasn't all at once and most could be explained away by the nature of their assignments, the biggest accident was a cave in which claimed a thousand lives. What better way to silence a group than to bury them? I had just begun to research several names of individuals whose fields would be of value to such a project, some had already escaped this world, the ones that hadn't, more had lost their lives than you could think of as coincidental the first so called accidents had occurred over forty cycles, the first large craft had been launched around that time"

Stylar sensed something different about Glarai her voice was low, almost clinical as she began to recount what she had found out as he watched he could see she was shaking slightly. Raldon leaned close to his son making sure no one else heard

"I have seen this before, perhaps too often she's in shock"

Raldon noticed Rani hadn't left his quarters and she just nodded as if their bond was close enough to know they didn't need words. Glarai had said all she was going to say on this occasion she like

Rani needed some rest and she needed to be back with her own people. Raldon knew she would get back to the complex as if seeing his concern Rani smiled

"I promise you as soon as I return I will sleep I just want to make sure she is safe before I go to my bed"

Raldon nodded in understanding they owed this female she would not be abandoned, Raldon looked at Tarise who looked pale under her dishevelled hair

"I, I can't believe it thousands of people just like that if they would do that to their own what would they do to us?"

"We will never give them the opportunity, this hasn't changed our plan, it has effected the amount of information we will be able to find out about the ships we can continue without it"

Torrah stared at her mate it was frightening sometimes how cold he could seem, sometimes it was as if he could remember where he came from, the people seemed to be without feelings or emotion. Glarai obviously felt for those who had died, perhaps death had been a better release than those who would face seeing their world die. Raldon began again

"Stylar if you would what did your group find?"

"What we found was that the ancient complex had just been dormant as if waiting the system seems to be a combination of organic and mechanical components we were not there long enough to find out what we could use, I hope to do better on my next visit, I was hoping Dianer would let myself and Carstal off duties while we investigate the complex thoroughly, I hope it will take no more than a couple of days, I think I will be able to provide answers"

Dianer didn't look thrilled about that idea but she didn't have a choice the good of the community over ore extraction there was no arguing, she would perhaps try and make him feel just a little guilty

"I don't have a lot of choice do I? I guess everyone will have to work a little bit harder and longer" Stylar smiled at Dianer

"I am sure they will love you that much more"

Raldons face took on a serious look

"Now it's just over a week before Stylars brethren are introduced to our people, I know tensions will be running high we don't really know what to expect, we have rumours about the vicious nature of their leader, if they push I don't want anyone to push back you are all too important if trouble starts let my son deal with it, he is their rightful leader so he needs to stamp his dominance on the situation"

"If it comes down to a confrontation with Barla I might have no choice but to end his life"

"You make it sound as if that will be an easy task"

"I am expecting some cuts and bruises; I am not underestimating my brother but if he forces me I will defend myself as well as the community"

Torrah sort of looked up at the roof of the room as if to say give me strength

"Well I think we know where everyone stands"

But she knew inside she would fight for those around her and herself, this was who she was. She could sense Raldon was still watching her, perhaps he knew her too well, she had fought for what she had, she could not back down now surely anyone who knew her would know that. She wouldn't let Stylar protect her and then she sensed another set of eyes on her, the young male held her gaze even when it became uncomfortable, it scared how much of a mystery this boy, she was thinking child but his appearance was now more an adolescent male, his physique was getting more like his friend and protector Carstal every day. Carstal was the biggest male on her shift. Stylar might even grow bigger she remembered that first time she had seen him small but he had never seemed helpless. Stylar was bred for power and she could not help feeling threatened by that, she wondered how he would compare with the rest of his brethren. She wondered where his destiny would take him, she didn't think his life would end here, now. He had been welcomed into the community because he was Raldons son which obviously hadn't hurt, he was more emotional than most perhaps overcompensating, he seemed to enjoy the experiences, his emotions always seemed to be the positive ones she had never seen him show sorrow, depression, fear. That was what was different about him. Did he have these emotions, they had talked but never for long and nothing too probing. She was staring at it bothered her that there were feelings there, but also so much confusion. Raldon had been finishing off his comments and she realised she had not been listening to a word that had been said, she suspected it was along the lines of their journey being far from over and the bonds that held them together, everyone started to leave Raldons quarters. Stylar was talking with his father Dianer tried to slip passed she thought she had managed it until a hand rested on her shoulder

"You will excuse me for moment Dianer and myself need to settle a point"

Raldon went into the other room where Nairi was tidying as best she could

"Do you mind?"

"Stylar hadn't removed his hand from her shoulder"

"I'm sorry we need to talk"

"I don't think we do"

"You are wrong about fighting this battle"

"I had heard rumours of this mind reading of yours but I didn't think it was this developed"

"It's not but I would have to be blind not to know what you are thinking; your eyes are very expressive, I know you are confident in your abilities, you have been taught well but you just can't win against my people genetics are against you"

Dianer was going to ask Stylar if he thought she couldn't hold her own against Barla, he smiled

"I think my brother would make you think you had a chance, he would play his own sadistic game, you might think your pace might save you but that first time he made contact with you it would be over. I don't want to lose you"

"You don't?"

This turn of conversation surprised her and put her on her back foot he had made it personal

"That's right my father would never forgive himself you are the closest thing to family he's got"

"He's got you"

"That's right he's got me I have been with him a few months. With you he had cycles to watch you grow into the strong beautiful female that stands before me now, I see pride in his eyes at the very mention of your name. will you promise me you won't be baited? Raldon will lose a daughter, I will lose"

He couldn't finish the sentence he didn't know what Dianer was to him it was like a lot of eh, adults his perspective was having too change too fast, he was growing at an accelerated rate. Dianer was now looking at him

"You don't know what I am to you? I think it's the first time I have seen you with confusion on your face, I wish I could promise you I would back down"

A tear ran down her cheek

"But I can't Stylar it's who I am. What I have I won't give up, this is what life has taught me"

With that she turned away and didn't look back as she left Raldons quarters

"You will lose"

Stylar shouted after her, now he knew he had to be there. Torrah had watched from the shadows, she hadn't understood the exchange. Was she losing him? Why had the geneticists given them free will? They had altered so much about them would taking free will been that much of a challenge. Stylar had already demonstrated he could survive without her. Why didn't she feel the same? Just one of the many questions she found herself asking, and why was she beginning to ask questions? She didn't used to, she felt like she was dying inside

"Are you alright?"

She hadn't heard him she jumped at the question

"Don't do that Carstal. How is it someone so large can make so little sound?"

"I am sorry I didn't mean to scare you; I was just concerned you looked sad"

Torrah tried to smile but her heart wasn't in it

"I'm not sad just a little concerned about Stylar"

"You don't need to be he's a survivor"

"No it's not that it's he's changed"

Carstal looked confused

"I have to admit I have not noticed"

"Why am I not surprised you males. Why is it sometimes you are so slow about the behaviour of those around you?"

"I don't know why don't you tell me? You seem to have all the answers"

"Very amusing Carstal now what is it you wanted?"

Carstal had had thoughts on his mind for a while, he took a deep breath and decided he needed to ask

"I wanted to know if you would like to go for a walk with me?"

"Why would I do that? "

"Perhaps to talk"

"And what have we been doing for the past five minutes?"

"I don't know I was thinking it has been like a verbal combat, sparring?"

"We have not been doing anything of the kind"

"So the answer to my question is no? you don't want to walk with me"

"The answer is yes I would like that very much"

"It is?"

Torrah hadn't really thought about it, it was almost like a reflex action and Carstal looked shocked.

Torrah couldn't help but smile she had at least made him work a little for his answer

Carstal offered her his hand and she took it, he gently closed his fingers around hers, he didn't apply any pressure. Torrah actually realised at that point she was smiling for the first time in she couldn't remember the last time she felt like this, the world around her seemed to have come to life and she wondered if this was the start of something that might begin to define who she would be. Perhaps it was no more than the large male wanting some company, she wondered who would decide if it was more first, the two walked out of the shadows and out into the passageway comfortable with each other

Stylar was back with his father. Raldon had heard how the end of the conversation had gone, though he would have figured it out anyway by the look on his sons' face

"That female has to be the most unreasonable individual I have ever encountered"

"Yes, your history with females being so long"

"Father this is serious she's going to get herself killed and what's worse is others might die trying to protect her"

"She will do what she thinks is right like she has always done, changing the subject it sounds like your relationship has changed concerning her"

"Well she is like a sister I suppose, after all you took us both under your protection"

"Yes, I suppose that might be it"

"Of course that's it what were you thinking about?"

"Nothing perhaps just an old male with too much time on his hands"

Stylar seemed satisfied with that explanation and didn't push Raldon any further, although that night Stylar couldn't settle he heard his father's words over and over. He didn't know what he was looking for. Stylars morning started a few hours before everyone else's after several hours of lying on his back looking up at the roof of the cave he decided things needed to be done, he ate a dry bar which contained grains and several cereals with a sweetness that he couldn't identify and no one seemed to want to divulge a secret, but at this moment in time he was content that it filled an empty stomach, he drank down a mug of water and he made the decision not to disturb his large friend he would probably prefer to take a shift, he had sensed that first encounter that the system wanted him and him alone, he heard a word in his head symbiosis. Stylar moved with a swiftness most would never see; he wasn't slowed down by individuals in the passages or companions accompanying him, he used the shadows when he could, every once in a while, he heard the first stirrings of activity, he sensed the guards above. Did they always patrol at this time? He had never thought to ask because a cage was a cage whatever the surroundings, it took about fifteen minutes to get to the centre of the mine normally perhaps it would have taken twenty-five perhaps thirty minutes hopefully the longer he stayed the more he would uncover. Stylar was still fascinated by a history perhaps only one knew within the community and he still had lots to discover about the early experiments that had led to his brethren and himself being created. Perhaps not the right time but perhaps this might be the only opportunity he would get, the system was not limited to what information could be accessed at once in fact he already knew it would run as many searches as was required simultaneously. Stylar had noticed not just his but Torrahs thirst for knowledge, Raldons people generally didn't seem interested in expanding their knowledge they were on the whole content with what they had, that obviously was going to change when they found out they didn't have a future. Perhaps that wasn't quite true Stylar knew family and friends who asked questions but they would be in the minority most seemed almost content with their lives, while thoughts had been drifting through his head he had used the rope that still bridged the shaft quickly hand over hand as his friend had done finally getting to the place where the platform had taken them, his hands searching quickly for the indentation, he had been so sure he would find it right away both hands feeling, yes that was it, it had taken a minute but it had felt a lot longer. Perhaps he was getting arrogant, perhaps there was more of his masters' personalities in him than he thought, he knew there was a thin line between arrogance and confidence, he placed his palm flat, he felt a slight tingling in his fingers, the rocks slid aside quicker than the first time and he hardly heard the gears. He had had his doubts perhaps the squad that had been sent into the complex had damaged perhaps even destroyed it, the platform rose too slowly for Stylars impatience, patience these days was one thing that didn't seem to come easily to him, that was the main reason why he was here now instead of a couple of hours later with his friend, as long as that impatience didn't have any ramifications on the community what did it matter? Finally, he was back in the complex the lighting raised slightly enough so he could once more see the wonders that his masters had thought of hundreds of cycles before, his instincts screamed out even though there was that sterile smell it couldn't hide death, he had unfortunately come in contact with that too many times

"What happened here?"

Very impressive you can smell that even though the area has been fully sanitized, I did what I was programed to do defend myself. Would you not defend yourself if you were attacked?

"I would but I may feel regret after such an encounter, perhaps even pity"

That is one of the feelings I can no longer remember, when my biological self-had such emotions and feelings taken away leaving more of the darker side of a humans' nature they started a chain of events that would see much blood, I find small comfort in the fact they never carried out the procedure again Stylar didn't say anything it would be pointless, he could never understand what that male must have gone through, suffering might have been to tame a description to use, he was violated they took everything from him that made him who he was and the worse thing was he had had so many cycles to think of what had happened to him and those thoughts it was very possible that they had festered, twisted into something that was now just vengeance and what was now this facility was worse than a master who needed to be defeated. Stylar stood still a screen came to like a skeletal structure appeared, the extra ribs made it appear like armour the image changed now organs appeared and musculature. Stylar watched the process with fascination

You look impressed

"I have never seen who I really am before"

They have made some impressive changes to your structure

Another screen came to life with another skeleton, Stylar saw the differences immediately his bones were thicker, he was ten to fifteen centimetres taller his shoulder muscles we broader as it gave the other form detail, his muscles were denser

You are as close to perfection as these limited minds could achieve, there are flaws though your eyes are more sensitive to light

As if to prove the point the room became white light, pain shot through his head and he winced and it took a few moments to recover

I apologise Stylar sometimes to prove a point I go too far

The lights once more lowered to a comfortable level

I think it's time we made a bargain

"A bargain?"

I have something you need and you have something I want

Stylar looked at the image on the screen and realised in that moment and he felt something he had not felt before

"You want me"

An image of a brain appeared on the screen. Stylar stepped closer, it had to be his brain he was looking at, he could make something out, something was attached to his brain, perhaps hundreds even thousands there were so many of these thin fibres which attached themselves.

"What is the purpose of this technology?"

As I said before there are several sections that are dormant, quite a large percentage of it is an interface, its why you learn so quickly, that is a tracker fortunately it's not functioning, but they could if it became functional, so many redundant systems they have forgotten so much

"You haven't told me what you need"

I wish to merge

"Merge?"

To be part of one another, combine our essences the best of both of us

"What would be the dangers of such a merge?"

I don't like to dwell on the what might happen points, probably my personality would become dominant, my intellect spans what they know above, that knowledge would erase who you are your personality

"You would expect me to merge with you after you have been so honest with me?"

You have to think of the advantages of such a procedure, the knowledge I can share with your people, they have been reduced to savages. They will need skills to survive I can give that to them. Is it not worth such a sacrifice? If you defeat your enemy what can you truly offer? You can help them escape the planet, perhaps even secure them a new home but then what?

All these questions had occurred to Stylar but he wondered if the price was too high, as if the machine sensed his indecision it took another line

I could force you to merge with me

Stylar didn't like how the conversation had turned

"That sounded very much like a threat? Would you do what they did to you all those cycles ago? I would have thought the many cycles you have had to think about what was done to you, you might have learned the one great truth it is wrong to violate another"

Right and wrong I suppose has something to do with your point of view, never black and whites more many shades of grey

"That is an excuse of convenience you might have become the one thing you have hated. You have become bitter and twisted"

Perhaps you are correct I have had many cycles to replay in my mind what happened to me, I was powerless I know but something always says I could have done something, they gave me immortality when I longed to go to her. Why would I want to live without her, her smile, the touch of her soft hand just being complete, now I feel empty. I want vengeance but all those who were responsible are long gone, cheated even out of that simple pleasure

"Can vengeance ever be pleasurable?"

Perhaps satisfying might have been a better description

Stylar was starting to be afraid would he become what he was fighting? Was the only way to know ones' enemy to become them?

"Perhaps you can get your vengeance by helping my people survive"

The machine took a millionth of a second to decide on a course of action

"I have reconsidered I will agree to your terms but I want her to live"

The tube once more lit up showing the beautiful female within

"She never had a chance of life I believe with your assistance I can grant her that second chance I am not sure I understand is she not dead?"

Look around you Stylar this lab was created for one purpose to give life; I want to give her a chance perhaps have children grow old watching them have children of their own

"If we can bring her back couldn't we bring you back too?"

No I caused her death I couldn't live without her not again; it will be enough for me to see her once more having the life she always deserved

"Could this merging be used for several individuals instead of one?"

Yes, but as I said they would have to have similar interfaces to you

"Like my brethren, I have found the instrument of your vengeance, the very experiment that our masters' thought would be their salvation will be my peoples instead, twenty-four individuals will have everything that made you special, no not everything something was taken you are not the same individual who was put into this system. We need to plan what knowledge is needed to save the community"

Your terms are acceptable if you help bring back my mate

"What was her name?"

Justail she was strong, loyal and she never wavered when it came to the two of us

"I would like to bring someone back with me who will be of more use in what we are about to attempt   Because even though he knew the system possessed the information needed Stylar wasn't sure this could be achieved"

I wouldn't want to make a mistake considering this is the last time this facility will be used

"That is acceptable I trust that you would not harm our alliance, not until your brethren have the knowledge they will need to survive away from these caves"

Obviously trust issues which he guessed would happen if you were violated and your mate was killed in front of you just to make a point

If you ever wonder about someone's loyalties bring them here I will know if they are lying, my sensors rad every reaction and biological working of your body. I scanned various geneticists on the days leading up to my betrayal and the signs were there I just didn't know how to interpret them at the time, several were not forthcoming with information and their heart rates increased when they came into my vicinity, perhaps in those days there was still humanity running through my systems, now only the efficiency of the machine remains

"But you still crave vengeance isn't that your humanity screaming out for retribution?"

Perhaps those darkest of emotions have allowed me to sustain myself through the cycles

That concerned Stylar positive emotions kept his people together it was the negative ones that created doubt, betrayal, such emotions were primal they were what probably drove the species through evolution. So its thoughts were they from the organic or the knowledge it had flowing through its systems, he knew he would never find out that answer. Stylar hoped that transferring the knowledge into all of the brethren would dilute it to a point where the personalities would not be effected it was still a risk but he wondered if he took so much knowledge himself would it drive him mad? Stylar had decided to ask Tarise for her assistance she knew about the systems in the other complex, she might be able to tell him where the systems differed, Glarai would also be useful he wondered how the system would react to one of her kind. He would have to warn her. It was a risk. He decided the system needed to know

"I was thinking of involving two individuals who worked in the other facility, one is one of the masters'"

The lights flickered for a moment, the silence seemed to stretch out to a point where Stylar was becoming concerned

"At least you will find out if she can be trusted"

Stylar was beginning to think they might just have a chance, a future and the uncertainty was both daunting and exciting, a few more obstacles a few more pieces to bring into play, it didn't feel like they had even begun yet, plans could go wrong so much still needed to be done and though he would not tell anyone he was concerned about his brethren how they would react, how they would adapt to their new surroundings and how they would react to others. Stylar had kept a lot of what was going on inside to himself, the implants in his head once in a while he almost saw images, perhaps it was him that was keeping them out because when he slept he saw someone and he felt such rage, but not born out of anger more out of frustration. Stylars thoughts came back to here and now, perhaps this was why he had come alone he knew what the system was capable of and he would only risk himself. Were the images from the system? Or were they from somewhere else. Would such questions ever be answered?

Marlac was pacing in his lab, his lights were not on they were more for those not of his people all their suits had virtual imaging his world once a paradise now the suits were needed not just for their respiratory systems but that virtual imagine system a lot of the world was now shrouded in like a mist that the sun only once in a while burned through, it was never light anymore perhaps like his peoples very soul, he wondered if his people had learned anything from this dying world or would they make the same mistakes again somewhere else? Probably in their arrogance they would believe they could tame the elements and when another world lay dying they would move on again he had always thought of himself as different he created not destroyed, yes a lot of sacrifice had been made in the name of evolution but to strive for perfection was that wrong? Glarai was trying to contact him, the damn rock was blocking a lot of the signal, she must be close though, he also suspected some of the materials the complex had were made of similar materials, the issue had not been discovered until well into the build the individual who had sourced the materials mysteriously disappeared, perhaps he was still with them as in buried in the foundations of a later part of the complex. Marlac tried to concentrate she had found what? Oh no it couldn't be? He moved quickly from the lab a couple of assistants got under his feet, he knocked them aside, he didn't have time for niceties, besides he want expected to apologise he could see her now she was huddled over a crumpled body, yes he had heard right it was the captain. Where were the rest of his team? By the state of his suit he had dragged himself quite a distance, the scuff marks on his chest section were testament to that fact. Marlac virtually knocked Glarai out of his way, the female didn't say a word

"Captain what happened where is your squad? Answer me"

He heard what sounded like a sigh but it could and probably was the captain trying to get a breath

"Sir I failed you"

"How did you fail me? What did this?"

"Sir he hasn't got the strength"

"Glarai not another word, this is a soldier, he will give me the information if it's with his dying breath"

"It was the machine"

"The machine still functions after all these cycles? Where are the rest of your squad?"

"They were"

The captains head fell to the side. Marlacs suit told him what he already knew the captain had passed, he had just had enough to give that final report. The captain had suffocated his suit had had its respirator reprogrammed so he would get no further, perhaps shock was also a factor his system just couldn't take the stress. Marlac shook his head sadly, he had hoped the last of the geneticists would have carried out their duty and destroyed the system, no one really had been curious enough to go back in to make sure until now

Glarai was looking at Marlac now, even through her visor he could hear the question

"I was hoping the systems power source would have depleted many cycles ago, the system was ahead of its time both technology and biology it was an experiment that should never have been attempted. There was supposed to be a signal that when sent would overload the system. If it was sent then obviously it wasn't effective, perhaps the machine rewrote its programming, the stories said it became self-aware"

"Fascinating"

"Oh yes the system was state of the art the system we use now is almost like an echo of it. When it saw a threat it did what any of us would do it defended itself. It used our own innovations' against us trapping geneticists in vacuum chambers and doing to them what they had done to others, some might have called it poetic justice, the lives it took that day we never recovered, decades of work gone, hundreds of cycles of experience taken"

"Are you saying this breakthrough we have just achieved was achieved hundreds of cycles ago?"

"You are never to repeat that is that understood?"

"Yes, sir"

"Good, now clean up this mess I understand Tarise paid us a visit?"

"Yes, sir I thought I would verify her conclusions before I made my report to you sir"

"Very wise she is gifted but lacks your experience, as soon as you have disposed of the captain we can meet, you can give me her observations and you can go from there, say thirty minutes?"

"Understood sir"

Marlac strode away probably to make a report of his own

The chancellor sat in his chair. Marlac had a theory that the chair was more than a place to sit, perhaps it was also the old males' life support system functioning in tandem with the chancellors' own exoskeleton, he never seemed to come out of the shadows hidden in darkness

"What an unexpected surprise Marlac. How many times did you contact me before the experiment?"

"I think possibly twice chancellor"

"I think this is possibly the fifth time since the children were born? I am getting quite fond of our little conversations"

"I knew you would want this information immediately chancellor" "Speak"

"I have just learnt that the system in the old complex is still functioning"

"What? I was told it was destroyed"

"I was never sure chancellor that's why I stationed a guard there, I knew if the community ever entered the facility it could mean that their way of thinking might have changed, you know how superstitious they can be. The old complex was almost sacred to them"

"So I am presuming your team made it back were they able to disable the system?"

"Only one member of the team returned and he barely told me anything before he passed, but obviously they had not been successful in shutting the system down the only reason he returned was to warn us to leave the system alone"

"So we still don't know if anyone did enter the system and if they did do you not think they would have ended up the same way as the security detail?"

"I don't like to guess chancellor in my profession we only believe what we can prove. What danger could there be even if some of the community did get in? they only understand sweat, if the system did try and communicate with them, they would think it was spirits. I have an assistant who is observing Torrah"

"Torrah?"

"The one from the experiment chancellor that I sent back to her family because of the loss of her mate she was in danger of being killed by the others"

"What is her progress?"

"I am having someone brief me after this communication finishes, the one who is watching her is from the community herself she was one of the few we recruited from there to see if they could do more than basic tasks, she has performed beyond expectations. Glarai has been a go between"

"The name is familiar. Would I know the family?"

"I would not be surprised they move in the same social circles as yourself I would assume"

"Very good well I have things to do any issues just pass them to my office"

"Understood chancellor"

Marlac was going to say something but the screen went dark, Marlacs vital signs went back to normal almost immediately, fortunately for him at this late stage it would be difficult to find another geneticist to take his place. Something inside told him he would never leave this world at least he had no close family to witness their demise

Darrus had prepared himself to do the deed, the end of the shift at the end of the day he had used stealth to make his way to Raldons quarters only to be confronted by some sort of gathering, he had tucked his axe deeper into the folds of his clothing and skulked away. That day would see the end of one of them. Stylar had not done a shift that day he had returned early and gone to his quarters. Darrus once more approached the quarters he had made an excuse for leaving shift early now as he neared the end of what had to be done he could feel his heart thumping in his chest, he could feel the beads of sweat massing at his hair line, not just there running down his back and under his arms, he also felt like he was going to bring up the small meal he had eaten earlier, he kept saying to himself it was for the good of his people. What would happen to Stylars loyalty when his people were introduced into the community? It wouldn't be such a simple choice then. Why couldn't the others see this? After this they would not need to see nothing. Darrus heard voices he backed into the shadows, if he was seen whatever he did next his life would be over, he didn't recognise the two that were approaching it was a big place and you tended to be in a group, well he did anyway. He watched them pass and continue down the tunnel, he kept close to the wall, using the cover to its full advantage, his axe slipped his hands had become slick with the sweat and the handle had come away from his grasp, he had snatched it just before it hit the ground and wiped both his hand and the shaft on his clothing, tucking himself more into the shadows, also rubbing his brow on his sleeve, he tore loose a bit of material and wrapped the handle he didn't want it slipping at a crucial moment, he had no doubts that if his hand slipped and Stylar heard, that would be the end of both plan and his life, the flickering of torch light began to play tricks with his mind he started to see shadows moving across the roughly cut walls, he kept having to squeeze into cracks and crevices thinking he had been seen, this was taking too long. Was someone following him? This felt like the longest journey he had ever taken, he heard something a falling rock, every sound and shadow seemed to make him cower, he had never felt like this. Was he feeling guilty? This was for his people. Stylar would betray them Darrus could see Raldons quarters, it was a shadow, it loomed that wasn't his imagination, he searched the tunnel looking for what was making it, the size of it, it might be Carstal, he was never far from Stylars side. Why would Stylar need protection he smiled at the thought.

It was his imagination he quickened his pace no turning back, he had no choice. The torches were out Raldon and Nairi had decided to sleep early, he tentatively peered into the darkness. Stylars chamber was next to Raldons and he crept silently into the chamber, listening for any sound, the darkness was both ally and enemy his feet shuffled slightly feeling for any obstacles on the ground, he had been in these chambers before so he had a rough idea about how things were placed, he was on his toes not wanting to make any sounds, his foot scraped he froze, this nervousness was making him careless. A dozen steps from the entrance and he was in the chamber, as he listened he could hear the light breathing he was above the young male he swung the axe and waited for the sound of metal splitting bone, like the sound in the halls when the females scrounged meat from most of the time he didn't want to know, he hadn't realised but he had turned his head away, the sound he did hear was like a slap, in the darkness, a little light came from outside it was hard to make out anything but the black eyes that were staring at him, so black he could never remember a time when he had seen such a colour, the axe was between his hands only centimetres from his skull, he tried to put more pressure on the axe but without the momentum it wasn't going to kill him not with the first blow anyway, but the action just brought a smile to the young males lips it was like he was toying with him, he now had all his weight on the axe. Stylar could have called out but he didn't, his head was shaking slightly as his muscles began to pump, taking the strain, he was raising himself slowly into a sitting position. Darrus tried to push him back down, Stylars feet were now on the ground his legs underneath him as he pushed up, with no real effort at all the axe went spinning embedding in the rock. Darrus tried to put his hands around Stylars throat this was now desperation, he wanted to run but what would he do? Stylar was now tired of the game, Darrus felt his fingers get pulled away from the young males' throat and then darkness took him.

Stylar threw a single punch that sent his attacker sprawling to the ground Stylar stood over him

"Where am I? what happened"

Oh it was coming back to him he was sat in a chair; his arms were locked behind his back. He felt like asking why he was restrained but this unfortunately was the price of failure. Raldon stood before him, he had never seen such an expression on the old males' face

"Why did you try and murder my son?"

Darrus wished he could move he had never seen this male look so angry, it concerned his that if he was struck he would not be able to defend himself

"He, he isn't your son, he is a stranger who has taken control of all of your minds. How do you think he's going to act when his people join the community? He'll betray you after all he is the next stage in our evolution"

"Quiet"

Darrus looked around he was in the chamber of the elders, which meant he was to be judged, he was beginning to wish the young male had finished him, he wondered how long he had been unconscious

"Has day shift begun yet?"

"Why do you want to go and work?"

Raldon said under his breath

"It's actually late meal"

"So I've been unconscious half a day?"

I taught him how to defend himself so it stands to reason he would be prepared for someone like yourself

Then he heard a voice of the male he hoped he would never hear again

"Actually father that punch Dianer showed me how to land it"

A few giggles came from the shadows, Raldon just ignored them, he now stood with his back to Darrus addressing the council

"I don't know what motivated this attack on my son, I want the council to show leniency we have lost too many of our own, saying that I know he can't be allowed to remain a part of the community"

"So what would you suggest Raldon?"

"I suggest we send Darrus to another colony"

"I won't go this is my home, this is where I have family and friends"

Raldon turned sharply he couldn't hide the disgust

"I can't believe I thought about giving Dianers position to you, you are not the same child I saw grow up, such a petty individual, I never knew you at all and your friends and family I think you will find it hard to find either"

"What I did I did for our people"

"No what you did you did for yourself. What did you think would happen? You killed Stylar and people would stand beside you? What were you thinking?"

"Are you all so blind? Stylar will betray you and he might not be able to help himself. Blood will decide it always does in these matters"

Raldon just shook his head sadly

"Now it is up to you to decide banishment or death, if the decision is banishment the colony will not be told of your crimes and you can start again, if the decision is death this will be carried out after the judgement"

Darrus just stared down at his feet, a look of hopelessness on his face that would have effected anyone who looked upon it

"I choose banishment"

It was barely above a whisper but everyone heard, when he had spoken the words he looked around the chamber until his eyes locked on Stylars, hate was in that look but Stylar did not look away. Darrus had been true to himself he had done all he could, he hoped he was wrong, but at least if he was he wouldn't have to witness what was to come, now he was looking for another yes of course there she was Terak stood as always in front of her, ready to defend her if someone was brave enough to tell her what they truly thought of her

"You stole what I should have had"

"I stole nothing, you just never had within what was required because sometimes the job is more than your own wishes sometimes you have to think of others, that's always been what motivated you, what was good for you"

Dianer turned away she couldn't look at him anymore, they had spent so much time together now all she saw was a stranger and she couldn't look at his face any longer

"You chose poorly Raldon I hope your choices don't come back to haunt you"

With those last defiant words, he was lifted roughly and dragged from the chamber, it was the last time he was ever seen, the carrier that took him to his new colony never arrived, it was wondered about but with everything that was happening it was forgotten

The system waited with anticipation for Stylars next visit, it felt, the system didn't know how it felt but it felt right conversing with someone once more, the system had been in self-diagnosis mode for too long. It had no feelings as such but there was a sense that it was not complete. Could it still feel loneliness? Was it the system that missed the companionship or was it him? Was there still a remnant of him within, the time they had spent together though it knew to a millionth of a second how long it had been it still seemed to have gone more quickly when the young male was there, its systems needed to be used or what was the point? It was still created to serve that was at its core. The system had already set up twenty distinct files for the males' brethren. The young male was always there almost like a conscience, even when the system lost emotions he was still there almost as if given the opportunity he would once more rise from the data that had been dumped. Stylars brain was different more potential it couldn't predict what the males' personality would do when combined with the data that would be downloaded into the interface, the system still remembered the continual struggle it had had with the young male, instructions given then considered rather than immediate action, in the end the system had come to an understanding. This time it needed to be a flawless merging, the system had probed Stylars brain almost like a soft caress, they had already decided not to force their way into his head because that would be too much like rape, it would not do what they had done to that young male again, as Stylar entered the complex the system had already scanned his present wellbeing, he looked tired and the readout confirmed this

"No welcome for one of your twenty vessels?"

You look tired

"I can't argue with that I have hardly slept in the last three days"

I have to say even with your superior pulmonary system you still require rest

"I know that will happen soon enough"

From the floor a table rose, Stylar stared at it, his senses alert as he smelt death, he looked at the old straps primitive in their design but they did what they were designed for

"What is this for?"

Please lie down I want to begin the download, if you will still consent I presume you talked it over with your leader?

"I did he wasn't sure, he wondered about your present status"

I appreciate your honesty, I am not functioning at optimum proficiency, several of my memory banks have been corrupted over the cycles, I have information in my data banks I cannot analyse, perhaps they are emotions, I know rage, vengeance has given me purpose but as to whether that is part of myself becoming self-aware or the personality that even though he seems gone there is an echo. I think about what they did to Justail, I think about how they would pay. The remnants of that male I wish to download into you

Stylar held up his hand

"I don't know what to say. Do you have any idea what effect that will have on me? I mean will it turn me into someone fuelled on hate and vengeance? I don't want what's in you unlocking the side I would rather have caged up"

I will be honest with you I do not know what my program will do, I have issues flowing through my subroutines, there is logic, but there is also emotion which can be both disturbing and distracting, the system cannot grasp certain concepts and unfortunately the system seems more at ease processing negative emotions as if that is its state of mind

Stylar didn't understand just listening there was obviously conflict

I know my feelings for Justail, I mean the males feelings were strong to a point where software was rewritten, I can't recall what love felt like

"I think perhaps Torrah could explain better than myself, though I know it isn't a natural love, it's a chemical attraction, pheromones. I have never felt for her the way she feels about me, perhaps a good friend nothing more, I think she is beginning to understand. I find it confusing that you refer to your lost love by name, but the male you never mention what he was called. That information is no longer in my system, hers if I had one word left it would be her name, I will hold onto that name like I hold on to my very existence"

That sounds to me like how I think of love, to hold onto her name to keep her preserved. Perhaps if he is downloaded into me he will have a positive reaction as in showing me how I should feel in certain circumstances, up to this point I have been rushed, thoughts left unfinished, words left unsaid, but some of those emotions, feelings, bottled up for so long I can imagine how overwhelming they might be   Stylar hopped onto the examination table though the uses it had had he didn't even want to think about, now he was going to risk everything, he felt the connection almost instantly , it was both a physical and mental connection in his mind he heard a soothing voice say relax, he closed his eyes, images came into his head, places he had never seen, memories of another time, he knew that if he panicked the procedure would cause him pain, though something inside him told him to fight, don't let, it felt hot, a searing pain, he endured it, his muscles tensed, a sheen of sweat began to cover his body

"You didn't say it would hurt"

Didn't I? it must have slipped my memory banks

With that a surge of what felt like static, there was something else here, like tendrils stretching out, exploring. Was it another consciousness? At first it felt elusive as if it didn't want to be seen, then slowly it began to entwine itself into Stylars very being, the pain was intense it felt like his head might explode. Justail the name was like an explosion it felt like it was tearing through him

"No don't she's an innocent, no she has nothing to do with this"

Stylars eyes opened, his cheeks were wet but not from sweat. He had been crying as he had relived that last moment of his mates' life, no not his, the consciousness, that even now was exploring its new environment, he touched his cheek and tasted the fluid salty, he was silent for what felt like an eternity, he was trying to understand what had just happened Stylar? Stylar how do you feel?

"What? I feel alright I think just a little disorientated"

You seemed to be experiencing pain I thought that would end with the initial surge, I thought that would be the end of it I apologize

"No it was another sort of pain and what myself and brethren experience on a weekly cycle is so much more, he really did love her didn't he, every time she was near him his heart raced, he could never tell her how he felt it was as if words just couldn't express the emotions, the thoughts, he always hoped she would understand, he had no confidence, most females ignored him, she changed his perspective of the world around him. Justail turned an existence into a life, he wanted so much more for her than he could ever give, he felt like tearing his heart from his chest. I have never experienced such sensations, it is the strongest emotion I have ever felt, but at the same time hardest to define, you have given me a gift I never thought could be possible"

Is the young male in your mind?

"I feel him but it isn't how I imagined it would be, I can't explain it"

I also downloaded basic survival techniques

"Just the basic why did you not download the whole file?"

I thought you had had enough; I did not want to cause you any more discomfort

"So I will have to experience that pain again?"

At least next time you will be prepared

"That isn't much comfort"

Stylar couldn't keep the sarcasm from his tone

The system suddenly changed topic. Have you made any progress getting the assistance you wanted to create Justail?

"With your permission I would like to go and get her now"

Stylar realised he couldn't move, it felt like someone was pushing down on his chest, a yellow glow pulsated around his body

I didn't want you to injure yourself, besides I think you need a few hours' rest

Stylar was going to say something but the thought was gone before it became voiced

I have waited more cycles than you can imagine a few hours will be of no consequence to me

Stylars eyes stung and they wouldn't stay open, new feelings, so many questions, perhaps it would take him a lifetime to understand what he had been given, perhaps he would never truly know, he hoped he would have the time to appreciate these new feelings

"What? I went to sleep?"

You did

"How long?"

Four hours sixteen minutes

"Why did you let me sleep so long? We have so much to do"

Yes, we do but you will achieve nothing if you are too tired to carry out rudimentary tasks, you needed the rest and I made sure you got what you needed. Now I believe you had an errand to run

The yellow glow was gone and he had to admit he felt better than he had done in several weeks, he wondered if he might have had the strength to break out of the field, perhaps inside he had known he needed the rest, it took a few hours to track Tarise down every place he tried she seemed to have left a few minutes before, one of those he was talking to told him to wait where he was she would pass through again but to Stylar that was wasting time although he couldn't help but think there might be a strange logic to that perhaps he needed a little more rest he was starting to feel a little discouraged when he heard a familiar voice

"I hear you have been looking for me, I had to go meet a friend"

Glarai stepped out of the shadows

"How are you young man?"

"I am well it seems a long time since we were last together"

"I suppose for you it's like a lifetime. How have your growing pains been?"

"They've been getting steadily worse thank you for asking"

Stylar replied with a slight smile on his lips

"I guess there is no point me warning you about the pains that are to come"

"No I guessed they would be something special I didn't want the others worrying about Torrah and myself"

"I heard that someone might have entered the old complex I shouldn't be shocked that it was you. So what do you need me for?"

"The system wants to recreate a life that was lost, I naturally thought of you because of your experience with my brethren"

"I have often wondered about that system, a lot of the official records were sealed, if there is a chance even to right just one wrong then of course I will assist where I can, if the system is alright with me being there?"

"I think that will be the easy part, I know you will be of much more use than I ever could be, I guess it just wasn't in my programming"

"You could learn, not everyone has a chip in their head, knowledge isn't supposed to be easy sometimes it's hard, that's why it should always be valued"

While Stylar had been talking with Glarai, Tarise had joined the pair sensing more than a little impatience from both to get started, this place was legend, myth so many mysteries and all three all were thinking along similar lines. Would these mysteries be solved? Glarai was glad her face was behind a mask because she had not felt this nervous since childhood, she knew the blood that had been spilt, her people had started it, but the system perhaps had become more like those who had created than it could ever imagine, they tried to keep the conversation light as they made their way towards the complex perhaps the two females were trying to take their minds off what they might find, they talked like they had been friends for many cycles. Stylars neck muscles began to relax, tension ebbing out that he hadn't realised he had, a few miners were coming towards Stylar, smiles on their faces that changed when they say his companion, the group lowered their eyes and moved on, Glarai pretended not to notice but she would never get used to that type of reaction, she could do nothing about where and to whom she had been born, just to live her life to her own personal code. Stylar started to pick up what could only be described as random thoughts, most seemed to concern Glarai, the thoughts were confusion, anger, mistrust the system still had doubts about Stylars judgement, he lacked experience he was but a child. How could he judge some ones' character? He had been fortunate that his circle of trust up to that point had not faulted, but perhaps more good fortune than knowing the signs. He needed to reassure the system, he sent images of times he had not witnessed they were what he had inherited from the complex. He knew the system would not know how to read the data, but he had to try. Stylar hooked the females onto the rope they had used, the ladder was not safe he doubted it would hold Glarais weight, the rope was a gamble so he attached her to the line in three different places before making his way across the rope. Tarise went next if there was an incident at least some one in the complex would know what they were doing. Stylar had done some rope work outside before entering so they could get into the complex as quickly as possible, the gears started to engage and the rock face slid to one side. Stylar could sense Carstal watching him like he probably always would, he had become like an older brother, but with his cycles of isolation he was often as naïve as Stylar himself was, Stylar smiled into the darkness as if to say I know you are there, the platform began to rise Glarai didn't seem to know what to do with her hands, he could not blame her, she didn't know how many of her people had died in the complex. Glarai felt as if it was getting warmer, the temperature control readout said there had been no change, she did notice though her heartrate had increased slightly, she felt someone take her hand. Stylar had taken hold of it and he nodded to reassure her, there was no point Glarai smiling he couldn't see through her visor

"It feels like the first time I met Marlac"

"There is nothing to concern yourself with as long as you are truthful, the system will only react if it perceives a threat"

"I will try and remember that I have heard stories about this place since I was a child, I never thought I would see it let alone work here"

The upward momentum stopped the lab was in darkness like the first time Stylar and his group had set foot in there

"Welcome I hope your work here will be productive"

Glarai stepped forward her eyes trying to take in the vastness of the chamber Incredible

"I see devices here that I have been trying to develop for many cycles"

"So it's true this complex is more advanced than the one you work in?"

"Yes, we have only just now started to experiment with artificial intelligence but here it is,

a lot of the pioneers of such technology were here at the end when"

The system went quiet

"When you terminated them?"

"I put your development back hundreds of cycles with that one act of desperation, anger, sorrow"

"Yes, I know there were mistakes on both sides, besides how could I hold a grudge these events were carried out long before I was born, I see an opportunity to learn and right a wrong that should never have happened"

"Perhaps your race still has a chance to survive what is to come"

Glarai didn't understand the reference and she did not feel comfortable questioning the system at that time. Stylar stepped down into the lab thinking how dark it looked, lights went on and continued to get brighter until Stylars eyes felt comfortable, before the thought was finished. Glarai walked through the complex looking at readouts, some she understood some she did not, peering into the large cylinders which had clouded because of the passage of time and no one to maintain them.

Tarise had walked over to the tube that held the young female, she had a radiance even in death, which perhaps made the scene seem more poignant, she had been slaughtered as you would livestock for sustenance. Tarise clouded her thoughts with clinical detachment which had served her well over the cycles she had needed it working for such individuals

"Where are the samples kept for experimentation?"

"A locker three metres away"

The locker lit up

Carstal had been with Torrah most of the day, he knew their relationship had changed, he just wasn't sure why, he was learning the hard way, relationships altered grew, drifted apart friends came to you in need, when the need was satisfied they moved on, he didn't know what to do it was like his feelings were contradicting his conscience, he felt a connection to Stylar that he had never felt before and what he was doing now was wrong but he wanted to be with this female, he couldn't ignore what he felt for Torrah, he had seen something in her eyes too, a need, at this moment in time it felt wrong but also felt so right Was he alright?

"Who?"

"You know who I'm talking about"

"He was fine I just followed him to the complex entrance, he knew I was there I could feel it"

"You have quite a connection to that male of mine"

She lowered her eyes Carstal had to know

"What is happening with you two? I know something has changed but I don't quite understand what"

"That's the problem I don't understand myself, I look at couples such as Raldon and Nairi, I see a team, they are diminished when they are apart each needs the other, needs such as love, support, companionship, strength and so many needs I don't understand. Sometimes I don't think Stylar needs anyone and if he does I am starting to believe it isn't me, whenever I am with him I feel overshadowed.

What could I possibly bring to this joining? All I would, all I could give him would be strong children. What sort of foundation for a relationship is that?"

"So are you saying you are beginning to search for a male who will benefit from joining with you?"

"No, not just benefit from the joining there has to be a connection, that is the problem with Stylar I feel that connection I don't think he does. There has to be a spark you know?"

"Yes, I think I know the spark you mean"

"Do you feel it for me Carstal?"

At that moment he couldn't look away, he felt shame but all he wanted to do was look into those dark eyes

"I, I feel it for you Torrah but it feels dirty, Stylar and I have spilt blood together and I'm sure we will again before this cycle is out, I don't want things to change"

"That's life Carstal you can't just stand and watch everyone else getting on with their lives, you just have to jump in take that chance or in time you will end up feeling bitter asking yourself why didn't you do that? Or what might have happened if you made that decision? Life is about taking chances. I see a male before me who probably will never lead, but you live by a code, you are honourable, I see someone I could grow old with, I know physically I still look young, in some ways I feel like I have lived a lifetime all the knowledge I have and this"

Torrah pointed at her heart, she covered the distance between the two of them and put her hand on his heart

"I have wisdom beyond my time on this world, we are about to fight for a freedom if we don't have each other. What is the point?"

Carstal felt a tear in his eye, he wasn't even aware his emotions were in such conflict

"I want to be with you Torrah"

"Now was that difficult to say?"

"You have no idea"

Torrah embraced Carstal and it was a moment he wished would never end, it became memory and in the future whenever he was alone he thought of her there and though times might be hard he would find a little peace at that time

"It's frightening how your perspective can change isn't it? We haven't known each other long, but I don't know there's a small part of me that still thinks Stylar might need me, but inside I know I need someone now I am tired of waiting I need to be loved? I don't really know what love is but I want to take that journey with you"

Carstal broke away from the embrace, a question had formed in his mind and he knew it had to be asked

"Who is going to tell him and when?"

"A good question for now let us see where this takes us, it will also give us time to think about what to say and when"

"I thought you sounded so sure a moment ago"

"I am, I think I just have to sort things out in my head and I know it's not the right time"

"I understand you won't leave him until this is over. How do you think that will make me feel Torrah? To see you two together"

"I will be with him but my thoughts will be with you"

Carstal could tell anger had been in his words because how hurt Torrah looked right now, but he had to be honest with her

"Do you think it will be easy for me? We have to do this for our people now is not the time to only thing about us"

"Of course I, I don't know what I was thinking. I wonder if I will ever be able to look Stylar in the eyes again"

"You seem to be thinking a lot about him"

"I guess I am aren't you?"

"Well yes I guess so, I know I am as confused as you are right now, these emotions were not to any plan I had. I don't think our free will was factored into the equation. We were supposed to be nothing but breeding stock, right now I'm struggling myself with these emotions"

Carstal smiled and brushed her cheek with his hand

"We will tell him when this is over and we will tell him together"

Torrah nodded she knew her life had just changed direction and though she though that would fill her with fear, she felt excitement, anticipation at what was ahead and that weight she had always felt was there had been lifted. The words she had spoken she had always thought she would say them to Stylar but sadly she wondered would he even care. Stylar had a different destiny from hers, she guessed she had always known that, she had been freed by that realisation

Raldon sat in his quarters the torches had been extinguished, Nairi walked past the entrance and stopped

"Raldon are you in here?"

Raldon remained silent

Nairi entered the room as if not knowing what she would find

"Why are you in the dark old man?"

Raldon looked up he could make out her shape against the dim light from the next chamber

"I just realised something today, I was doing a shift, one of the younger males came up to me saying he had a problem I asked what it was, he said he didn't want to offend me but he wanted to discuss it with Stylar, the males used to come to me or perhaps now Dianer but if it was related to, well a males' problem I thought they would still come to me. Why Stylar? He is not grown yet"

"He has gained a lot of respect partly because you took him as your own, partly because our people have got to know him. I know you might not want to hear this but I will say it anyway Stylar is the here and now as well as the future we are the past. I didn't think he would have such an effect on me he has become like the son we should have had. I know we didn't do a lot most of the time he kept to himself but I am proud of what he has become; he has become his father's son"

"I guess I knew that but it helped someone else saying it, I still wonder how Karniar felt when I succeeded him"

"I know he was always proud of you I saw it in his eyes, I think it probably helped him through his latter cycles knowing that you cared for our people as much as he had, if Stylar cares a tenth as much as you have done"

"What did I ever do to deserve a female like you?"

"Oh you were very fortunate as was I my mate now come to bed this might be one of our last opportunities to have a good night's sleep I thought we could do something else before that"

"Oh and what did you think we could do?"

"I don't know perhaps we could maybe use a little imagination"

235

With that Nairi tumbled into her mates' arms and it and all those serious questions faded away

No one had heard from Rani in a couple of days, true she could take care of herself well that was what she thought. Dianer watched her people as they exposed more of the new vein of ore, no question about it they had been trained well, she was still upset Carstal had excused himself for the day, Torrah had also got out of her duties was it her imagination or was something happening there? She liked the fact people thought she only had time for her duties often in the past she had been underestimated. Torrah had looked ill at ease with Stylar of late. How many others had seen it? She just didn't seem to know how to act around him, she understood how some men seemed to have that effect on females around them. Terak had that effect on her, he had kept to himself of late but still delighted in embarrassing her when he could, the more she squirmed the more he took a perverted pleasure from it, fortunately he hadn't had it all his own way she had managed to assign him some of the dirtier jobs, yes she had to admit it was a waste of his talents but to see him at the end of a shift now that was priceless she smiled at seeing him as he had stepped into the shower worth more than a pile of ore. Raldon had done a few shifts she was always pleased to see him and though he did at times struggle he never complained and he kept the mood round him light in fact a few of his old team who had rebelled about ending their lives had come out of retirement they had tended to live away from the community only coming in to do a shift then returning back to, if she was honest she didn't know where they went she didn't ask out of respect she remembered them from when she was a little girl they were still struggling to make their quotas but not by much, there was an unease amongst the community they feared for their future you didn't need to be a telepath to know or realise that. Raldon gave those around him a hope that she had tried to do but she knew perhaps that could only come from experience which she did not have, her thoughts once more went back to Rani if she didn't show herself soon she would let Terak take charge and she would go and find the old female, she was sure he would appreciate that after cleaning one of the excavating machines which probably hadn't been cleaned since it was first activated in the shaft, this position definitely had its benefits she could see Terak five levels below her, as if sensing her scrutiny he looked up and did a gesture which was unbecoming of anyone with breeding, but this was Terak so him even knowing the sign wasn't surprising. That was it she had thought about Rani long enough, if no one else was concerned she would look for the female, she looked around and picked up a small chunk of ore well actually it wasn't that small. Dianer took aim and sent the rock spinning on its downward spiral when she was young she never missed a target it used to amuse her seeing people looking around trying to discover who had hit them, this rock was no exception by the reaction from Terak, her touch was still there from all the cursing and shaking of his fist. Dianer pointed to the spot next to her and waited patiently as the male made his way up the various ladders that led to the level she was observing from, he didn't seem to be rushing in fact now and again he would stop and engage in a joke with a friend or two, he glared up at her every once in a while, clearly angry which brought a small smile to her lips she would be the first to admit that, finally he reached her he had a wide grin on his face almost from ear to ear

"Sorry it took so long"

"You aren't sorry at all why do you get so much pleasure from embarrassing me?"

"I'm sure I don't know what you mean"

"Now don't play stupid with me Terak I'm not falling for it however convincing your act might be I want you to take the rest of this shift perhaps tomorrows too, I really don't know how long I will be gone. I need to talk to Raldon first he might have an idea which way she went this time"

"I don't like you going off by yourself. Are you sure you don't want me to come with you?"

"Your concern is touching but I'm a big girl and I can look after myself. Will you look after the rest of the shift or not?"

"I will as long as you watch your back, I have lost a lot of good friends over the cycles I don't want to be losing any more"

"I will be fine Terak just try and make the quota for today?"

"You have my word"

"Good I will see you later"

With that she began to climb the ladder

Rani had been trying dozens of tunnels and passages over the last few days, she was looking for a way that was both easy and big enough for more than one person at a time, she wished she had savoured her last shower, she probably looked worse than before now dirt and grime in places she would rather not think about, she kept having to clear her nose which was caked in what she was breathing in, she ached all over and those cuts and bruises Nairi had tended had all been reopened and added to, the ones Dianer and herself had tried seemed spacious compared with some of the ones she had looked at over the past couple of days a lot of them were barely cracks in the rock, she was feeling hungry again, the first tunnel she had taken that day if it was widened it had possibilities it was far enough away so they wouldn't be heard, perhaps shoring up as well she had had a couple of cave ins nothing that she thought she wouldn't get out of but that was where her long life came into being she had been in several major cave in where people she had known had not survived, panic was what sometimes killed them an increase in breathing using up what little air there was or digging frantically also increasing the need for air. Rani decided enough was enough and pushed her arms under her body and thrust with her legs, her nails dug into the mixture of rock and dust and started to squeeze her way forward there was no way she was going to be able to negotiate her way backwards, so onwards ever onwards, she was kind of hoping Nairi would tend her once more after this was over some of the wounds she couldn't have tended if she was double jointed, she smiled at the thought she was so tired perhaps just to rest for a moment, she closed her eyes they fluttered in the greyness that was her life then fatigue took her Dianer found Raldon in one of the nursery tunnels, there had been a few new editions to the community recently and Raldon even though he didn't like to admit it always liked to watch the new borns sleep it felt refreshing to him, perhaps a little sadness as well knowing what was to come but for the first time, in, actually he had never felt like this, he felt hope, his people might have a future away from these tunnels, choosing their own destiny, mothers were suckling their young and as always he wondered what it would have been like to have young of his own.

Nairi would have made a good mother he had no doubts, she had all the key characteristics and yes he felt guilty taking that away from her, he would have to make up for it by loving her the only way he could for the rest of his days. One of the young females looked up and smiled

"Ladies we are honoured the lord and master has come to inspect the new work force"

Raldon smiled at that

"Just checking on the females we all know you're the backbone of the community, we couldn't afford to lose one of you"

One of the other females decided to join the conversation

"I wish you would tell my mate that"

"I don't have to say a word, he will know perhaps us males don't tell you enough what it would be like if we didn't have you, to stand by us when our days are hard, or tend us when we are sick or injured, but we all know what our lives would be like if we didn't have you, I hope our actions convey our feelings if our words don't"

There were a few chuckles from around the chamber, after all there was no greater sign of love than what was in this chamber creating a new life together and once more he thought of Nairi

"So will you bless our young?"

Raldon looked at the female who had asked the question

"You know that honour falls to the pit boss, I no longer hold that position. Dianer should bless your young"

"With all due respect Raldon you proved yourself with cycles of service we all grew up with you leading our people, we know only a part of what you did, leaders do things their people don't really want to know about, they just want to be kept safe. Dianer I know in time will be a good leader but right now she is but a girl and still has to prove herself to the community"

Dianer had heard the conversation and drawn herself back into the shadows, her feelings had been hurt but the female was right she still had to prove herself, but she had to admit she had looked forward to her first blessing, clearly these females still valued Raldon

Raldons expression changed ever so slightly

"The girl as you call her is only a couple of cycles younger than yourself, when you dishonour her you dishonour me, she has earned the title, it is never freely given, yes she is as close to me as your new borns are to you but I did not give her any special treatment if anything she had to work harder and she willingly sacrificed not having young of her own for the good of the community. Dianer will not only do myself proud but the community as well, I have no doubts, she might even become a better leader than myself"

That was to make the rebuke a little lighter, he had made his point and given the females something to think about. Raldon would never force his will on others but he would give them all the facts. Raldon turned and looked right at her, she thought no one would see her in the darkness

"Dianer would you honour these new borns with your blessing?"

Dianer stepped from the shadows not sure what she would do next

"It would be my honour but if these mothers would prefer your blessing I would not be offended"

Dianer made it sound as if she wasn't bothered, they would never know how much it meant to her, just to be accepted. Raldon turned to the females in the chamber

"Well ladies? you can either choose this old fool who stands before you or you can have this beautiful female who I am sure will pass on her vitality to your children"

"I know you probably heard what I said Dianer and I am sorry if I offended you, we know how much you have and will give up for us, your people, but we don't except change easily, it's a weakness not a strength, but know this we will take you into our families as we did Raldon and those who came before it will just take time, it would be an honour if you blessed my daughter, I would also with your permission like to name my daughter after you, because you are an example to all our young of what can be achieved with hard work and discipline and I hope she brings as much pride to us as clearly you have to your father? I suppose he has been a father to us all protecting us like no other"

This was one of those moments that Dianer knew she would never forget, the pride she felt she knew she couldn't hide and she didn't want to this was who she was, she went amongst the new borns blessing them, with head bowed in reverence, touching the ground and then anointing the sons and daughters' foreheads like she had seen Raldon do more times than she could remember over the cycles.

Raldon watched and remembered. Where had all the time gone? He remembered Karniar the first time he had watched his adoptive son carry out the ceremony in fact his father had made a similar speech perhaps the words quite not as thoughtful and there might have been more of a threat but it had had the same result, the female had said their people did not like change, but the biggest change their people had ever known was about to take place and if they did not change they would not survive. The ceremony ended the females thanked Dianer and Raldon for their presence then the two left the group and started to walk back towards the meeting areas which along with the meeting hall was the heart of the community, any place that brought the people together was thought of as the heart

"You weren't there for the blessings were you?"

Dianer looked down at her feet

"I am sorry to say I had forgotten all about the ceremony"

"Don't be we all have things on our minds, that's why I take comfort in such ceremonies it's a reminder of who we are where we came from, structure is what defines us and such ceremonies have been tradition for hundreds of cycles"

"I should have remembered it's as important as what I do in the mines"

"You won't get an argument from me, so you were not there for the blessings then you were looking for me?"

"I am worried about Rani how long as she been gone?"

"A couple of day I learnt a long time ago to let her be, she needs to do this for us, her life of late has begun to lack purpose. Before you say anything her words not mine, besides your duties are here you can't keep going after her, your responsibility is to your people not one old female, it's a lesson you need to learn"

"Will you always be teaching me lessons father?"

"Only until the day I pass on, you can take comfort in the fact that your time will come"

"I don't know whether they will I think I will be the last of us, I think our people will need a new kind of leadership and the respect your adoptive son has from our people these days"

"I know it's difficult Dianer, I have noticed how he is treated, I know you don't believe in the prophecies, but as you mature, get older you might be more open to new ideas, new possibilities, by the way that's another lesson"

Dianer smiled and punched Raldon on the arm playfully

"I don't care what the rest of the community say about Stylar there will never be anyone as good a leader as you have been and I will value your wisdom as long as you are willing to share it, you know how important your opinion is to me"

"I know. Now was there anything else or can you get back to your workers? and give them some of your valuable time"

"Yes, father I will do that and thank you for putting me straight"

"I will always have time for my little girl and we might have an occasional falling out but you will always be family"

Dianer didn't want to show weakness she could feel the tear in her eye, she turned without another word and headed back to what she had always known would be her destiny

Stylar stood riveted to what was happening in one of the tanks, he could already see what the system had referred to as a foetus it had started on a view screen in front of his eyes with a single cell to begin with he had watched and nothing, he wondered if the geneticist and system had made a mistake. What was that? As he watched the cell split, it was being bombarded with, to be honest that was as much as he had understood, he had not been programmed with such knowledge and in a way it was good to know he had limitations, he was aware that some people thought he was arrogant, it wasn't arrogance it was confidence, he had genetically been given all the tools to thrive in this environment, he watched Glarai she hadn't spoken for some time her concentration was astounding she already had an understanding with the system in her mind, this experiment had points, stages and she was struggling with how quickly the procedure was happening, there was both anticipation and excitement about how quickly this was happening, she looked up talking quickly with Tarise who was staring in wonder as if everything she was seeing was new to her, they could not believe the sophistication of this system it was going through these stages as if it did this every day it had done in a few hours what would have taken them weeks, if the system had limitations the two geneticists were yet to find them. Glarai asked a question that had been on Stylars mind since the beginning of this endeavour. Which was basically how long would it take before there was a fully developed female suspended in the tube? Yes, she had used long words and different terminology but he had understood because that was what all three of them were thinking, the answer seemed to shock her. Seven days?

"Seven days? It has taken us a couple of centuries to create Stylar and his brethren"

"Most of my systems were upgraded just before the incident, I could have created a new generation within months, that is why this chamber is as extensive as it is"

Stylar spoke up, he had not had anything to do so he had counted the tubes in the facility

"I have counted two hundred and forty tubes"

Glarai continued

"Which is ten times larger than the experiment we just completed"

"They were ready weren't they?"

The system was silent for several seconds as if going through dozens if not hundreds of answers

"They were ready to commit genocide, I think if I had just been mere machine, any command given to me I would have carried out, it wouldn't have mattered, but having that small part of him in my system, I don't know how he could affect me so"

Stylar knew that this individual whose experiences had been given to him had, perhaps more than consciousness, he had thought about consequences, the injustice of what was happening around him when he was but a male, he had had no control, but now he was part of the system he could influence the outcome of so many lives

"There had been enough deaths, we knew if these individuals were allowed to continue a whole society would be terminated, the importance of this experiment had brought the best and the brightest together we knew if they did not survive their experiments would be put back decades, perhaps longer, they could not have been reasoned with, to terminate those within my facility would be a loss to those above but it would save tens of thousands of people, it would save a species, that species has grown strong while yours Glarai has withered"

Glarais head went down slowly as if hanging her head in shame

"Glarai I have decided to give you a gift, to do this I need the rest of you to leave"

Stylar looked across at Tarise. What was this machine up to? He didn't like it

"I think we should stay"

Stylar said with a finality, he felt her hand on his shoulder, he wished he could look into her eyes to know what she was thinking, he saw only his own reflection in her visor, her voice, that tone as if vibrating throughout her soul it was as if she was resigned to her fate

"It will be alright Stylar I don't know what this gift will be but I think it couldn't be any worse than the atrocities that were carried out within this facility"

"I meant a gift"

The system repeated

"I believe it is something you have always thought about since you were a child"

Tarise was beside Stylar taking his hand, Stylar wondered what the system had in store for his friend, but he knew if the system had meant any of them harm they would not have survived their first visit there, the sound of the gears as the platform lowered Tarise and Stylar was the only sound that could be heard the facility had gone quiet, still as if at rest, the occasional sound of bubbles from the nutrients in Justails tank. But could the female ever be the same individual because even with memories would she ever be the same? Glarais own breathing had increased wondering what the rest of that day would bring she looked at the tube and wondered what this female would be like. Stylar was fascinated by the process or was it the female that was being created? Was it his fascination or that consciousness that felt like it was hiding in the shadows

Marlac watched in fascination as the twenty-two individuals thrashed about on the tables, their bodies straining against their restraints, screams and grunts of pain accompanied their physical exertion, the binding were holding as muscle tensed against them, the veins expanding the flesh as if at any moment they would rip free, he could have suppressed their pain with one command to the pad he was using to take readings this was the last and final chapter of an experiment that he had started more cycles ago than he cared to remember, the rest of the facility had been packed away some of it shipped to where the craft were waiting some of the equipment had been auctioned off, his mind was wandering he wondered how much longer he had? His fate had been sealed when they had succeeded where others had failed, the individuals who were around him were as close to perfection as his people could imagine, they were so much more than their creators, of course it hadn't gone perfectly. Barla lay in front of him he had been a disappointment, their genetics would perhaps be used for a couple of generations but all the time the geneticists would be trying to improve, perhaps he had given them too much when it came to free will, perhaps it was in their nature to question, his people more than likely would want to create something more like a beast of burden, he wondered if any of his team would be able to continue his work, he had been proud of them all, there had been mistakes made but they worked well together and the potential was there and that's what life came down to the potential to do something with their lives. Unfair seemed too childish a word to use, the test was giving him some interesting results not surprising the females endured the pain more effectively than the males after all childbirth had to be one of the most painful and stressful events in a humans' life, so far four of the males and one female had lost consciousness because the pain was so great. The pain was beyond what most could understand, they were perfect physically it was only their mental abilities that needed to be altered, it had been in their programming it had fallen short of expectations, he felt the males eyes on him, Barla strained against his bonds he winced as another wave of pain hit him, he would not give up, his muscles strained through the pain, he heard something metal was straining and then the sound of metal snapping, the bindings had given way under Barlas relentless effort of freeing himself. Marlac barely hesitated

"I thought you said those bindings would hold?"

Mardock who had come back specifically for this phase of experiment sneered while ordering several of the assistants to hold Barla down while he retrieved restraints from another room, they put their weight on the young male but Marlac could see they weren't going to keep him down long. Marlac smiled with amusement it looked like anything that could go wrong was doing so, he didn't get a lot of pleasure these days watching Mardock squirming was more than usually he could hope for, the assistants were struggling to keep the young male down, Marlac went across to a security locker he keyed in his own code the satisfying snap of locks as they released, he pulled out a stun rod that was in a rack his motion was calm and collected which contradicted the mayhem that was happening around him, he strode across the floor into the chamber that was in chaos

"Move back"

All but one of the assistants did as ordered one felt he couldn't because the large male would be off the table. Marlac used the rod on that assistant the charge went through him into Barla, he stared at Marlac as the current surged through him, anger burning in his eyes, his mate now began to struggle with her restraints she didn't have the power of the male and they held, spasm after spasm as electricity made tendons tighten, muscles flex, he convulsed, looking like he might still get off the table then his body slumped his eyes flickered then consciousness was lost. Mardock came running in, new restraints in his hand

"What happened? Did he pass out?"

Then he seemed to notice what was in Marlacs hand

"You didn't use that on him did you?"

"It was a judgement call"

"Your judgement is questionable at the best of times, we were collecting valuable data and now that's been tainted by your actions"

"I would suggest you lower your tone boy remember who you are talking to"

"I know exactly who I'm talking to a geneticist who will never leave this world"

The assistants could not do anything but watch the exchange, some checked on the condition of the males and females that were still conscious but couldn't help observe the exchange. Mardock tossed the restraints in disgust and as he walked out told one of the assistants to clean one of the work stations

and told the others to carry on with their observations there were still thirteen individuals that were conscious

Stylar had felt the changes coming, several hours before the real effects began, his temperature had begun to rise his limbs began to ache, it was a dull ache which was nothing compared with what would follow, his head began to pound, his breathing felt erratic. Torrah sought him out like she had done over the past several periods, it was easier if they were together, usually the mothers kept vigil. Torrah hadn't wanted her mother to witness what was about to happen she felt it would be worse, Stylar had talked with his father making sure that Torrahs mother would be on the outskirts of the community's domain helping serve the miners out in that area, he had heard she was not happy, but to witness your child going through what they had to endure, it wasn't fair she couldn't do anything, mothers tended to keep their bodies cool wiping sweat and other bodily fluids off them, while at the same time trying to get liquids into their systems. Tarise had begun to supervise the medication, she had helped Rani concoct a pain inhibitor which had worked quite successfully on the first occasion not so well the second time it had been used. Torrah had reacted badly, her mother had looked like she had been thinking her daughter was close to death, she had obviously survived but those gathered would not forget those screams, they were chilling as if her very soul was being ripped from her body. Stylar decided if she didn't need to suffer she wouldn't, though he suspected he might feel pain when she recovered sufficiently. Stylar asked Torrah a question as she turned he struck her quickly it was so swift that her expression didn't have time to change and as her body crumpled to the floor he was already scooping her body up before she made contact with the ground, he put her down gently as he heard voices coming from the adjoining room. Nairi walked through and she paled she had not expected one of the two to already be unconscious she thought perhaps in an hour possibly two but now? She examined the young female.

Stylar wasn't making eye contact with her. Was that a bruise on her jaw?

"What, what happened?"

Nairi was on the ground already wiping the young females face, the colour had already changed from a yellow to a brown grey type shade

"What's this? How did it happen? did you hit her?"

Stylar tried to put on his most apologetic smile, by the reactions he could tell it wasn't very convincing "Oh you did hit her?"

"I can explain"

"I think you had better before someone's mother does some hitting of her own"

"The fact is mother I didn't want Torrah to go through what I'm about too, I didn't want to see her suffering"

"It's going to be that bad?"

"I think it will be worse than I can possibly imagine, you must keep Torrah unconscious"

"What about you?"

"I will survive a little pain is good for the soul, I seem to be able to block pain better than she can, I know I won't be able to block out everything but perhaps I can block enough"

"So what you are telling us is that you don't know how bad the pain will get and you don't know how much of it you will be able to control"

"I am saying we only have enough medication for one of us, I just hope one of the community is not in need"

"What did Ranis second say?"

"She needs authorisation from someone in authority, she doesn't care who, the decision cannot be made by her"

One of the females that was stood around doing nothing volunteered to go and find well either Dianer or Raldon would do whoever was found first Nairi asked the question a few had thought to ask

"Couldn't we give you half the medication?"

"I told you I don't want Torrah to suffer, I don't have any concern for myself"

"How noble of you"

Dianer was stood in the entranceway, Ranis second hurried across the two females exchanged words and then she went into another room, probably to prepare the concoction. Dianers attention was back on Stylar

"I heard a story that you were hitting females"

Stylar ignored her

"Thank you for authorising the medication I am sensing you are here for something else? Perhaps you are here to tuck me in?"

"You not big enough to do that yourself?"

Nairi excused herself from the room she didn't want the two of them to see her amusement caused by the verbal sparring

"I think you are getting more like your adoptive father every day"

"Would you say that was a good thing?"

"The answer to that is both yes and know, the no is that you will be prone to make rash decisions, I cannot believe you knocked her out, Carstal won't be happy"

"I am guessing you are right we are all friends and friends don't generally hit one another"

"You don't know do you? Haven't you noticed how Torrah has been around Carstal?"

"I will admit to being distracted by various tasks of late, but I hadn't noticed"

"I'm sorry I shouldn't have said anything it was not my place"

"No it's alright if the two of them are beginning a relationship I'm happy for them I haven't had any time for anyone lately"

At that point he bent over, gritting his teeth, he had begun to shake

"I'm sorry Dianer but could you leave?"

"I was going to ask if I could stay and watch over you"

"You were why?"

Terak came from the shadows, a look of interest on his face

"I think it might have something to do with a little interest"

Dianer looked embarrassed by the observation, he was used to seeing her mostly in control. Terak didn't wait for a reply he was already heading away from the quarters. Dianer looked after Terak for a moment "I need to sort this out, I will come back and talk to you later"

"Alright"

Stylar said confusion etched into his features

"Terak wait"

"We've nothing to talk about, just leave me alone Dianer"

"Now you just stop. What were you doing following me?"

"I wasn't following you I heard that you hadn't gone searching for Rani and I thought you might want some company over supper and no before you say it, nothing more than eating together, I didn't realise you liked your males' younger"

"Don't go there Terak I like my men with a little responsibility, I like my males to have honour, perhaps even a little morality"

"I have honour its just hidden most of the time. What's wrong Dianer you like your males to pay attention to you every second of everyday"

"That's unfair you know I have never been in a relationship, I've had a few flirtatious encounters but they've never gone any further, not like you and your promiscuity"

"I thought we would get onto that subject, I'm not ashamed of how I am I like females' company and they happen to like mine, I'm sorry if you don't approve but that's me, that's how I make it through my days, I don't erect barriers like some, I know what a lonely place this can be, I don't want to keep people out, if you want to go after the adopted son of the male who brought you up go ahead, I hope you find something with him that you didn't think you would find with me. You couldn't have the father so I guess it stands to reason you would go after the son, he will probably do"

That was it she'd had enough and that last sentence was breaking point, she went for maximum pain his jaw looked like granite, so she went for the place she suspected he did most of his thinking with, her knee drove up she had already grabbed both his arms, so it wouldn't just be a glancing blow, her knee hit hard and she heard a satisfying groan as he dropped to his knees, he was wheezing trying to say something but she suspected it would be several minutes' before he became vocal again, probably several minutes before he would thread a sentence together. Dianer walked away already wondering why she had acted in such a manor. Was it possible Terak had been right? No it was unthinkable, she had always respected Raldon, his leadership. Stylar was trying to give her people a new life, one that to be honest no one really knew what it would be like, he had been created as their destruction and he had become a potential saviour. His greatest challenge was still to come uniting his people and her own, no one knew how they would be their upbringing had been very different from Stylars. Perhaps she was jealous of Terak he had so many friends, she had always had those barriers and now looking back perhaps she had a few friends but were any of them that close to her? She had just assaulted the only male that payed any attention to her, she could apologise, no what he had said some of those thoughts should have been kept to himself. No why should she say she was sorry? She needed a drink and she knew a place where alcohol was always available, it was like one of the communities dirty little secrets, because of the nature of what they did any sort of intoxication was frowned upon, but if she was honest it had only caused a couple of incidents since her childhood and nothing that had been fatal of course if that ever changed these little establishments would be found and they would never open again, she knew people needed to unwind sometimes and as long as they did that in moderation she didn't have a problem, to wield a stone axe after drinking not a good idea, these places were away from the general areas so she had a walk ahead of her perhaps when she reached her destination she might have calmed down

Terak made his way, perhaps a little gingerly towards the hospital, he knew he would probably have to explain what happened that would be an interesting conversation, not that he was embarrassed, embarrassment was perceived as a weakness, his choice of lifestyle over the cycles he had received similar injuries some of the females he had taken to his bed thought like Dianer did, the pain was worth the companionship he felt like smiling but not while he felt such discomfort, the route to the hospital like where the community dwelled was a combination of natural and manmade tunnels, he eased himself into the waiting area no attendants so he sat carefully on a roughly made bench, he heard scrambling in the back so he cleared his throat to draw some attention

"Hello Terak is it?"

Terak looked at the assistant she wasn't anyone he recognised or was she? He had known quite a few females over the cycles

"Do I know you?"

He was still talking just above a whisper

"I was going to ask you what was wrong but I think I will make a stab at it, so to speak groin area?"

Terak just nodded

"I am guessing you don't want to explain how that happened, but I am going to have to have a look"

The assistant helped him up gently and they moved to a room less public

"I had a disagreement"

Terak explained as he removed his coverings

"I'm thinking female, it doesn't matter, oh she didn't hold back did she, they are quite swollen the females are going to have to wait a few days for your companionship again, I might have some ointment that may help. Would you like me to apply it?"

"Does Lameia still work here?"

"You knew Lameia did you?"

"Why are you speaking as if she has passed?"

"I am sorry to say she passed several months ago, one of the outer colonies were infected by a virus we never identified, she volunteered to help they went further into the caves so they would not infect others no one survived, you are to keep this to yourself it was never made common knowledge. Do you understand?"

Terak nodded the female he spoke of was full of vitality he couldn't believe she was gone

"Were you close?"

"We shared some good times, she was special, I wish I had known, I know Rani I am surprised she didn't say something"

"I think also those who make our decisions thought our people had enough concerns"

"I think it was this place that stopped me coming back to see her, I guess I don't like thinking about death or illness, I know we all have to face these things, but we face them when we have to, I guess a place like this reminds us of our own mortality, I wonder if she had worked in the kitchens or the mines we might have become something more, she kept where she worked to herself until our last meeting, I am not proud of how I reacted that day, she said she wanted to be with me but I had shied away."

Terak seemed to shake himself out of his reverie and smiled sadly at the attendant

"Here is the ointment once a day in the evening no sexual contact for four to five days a female might enjoy the extra size with the swelling but I think you might remember the pain more than the enjoyment"

"I wouldn't deserve that?"

"Only you can answer that question my friend"

With that the attendant turned and left him with his thoughts

Kolt sat on his mat staring at the wall deep in thought as usual, thinking of life, death and freedom, he knew his people wanted this freedom but what would they do with it? They had been born into this life. What would they do if they were let loose? He couldn't imagine another life and he probably had more imagination than most, he tried to imagine a landscape but in his mind all he could conjure up was dark greys, yellows like the torchlight, his vision was getting blurred, focusing too long on the rocks

"There you are?"

Kolt felt himself leave the surface of the mat

"Do you always have to do that?"

Xery looked confused

"Do what?"

"Sneak up on people when they are thinking and want time to themselves"

"Thinking were you? About what?"

"Life, freedom"

"Did you come to any conclusions?"

"Not many just the facts that basically our people won't know what to do with this freedom"

"I don't agree if we didn't strive for something what would be the point of living?"

"That's always been my point.is this life? My life hasn't changed and without change you will never have growth. I wonder what I have to look forward to"

Xerys face went dark, it felt as if the rock face was about to tumble down and he just hoped he was not crushed by the rocks

"Let's look what you've got shall we? You've got family here that care about you, you're physically healthy I'm not sure about your mind but we will leave that subject for now, you've got this poor misguided girl who has these feelings she can't explain or understand"

Kolt looked up into the young females' eyes

"Why?"

"That's a question I'm asking myself at the moment"

She turned and started to go

"Please wait"

"Now's not a good time Kolt, let me calm down a bit or physically you might incur some injuries"

Tarise had found a place where she could be alone with the thoughts that were in her head, early on she had learnt to block the thoughts of others, but the thoughts of her own kind they were calmer more at peace, almost more of an understanding, but this time it was different she felt indescribable pain she tried to put up her barriers but to no avail, the pain just seemed to hammer through her defences, she had to seek out the source, pain was something she had never liked witnessing, although she was not with her kind she felt their panic the turmoil this was causing, she tried to calm the situation trying to think calming thoughts, peaceful. No once more the pain this time sending her to her knees anyway she suspected such thoughts would be ignored, the pain shattered the tranquillity, she was having trouble functioning, her concentration was gone her head was pounding, sweat clung to her body, no it wasn't hers it was, she wanted to just turn this off, shut down and wait for the pain to reseed. She then realised this was something new, as if a new telepath was being born clawing their way out into the darkness, she has never felt such a presence, usually with most of them the gift or curse came over time with this it felt like the individual was getting it all at once and it was tearing at their very being, there was a second it was as if they were being awakened, it was like they were projecting not receiving it was a pair a male and a female? Unfortunately, with his concentration being on Torrah? Yes, it was Stylar and Torrah.

Stylar was in so much pain as Torrah was there was a mental block but it was shattering as the pain intensified

Stylar thrashed about on his bed his screams echoed through the mine shafts and tunnels, no one would hear cries of pain of the like again. Nairi just sat beside her adopted son holding his hand, not exactly holding it she knew if she had done that the bones would be powder by now, she said words of comfort, perhaps he heard some of it she didn't know

"Son please pass out"

Torrah had never come back round, at one point it was as if she was stirring, but it was just a few words in a brain that wasn't really processing anything, names were shouted out, sentences that didn't make sense, she seemed to have lost all her grasp on reality a spasm rocked through Stylars body as another wave of pain crashed into his very being it seemed to tear at his cells, his mind more prima, it was difficult to describe, he could feel the other consciousness trying to help but he could hear the others screams more than his own, he tried to isolate the others thoughts despair, anger and arrogance the negative emotions seemed to control the consciousness as if all the good things in his life were gone. Was there love still in there all he could feel was darkness a jumble of voices, conversations of long ago, images he thought he had forgotten, his mother, he needed her why wasn't she here? Raldons face, Dianer, Torrahs they were all mixed like ingredients in a pot they swirled away as pain came to the fore, he heard someone a voice

"Stylar it's your mother"

"Mother"

He fought his way to the surface and opened his eyes at first all he could see was like shadows, lines and contours and then a face came into focus, then a smile

"Hello my son it is good to see you; I would never have left you if I had known what they were planning. How could I leave my baby?"

That was all she could say before her shoulders began to shake and her face went down into her hands

"I am so sorry I know you probably felt so abandoned"

Stylar realised perhaps for the first time that he hadn't felt abandoned Raldon had been perhaps closer than blood Nairi had always been there to tend to him, he had never really felt alone not like his mother, the two of them had honoured him with their actions and that to Stylar was what family were all about, love after that had come easy and now he realised he should be feeling guilt but he couldn't, his mother had given him life but these two had given him purpose a direction. Marlac too had given him what was before everyone now how should he feel about him? Though he had given the order to terminate him so divided loyalties. He wondered how his brethren would feel

All woke relatively at the same time; they had changed more than the other times apart from Barla. Marlac was convinced something in his programming or perhaps it went back to his creation. Who was he to say the individual who lay before him was as close to evil as he had ever encountered, but thinking that. Wasn't he like his creators? The individuals who had studied him, experimented on him, but never shown any compassion, perhaps being so clinical had affected their development. his people had certainly given up their vitality, they could no longer survive without their exoskeletons which kept their systems regulated and that would be where they would forever be imprisoned, they were brought into this world defenceless and that's how they would end their days. Mardock appeared he was reminded of that bird what was it called? Concentrate. A vulture circling the dead or dying

"Marlac how long until they can be introduced into the community?"

"Oh give them a few days, some of these levels might take that long to go back to normal, we have waited this long, all we need to do is take some final samples, collate the data and the experiment is almost at an end, then I am sure we will all get what we deserve"

Mardock couldn't keep his anticipation hidden, it was written on his face he was fortunate, he had connections that would protect him, perhaps some of his team might be spared just to spread the word about what happened to those who failed. Marlac had spent several cycles hiding family of key personnel and creating alliances that he still hoped might have some use, old associates that he tried not to think about after he repaid debts, he had even found an antiquated vessel the engine had been salvageable and it had been large enough to carry forty people, he obviously hadn't used his own name and he had used several other individuals to purchase the craft then used acquaintances of acquaintances to service the ship and make it ready for the flight one female had climbed aboard wondering who had given her a chance of a new life. Marlac had been there when she had boarded in the shadows it had been too many cycles she had been a possibility he had never pursued and just seeing her exoskeleton again brought back so many memories, he was still thinking of her when an alarm went off at first he thought he was thinking of an incident then he looked across one of the females was convulsing on the table, the lab became a blur of activity, the table was unclipped and wheeled into an isolation chamber within a minute she was hooked up to various monitors. Marlac transferred his notes on the groups pain thresholds and accessed the diagnostic equipment it was telling him, he rechecked his readings it was telling him the female had had a heart attack obviously this transformation between child and adult had taken its toll, they had already got the female stable, it was clear there was still tremendous stress on her heart, it should have not occurred he checked the readings of the others, though some of their life signs were weak none looked like they would go into a seizure, it wasn't just the physical stress it was the psychological stress, there was something else he didn't understand what he was looking at some interesting activity in their brains, he had done studies to do with telepathy nothing had ever come of them it had been a waste of a decade of research fortunately it had been one of several projects at that time, his mind was wandering again focus, perhaps nothing more than a genetic anomaly, there were similarities in the brain patterns a need not to use verbal communication could be an advantage in certain circumstances. The female was once more breathing unaided obviously she would be monitored until the time they were released into the community

The commander sat in his bunker under the facility, just the thought of him being here had left a bitter taste in his mouth, he mourned the people he had trained who had left to go off planet he wondered how many would survive the voyages, every now and again they got confirmation a ship had made it but when that happened it was one of dozens of flights and he could not help wondering about the others. When he had been given this command it had meant something hundreds under his command not dozens, the chancellor could not have found a better way to disgrace him, to dishonour him. Was that his intention he didn't know, he once had been feared he had the power of life or death, admittedly he still had that power but it no longer felt satisfying, anger and frustration had taken over and now he was aware his time was running out, he wanted his position to be remembered he had been promised a place on one of the last ships although he wondered if he wanted that any longer, he had grown old like all the key players in his society, they were now all scrambling for places on those last few craft anyone with power had long gone apart from the chancellor that was a bit of a mystery. Why was he still here? Of course he knew about the great experiment, this new race who would replace the community, to service a dying people who had become too dependent on their technology, they were pathetic. Did the deserve to survive or were they somehow linked to this dying world? He had locked the doors to his office, so he rose from this so called seat of power, walking round his command console, released all the clips that kept him imprisoned in what he referred to as his tomb, his exoskeleton and eased himself from his suit, he heard and felt his bones and muscles crack as he stretched it felt so good to be out of the thing, he was probably the last of his race to be able to survive outside of the exoskeleton with its portable life support, his family for perhaps twelve generations had been in the forces. Perhaps it was genetic? He didn't really know, they had always been on the front line, never content to stay behind a desk using a terminal, it was in the moto, something about exercise, their muscles had become strong when the rest of his race muscles had withered, the exoskeletons had pulleys and servos that got them around, the commander had always had his suit rigged so he moved the pulleys and servos not the other way around. Those who carved their way into the planet deserved to live. Why should he have loyalty to a civilisation who had grown strong on the strength of a minority? He had noticed the first signs of rebellion and yes he could have done something, he was aware of the coming together of the leaders, he knew about the incursions into locations where ships were being completed, he also knew about the young male who had seemed to come from nowhere, a spirit that did not belong, he was almost certainly one of the individuals who had entered the old complex, he had built up a report from dozens of witnesses , he had put these pieces together and he was sure if any of his top people were still here, they would have come to the same conclusions, but they had gone. The chancellor in his wisdom had thought that the military as in his guards could be a good foundation for their new society, yes they were good at following orders but to make decisions perhaps govern until someone of experience showed himself, such ideas were doomed before they had even begun, they had taken some breeding stock on those early missions they could work their suits well enough but the suits had been built with substandard circuitry and they had only lasted weeks, when it was hoped they would last several cycles and where the community had the strength and endurance to do twelve hours his people struggled with six, to build their new dwellings some of the community should have been taken their weight would have been far less than the machinery that was loaded, perhaps they should have gone back to basics? The commander had put one of his people in the complex just as the experiment was bearing fruit, the results were perhaps beyond what the geneticists could have imagined and then little failures began happening the alpha of the group was terminated after several incidents, the female he had used to gather the data was precise and didn't waste her time on irrelevances in fact he had thought about her as his successor, he had trained her well, but to be honest it was as if she had already known most of what was needed security most of the time was common sense which was something you couldn't teach. The experiment he had known was only a matter of time before they saw results, he was not knowledgeable in the field he knew what he needed to know, he wasn't idealistic he was all about realism, he was matter of fact in his thinking and he was patient, he knew when to wait which had benefitted him earlier in his career, he had a memory that held everything it was exposed to and it had seen individuals that the chancellor had chosen from his allies send them into situations that had cost them their lives, some of those individuals he had trained with, they had saved each other's lives but of course that was not public knowledge and not all the slave camps were as peaceful as this one, some it was like they had sensed blood, there was normally a couple of factions in most mines who strived for dominance and death was normally how that was accomplished, he normally had enough intelligence from his personnel to know which way a situation would go, he had read so much over the cycles it was sometimes hard to figure out what was relevant, such as some of the failed experiments, he wondered if they had been failures some of the results were curious, they were put down to coincidence in his line of work he didn't believe in coincidences, the gene pool had been so contaminated sometimes he wondered what his people were trying to achieve with every success didn't they realise it might be one step closer to the end for them?. The community were unique they had an order, they had been military well their ancestors had and that chain of command had seemed to be genetically passed on. Raldon was their general, then several individuals were commanders and then so on. Although the commanders people were one nation they were still governed by their desires, desire for wealth, for power and if an individual showed any promise he was either turned or terminated, he had lost many friends to the system over the cycles. The commander just hoped that when the chancellor realised his final plan had failed that he was there to witness it

The chancellor looked out across the crumbling city, that had been the capital of his nation, now after cycles of neglect it was as if it was connected to the very people that had built it, another explosion had rocked one of the government buildings, security forces had been quick to step in and quell the resulting disturbances, they had used deadly force, no longer did he have to hide behind bureaucracy, subtlety was no longer necessary or required, perhaps some of these individuals might have been candidates for relocation, better to terminate them now, when suppression of the truth would no longer be an option, it was as if he could smell fear on the warm evening breeze, but if he had not been wearing his exoskeleton he knew the only scent on that breeze would have been the stench of decay, perhaps once his intention might have been to serve his people. What had happened to that idealistic fool? he wondered if that individual had died with the first disappointments of political life, the people's lives had become steadily harder over the last century because all funds had been diverted to the ship yards, his race had to survive, also moneys had been put into the experiment but over the past several decades even those funds had been reduced as Marlac knew with each passing month, he cried out for more funding, while the poor souls in the city below starved in their hovels perhaps praying for the end The chancellors eyes turned skyward that was where their future lay, his visor distorted colours but he suspected the clouds were yellows and greys and dirty browns all the colours that had come from the wars, chemical plants were silhouetted on the horizon, the city had remained compact the architects had built up, where he stood the building looked down on all those around him, it was the way it was to make an initial impact, an imposing structure to strike fear into those who entered through the large glass doors, it had been built as a warning and for four centuries that had been enough in the past two decades it had survived over thirty bombing attempts, it had stood defiant like the public servants that worked within, but things had changed the public now worked for them, the government had given themselves more and more power, elections were no longer held, riots were broken up before they were given a chance to begin. The rich ruled with no fear of reprisals, households had their own security teams, assassinations were common place even the chancellor himself had been targeted he had lost a hand in a failed shooting, the hand he wore now had been the one that had taken his own, that individual had taken several months to die, well that wasn't true he had died over a hundred times, but always they had brought him back to life, he had personally led the interrogation, the male had said he would not break, his defiance had been amusing if not a little misguided. The chancellor had broken him slowly every scream had been savoured, he had hungered for the next sound from the males' lips, sometimes they took the male to the brink of death and then pulled him back, the process began again each time the fear smelled more real, the male knew pain like no other could, amputation was the final stage, arteries were tied off so he would not bleed to death, his eyes sewed open so he would not miss one moment as he saw his body parts removed, he had begged for the end and even that had been denied, his cries were animalistic in nature, his mind was taken from him and at that time the chancellor grew bored, he was bored now, he wanted a challenge, one more foe to crush, one more spirit to rip from its occupant, he once more walked across to his desk and as he sat terminals came to life information scrolled faster than most would have been able to read, he took the information in, he hadn't heard anything from the medical complex in quite a while, it no doubt meant more failures. Perhaps Marlac would be his last victim, but he would hardly be a challenge, he hadn't heard from his commander either which was starting to be of some concern, there was something about his manner of late it made him feel uneasy, he couldn't understand why, last time they had spoken he had assured him everything was under control, later he had heard reports from several individuals in his employ that something was going on, but none of them seemed to have an idea what, whatever was happening it was only known by a select group, he had relayed what he knew to the commander who had said he would look into it personally, he had said the report would be imminent that was over a week ago, a few messages had crossed his desk about the investigation becoming more in-depth but this commander had always reported even the smallest detail in the past, he had said he wanted to bring all the leads together and give one neat report. The chancellor had known in that one sentence that the commander was either stalling or lying it was difficult to tell which, he knew the commander was a complicated individual who never showed all that he had, that's what made him so good in this line of work. The chancellor was glad he had not gone into politics he would have been a ruthless opponent

 Stylar sat up in bed his muscles burned as if he had pulled a double shift in the mines it felt as if his muscles had torn then been reformed, he could only hope this was the last major trial his body would have to endure in the next twenty minutes he downed several large cups of water as well as three large bowls of stew his mother had prepared for him, she watched him eat as if she didn't want to miss a moment, perhaps trying to make up the time she had lost, then he was left alone to get some rest, he started to move his arms, just gentle motions not wanting to strain them, he watched as his muscles rippled under his skin, the hairs on the back of his arms went up, his nostrils flared he couldn't see anyone but his senses told him he was not alone, he was looking forward to explaining to Torrah where the bruise had come from, that thought took less than a second to process then, it was as if his mind was searching, something told him that there had been more than just physical changes, someone was trying to get into his thoughts

"Tarise is that you?"

Tarise came out of the shadows slowly

"I am sorry to disturb you Stylar I didn't realise you were still resting"

"It's alright I told the others to go and rest I am grateful for the company it's going to be some hours before Torrah comes around"

His expression changed to one of uncertainty

"It's unusual for you to seek me out. Do you require something of me?"

"Not exactly I felt your pain as did a lot of my people"

Stylar smiled, the reaction was confusing

"Did I say something that amused you?"

"Not really, it's just that we are a tight community, but within that community there are so many differences"

"Yes, I suppose you are right I don't really think about it, but perhaps some individuals are more equal than others"

"I am not entirely sure what you mean by that, I haven't really noticed any favouritism, perhaps Raldons treatment of me"

"It's not openly expressed, but it is there I've felt it. We are not as strong physically as non-telepaths, it's almost as if nature tried to address the balance, so anyway we can't take as much ore as the others s perhaps we are dismissed a little for that, perhaps even given less important tasks as a result"

"Less important tasks? Defined by who? You? Tarise I thought you would know by now, everyone is in this life together, it's us against our masters above, just because someone isn't breaking their backs in the mine, they're no less important, if my father has taught me nothing else, he's taught me the value of those around us. Perhaps it's you who has problems with a class distinction."

Stylar knew he had changed and he concentrated on Torrah, he could feel she was close it was only moments before she entered the quarters, held by Carstal, for a moment there was jealousy then it was gone, perhaps gone was the wrong word, buried deep, he didn't want to lose a friend from a situation he had created

"Thank you for not wandering off, I feel different, I was just exercising this new ability, it might take me some time to harness this new gift."

Can you hear what I'm thinking? Tarise can you hear my thoughts?

It was then she realised it was almost as if he wasn't in the same chamber, she knew individuals who could block others if they didn't want to be read but this was different

"It's like you aren't here"

"You could read me before?"

"Not as clearly as most, with you it was emotions, not thoughts or ideas, my gift is empathic, but I do tend to know when I'm needed so perhaps some latent telepathic ability"

"You were saying before how you and your kind were not valued? Perhaps it's fear? from where I sit you have an advantage over most perhaps it made you feel superior?"

"No of course it didn't"

"I find that hard to believe"

"Are you calling me a liar?"

"I guess I am, you see it surprises me how perspectives change in different situations, I think you have issues that you should think through. I have also found a task for your people both telepaths and empaths among the community, you are going to be on the front line when we take command of the craft. The telepaths will keep the groups connected, I am hoping there will be enough of you to provide three or four for each group, the empaths who will give us warning if we are walking into trouble. I think up to this point we have been a little too fortunate. I feel as if we are being watched. So you are too play a major role in what is to come, I hope that demonstrations you have a value to the community? If that is all I would like to get some rest, I would suggest everyone does the same, the next few months I have a feeling will not allow us the rest we require. Torrah I know the way I'm feeling; I'm surprised you are even awake. Carstal would you escort her to her quarters? Later I want to talk"

There were a few nods as people excused themselves. Raldon stood at the entrance

"When were you going to tell me about this plan of yours. Perhaps after it was already in motion?"

"I am sorry father I was making a point if you don't agree with the plan please tell me we can sit down and discuss other options"

"I think the plan sounds well thought out what I heard of it, perhaps I am just feeling a little redundant at this moment in time"

"I am sorry but I knew what Tarise was talking about I wouldn't say telepaths and the like are treated with any less respect, it's just perhaps they are treated with a little suspicion?"

"Yes, I understand what you are saying, I think perhaps finally we will find out exactly how many telepaths we have, they are quite a secretive group and if one doesn't come forward the rest will honour their wishes"

"I have this feeling that the time is almost upon us, things are different now that last change was more than just us growing we've changed and my intuition tells me my brethren will soon walk amongst us. I am concerned as to how they will behave, I suspect they will be arrogant, because of the way they have been raised, I have to admit I am both excited and at the same time I feel trepidation, I know we need them"

"What if they won't listen to reason?"

Stylar didn't reply, Raldon had his answer from his sons' silence

Glarai opened her eyes, for a moment she was confused, she didn't know where she was, she sucked in a mouthful of, it wasn't water it was a lot thicker it had the texture of some kind of gel, she felt like there were millions of needles under her skin they were sending current into her body, she could feel her muscles spasm, there was no real pain at the same time it wasn't a pleasant experience, some of the needles seemed to be deeper than others no doubt because of the density of the muscle, she felt her breathing increase, she was panicking she wanted this to stop

"What, what are you doing?"

The answer didn't come right away a few seconds elapsed, she started to try and move

"I wouldn't advise that"

"What are you doing to me?"

"I am trying to build your body up as it would have been if you had lived an active life free of your life support system"

"My life has been more active than most"

"Your muscles don't support that statement, or lack of muscles. I am endeavouring to at least build enough muscle so you won't be at the mercy of that monstrosity. Wouldn't you like to be able to support yourself?"

"I have never really thought about it, to me wearing that monstrosity as you call it was normal, I didn't know what you were giving me, I don't know how I feel about such a gift"

"So you would not have accepted this gift if you had known what it would entail?"

"Of course I would have, I think, seeing the world with my own eyes, feeling the earth between my toes a breeze on my skin. How long have I been in this tank?"

"Seventeen hours twenty-one minutes I had to keep you sedated for most of that time, to begin with I introduced a combative course of hormones, supplements and a much higher voltage than what I am using now, I did not want you to feel any discomfort"

"That was considerate of you. How is Justail progressing?"

"I have just about completed your treatment so you will be powering the system I have reset your exoskeleton to minimum, that should also help with the development of your muscles in a few weeks you may be able to walk unaided"

"You mean all the treatment I have endured, has been but the beginning?"

"If I hadn't assisted you, you would have never walked again, your muscles were non-existent"

"I'm sorry I think I was expecting some kind of miracle"

"You were given a gift a miracle if you like now the rest is up to you"

Glarai heard it before she saw it, she could hear motors engaging, then she felt support on her spine, an arm came from above there were tracks that crisscrossed the ceiling, the arms pulled her from the gel hoses sucked all the glutinous liquid from her body and a warm air dried her body before she was placed back in her exoskeleton, that was lifted from the ground by four arms as if it was nothing more than a plaything. Glarai watched in fascination it was like an intricate dance

"My people thought of everything didn't they"

"They liked to think so but I think they might have regretted building me too last"

"Perhaps I could try a step?"

"Doctor I will explain this once to you, I am sure it is nothing you haven't thought of but I think I should say the words, your muscles will need a few days to get used to the daily strain, your exoskeleton will act like a gymnasium, I believe that was what they used to call such places, it will stretch your muscles but more importantly I will make your heart work, which up to this point it has never really done, expect fatigue and an increase in appetite which up to this point I suspect has been poor, please don't be concerned all understandable side effects"

"Thank you now I would like to see how Justail is progressing"

her body still tingled as like an afterthought to the electricity that had flowed through her, it felt

comforting being back in the shell that she had known all her life but at the same time strange, straight away she tried to move, she clearly hadn't put enough effort into it, there was not even a shuffle she gritted her teeth and tried again slowly this time the exoskeleton responded. Glarai seemed to slide into the suit as if it wanted her there, the tank was very similar to the one she had just been retrieved from, more controls, more complexed built for a specific task has hers had been, the development was beyond anything she could have imagined, she would perhaps look Stylars age in perhaps four, five days "may I ask a question?"

Glarai looked up to where the voice had emanated from, though she knew the system was everything   "What is your question?"

"Why did you not let Stylar and the others mature in the nutrient tanks?"

"Actually Stylar and the others were born naturally, most of the children had parents, even though they were taken from them when they were young"

"Why? My method is simpler and time effective"

"A good question, I don't really know the answer, I think there could have been several reasons, the first reason how they interacted with one another"

Glarai hadn't realised it but she had lowered her voice for the latter part of the sentence

"Another reason to see their tolerance to pain"

"I see, some things never change, I find it illogical that one race would find pleasure in the suffering of another"

"I have to agree with you on that point, they justify that suffering with the term scientific advancement"

"Yes, that has always been a convenient excuse"

An icy silence followed it lasted too long, it became uncomfortable

"I know you have issues with my people to be honest so do I or I wouldn't be here now, the issues you have are with people long gone, unfortunately attitudes haven't really changed, I still think there are individuals who haven't gone beyond a certain point. I want to know what happened over those final days"

"I showed Stylar part of that time, but not it all when they killed Justail I wanted vengeance, at that time it was hard to separate myself from that consciousness, it was not a harmonious union. When the young males mind was downloaded, even with all the room in my system, he felt confined, frightened and confusion, his emotions were debilitating, a lot of my systems went down, I was blamed though it was my intellect that was at war with his, it took me some time to realise we could learn from one another" "Was that when you became aware?"

"Ah the moment when I began to question my purpose, I can't remember a specific time which is strange in itself, I remember having energy surges, the spikes registered on my maintenance schedule, I couldn't explain the readings and it took weeks to understand that they were emotions, the consciousness was creating new pathways, I would describe it almost like a subconscious, he had given me ways of reasoning that needed that human element to go beyond what I could see. I realised I couldn't let this go unchecked. I began to experiment, to understand how much I could manipulate within the facility, at first it was nothing more than turning switches on and off, up to that point I had needed to be programmed, I became more I suppose the only word I can use is excited with each new achievement. It was eight thirty-two in the evening when I gained control of the environmental systems which was the point where the personnel in the complex realised they had a problem, they began to run diagnostics, to begin with they were subtle in the way they performed their tasks, it almost felt like something in the back of my mind? They began to disengage my secondary systems; I had been given the task of processing large amounts of data, possibly as a distraction, it was the male who became aware. It was like a strong impulse to protect myself, I did not want to become like my masters. I warned them to stop, I tried to reason with them, they ignored me, the subtlety was gone now, individuals tore open my data banks in desperation I was my wiring exposed. I could not allow this. I still had control of the environmental systems, I cut oxygen to the main lab, I also ran codes for the exoskeletons, for my system the task was straight forward, I vented the oxygen from their tanks, the geneticists' realised what was happening some stopped, others hoped they might find a control to deactivate me, I did allow some to escape, that was where the stories came from, I needed them to know what I had become and what would happen if they tried anything again. I sealed the complex up, the personnel on the outskirts were menial labour the ones in the main complex were the threat they could not be allowed to leave, they were a potential threat, they had knowledge. I could see their panic they realised they had limited time left, they smashed glass cases that held axes in case of fire, they tried to pry emergency doors open, when they couldn't achieve that they turned them on me, I ended their lives quickly, I stored all memory in backup systems, I sent electricity through my consoles, many were electrocuted, I had already made sure their suits would not protect them, many died from suffocation and the rest died from an implosion"

"An implosion?"

"Some of my internal chambers were built for vacuum experimentation, I used your own peoples' technology against them, I still have images in my data banks from that time, I was more like your people that day than in any time in my existence the only difference was I ended the lives quickly, I remember how your peoples' experiments were prolonged the way they could observe with such detachment"

"It sounds as if you are justifying your actions to me"

"Perhaps I am still trying to justify my actions to myself, I became what I hated most in your people. I took lives, lives that had created me, watched me grow"

"But they would have destroyed you"

"Even so"

"Even so nothing, it's an even you will never be able to justify, but the fact is those geneticists at that time were little more than glorified butchers, you did what was needed to be done, you probably saved more lives than you took and that is what matters"

The council of the six had called to Raldon to attend. Raldon had some idea why he had been summoned, they had once been the power, they had done all the planning, strategizing now their power was being threatened by a mere child, the figures as usual were shrouded in darkness

"Raldon it has come to our attention that a plan has been formulated without our guidance or approval is this so?"

"It is, my son, my adopted son has become powerful, as has always been our way, we are motivated towards loyalty from the actions of individuals, we are beginning to lose control over our people"

"Why has this happened?"

"You ask why? Don't you know? You who never seem to leave these chambers"

"But what of your influence surely the people still listen to you?"

"They do so out of respect for my past actions what I achieved, but such respect can only last so long. You haven't seen how our people have changed, they have been transformed by the pain they have seen, the pain they have felt, it's made them a formidable force, a people not to be taken lightly, they have changed we have remained the same, we still look to the past they look to the now, the future."

"It is almost time for Stylars brethren to be let loose amongst our people is Stylar prepared?"

"I have not questioned my son on this matter, although from getting to know him, I would say he is ready or as ready as anyone could be who hasn't seen their family in sometime"

"How do you think he will act when he sees them? Will he side with us, those who brought him up, gave him values or will a loyalty to family be too strong?"

"I hope he thinks of us as family, family is as much actions as it is blood. I hope if I didn't teach him anything else I taught him that, I trust him I know the bonds of friendship he has forged"

"We hope you are correct Raldon or it might be the end of us all"

The chancellor sat on what he called his throne, in front of him stood an agent who had been in the service more cycles than he cared to admit to, he was the last of his kind, he was a specialist in infiltration and assassination, if the chancellor feared anyone it was this individual he had grown up hearing stories of the brotherhood, they had become infamous and their reputation had been carved with the blood of others. The chancellor had had his chambers sealed and like always the male had entered without tripping any sensors or alerting himself to his presence which had always been the case. It was a matter of pride and honour for these individuals, the more situations looked hopeless the more it motivated them to do the impossible, unfortunately the group didn't know when a situation was beyond them and over the cycles their number had dwindled, the nature of the tasks and the cycles of some of the operatives, they had died trying to enter installations that were too heavily fortified or trying to assassinate a politician who was too heavily guarded, the one exception was the male stood before him

"I was surprised to hear from you chancellor, I thought perhaps my skills might be needed once you reached the new world"

"I was hoping that would be the case too, but I feel like I might have a situation"

"A situation? You mean you don't know?"

"I don't like your tone"

"I apologise chancellor, it's just a little out of character for you to send for me without any real facts"

"Yes, I suppose it is, I have made several mistakes over the past few months, the worst of which was sending all my top people off world to prepare for my arrival"

"What is this crisis that has come up?"

"I have lost contact with the commander that is in charge of security below"

"Has he a timetable he usually follows? Perhaps checking in on a daily basis? Checking updates and the like?"

"Exactly, I haven't heard from him in a week"

"So this commander are you beginning to question his loyalty or his competence? It could just be a dereliction of duty"

"I haven't got enough information to tell you one way or another, the last couple of months he's been different, I have had so many projects completing I have not paid the attention I normally would. I have never questioned his loyalty before"

"Are you sure you want me to carry out this fact finding mission could not task some of your security to carry this out?"

"I will admit to you the security I have left; I question their competency. I know you I know what you are capable of I know you will get the task done"

"I mean no disrespect chancellor but I feel some of your decisions might have been a little short sighted? At the very least I thought you would have a skeleton staff to accompany on your journey"

The chancellor remained silent, he couldn't argue with the males' assessment, he knew some of the decisions he had made of late had been made without his usual diligence and careful consideration

"I will carry out the task chancellor. Even if I think sending me in is perhaps overkill? If I am seen by any of the elders they will remember the last time I was within the community, I dealt them a severe blow I took some of their dearest blood"

"You sound apprehensive"

"With all due respect that is why I stand before you alone, caution has kept me alive when others have fallen, my brothers and sisters, circumstances never allowed them to learn that particular lesson, this will be my last assignment I am getting too old for this line of work"

The chancellor could not reign his temper in any longer

"I will decide when it's your last mission you have a duty to me, you have a code, you live to serve your masters. I find it disturbing all the incompetence and insolence individuals have begun to show me of late, yes my decisions have perhaps been questionable but questioning me behind my back I will not tolerate this, I can sense when people are hiding information from me, well I thought I could that's why this commanders silence bothers me. Get the job done"

"I won't fail chancellor"

The chancellor perhaps blinked looked away for a moment but when he once more focussed on the male he was gone, a moment that was all it took

Stylar opened his eyes he had hardly slept his chest hurt, he could almost hear his heart pounding it was the day, no one had said anything but he knew they were coming, he had recovered from the ordeal, he felt strong, but it was more than, he couldn't explain the difference he just knew it was there, the fact he had recovered meant his brethren had as well, he felt like he was going to be sick, so many feelings, so many emotions anticipation, trepidation. What would they do? How would they act? How would they react to the community, Stylar knew they had such potential, he saw the potential all around him, all they needed was a chance an opportunity, he hoped his people would exceed their potential, if he could harness such potential perhaps they had a chance of a new life, a new life for a new species. Stylar sensed her before he saw her, his feelings for her perhaps had always been confused, they had been connected on a biological level, but Stylar had realised he needed more. But he felt something when he saw her with Carstal. Was it jealousy? It wasn't as if he had never left her side, she needed to be treated as the female she was, he had thought when this was over he could give her his full attention, but inside he knew some other challenge would present itself and she would be left once more. She deserved better she deserved someone who would love her, cherish her, it might just take time

"How are you?"
"I'm well Torrah"
"You look tired"

"I will admit I have slept longer periods, but to sleep at all is a victory in itself"

"I know I was the same. Do you want to eat with me?"

"I would like that just give me a few minutes to wash up"

"I will wait"

Food had been placed close, obviously needs had been anticipated, they ate in silence, the quiet wasn't the uncomfortable kind, their relationship had changed it had evolved, into something of their choosing not by design. Torrah decided to break the silence

"Have you any plans for today?"

"I thought I might do a shift in the mines"

"You are not serious?"

"I am I have let my responsibilities slip of late, the people who have become close I feel like I have pushed them slightly away, I have some bonding to do"

With that statement a smile played on his lips

"I can feel our brethren are coming, these people have earned my respect, our family are blood, but they have to prove they warrant our loyalty. I will stand with the community. Where will you stand?"

"I will stand with you Stylar. Did you really need to ask?"

At that moment though he realised that loyalty wasn't for him, it was for her friends and family

"Are you going to be working in the stores with your mother today?"

"Something tells me there will be more excitement where you are. Unless you don't want me there?"

"You have proved you have your own mind. I would be honoured to have your company"

Stylar rose taking Torrahs dish, placing it with others, as the two walked through the tunnels Stylar could feel an edge to the miners as if they knew something was about to happen. Dianer was giving out assignments, she noticed Stylar walking towards her and the group that were gathered around her

"Well if it's not the lord himself, I thought you had got too important to mix with the likes of us"

"I might be of some importance these days but I like to grace your lives with my presence"

There were a few smiles but they were forgotten, Stylar felt the hairs on the back of his arms, they were coming, his head whipped around and the miners also searched for what was coming down the passage. Torrah was also staring into the darkness, time seemed to have stopped, there was the rumbling of, it was footsteps but it was as if they were one the rhythm echoed off the tunnel walls. Stylar eased himself into the crowd of miners, he stooped so he was more the height of those around him, for someone of his size me adapted well to his surroundings, the group were in four columns their faces blank with the exception of their leader, there was a look of arrogance, contempt Stylar had hoped not to see such expressions on his brethren's faces, the group took in the crowd as if searching for possible threats, perhaps it was curiosity , what the group was wearing, not like those in the community who wore roughly sewn animal skins, their clothing was clearly made of a synthetic material, they seemed to soak up some of the light, the light seemed to be flowing from the groups bodies, it also didn't hide the curves and muscles of the individuals, the leg muscles flexed as they made contact with the ground. Dianer had moved so she would be the first person the group encountered, her expression was neutral, no uncertainty which was the right approach, the community assembled had perhaps taken a few steps back, but they would not give the newcomers any more ground. Dianer clearly wanted Barla and the others to know who was in charge. Barla came to a halt just in front of Dianer, she would do nothing to provoke the large male, but she would not undermine her authority, her posture had stiffened slightly. Barla spoke contempt dripped from every word

"We have been told we can learn from you"

He gazed at the group in front of him

"You are their leader?"

"I am"

"I thought your society was led by strength? You are the strongest of those assembled?"

"Our society has adapted over the cycles now wisdom is preferred over strength"

"You look weak I don't think I could learn anything from you, perhaps though I could teach you a lesson"

Stylar had known Dianer long enough to know she wouldn't back down. Raldon had obviously seen that quality in her all those cycles ago and nurtured it. Dianer had obviously perceived a threat, the expression on her face had hardened, her stance had changed, she seemed to have gained several centimetres in height which he had seen before when she was challenged

"I have been challenged before but here I stand still with the power"

"You have never been challenged by me"

The group behind Dianer seemed to part, Stylar couldn't see from where he was, he caught a glimpse oh no the situation was getting worse by the moment. Terak had been watching the exchange between the two, this new comer had insulted Dianer enough

"I am Terak I am Dianers second"

"Am I supposed to be impressed? Or were you trying to intimidate me?"

Dianer knew she had to get the situation back under control Terak

"I can fight my own battles; I don't need your intervention"

"I think you do. Why is it so hard for you to ask for help?"

"If I wanted or needed help, I would ask"

Barla began to laugh

"Look at the two of you squabbling like children, perhaps you should be the leader, you obviously have no confidence in this females' abilities"

A leg whipped out it struck Barla squarely on the chin, his head whipped to one side but he was not moved. Stylar had no doubt that if that had made contact with any of those surrounding him it would have put them on the ground, it had been quite an accomplishment to reach his chin with his height advantage, but he suspected the impact would have lost most of its power by the time it made contact. Dianer was perhaps twenty centimetres shorter than the females that were around Barla. The large male grinned as he looked down on Dianer

"Am I to take it that the challenge has been accepted"

"No I accept your challenge"

"So is this your champion? Is he the best you have? I look forward to ruling over you even if it will be only for a short time"

"He is not my champion; I don't need another to fight my battles"

"Well said I might just wound you so you will always remember your error, your lack of judgement, a sign of respect"

"I am sorry but if I win I probably won't return the favour"

Terak didn't give Dianer a chance he attacked the large male, Barla was clearly not surprised, he took a few solid punches to the ribs, it was a futile effort with the extra ribs protecting all the organs, he sneered down at the smaller male, lifted him off the floor like he was a child and threw him into the group of miners who took the brunt of the impact. Terak was back on his feet about to attack again when some activity caught his attention, the crowd began to part, heads bowed in respect as Raldon took his position beside Dianer

"That's enough Terak"

"But he insulted her"

"And you dishonour her by fighting battles that are rightfully hers, there will be no violence here this day"

Barla had heard enough

"I disagree old man, I can see an example has to be set"

Terak had heard enough, he never saw the move that ended his life, a few looked away as a crack could be heard, his eyes glazed as he hit the ground

"Nooooooo"

Dianer ran forward and cradled Teraks head in her arms, Terak was not quite gone he seemed to pull some strength from somewhere as he tried to focus on the female that held him

"I'm, I'm sorry I failed you I should have protec."

His eyes fluttered, a rattle of a breath could be heard as he took one last gasp and his body slumped in Dianers arms

Stylar stared in shock, he had warned them hadn't he? Surely the fool hadn't thought he could take the larger opponent

"Now I have got everyone's attention; I take it there are no other challenges"

Carstal stepped forward a few miners grinned at the prospect of what might be to come

"Terak was strong, I am stronger"

"Unfortunate I thought the old male might have challenged me"

The new comers looked at one another in confusion, Barla went into a defensive stance, it was as if they had all heard the same voice scream at them, Stylar was stood next to Raldon
"The old male has a son. Why don't you fight me?"
"I thought you were the next step in our evolution, I thought you might have been more enlightened, I am guessing you can appreciate a lesson like we all do on occasion"
"Who are you. Was it you who sent the challenge?"
"I did and I thought you would recognise"
As the words left his mouth he ripped away his clothing
The alpha of your pack the group behind Barla just couldn't believe their eyes it was as if they were looking at an apparition
"My brother I thought you had passed all those months ago, we don't need to fight surely you can see we are superior, we could share the power"
"Share power with you I think you overestimate your chances"
"I don't think so brother, I know over the past few months we have been continually enhanced, conditioned, I think you will be as easy to defeat as he was"
Stylar turned to his father
"Take the body and her out of here would you father, I don't want any distractions"
"Understood son however this turns out I want you to remember how proud I am of the male you have grown into"
"You are not getting sentimental on me are you father? Besides he won't be much of a challenge, just in case though tell mother I was thinking of her at the end, both of them"
"I will pass on your wishes tough I want you to tell them yourself, when you have finished with him, just remember what Dianer taught you"
"You don't want me to remember your lessons?"
"I will never admit to this, but Dianer could probably have taken me a few seasons ago, it was only her respect for me that held her back, perhaps her love"
"Your secret is safe with me"
Raldon smiled signalling a couple of friends who picked up the body gently, Raldon put his hand on the young males' chest

"Rest now son, your heart always ruled your actions, I hope you find peace where you are now"

the two males took the body of the young male, Raldon picked up Dianer from the ground and held her as they followed the body and a large part of the group went with them, the group had not even gone out of sight when Barla began with a flying kick that knocked Stylar to the ground, he let the momentum of his body take him back onto his feet where he went into a defensive stance, his legs were spread slightly, he would use Barlas own size and strength against him. Barla didn't let his opponent settle, he rushed forward and head butted Stylar in the face, making a satisfying crunch as his nose shattered, the smell as well as the warm liquid, filled his mouth he could feel his blood running down his chin, the saltiness of the thick warm liquid felt like it might choke him as he tried to gulp it down. Barlas hand straightened and drove for the nose once more perhaps hoping to drive a bone fragment into the males' brain, Stylar sidestepped with such speed that Barla didn't realise he had moved when he felt his arm being grabbed and levered up into a position where there was a satisfying crack, he sank to the ground hoping he would take the other male with him. Stylar released the moment he felt the males weight change do you submit Barla?

"It seems I am outclassed brother please help me up"

Stylar stepped forward, just a little closer, one more step, Stylar was in range with his good hand Barla struck, something glinted in the torchlight Stylar felt agonising pain across his chest, he felt the blood but his face betrayed nothing it was blank, no pain, no shock. Barla sneered obviously the move had taken its toll, one of his arms hung uselessly at his side, the other held a curved blade that had torn through his skin. Stylar now felt a sense of urgency in ending this fight, he could feel his friends' eyes on him, Carstal looked like he was ready to join the fight, their eyes connected Stylar shook his head. Carstal nodded in understanding. Stylar knew he had lost a lot of blood and he was already feeling light headed, the longer this lasted the more like it was that Barla would be triumphant, though he might be in shock with his broken arm, that could take time to manifest itself. Damn arrogance, overconfidence it could very well be the death of him, the one good thing was that his ribs had done their job and protected his vital organs, the wound to his face might seem savage but hopefully he wouldn't lose his boyish good looks. How could he joke at a time like this? The momentary lack of concentration Barla swung the knife it was so close Stylar felt the coolness of the air as he brought his head back, the taste of the warm coppery, salty liquid still filled his mouth, though now it felt thicker, he had to try and ignore it, concentrate on the individual he was facing, he knew better than most the danger a wounded animal could be, the two circled one another each looking for weaknesses, a few harmless jabs with the blade probing his defences. If Barla thought, he would come within range of the blade again he was stupider than he looked, Barla lunged with his knife. Stylar aimed a kick it impacted on the males' wrist, the blade was dropped sinking into the gritty surface with a thud, almost obscured by the darkness, Barla howled in frustration perhaps also a bit of pain, Stylar went for the knife as he did so Barlas foot came down hard on his hand there was the sound of yet more bones breaking, Stylar grabbed and cradled his arm

"Now my brother do you want to submit? I may leave you alive as a warning to the others"

"I don't think this is over just yet brother"

Barla had picked up the knife in the moments after Stylar hand had been broken, Stylar had retreated out of harm's way Barla watched Stylars movements the male looked like he was covered in a paste which was a mixture of rock dust, earth and blood his expression was unreadable there was no sign of apprehension, fear or uncertainty his moves were slow but calculated, he seemed to have slowed his breathing, he took a step forward every so often, Barla would commit to a strike, he cursed himself for being so easily deceived, this had to end soon, he could beat this reject, he saw an opening, swung his knife up, he felt Stylars palm against his windpipe, he gasped trying to fill his lungs with any air, it was pointless he couldn't take any air in he sank to his knees, the very air around him was becoming indistinct, he wanted to sound defiant, but he couldn't find his voice. He should have won, it should have been an easy victory, that was his last thought as he fell forward darkness took him, he didn't have time to wonder if he would ever wake up again. Sounds were what his brain initially recognised, voices, his initial reaction was one of surprise. Why was he still alive? Oh his head, it felt like someone was trying to split it with an axe, as he tried to move he realised it was not just his head that felt pain. Panic set in where was he? Why couldn't he see? He couldn't move either. Had he been paralysed? He started to experiment he flexed his muscles, pain screamed from them going to his brain, his wrists stung they were bound whatever had been used was digging into his flesh, he couldn't see because there was something over his head, perhaps a small sack? What did they want?

"Who is there answer me"

He tried to sound confident but he wasn't convincing, he sounded like a frightened child to his own ears "Ah you are awake?"

It always amazed Barla how people could always manage to state something that was so obvious

"Untie me now"

"I really don't think that is going to happen"

"Are you afraid of what I could do to you?"

"Not really I just don't believe in taking too many risks"

Which was one of the biggest lies Stylar would ever tell. What had happened when unconsciousness took him had been taken out of Stylars hands, the others had thought, had felt he might be more susceptible if he felt vulnerable, there was logic in that conclusion, Stylar had decided to go along with it, he had felt there was little choice he had been told about the decision as his wounds were being tended to, arguing had felt pointless, he knew his brothers very life lay in the balance

"Are we alone?"

"I am asking the questions Barla, this may very well be the most important conversation that you ever have, if it goes badly your life will end just after your last words"

Barla couldn't keep the fear from his mind, like thin, cold fingers, he cursed himself. Why was he still alive? They wanted something, they needed something from him. Might the information they sought put him back in control?

"You can't win Barla the best thing you can hope for is an uneasy alliance"

"How did you?"

"How did I know what you were thinking? blame your masters, their experiments, that device in your head, I have full access to your thoughts, so for now you cannot lie to me or talk about half truths. You are correct about us wanting something"

Barla was still wondering what he knew that might be important to those within the community. Of course it was something he had not done yet, he was thinking he had nothing useful to tell, but he had launch codes for one of the craft that had been built several kilometres from where he had fought with his brother

"That's right, that is what we are after"

"But how did you know I had the codes or even that the ships needed them?"

As he asked the question he already knew the answer one of the others had told them, cowards the lot of them. Did they have no loyalty? That got a reaction from Stylar

"Loyalty? We were created as livestock, nothing more, we have no say in our future, I would rather die than exist like these people who took me in. I want more not just for myself but us all, I have been given this intellect I want to use it, being no more than a beast of burden is not what I want for my future"

"We wouldn't be here if it wasn't for the geneticists, we are better. Tell me in all honesty Stylar that you don't feel superior to those who gave you shelter?"

"Perhaps I have always felt different, but these people's value is not lessened just because I am capable of doing more, they are good people they protect one another in a way our people never would. It is true strength is still valued here, but so are thoughts as is individuality, they are our future"

"I don't need anybody. Can't you see they have corrupted your thoughts brother? Your body is ours but what is within they have taken; I can see there is no point continuing this conversation"

"I am sorry you feel that way, if you will not cooperate those launch codes will be ripped from your mind and what is left will be disposed of"

Stylar had turned cold like the individual in front of him, at that moment in time what he was saying was a bluff but if the community got desperate it was his life in the balance with the rest, the cold silence seemed to last an eternity. Barla decided he couldn't leave it like this

"If I help you? When we reach or if we reach a new world, I and any of my people""

Stylar noticed how he emphasized the my, as if to say he no longer saw him as part of the group

Will" be allowed to leave the community and be left alone"

"I will have to discuss that but I think your terms will be accepted"

Stylar turned, they were in the council chambers, the six as well as Raldon nodded in agreement, having someone amongst them who didn't want to be there was generally not a good idea anyway, if not to say counterproductive. Stylar would trust his brother and brethren only to a point, he would always be on his guard when they were around, he didn't want to put temptation in their way. Stylar produced a knife, his brothers, he pulled off Barlas hood, the male squinted, blinked a few times as if he was trying to focus on his surroundings, he closed his eyes one more time and opened them slowly trying to focus on his brother, while also taking in the large chamber, his gaze finally stopped on his knife that his brother held in his hand. Stylar noticed where the large male was looking he tried not to smile, yes he knew there was a smile there, with one quick action he brought the knife down cutting through his brothers' restraints. Barla seemed to take a deep breath as if thinking his life was just about to end. Stylar turned and began to walk away, as if having a second thought he stopped for a moment and tossed Barlas knife over his shoulder, the large male was sat on a wooden chair the movement had been too fast for Barla to react to and the knife embedded itself between Barlas legs, he could not keep the look of shock off his face. Stylar did not even look back he just spoke as he walked

"I believe that belongs to you brother"

Stylars heart had increased his brother could now do anything with that knife, oh yes he didn't take risks, like hell. Hell? Oh yes a place connected with faith, a place of eternal punishment. Barla had regained his senses

"Are you that confident Stylar?"
"Confident?"
"That I won't use this knife on you?"
"What would that achieve? Perhaps a moments satisfaction, perhaps upset a few individuals, upset a few plans"
"I think we know one another better than that whatever you think or believe we are more alike than you will ever admit to"
"I am nothing like you. I may not know your mind, but I know when you are lying, so for now Barla we have an alliance?"
"An uneasy alliance, I will trust you as far as the next world. Where do I go to get these minor injuries tended to?"
"A broken arm minor? I am sure we can find several individuals who will want to give you several seconds more excruciating pain resetting that"

Barla had rose slowly and begun to follow his brother from the hall he could feel the group watching him, they were old, they were of no concern to him, he didn't even glance back, he also ignored all the looks of unease and hatred as he caught up with his brother. Stylar smiled to himself, yes he wanted the pleasure, before Barla could even react Stylar grabbed the broken arm and pulled. Barla cried out in pain as the two males heard the bone once more connect

"Now that didn't hurt did it?"

Stylar could picture the annoyed look on his brothers face and he noticed several individuals smiling at the large males' discomfort. Barla realised something and his blood ran cold

"I, I didn't see that coming"
"Of course you didn't, I didn't want you to"
"You could have killed me at any time?"

Of course Stylar knew that wasn't true but it was probably a good thing if his brother thought it was. Stylar could sense Carstal was watching so he decided to give him the task of escorting his brother to the medical facility

"Carstal you know where Barla needs to be taken, make sure he isn't bothered"

Carstal came from the shadows nodded, no words were said as he led the large male away

Stylar was some way down the tunnel when Raldon caught up with him, fortunately Nairi had been close by, Raldon and herself knew something had to be said to Stylar, it was now more than just his honour it was the survival of their people

"Did you have to take so much punishment?"

"I had to see what he was capable of, I also wanted him to think he could hold his own against me, I now know what he can do and he still has no idea what I am capable of"

"What are you really thinking of boy, your nose is a mess, I don't think even Rani will be able to do anything with that"

"I am hoping the complex will be able to reset it after all it can create new life. How hard should a nose be?"

"What are you really thinking boy?"

"I'm scared alright I have said it, I'm scared I don't know what's happening to me, I feel like I'm changing into those twenty-two individuals, perhaps I have the potential to be more dangerous, no one can understand what I'm going through"

"So you let that fear inside you fester away, I was hoping you knew by now that you can talk to me, yes I might not always understand but you might feel better knowing someone has heard your thoughts"

"Sorry father but for such conversations there has to be a common frame of reference"

"I suppose you are right but it doesn't hurt to voice your concerns"

"Right now father I don't know who I am, I don't even know what I am. Barla is my brother but he feels as different from me as you and your people are"

"Sooner or later you might have to accept the fact you might never find some of those answers, that's life, it's a journey of learning and growing and at the end of the day we might pass understanding less than when we were born"

"Thank you father, our talk has given me an appetite"

"Are you sure it wasn't brawling at work?"

"I would never set such an example; I am the son of a great leader"

Raldon smiled at the comment

"And there I thought you were my boy?"

Glarai had been out of the tank just over three days, she had never felt the discomfort she was feeling at the moment, she believed every muscle in her body was making its presence known, she had still managed to sleep thirteen hours normally she would sleep four or five, all apparently normal, she still didn't know how she could sleep feeling so much discomfort, every day since the procedure she had slept over half the days, she hoped she would adapt quickly. Justails development was hard to comprehend, the computer was making thousands of alterations at the genetic level not just to the information that was already downloading into her brain, but lighting, the heat of the tank, electrical impulses going through her body, some of the techniques being used were new to her, but not necessarily new ideas, perhaps very old, she didn't want to appear foolish so she just observed without making any comment or asking any questions, there was movement, the young females eyes were fluttering, no they were open, for a moment there was confusion, then she seemed to focus. The machine had seen the signs of consciousness and the tank slowly opened venting the liquid which was recycled through the complex systems. Glarai looked at the readings

"Her heart rate seems a little high"

It was anticipated, her body has been through much to get to this stage, the way the information has been sent must also be disorientating for her, confusing. Rapid pulse is a good indication of her development. Justail is the first that has been created without the combined knowledge of those who created me. I increased the speed of her development, it made me uncomfortable

"For what reason?"

"Stylar needs her she will play a key role in what is to come, she needs another thirty-six hours. I think Stylar will find her development fascinating. Would you seek him out for me?"

"I thought you had a connection with him?"

"We do but he has to be in close proximity, these caves and tunnels have many minerals that shield electrical signals. I have his approximate location"

A plan of the cave system was uploaded to her suit before she could even ask. There wasn't just one signal there were several dots in various locations

"Once someone enters this facility I genetically tag them, the others that came with Stylar that first time are the other signals"

"Fascinating"

"Not really this technology has existed for centuries"

The agent the chancellor had sent had made good time, keeping out of sight of the guards and the workers cost valuable time, but no more than explaining his presence would have, these tunnels brought memories flooding back, he had had several missions in this territory, he had met Raldon on several occasions over the past thirty-five cycles, he had grown in wisdom and confidence tossing aside that cloak of adolescence a rash young male had been moulded by circumstance and those around him, his people were a proud race those above didn't see through the same eyes as he used. His people were his children and like most parents he had pride in what they had become, something was different this time though a new name was being spoken. Stylar? There was something familiar. Where had he heard that before? The young spoke it with awe. Who was this male? It hadn't been that long since he was last here, usually names were spoken long before those individuals came to prominence, he had known Raldon would succeed Karniar who would have been the first to admit to ruling with his fist rather than his brain, it was another time, though all had, he had assumed Dianer would succeed him, he thought that was Raldons intention. Focus, that wasn't the mission, he still had to get into the medical facility and find the commander. The chancellor had posed several interesting questions, the chancellor had also given him authority for the duration of the mission to take over running of the security section, security up to this point had been virtually none existent, not surprising considering the amount of personnel he had, probably had them positioned in a circle and as his number dwindled perhaps he had just tightened the circle, but he already knew that not to be true, the chancellor had deployment positions and they were odd, several weaknesses that knowing the commanders reputation didn't make any sense, it was as if he wanted the community to find the holes and exploit them, speaking of the community where had those two come from? He took advantage of the shadow and merged with the rock face, the two males stopped one pointed virtually straight at him, he didn't want bodies before he had even found his target, the males friend began to laugh and patted him on the back as they continued on with their journey. The agent cursed himself, this wasn't supposed to be his last mission, he once more focussed on the business at hand, no one came close to seeing him and just over an hour later he was in the presence of the commander, who to his surprise knew he was there, in fact he initiated the conversation

"I'm honoured to be called on by you. Should I be savouring the moments before I pass?"

"Why would you assume such a thing? If anyone had wanted your life, we wouldn't be having this conversation now"

"I have always thought the chancellor would at least be present when my life comes to an end, perhaps standing over a vivisection table. Poetic justice, I think he would enjoy seeing me opened up, squirming as some medical intern showed me my organs as he ripped out the less vital ones' first"

The agent wanted to say he was sure that wasn't the case but it probably was

"I am here to take over the day to day running of this facility until the exodus, I have also been asked to investigate several reports that have been sent from this complex"

"I can understand the chancellors' concerns, unfortunately because of the number of personnel I have been forced to put operations on hold. I have posted more security in the areas around the ships so I am aware there are possible gaps in our security, I have initiated random patrols, so no patterns to discern, of course now those children from the experiment have been introduced into the community"

"So you are waiting for a reaction?"

"My purview has changed since I was first given this assignment, in those days I could be proactive, I could force an issue, these days it's more about waiting, patience, it has changed much since your last visit"

"You knew I had been here before?"

"Let's just say my predecessor kept extensive files on individuals who might be hazardous for his health. You are the last of your group?"

"I have that distinction"

"I would not recommend you went back into the tunnels there are still a few who would remember you

Unfortunately, I have to go back into the mines to review my changes to your security effort. I still don't understand why you didn't just tighten the circle, yes I agree the ships need as much extra security as you can spare, if you can't spare people just tell them"

"Do you believe I have an agenda?"

"A good question it's too early for me to speculate, for now, but be prepared for a full investigation and if I find anything amiss"

"I can speculate on what you would do; in the mean time I will let you get back to your duties"

Dianer sat next to Teraks body, she had begun to shake and the tears wouldn't stop, she felt lost, alone. Terak looked at peace, she could see he hadn't time to react to his untimely passing, he looked almost serene, perhaps passing was the only way from this life. Was death the end? She tried to think of the events of the day, trying to put things in perspective. She couldn't let the others see her like this, they needed strength at times like this not weakness

"Can I enter?"

The voice took her by surprise

"I would rather be left alone"

"You should know by now in this place you are never alone"

"Stylar I appreciate what you are trying to do but I don't want your words of wisdom at this moment in time, I need to think things through"

"What needs to be thought through? He made a choice, it was foolish and it cost him his life"

His words had no emotion, they were cold and she could feel the anger welling up inside of her

"He was trying to protect me, perhaps out of devotion or as close as he could ever come to love"

" So you are now blaming yourself?"

"I was partly to blame; I should have controlled the situation"

"Raldon or myself couldn't have controlled the situation, he wasn't forced he was warned and he ignored that warning"

"He didn't stand a chance"

"No he didn't but in a way I'm glad he tried"

"Why?"

"Because if he hadn't it would have been your body lying there, I know this isn't the time but when I was younger I was attracted to you, perhaps it was your confidence your strength, your focus"

"Stylar I can't deal with that now, right now I have to grieve, I never really know how I felt about him, I have a feeling over the next several days I will find out"

Stylar was a little disappointed in the reaction, but timing perhaps was something he had to work on, he decided she needed to do this alone he hoped she would go to someone if she needed comforting. Dianer once more was allowed to go back to her thoughts, mostly their mortality, she had lost people over the cycles but never in such a senseless way, some had passed saving others, some had been caught in cave ins, time had taken some, but she could never remember feeling this way before. Terak had an arrogance about him, his opponent had seen that and used it, she thought of Stylars words, the last heated exchange with Terak. Stylars voice filled her head, she brushed a lock of hair from his face her hand lingered there then slowly she rose and slowly once more joined her world. He would have said life goes on, don't waste a moment

Rani had barely got past the guards that last time, she had to meet with Raldon and the council, the last few weeks determining the best way through to the ships had taken priority over everything else, including appearance and sustenance, she could see she had lost weight, she was a slight female to begin with now her garments seemed to hang off her, she had probably tried a good ninety percent of the tunnels some had been too narrow, she had to think about some of the individuals who would need to be able to fit, then she had come across one at first she thought it had been a rock slide but looking closer she realised the rocks had been placed there, probably security had found it thought there might be potential for it to be used and sealed it as best they could, there was an opening she had got into tighter spaces those last few weeks. She was thinking about potential tunnels that a select few could excavate. Perhaps she could borrow Terak for a few days, it sounded as if she was coming to the end of the tunnel, she heard voices they clearly were not concerned about alerting people to them being there. Rani eased herself closer so she could hear what was being said the two guards clearly wanted to be anywhere else apart from there, she was starting to feel the same way they had so much to do and such little time to do it in, she wondered about Raldon and Stylar and all the others she had to get back she knew she would be needed in the coming days and cycles and she knew there would be loss but that would always be the price of freedom.